PRAISE FOR *THE* ... *CURE*

"Huge applause to *The W*... ...rothy's brilliant work to the forefr... ...en have *always* been in science—d... ...rwise."

—Bonnie Ga... ...uthor of *Lessons in Chemistry*

"This timely and important novel will touch you, inspire you, and leave you with a sense of hope about what dedicated scientists can achieve."

—Stephanie Dray, *New York Times* bestselling author of *The Women of Chateau Lafayette*

"Without Dorothy's determination and courage there would be no vaccine for polio, and in this engrossing, timely read, we finally know how much she and so many other women like her sacrificed in order to accomplish the impossible. HERstory at its finest."

—Melanie Benjamin, *New York Times* bestselling author of *The Aviator's Wife* and *The Children's Blizzard*

"A rewarding read that both enlightens and entertains."

—Pam Jenoff, *New York Times* bestselling author of *The Woman with the Blue Star*

"An enlightening and immersive read. . . . Powerful, visionary, and inspired."

—Patti Callahan Henry, *New York Times* bestselling author of *Surviving Savannah* and *Becoming Mrs. Lewis*

"A compelling page-turner of a novel. . . . I could not put this astounding story down."

—Meg Waite Clayton, international bestselling author of *The Postmistress of Paris*

"The research that must have gone into this novel is mind-boggling and yet Cullen delivers it with the skill of a masterful storyteller. I was rooting for Dorothy the whole way through. Her journey will inspire and stay with readers long after the last page is turned."

—Renée Rosen, *USA Today* bestselling author of *The Social Graces*

OTHER TITLES BY LYNN CULLEN

The Sisters of Summit Avenue
Twain's End
Mrs. Poe
Reign of Madness
The Creation of Eve
I Am Rembrandt's Daughter

THE WOMAN WITH THE CURE

LYNN CULLEN

BERKLEY
New York

BERKLEY
An imprint of Penguin Random House LLC
penguinrandomhouse.com

Library of Congress Cataloging-in-Publication Data

Names: Cullen, Lynn, author.
Title: The woman with the cure / Lynn Cullen.
Description: First Edition. | New York: Berkley, 2023.
Identifiers: LCCN 2022025642 (print) | LCCN 2022025643 (ebook) |
ISBN 9780593438060 (trade paperback) | ISBN 9780593438077 (ebook)
Subjects: LCSH: Horstmann, Dorothy M. (Dorothy Millicent), 1911- Fiction. |
Virologists--United States--Biography--Fiction. | Poliomyelitis--United States--Prevention--History--20th century--Fiction. |
LCGFT: Biographical fiction. | Historical fiction. | Novels.
Classification: LCC PS3553.U2955 W66 2023 (print) |
LCC PS3553.U2955 (ebook) | DDC 813/.54—dc23/eng/20220624
LC record available at https://lccn.loc.gov/2022025642
LC ebook record available at https://lccn.loc.gov/2022025643

First Edition: February 2023

Printed in the United States of America
2nd Printing

Book design by Daniel Brount

For the children in my life, Keira, Ryan,
Will, Maeve, Vivi, Olivia, and Sloane,
with thanks to Dr. Dorothy Horstmann
for her hand in protecting them

All truths are easy to understand once they are discovered; the point is to discover them.

—GALILEO GALILEI

THE WOMAN WITH THE CURE

1940–1941

A WIFE

1940

Arlene would never get over the empty swimming pools. It was July 1. The water should have been frothing with kids. A lifeguard should have been twirling his whistle up on his white wooden throne. Moms should have been unpacking egg-salad sandwiches wrapped in wax paper and Kool-Aid in a thermos, and whisking grit from the concrete skirting from their toddlers' saggy diapers. But now the pool gaped open like a gum just relieved of a baby tooth, its only visitor a short-haired black dog eating a candy wrapper.

Their dresses already damp with sweat, Arlene's little girls, ages two and a half and four, were trying to mount the seatback to invade the front. She blocked them with her arm as she read a sign nailed to a telephone pole:

DANGER!

INFANTILE PARALYSIS!

POLIO!

POOL CLOSED

BY ORDER OF THE NASHVILLE MUNICIPAL HEALTH DEPARTMENT

NO SWIMMING ALLOWED

"Girls! It's closed. Get back!"

She didn't think it would be open. It hadn't been most of the summer. She'd paused here on the way to taking her husband lunch at the hospital only so they'd see for themselves and stop begging her to go swimming.

Arlene drove on, through the wooded park, past empty swings, past a motionless merry-go-round, past teeter-totters frozen at a tilt. Soon they were in a neighborhood of white frame houses, where aproned women hung clothes in their backyards, cats sat on side porches next to the milkman's wire basket, and men pushed mowers over their lawns. There were no children anywhere, a Norman Rockwell picture with the kids painted out.

She remembered reading in the paper a few years back of towns hit with polio being quarantined like plague villages in the Middle Ages. She'd been horrified to learn of policemen stationed at roadblocks at the edge of town, sealing the polio victims in and the healthy out. They didn't do that now. You could travel around in the summer all you wanted, as long as you didn't mind being terrified for your kids.

The kids scuffled in the backseat as she waited at a stoplight. Through her idle thoughts paraded Mikey Brown clanking into church in leg braces and a little girl being wheeled into Kroger by her staunchly smiling mother. She recalled one of Barry's little patients in an iron lung, watching her from the mirror angled over the contraption. There but for the grace of God go her girls.

At the hospital, she parked along the curb, then coaxed her oldest, Suzie, off the coveted shelf under the rear window. She straightened her daughters' hairbows and fluffed their topknots and skirts, then dabbed her own perspiring neck with her handkerchief before grabbing the brown paper bag with Barry's lunch.

On the way up to Barry's floor, a stern lesson was delivered to the girls about the importance of being quiet in a hospital. They must not wake the sick people. The elevator operator pulled open the door, revealing Barry at the nurses' station, grinning in the lab coat that she'd bleached, starched, and pressed. The girls clattered out. "DADDY! DADDY! DADDY!"

With a child clinging to each leg, he stumped over to the reception desk. The secretary behind it stopped her typing. "Aren't they cute?"

"May I?" Barry indicated the cut-glass bowl on the counter.

"Go ahead."

He fanned out two lollipops for the girls. "Who wants a sucker?"

They grabbed them greedily. "They're new," he told Arlene as they handed them to her to open after a brief tussle with the wrappers. "Saf-T-Pops. The handle is looped so if a kid falls on it, it won't jab the roof of their mouth."

"Clever."

The family strolled down the hall thick with the tang of rubbing alcohol and iodine, the girls sucking on their candy, Arlene listening as he told her how busy he'd been. Oh, she knew. He came home late many nights since he'd started his two-year residency last July, too tired to do anything but eat the dinner she warmed for him on the stove while he showered, and then crawl into bed. Another resident was expected to join the program today. "Some guy named D. M. Horstmann," he said. "Old D. M. had better hurry up and get here and help me, before these kids' dad drops dead."

"Barry." She felt strangely tired herself today, as if a war were being fought on a cellular level in her body. Fear extended a sickening tentacle through her gut. She had felt this way twice before.

Funny how pregnancy was like polio in that the only tool you had to fight it was physical isolation.

The girls had found a stand-up scale and were hopping on it to make the base jiggle.

"Girls!" But no sooner than she pulled one child off did the other scramble back on. They were having a grand time, rattling both the instrument and their dad, when two-year-old Trixie, chortling in another attempt to climb on, toppled backward. Her head thudded on the hard tile floor.

Arlene screamed, "Trix!" Even as she scooped her up, the baby arched and flailed, eyes bulging, face red, voice stoppered.

"Barry! She's choking!"

Arlene felt a draft of air. A woman swept up and, in one smooth motion, snatched Trixie, dropped to her knees, bent her over her forearm, then rapped the heel of her hand between Trix's shoulder blades.

A red disk popped out, its looped handle softening its click on the floor.

From behind Arlene a deep voice said, "Nice work, Miss—"

The woman gave Trixie back to Arlene and unfolded herself to her considerable height. In fact, Arlene had never seen such a tall woman. Barry looked like a schoolboy next to her. She was adjusting her beret over honey-colored clumps of hair while reading the blue stitching on the pocket of the speaker's lab coat when a smile lit her face. "Dr. Morgan! You're just who I was looking for."

Arlene's gaze shot from the lab coat pocket to Barry. Hugh Morgan was the chief of medicine. Barry's boss.

Dr. Morgan cocked his head. "Have I had the pleasure . . . ?"

"I'm Dorothy Horstmann."

The flesh bunched on Dr. Morgan's bony brow.

The woman drew in a breath. "Dr. D. M. Horstmann." She added, "Your new resident. I'm sorry I'm late. My bus had a flat."

Arlene stifled a gasp. D. M. Horstmann was a *woman*?

Dr. Morgan's skin seemed to have become too tight for his face. "We spoke by phone last winter."

"Yes!"

"And I regretted to tell you that our program was full."

"Yes, you did." She opened her purse. "Imagine how surprised and grateful I was when I recently received this letter of acceptance." She produced a folded sheet of stationery.

He looked at it, then gave it back, wavering as he stood, like a tree chopped at its base and ready to topple. Had he forgotten who D. M. Horstmann was?

Barry took Arlene's arm. She grabbed the girls' sticky hands as he guided her away from the confrontation.

"Thank you, Dr. Horstmann!" she called over her shoulder. "Do you think she heard me?" she asked Barry.

"It doesn't matter," he said. "She won't last."

1

NASHVILLE, TENNESSEE, 1941

"Say, Horstmann, want to meet a jerk?"

The voice seeped into the melee in which Dorothy, a modern-day Gulliver, was being roped down by tiny little men. Apparently, she'd stumbled into the little guys' mysterious world, and they were hopping mad.

She peeled open an eye. In front of the cardboard boxes in the storeroom where the residents liked to steal a nap, a baby-faced redheaded man was peering down the front of his white gown at her. Probably not a dream. Barry Montgomery was a resident at Vanderbilt, same as she. But she wasn't sure. She'd slept thirty minutes over the last forty-eight hours—not uncommon these past ten months at Vandy—and her senses couldn't be trusted.

She shut her stinging eye. "Do I?"

"Oh, I think you'll want to meet this one, if the nurses are any indication."

Over the radio that Dorothy forgot she'd turned on, the sound of clacking typewriters announced the end of orchestral music and the start of a news program. She pushed herself upright and snapped off the receiver.

"Don't you want to hear the news?" Barry had a newborn baby and two kids, but with his carroty cowlick and ruddy cheeks, he looked like he should be carrying a slingshot and harmonica in his pocket, not tongue depressors and an otoscope. He was thirty, a year older than she was—did she look so young? "What country do you think the Germans are invading today?"

Even half-asleep, unease slithered into her gut. On another side of the planet, horrible things were happening, yet they were carrying on here in the States as if this were not so. This was not sustainable. "*Are* there any more countries in Europe left for them to occupy?"

"Russia." Barry's stethoscope bounced against his white gown as he pulled her to her feet. "Upsy daisy! Come get a look at this character—if you can see him through the wall of panting nurses."

"I can't believe I'm giving up precious sleep for this."

"Yeah, yeah. You can thank me later."

Her dream hadn't quite left her as Barry prodded her down the hall. It must have come from studying Group A streptococcus under a microscope earlier. What robust lives bacteria lived! When they found themselves in a favorable new situation, like a plate of blood agar, the happy little hedonists rejoiced at their good luck and threw themselves into a frenzy of feasting, after which they procreated, then procreated some more, until there was nothing left to squeeze out of life and then they died. She was almost fond of the tiny terrors, so bold, so hungry, so hell-bent on having it all. She would have been fond of them, had they not claimed millions of human lives.

An ominous mechanical *whooooooossshhh*-GROAN, *whooooooossshhh*-GROAN broke into her thoughts. Behind the windows of the polio ward, nurses could be seen rushing between toddlers crying in their cribs and kids laid out in full-body casts. Other nurses tended to the source of the metallic moaning, the ventilators containing individual children.

In medical school, Dorothy had asked, once, to be put into an "iron lung," to see how it felt. A tall teenage patient had just graduated to a cuirass respirator, the kind that fits on the patient's chest, and had vacated his extra-long chamber model. Two nurses hesitantly agreed to Dorothy's request, glancing at each other when she laid herself down on a gurney.

"Transfer me in!" she'd said. A crinolined lady taking a picnic to watch the first battle of the Civil War could have been no more jovial.

The nurses wheeled her next to the ventilator and, in a real-life *Gulliver's Travels* situation, heaved her up from the stretcher and dropped her onto a cushioned tray. They then slid the tray into the tank and closed the coffin-like lid, latching it shut with just her head jutting out.

"Ready!"

Someone turned it on. With a clank and a groan, the machine wound up. Pressure bore down on Dorothy's chest as if an elephant had sat on it. Then, after every scrap of breath was flattened out of her, the elephant got up; a tsunami of oxygen rushed in. She was drowning in air when the elephant plumped down again, vacuuming it out of her.

She pounded the sides of the tank. From somewhere in her lungs, she scraped together the wind to gasp. "Help!"

The nurse—Dorothy still remembered her name, Trudy—put her face inches from Dorothy's, her breath smelling of the Wrigley's tucked between teeth and cheek. "Go along with it. Let go. Let the machine do the work."

"I can't!"

Dorothy felt a hand grab hers—Trudy had reached into one of the portholes. "Yes, you can."

Humiliatingly near tears, Dorothy let the device squeeze the air from her lungs then release them to fill. She breathed, not on her terms, not comfortably, not naturally, not happily, but she breathed.

Even now, that fear still felt fresh as she scanned the row of machines, the mirror positioned over the end of each reflecting the terror, bewilderment, or resignation of the child within. Her job as a doctor was to fix these broken kids. Worse, they actually thought she could.

Barry plucked at her arm. "Come on, Horstmann. You're not going to beat polio today."

"What if I do someday?"

He laughed. "Sure you will. And I'm finding the Fountain of Youth."

Down the corridor, a crowd had formed at the nurses' station. The man in the center didn't seem much older than she was. He was almost comically handsome, with a matinee idol's dark hair oiled in waves and a dapper mustache. He even had a Laurence Olivier–like cleft in his chin. Judging from his expensive pin-striped suit, he could have actually been a celebrity, or else he came from money. Most people in her profession had money in their background, at least they did at the upper-echelon medical schools. Women were scarce in a place such as this; women from families like hers, even scarcer. In fact, she had so far yet to meet another person like herself in her field. She was the human equivalent of a unicorn.

Barry addressed him over the nurses. "Doctor, I'd like you to meet somebody."

The nurses, seeing that a physician was speaking, even if only a resident, cleared a path for Barry.

"Excuse me." Dorothy tried to get through, too, but the nurses were not conditioned to falling aside for a woman. "Sorry. Sorry." She squeezed a nurse's arm in apology after knocking into her, then held out her hand to Young Dr. Suave. "I'm Dorothy Horstmann. Nice to meet you."

He stopped talking long enough for his gaze to travel the considerable distance up and down her doctor's gown. She braced herself. *Go ahead. Say it.*

He put out his hand. "Dr. Horstmann, nice to meet you. Albert Sabin. This is my colleague"—he ushered forward the young man next to him—"Robbie Ward."

Dr. Ward, as big-boned and brawny as a football player, pulled back his chin to gawk at her. "You are tall!"

Ah, there it was. Somehow, seeing a six-foot-one woman pressed a lever in most people's brains, and those three words instantly shot out. It was uncanny.

He shook his head in appreciation. "You are a lot of blonde."

She supposed the bird's nest atop her head qualified her as a blonde. She smiled for Dr. Ward, not wanting him to be embarrassed should he realize how idiotic he sounded, then turned to Dr. Sabin. "Aren't you the one who advised doctors not to perform tonsillectomies in the summer because of their connection to polio?"

He bowed. "I am."

"How old were you when you wrote that paper?" Barry asked. "Ten?"

"Twenty-six," Dr. Sabin said. "But even a ten-year-old could have suspected that performing surgery in polio season might be a bad idea." He crooked a corner of his mouth. "More often than not, the obvious is true, yet we ignore it."

Oh, yes. He was *that* Dr. Sabin, the boy wonder. She'd heard about him when she was fighting her way through medical school back in San Francisco. While *he* was in medical school, he'd devised a test that doctors around the world still used to more quickly identify the type of bacteria causing pneumonia. Word was that he'd been offered the chance to head up pediatric research at the University of Cincinnati, a minor research institution until he'd arrived there. Many colleagues were said to be rubbed wrong by his cocksureness, irritated by his belief that he was leaps ahead of every other living being in his thinking, but Dorothy didn't see how that made him any different than most other medical men.

Now he started down the hall as if he were a chief showing off his hospital and not a young visiting doctor. Dorothy and the others followed three abreast, with Dr. Ward eyeing her as he walked next to her, as if to measure who was the taller.

"What brings you to our humble clinic?" Barry asked Dr. Sabin.

Dorothy detected sarcasm. There was nothing humble about Vanderbilt. People liked to think of the university as the Harvard of the South. Some newly minted MDs chose to do residencies at the hospital simply for its prestige, Barry among them. While she could certainly use the prestige, Dorothy chose Vandy because, well, it took her. Even that had been an error. Dr. Morgan had forgotten that Dr. D. M. Horstmann was a woman when he'd accepted her based on her record. He still hadn't figured out how to get rid of her.

Robbie Ward answered for Dr. Sabin. "Top secret."

"Not really," said Dr. Sabin. "I've been given permission by the NIH to conduct autopsies on every polio victim within four hundred miles of Cincinnati. You had a seven-year-old boy die here this morning, so here I am."

Dorothy glanced away, a shard of grief shivving the inside of her sternum. The child had been admitted for weakness in the arms and lower extremities. Within two hours, his paralysis had progressed so quickly that they didn't have time to get him into an iron lung to breathe. He died as Dorothy was desperately puncturing an opening into his windpipe. She'd tried to resuscitate him for twelve minutes after the attending physician had pronounced him dead. The attending had sent her from the room, telling her to "get hold of herself," which was how she had ended up in the lab, numbly watching the antics of the deadly microscopic strivers.

"Did you have to come all the way to Tennessee for a body?" Barry said. "Don't you have enough in Ohio?"

Dr. Sabin lifted his Olivier cleft. "Evidently, I don't."

"It's a four-hour trip here," said Barry.

"Three-and-a-half," Dr. Sabin corrected, "when Robbie's at the wheel of his convertible. If he ever tires of medicine, he could be a race car driver in *du Mans*." He pronounced it the French way, Dorothy noticed. A man of the world.

Robbie ran his hand through the peninsula of sandy hair left by his receding hairline. "Aw, I don't drive so fast. Though it is true that my wife refuses to go out with me if the top's down."

"Just be glad you're not on the back of his motorcycle in February," said Dr. Sabin.

"Say!" Robbie exclaimed. "It wasn't my idea to take the Harley to that case!"

"I assume full responsibility." To Dorothy, Dr. Sabin said, "Do you know the secret of staying warm on a motorcycle ride in February?"

She made herself smile. The chest-beating got tiresome.

"Newspapers!" Dr. Sabin replied to his own question. "You stuff your coat with them. Friend Robbie taught me. They're excellent insulation."

"I'd like to try that," Barry said.

"No, you don't!" Dr. Sabin exclaimed over his shoulder. "We looked like Tweedledee and Tweedledum."

"I meant ride a motorcycle."

"Easy as riding a bicycle," said Dr. Ward. "You just—"

Dorothy spoke up. "Why are you doing so many autopsies?"

The men looked at her, their boys' club talk interrupted.

"You're zipping around the country doing postmortems on patients who weren't yours—why?" She smiled. Always smile. Always disarm. "I can think of pleasanter reasons for a road trip."

Dr. Ward glanced around as if a spy might be hiding behind the drinking fountain. "We're working on something big. When we're done—"

A look from Dr. Sabin snuffed his colleague's speech.

"May I sit in?" said Dorothy.

"On the autopsy?" Dr. Ward exclaimed. "You want to sit in on an autopsy?"

"It wouldn't be my first." It wasn't that she enjoyed postmortems, although she preferred them to injecting mice with pathogens, for instance. An autopsy subject could no longer suffer; a mouse could. But since she hadn't been able to save the boy, she felt she owed it to him to find out what went wrong. Anything to help to get closer to the day when she didn't have to tell a mother that she'd lost her baby to polio.

Dr. Sabin shrugged. "I don't see why you shouldn't attend. You'll have company."

2

Dorothy peered through the window of the gallery. It was going to be a most peculiar autopsy. Not only was it to be performed in a surgical operating theater instead of in the morgue, but Dr. Sabin had brought his own instruments—medical bags full of them. Now masked, gowned, and gloved as if his subject were still alive, he reviewed his paraphernalia. Dozens each of scalpels, saws, scissors, and forceps were arrayed before him like the keys of a pipe organ that he was about to play. At his side, Robbie, the maestro's assistant, prepared stacks of slides and rows of vials. The body had not yet been brought in.

Down the row from Dorothy, the chief of medicine, Dr. Morgan (still recovering from allowing a woman on his staff), narrowed eyes deep within bony sockets. "This is ridiculous."

The nine other doctors in attendance agreed.

He leaned forward to speak into the microphone, the light of an overhead bulb reflecting off his rocky slab of brow. "Why the elaborate production, Dr. Sabin?"

Dr. Sabin glared up through the bright lights of the operating theater, visibly irritated at being held up by the arrival of the body. "Since we are experiencing a delay, allow me to provide some background. As you know, our esteemed colleague Simon Flexner tells us that the poliovirus enters the body through the olfactory neuronal pathway and spreads directly from there to the central nervous system."

"Yes, we know," said Dr. Morgan. "You can lower your mask so that we can hear you—you can't infect the body once it comes."

A few of the doctors chuckled.

Down on the operating floor, Dr. Sabin either didn't hear or pretended not to. "And since Dr. Flexner says this, what does the scientific community do? Chases ways to stop it from entering the nose. Installing nasal plugs, putting powdered zinc or picric acid up the noses of children—none of this works, or worse. Some of the children permanently lost their sense of smell. Our colleagues seem to have forgotten Hippocrates: 'First, do no harm.'"

"It's not forgetting Hippocrates," a doctor declared, "when you're trying to save a child!"

Dr. Sabin waited for the gallery to settle down. "Meanwhile, more children perish from polio. Yet no one asks, is it possible that Flexner's conclusions were based on flawed work?"

"But why should we think that?" Dr. Morgan exclaimed into the microphone. "Simon Flexner is the leading authority on polio."

Dr. Sabin cocked his head with a little smile. "If something is not working, shouldn't you ask yourself why?"

Behind the glass, the doctors grumbled. Next to Dorothy, Barry said, "Who does he think he is?"

Dr. Sabin scowled at the operating room door before continuing. "First of all, Flexner's conclusion that poliovirus enters through the nose was based on research using rhesus monkeys. What if they process poliovirus differently than other kinds of monkeys, or, more importantly, humans? I'm already finding this to be so—what is true for the rhesus is not necessarily true for us.

"Second, I realized that the autopsists in his studies were using dirty scalpels, with no care to sterility. The patients were already deceased, I suppose they figured, so what did it matter? But you see, it does matter. If poliovirus on a scalpel contaminated otherwise unaffected tissue samples, the wrong inference could be made." He surveyed the row of doctors. "Same goes for contamination by an autopsist not wearing a mask."

"Do you think you might have polio?" Dr. Morgan scoffed.

"Have we proven that is impossible? Gentlemen, when it comes to polio, we have proven essentially nothing." He paced now, his irritation growing. "Flexner's work was sloppy, but we didn't question it, because Flexner was the top man. All those years, wasted, because of an early wrong turn."

The chief leaned into the microphone. "How do you know that they were wasted?"

"Where is the body?" Dr. Sabin burst out. "Robbie! Go find it!"

Robbie trotted off.

Begrudgingly, Dr. Sabin returned his attention to the gallery above him and, scowling, took down his mask. "So far, in all of the sterile retrieval procedures that Dr. Ward and I have conducted, we've found that poliovirus in the nasal olfactory bulb is nonexistent. It's just not there."

"So you are saying that Simon Flexner was wrong," said Dr. Morgan.

"In a nutshell—yes."

"But how does the virus get to the nervous system to cause paralysis? What's the path?"

"Here's the interesting thing." Dr. Sabin paused as if reluctant to share this information. "The poliovirus may not be readily found in the digestive tissue of rhesus monkeys, but it *is* found in humans."

Dorothy sat back. It didn't make sense. Polio was a disease of the nervous system, paralyzing its victims, sometimes to the point that they couldn't breathe, like the poor child who they would be autopsying. Already other scientists were reporting finding the poliovirus in human stools. Was he saying the virus didn't just pass through the digestive system but grew in it? How'd it get there? How did it paralyze kids from there?

Robbie pushed into the operating room. "There's been a holdup on the release of the body."

Dr. Sabin flung up his hands. "That can't be. I have all the paperwork."

"The mother is refusing."

"Does she not know that this is for the benefit of science?" he exclaimed, as if that were everyone's main motivation in life.

"There are some nurses talking to her, but they can't bring her around."

"Do something!" he cried.

His ideas burned through Dorothy like a gulp of whiskey. To pull herself away now was painful, but someone had to help.

She made her way past trousered legs. "Excuse me. Excuse me." Dr. Morgan stepped aside, frowning, as she adjusted the chrome head of the microphone upward. Her voice twanged across the air: "Dr. Sabin."

He shaded his eyes. "Dr. Horstmann?"

"I know her. I know the mother. I can try to talk to her."

"Yes," said Dorothy's attending physician. "Yes, let Dorothy go."

Dr. Morgan waved her off. "Go. This is no place for a woman."

DOROTHY SAT IN THE WAITING ROOM NEXT TO THE PAtient's mother, a young woman whose delicate arms and wrists seemed to belong to a different species next to Dorothy's hardy Viking bones.

"Mrs. Brooks, I'm very sorry about your son Richard."

The woman lifted her face. Tender purple bags had swollen the woman's eyes into slits. "I remember you. You were the one who came out and told me he was gone." The words floated between them: *You were the one who lost him.*

"Is Mr. Brooks here?"

The woman plucked at the wilted flounces at her throat. "There is no Mr. Brooks. He died of a bleeding ulcer last year."

Dorothy had only meant that she didn't want the woman to be alone, and now she was making it worse. "Is there anyone who can be with you?"

"My sister Carolyn. But I sent her to find a lawyer." The woman swung her head back and forth on the thin stalk of her neck, her soft brown ringlets rolling along with it. "I know I signed papers, but I changed my mind. I can't do this to Richie." She swallowed audibly. "I'm his mother. Doesn't that count?"

"Yes. It does. Completely."

The mother stared at the snapshot in her hands. "I know you want him for research."

"Yes. To help others."

Mrs. Brooks's face crumpled upon itself. "Can't you just use a monkey?"

"They say that the study of man is best studied in man." Dorothy sighed. "I fear that is true."

Mrs. Brooks lowered the photo to her lap. "He had a temperature over 101 and was throwing up. He said he just wanted to go to bed. His legs and arms felt funny—he couldn't make them work right—but he just wanted to go to bed." She balled her fists, pinching the photo under her thumbs. "I wanted to take him to the hospital, but he begged me not to. He was scared of the hospital. That's where his dad died."

"I'm so sorry."

"I told Richie, okay, get some sleep. We'll see how you feel in the morning." She raised her face. "I killed him by waiting."

"You were doing your best."

"But it wasn't good enough!"

Nor was Dorothy's treatment of her son. Between her and this poor mother, the room was so thick with guilt that you could cut it into blocks.

"Do you have a child?" asked Mrs. Brooks.

Their eyes met.

"No. I wish I did." Dorothy had never told a soul that. She rarely admitted it to herself.

Mrs. Brooks touched the serrated edge of the photo. "Whenever there's been something difficult for me to do, I tell myself, you birthed a baby, Milly. If you survived the agony of giving birth, you can do anything."

Dorothy had delivered enough babies in her obstetric rotation to nod solemnly.

Mrs. Brooks saw that Dorothy knew what she meant. "But childbirth only lasts for hours. This— This is never going to end. What do I tell myself now? How am I going to keep living?"

Dorothy wouldn't look away. This woman deserved the truth. "I don't know. But you will."

They sat, the woman's suffering filling the empty waiting room.

Mrs. Brooks looked up from the snapshot. "Letting the doctors have him will help others?"

Dorothy nodded. "Yes."

"Then take my baby. Somebody's got to do *something* about this terrible disease." The woman lowered her gaze back to the photo.

Dr. Sabin wasn't the only hero.

THAT EVENING, NURSING A CUP OF SCORCHED COFFEE IN the diner across the street from the hospital, Dorothy waited as Barry fished another sugar cube from the bowl. The restaurant, hazy with tobacco smoke and steam coming from the cooking hamburgers, was filled with young associate professors with pipes and buckled briefcases, glassy-eyed medical students, and cigarette-smoking graduates with their shirtsleeves rolled up. Other than the two waitresses in white caps and aprons, and a nurse at a table with a doctor, Dorothy was the only woman in the place.

"I'm not sure what Sabin and Ward are up to, other than to attract attention." Barry splashed the cube into his cup and stirred. "Does it really matter how the poliovirus gets to the nervous system? What counts is how we treat it once it's there."

Dorothy glanced over the rim of her own cup. It mattered a lot. To beat polio, you needed to snuff out the virus in the body *before* it attacked the nervous system—it would help if you knew where in the body you were supposed to do the snuffing. How did he not immediately see this?

"At any rate, sorry you missed the production, Dot, but thanks for talking sense into that mother. There would have been no show if you hadn't tied her up until those characters got it done."

Her blood blazed. "I wasn't trying to tie her up. It was her choice to let them use her son. She wanted to make a contribution to research."

He tipped back his cup to get the last drop. "Well, thanks for taking the bullet. That sure was civilized of you."

She was about to say that her being civilized had nothing to do with it—did he not see this woman's sacrifice?—when Albert Sabin stalked into the diner.

3

Someone had put some Glenn Miller swing on the jukebox. The crowd of mostly young men raised their voices over the whine of the clarinets and plink of cheap silverware on ceramic plates. Above the cloud of beef grease and onions rising from the grill, a Kit-Cat Klock was ticking toward Dorothy's next shift, but what was the sense in going back to her apartment? She was too worked up to sleep.

Barry slumped against the high back of the booth. Wearing the open-collared plaid sports shirt that his wife had starched and ironed, and with his pumpkin-colored hair plastered down save for that recalcitrant tuft (for which she felt an affinity, seeing that her hair was nothing but recalcitrant tufts), he looked like even more of a kid than when gowned for work. "You really think you are going to prove that the olfactory pathway is not involved in polio?"

Next to Dorothy, Dr. Sabin paused with the sleeves of his immaculate pinstripe suit resting on the edge of the table. "Yes." He took a bite of hamburger.

Her gaze went to his hand holding the sandwich. A wedding band was on his finger. Figured. Everyone got married in college, if not straight out of high school. Except her. Oh, plenty of men wanted to bed her. She saw it all the time—the shorter they were, the more they wanted a crack at cutting her down to size. But no man wanted to permanently play Mary Todd to her Abraham Lincoln.

"Where do you think it enters, then?"

Dr. Sabin finished chewing, then swallowed. "Now, Barry, my paper hasn't been published yet. I'd have to kill you if I told you."

Barry's cheeks got pinker. That was supposed to be a joke, though it wasn't really. If every industry was a jungle in which only the fittest survive, the academic jungle had to be the fiercest. Everyone was fighting to be king of their turf. Sabin must think that he was sitting on a kingmaker.

"So what's your endgame?" Barry asked.

Dorothy spoke up. "He suspects that the poliovirus enters through the mouth. Which means we have to think of how it works in the body in a whole new way if we're ever going to beat it."

Dr. Sabin lowered his sandwich and turned to look at her.

"Well, good luck," said Barry. "Any man who conquers polio will be considered to be a god."

"Or woman," she said. Let Sabin stare. She was used to it. "I don't know about being a god, but they will have done something very good."

"Might as well go for being a god." Barry stood up. "Sorry to leave you two, but my wife is waiting for me, and I have"—he peered at the clock cat swishing its tail over the grill—"about six hours to prove to her and the kids that I'm still alive and then to get some sleep." He saluted and left, leaving Dorothy in the awkward position of sitting on the same side of a booth with a handsome near stranger, close enough to feel his heat as he went back to eating.

"Waiting spouses seems to be the theme of the night," he said lightly, an English accent creeping into his voice. "Robbie's seems to be keeping him on the phone. I shouldn't keep you from yours."

"Oh, I'm not married." She felt the blood vessels filling across her face. She was back in high school again, a lone telephone pole standing by the wall.

"Then do you mind if I stay here until Robbie gets back?"

"Not at all." She drank some water. Oh, yes, there was a bit of Englishness to his voice. She imagined a boyhood of nannies, pony rides, and privilege.

He slid his plate across the table and himself onto the other bench. "What makes you say we have to reconsider how poliovirus travels through the body?"

She felt her limbs relax with his distancing. "That's what you're saying, isn't it? At least that's what I thought you were saying by looking for poliovirus in the gut tissue in your autopsies."

"What makes you think the virus is in the gut tissue?"

"You said it was. What I want to know is, how do you think it got there?"

He narrowed his eyes and smiled, then picked up his sandwich.

Was this the top secret that his partner had mentioned? It would be news to the scientific world. He certainly was guarding it.

She pushed him anyhow.

"Are you thinking in terms of a vaccine?"

"A vaccine? Isn't that putting the cart before the horse?"

"I can see why you are cautious, after what happened to Dr. Brodie."

Just two years ago, researcher Maurice Brodie had injected seven thousand children and adults in New York with a vaccine containing poliovirus that had been killed by a formaldehyde solution. It was a catastrophe. Three kids were paralyzed from their shots. When Brodie died soon afterward of what was said to be a heart attack, many in the scientific community believed that, despondent from the harm he'd done, he had died at his own hand.

Dr. Sabin swallowed down his bite. "Brodie let people talk him into rushing it. I knew him—he was a good man. You shouldn't be spreading rumors about him."

"I wasn't spreading rumors about him. I just said I could see why you would be cautious about a polio vaccine."

He finished the last bit of his sandwich. "I should think that if we wanted to speak of medical advances," he said, wiping his fingers with his napkin, "it should be about penicillin. Two English gentlemen, Drs. Florey and Heatley, had success giving Fleming's drug to a forty-three-year-old policeman—"

"Yes, I know, who'd scratched his cheek while pruning roses and developed streptococcal abscesses on his face. He went septic and wasn't expected to live, so they pumped him full of penicillin." Dorothy read scientific journals, too. "He lived."

"Until he died a few days later. Still, he likely would have lived longer had they not run out of the drug before he was completely cured. Now that it's apparent that penicillin can save millions of lives, drug makers cannot prepare it for battlefield usage in Europe quickly enough. You do see how, once scaled up, penicillin will change the course of history." He drew in deeply. "Imagine how it felt to make that discovery."

She thought of the voracious streptococcus bacteria in her lab, gobbling up agar under her microscope. The little monsters would have met their match, as would staph and other bacteria. Fewer kids might die of strep throat. Fewer might succumb to a brain infection that had started as an earache, or pass away from something as simple as an infected blister on their toe, as had President Coolidge's teenaged son. Imagine not having to tell parents that you'd lost their child so nightmarishly often.

Over on the grill, hamburger patties sizzled. Dr. Sabin would be taking his leave. She took a last gulp of coffee and picked up her purse.

"Tell me about yourself," he said.

She swallowed hard. She hadn't expected that.

A new platter dropped in the jukebox; Billie Holiday crooned to the noisy restaurant. Dr. Sabin smiled. "Let me guess—you're from a farm."

She laughed in spite of herself. "I'm not."

He waggled his finger at her. "I don't believe it. There is something sweet about you—"

She wasn't sure on which level she was most insulted. Did he think she was so trifling that he could be over-familiar, or did he believe that she'd just fallen off the cabbage wagon?

He smiled. "It's just that I have spent some time in the country." Right. Those ponies and nannies. "It was a very happy time."

"Are you from New York or England or . . . ?"

He cut her off. "Where are you from, if not from a farm?"

She gripped the top of her purse. "San Francisco."

"Exotic. I have never been."

Remembered sensations passed over her: the stickiness of the lacquered wood bar on the undersides of her arms as she wolfed down a pickled egg after school. The metallic squealing of the Carl Street streetcar on the rails, its trolley pole crackling with electricity. Ruby light streaming through the stained glass of a mansion window as a child hit a sour note on the piano.

She closed her mind with a shiver.

Dr. Sabin watched her. "Where did you train?"

She exhaled. "San Francisco City and County Hospital."

"You went to medical school in the town where you grew up."

"Yes." She looked toward the door.

"I did, too."

She was going to say too much. She made a preliminary scoot from her bench.

"I was supposed to be a dentist," he said.

She stopped, genuinely interested. "You?" She was supposed to be a piano teacher. She liked music well enough, and in high school, her steady stream of paying students was her family's only source of income after Prohibition had shut down the bar where her parents worked. She had resigned herself to a lifetime of traveling to the homes of sweet, tone-deaf, rich kids, unless some lonely

Paul Bunyan type happened to tramp through her neighborhood in search of a wife.

Then one night, she was riding home with the physician father of a student, when he'd been flagged down to make an emergency stop; a toddler had eaten a fern. As Dorothy watched him dose the limp child with syrup of ipecac, restoring the little girl, after much vomiting but in short order, to tearful, grateful parents, it occurred to her that her aspirations might be too low. How wonderful to be able to fix someone! If only someone had been able to fix her pop.

A gaze around the doctor's gilded mansion while his daughter mangled Chopin the following week further piqued her interest. All this splendor came from making people well?

On the way home, she had asked the doctor if she could watch him at work sometime. He'd raised bushy brows over his round horn-rimmed glasses. Maybe he thought she'd think better of it once she'd seen him set a compound fracture. Maybe he felt sorry for Henry Horstmann's hulking daughter. Who knows—maybe he liked the idea of his own Mozart-murdering daughter making such a wild request someday. For whatever reason, he agreed. He let Dorothy follow him on his rounds at the hospital for a week. This did not exactly delight the other doctors.

It was when she witnessed a sixteen-year-old boy, locked in a fetal position and unconscious with meningitis on a Wednesday, and, after having been given an experimental course of the sulfa drug, awaken, uncurl, and smile at his mother on Thursday, that she had set her cap for medical school. *She* would work such miracles. She saw no reason why a woman couldn't. Her mother and she ran their household. Becoming a doctor in charge of others' well-being seemed to be the most natural progression in the world. Thank goodness she'd been so naïve.

"My uncle wanted me to join his practice in New York City," Sabin was saying. "But I found out in dental school that I hated working on teeth and quit. He disowned me."

"What did you do then?"

"Got my MD, trained at Bellevue Hospital, then eventually sweet-talked my way into the Rockefeller Institute to do research. I was a bit of a hard sell. I can be . . . me."

She believed it. But he'd gotten himself into the Rockefeller Institute, hard sell or not. Money will do that. She mentally pinched herself. *Do not envy him. You are what you are. Deal with it.*

"I've not been to New York yet," she said with a chuckle, as if it were amazing that she still had not made it there. Truth was, Nashville was the only city to which she'd ever been beside Spokane, where she'd been born, and San Francisco, where she grew up. She aimed to correct that someday.

"Oh, it's a tremendous town. I could show you around. Broadway, the Metropolitan Opera, Oscar's for a drink in the Waldorf, that new Rockefeller Center . . ."

Show her around! The man was married. She wasn't letting him show her around anything. But there was something that she'd always been curious about, as silly as it was.

"Have you ever been to a ticker tape parade?"

His face lit up. "They're a marvel. The honoree, the motorcade, the cheering crowd, even the skyscrapers—everything's obscured in a blizzard of paper." His English accent faded as his enthusiasm grew. "The noise of the sirens and the cheering and the ships blowing their horns on the rivers is deafening. You've never heard anything so loud. Can you imagine how it would feel to be the focus of all that adulation?"

Horrifying, she thought. "You can tell me about it after they throw you one for discovering the vaccine for polio."

He went still. She sensed it was important for her to not smile.

His eyes on hers, he leaned forward as if retrieving something he'd dropped under the table or straightening his trouser cuff. "I was at Lindbergh's parade, and at the one for the woman who swam the English Channel, Gertrude What's-her-name." He righted himself. "I went to Amelia Earhart's, and Admiral Byrd's when he got back from the Antarctic. All that confetti!"

He reached across the table and touched her hair. He left his fingers there for a long moment, almost a caress. Was it a caress?

"Why, I think you have a piece of it in your hair." A bit of white paper rested on his palm.

She patted the top of her head. "Now where'd I get that?"

"The parade they gave for you."

He got it from the floor. What a terrible pickup line. "I'm a mess, shedding confetti!"

"You are perfect."

Her heart sank. So that's who he was. Another vanquisher.

But before she could make a getaway, he began telling her about his life in New York. He told her about his fourth-floor walk-up apartment on Bleecker Street when he was a lowly medical student, about his wild times at the New York Department of Public Health, when he and his pal had to talk fearful tenement residents, foreigners, mostly, into bringing out their sick children so they could help them.

She forgot her need to flee. Sometimes his suave mid-Atlantic society lockjaw speech slipped into a little Edward G. Robinson Brooklynese. At other times, the English accent made an appearance, only to be hijacked by an Eastern European pronunciation. Had he picked up that accent from working in the tenements? She was an expert on accents. She'd banished any traces of her German one by high school but was still working on her grammar. Speech will give you away quicker than anything.

"When Will Brebner and I—"

She snapped to attention. "Will Brebner? Not the same William Brebner who—"

"—died after being bitten by a lab monkey while researching the poliomyelitis virus? Yes. He was talking to me when the monkey bit him."

"Oh, no. I'm so sorry."

Their waitress came over to ask if they wanted pie. He waved her off before Dorothy could say if she wanted some.

"Brebner was a great scientist. A great friend. Like me, he'd been inspired by the book *Microbe Hunters*. We called ourselves the 'Disease Detectives.' Corny, isn't it?"

"No, not at all. I love that part of medicine."

"We were going to solve the case of polio." Dr. Sabin glanced around the restaurant, loud with male voices and the clink of cutlery. "Now it's just me."

What did she say to that? "It's good of you to carry on for him."

"Oh, there's nothing good about me." He spoke quietly. "He yelped when the monkey bit him. By the time I fetched the iodine and he was painting his wound, he was joking about the creature mistaking his fingers for bananas. It got him here." He tapped between his ring and middle fingers.

Her gaze went again to his wedding band.

"I told him to go to the clinic. He wouldn't. He said no, he was fine, and he went back to his work."

The shirtsleeved grad students at the table next to them got up. Dr. Sabin waited until they had scuffed out before continuing.

"The bite marks seemed to be healing. Then, three days later, the site began to redden and swell. A nasty pink streak went up his arm. When he developed a fever, he checked himself into the Third Surgical Service at Bellevue, where they injected him with tetanus antitoxin and he improved. After another three days, we were sure he was over the hump. His sweet young bride even baked us a cake to celebrate. Strawberry."

Dorothy winced.

"He woke up the next day in severe pain from the waist down. He couldn't urinate. He had no reflexes in his legs nor in his abdomen. He insisted that we give him antibody serum, but it didn't matter. The next day he lost use of his lower limbs. He began hiccuping uncontrollably, and then he couldn't breathe. We rushed him into an iron lung, the very device into which he'd committed the sickest of his own patients."

The mechanical whoosh of an iron lung seemed to well up over the noise of the busy restaurant.

"For five hours, I stayed and watched Bill Brebner die, through the seizures, through the foaming at the mouth, through the death rattle. He was twenty-nine years old. I was twenty-six."

"I'm so sorry."

"You know what still haunts me? All I could think those five hours during which my best friend was dying was, this isn't polio. The symptoms aren't quite right. He has something else." He rubbed his mouth, clearly agitated. "What is wrong with me?"

"You're a scientist."

He smiled slightly. "I figured out that Bill had a brand-new virus—the first herpes virus known to cross over from animals to man. I called it B virus, after Brebner. As if that were enough."

"The world is better for the knowledge."

"Bill Brebner isn't."

Plates clattered in the kitchen. He wouldn't let her look away. "I sat in on his autopsy. My best friend's autopsy. I saw them take him apart. And here's the thing—I learned from it. I had to be a cold son of a bitch, but I learned from it. I'd sit in on it again in a minute." He lifted his chin in his maddening, bullish way. "Stick with clinical medicine. You have to be heartless to get anywhere in research."

"What if I am heartless?"

"You? Heartless? I don't think so."

A smile grew on his face as she stared back. She didn't return it. "I'm tired of polio robbing the Mrs. Brookses of the world of their Richies."

"What?"

"I'm saying that if I have to be heartless, I will be."

"I don't think you know what that entails."

The diner door swung open with a jingle. Dorothy jumped, her heart thumping.

Robbie Ward powered over to the table like a gridiron star with the ball. "Sorry! Emergency at home! My kid's pony was in a show, and I had to hear all about it."

"Go!" said Dorothy. "You gentlemen better get on the road with all those specimens."

Dr. Sabin took no urging. He was up and reaching into his suitcoat. "If you're ever in Cincinnati and would like to see my lab, here's my card.

"You've got a mind for research," he said when she took it. "The jury's still out about your heart." He fitted his hat onto his head, then spread his arm for her to lead the way.

She glanced down as she passed his side of the booth. There, by the leg, she saw a white paper napkin. A corner had been torn from it, the size of the confetti.

4

CINCINNATI, OHIO, 1941

Who wants a unicorn? Apparently, no one. In the past two months, all the other residents Dorothy knew, both at Vanderbilt and from her medical school days, had gotten job offers or fellowships for when their residencies ended. Even Barry had been called, to Baylor, his papa's alma mater. Dorothy's papa's alma mater was the school of tough knocks.

She would not think about this now. She was out for a Sunday morning hike in the leafy Cincinnati neighborhood of Walnut Hills, killing time before her bus left for Nashville, having come to town the previous evening for the wedding of one of her favorite nurses at the hospital. She stalked vigorously past lawns that smelled of maple trees and mown grass—she had no idea how to stroll—until she found herself at the Church of the Advent, where the wedding had been held. The sanctuary windows were by Tiffany, she'd been told. They must be stunning in the morning light.

She stood outside the stone building, angling to get a better view as organ music and endearingly inharmonious singing swelled through the open door. It seemed that she could actually feel the togetherness of the people gathered within—and her own terrible apartness.

She stepped inside the narthex, devoid of greeters now that the service had started, and was enveloped within the calming smell of candle wax, hymnals, and perfumed and pomaded humans. By the time the Gloria Patri was sung, she'd found a seat. By the scripture readings, her pewmates had forgotten the strange giantess among them. By the sermon, she was free to contemplate the windows.

Light shone through her favorite, that of the little boy Jesus and his gentle earthly dad working companionably on some carpentry. The jewel tones streaming from the glass, the familiar church scents, and the docile congregation around her softened the edges of time: she was a small child again, leaning on her papa as the minister droned on, her cheek against the rough wool sleeve of his coat as she played with the blond hair on the back of his hand. Love swelled so quickly in her chest that it hurt.

The rattle of a menthol throat lozenge against teeth jolted her back to the present. Behind her, someone was sucking hell-for-leather on a Vicks.

"In decades past," the minister was saying at his pulpit, "there have been pogroms in Poland. The last one"—the minister, a small shiny man in a big black robe, referred to his notes—"was just in 1906, in the city of Bialystok, when hundreds of our Jewish brethren were killed or wounded. Now, under Hitler's occupation, the terror has begun again. At this very moment, Jewish families in Poland are being ripped from their homes and herded into a camp called Auschwitz. Even as we are awaiting our breakfasts, mothers, fathers, and children are being forced into boxcars at the point of a gun."

The minister took off his wire-rimmed glasses. "Picture our correspondent, one Father Kolbe, a Catholic priest in Poland. He is sitting at his amateur radio in the cellar of his monastery near Warsaw, sending out Morse code. Father Kolbe knows full well that if he is caught sending messages, he will die. And if he dies, who is to spread the word about these desperate people?"

The minister hooked his glasses back over his ears, then leaned on his pulpit to look over his flock. "But we have received Father Kolbe's message. Here, in faraway Cincinnati, his little taps have been heard. What seems inconsequential, just a smattering of dots and dashes, can save people's lives. Father Kolbe is doing his part. Now we must figure out ours."

Except for someone's soft snores echoing from the vaulted ceiling, and the lozenge-rattler, the church was silent.

"Let us pray."

Afterward, on the church steps, someone muttered, "Dirty Krauts!"

The words shot like blow-darts under Dorothy's skin, where they released their terrible poison. Even as churchgoers greeted one another, she was five years old again and in a shoe store in downtown Spokane, holding her mother's hand. Mutter was haltingly speaking in the English that Dorothy was learning in school.

"Please, sir, may I have size seven of der shoe?"

Mutter held up the model in question.

The shop man recoiled from her. "'*Der* shoe? *Der* shoe? Out, you dirty Krauts! Come back when you learn to speak English!"

"You are tall!"

Dorothy blinked away the past. Next to her, a tiny cricket of a man was holding on to his straw hat to gaze up at her. In a voice rusty with age, he croaked, "How tall are you?"

Dorothy shifted her purse on her arm. "Too tall, I'm guessing."

She could feel the usual stares gathering upon her back as she loped from the churchyard and out to the sidewalk. She kept going, to her hotel, to—what? Go sit on her bed and wallow in her loneliness?

She took off her white gloves to dig in her handbag. A car rumbled by, tossing her skirt against her nylons in its gritty wake.

He'd said to come see him if she was ever in Cincinnati. As badly as she needed a job, she hadn't planned to. Even though Cincinnati Children's was becoming known for polio research, and oh, how she yearned to boot that bastard polio in the rear, she'd steered clear of that hospital and its pediatric chief. She was good at reading people. You got that way with a father like Pop, and she could not shake the sense that Sabin wasn't leveling with her. Confession of his heartlessness aside, there was something that he was withholding, something that she sensed would trip her up. Was she heartless enough—what baloney!

Yet here she was, stirring through her nest of handkerchiefs, lipstick tubes, and bobby pins. Well, she probably needn't worry about seeing him. Who would be in a lab on a Sunday?

She found his card.

A BLURRED FIGURE MOVED ON THE OTHER SIDE OF THE frosted glass door. He must be as compulsive about working as she was. She grasped the doorknob and pushed into a miasma of Bunsen burner fumes and formaldehyde.

Dr. Sabin pulled back from where he sat next to a young woman looking into a microscope, her face hidden by a swoop of shiny blond hair that had escaped her lab cap. The woman bolted upright. Dorothy stared at the woman's shoulder. Had Dr. Sabin's hand been upon it?

"Miss Horstmann?" Dr. Sabin stood, a genuine smile broadening across his face. "Is it really you?"

She considered reminding him that she was an MD. "I'm afraid so."

"What has it been, two months? What brings you to Cincinnati?"

"A wedding."

"Well, well. I'm glad you looked me up. Barbara," he said to the woman, "this is Miss Horstmann. She's a resident at Vanderbilt. I apologize—it's Dr. Horstmann, isn't it?"

The woman, pretty and young, younger than Dorothy, and

definitely not as big of a galoot, shook back her errant swoop of hair and put out her rubber-gloved hand—before snatching it back with an attractive laugh. "I'm sorry. You do not want to shake my hand, even with your dress gloves on. This particular strain of polio is a monster."

"Barbara prepares the tissues from my autopsies," said Dr. Sabin.

A tendril of interest unfurled. "Are you still conducting your procedures?"

"Yes. Until the end of the polio season. As a matter of fact, I've just gotten a call today to come do another one in Cleveland—they're having quite an epidemic. Ninety-seven acute flaccid cases, six deaths already. It will be my second autopsy there this weekend. I'm leaving as soon as Robbie gets here." He turned to Barbara. "You might finish rinsing the rest of the tissue that's in the cooler. You really should wear a mask, you know. I don't like this strain, even between slides."

"Yes, sir." Barbara's voice was rich with affection. "As miraculous as Dr. Sabin's studies are," she said to Dorothy, "it might be a bigger miracle that I'm here to tell the tale."

"The strain is that dangerous?" Dorothy asked.

"Oh, it's plenty bad, but the wild ride from here to Cleveland is worse." Barbara grinned at him. "Dr. Sabin is such a Mr. Toad behind the wheel."

Dr. Sabin's smile stiffened. "Toad?"

"From Toad Hall, racing around in your car. Mr. Toad was always my favorite when I was a child."

His voice grew cold and British. "I must drive fast. I have to get to the body."

Dorothy watched with interest. He was offended. He had no idea who Mr. Toad was. She herself hadn't exactly had the kind of childhood where she sat on her mother's lap being read to. Sitting on the bar while her mother washed glasses and avoided men was more like it. But she'd gotten her undergraduate degree in English to help with her communication skills before she'd applied to medical school, and taken a class on children's literature, so she was familiar with *The Wind in the Willows*.

"The insane car ride is worth it," Barbara said in a soothing voice. "Your autopsies are like no other. He never uses the same instrument twice," she told Dorothy. "When he opens his bag to set up, he looks like a scalpel peddler."

"And would you buy?" he asked.

"One of each, sir, I assure you."

He crossed his arms. "Put on your mask." He turned to Dorothy. "Would you like to go with Robbie and me today?"

Barbara opened her mouth, then closed it quickly.

"Barbara should go," said Dorothy. "She must know exactly what to do, having gone before."

She was eyeing the door to make an exit when it swung open. In bounced an older woman with an impressive bouffant. She let her glasses fall to her chest from their chain. "Dr. Sabin, you have a phone call."

"Tell them to wait. Dr. Horstmann, I think you'll find the procedure to be unique."

The woman would not move. "It's Dr. Larry Anderson at the Mayo Clinic."

"Tell him I will call him."

The woman stood her ground. "He says it's urgent. Also, Mrs. Sabin has been calling. She wanted to remind you of dinner tonight with a Dr. and Mrs. Salk."

Dr. Sabin pointed at Dorothy on his way out. "Go with me to the procedure." He paused. "Unless you don't feel heartless enough."

He was gone before she could answer.

Barbara tied on a mask and returned to her microscope, clearly done with talking.

Dorothy didn't know whether to stay or go. "How is it, working with Dr. Sabin?"

Barbara rolled her gaze up over the gauze of her mask.

"He seems to be very . . . driven."

"It takes a lot of drive to beat polio," Barbara said staunchly.

Dorothy's heart softened. The poor woman must be in love with him. "Don't get me wrong. Getting a handle on polio is a worthy motivation. It motivates me! But there's something else about him. It's like there's a devil knocking at his door." She saw that she was offending her. She lightened her tone. "I can just imagine him behind the wheel. He must be a terror."

"They all drive too fast to postmortems. You should see Dr. Ward."

"Oh? Have you been to many postmortems with them?"

Barbara resisted only for a moment. "Yes. Most of them."

"And you're just a technician." She felt Barbara bristle. "I'm sorry. I didn't mean 'just.' You are the wheels that carry the train. It's only that technicians don't usually go to autopsies."

"I plan to go to medical school."

"Do you? Good! Don't give up. It won't be easy."

"Dr. Sabin is giving me a recommendation."

As if that would be all it took for her to get in. Maybe it was, if you were smart, came from a good family, and had the head of the department's eye. So be it. You had to use whatever you had.

Robbie Ward shoved open the lab door as if he were a quarterback muscling through tacklers on the field. "Say, Dorothy Horstmann! I ran into Dr. Sabin in the hall. I hear you're taking a joyride with us."

"Actually, I'm not sure—"

"Oh, you're going. Sabin said so."

"But I didn't—"

"Get used to doing what he says. It's a whole lot easier once you do."

5

Steering a cocktail tray, Dr. Sabin's wife, curvaceous, porcelain skinned, and cheery, was making her way through the haze of cigarette smoke and Tabu in her living room, her full skirt brushing against the furniture. Her lovely smile as unwavering as a doll's, she seemed to be purposely avoiding her husband, who was leaning into his research assistant, Barbara. He could have been just trying to raise his voice over the Bing Crosby record crooning from the console. The pair could have been just discussing their findings in the lab. But judging by how studiously Mrs. Sabin was avoiding them, it appeared to Dorothy that his wife believed neither.

What an awkward party! A giraffe among zebras, she was used to sticking out in couples situations. She was no stranger to nibbling barbecue cocktail franks from toothpicks alone. But this was worse. This time, the host was actively peeved at her, and she'd run out of smiles to bring him around.

If only she hadn't agreed to go to the autopsy. She should have gone straight back to Nashville, but no, she was stuck now with taking the first bus in the morning. Not that the procedure itself hadn't been interesting. His method of keeping each tissue sample pristine was bizarrely efficient. But the drive back to Cincinnati had been unbearable.

They hadn't reached the Cleveland city limits when Dr. Sabin, still grinning from wowing a group of doctors with his genius, had turned around to where she was weathering the blasts of the furnace that was the backseat of Robbie's open convertible on a summer afternoon. "What'd you think?"

She'd held down her flapping silk headscarf. "About the autopsy? What did *you* think?"

She caught Robbie's glance in the rearview mirror.

"I think that I collected another piece of evidence to bolster my case," Dr. Sabin said. "And that the doctors from Case Western are second-rate."

Robbie shot a frown across the open front seat. "Why do you say that, boss?"

Before he could answer, Dorothy said, "When we visited the polio ward, I saw one of them being remarkably kind to a former patient. A teenaged boy had come back to find a girl he'd met while they were in iron lungs. The boy had even brought a rose—he had no idea that the girl had died."

Dr. Sabin gave her a wry smile. "We have nurses for that."

She tried to keep her face pleasant.

"I see you don't approve," Dr. Sabin said. "But if your strength is in research, you can't waste your time doing what others can do."

"Showing compassion is never a waste."

He shook his head with a smile. "I knew you weren't heartless enough for research. A good researcher has to bend every ounce of his concentration to the problem at hand."

She gripped her scarf, in its own battle with the wind. "Isn't there a difference between being heartless and being single-minded?"

Robbie rounded his eyes in the mirror.

Dr. Sabin turned around to face the front.

The convertible flew past cornfields. At a four-way stop marked with a grocery store that was part of a white clapboard house, Dr. Sabin turned back to her again. "Perhaps I might regret this, but I'd like you to join my team."

In the mirror, Robbie mouthed, *What?*

When she didn't immediately respond, Dr. Sabin said, "Unless you've taken another position after your residency."

She hadn't, and she was desperate. But still, something about him just wasn't on the level. And she did not like his cozy relationship with his lab technician, although it was hardly a shock—just ask any single nurse. Yet what other choice did she have? And she burned to beat polio. She was sick of facing the disease with quarantining as their only weapon. She might as well be a plague doctor, making her rounds wearing a beak full of dried rose petals and herbs.

"It seems as if you are having a difficult time in deciding. I shall help you with that. Never mind. I rescind the offer." He turned around with a squeak of seat springs, then ignored her for the rest of the way to Cincinnati. He'd not yet thawed, even after dumping her at his house before running back to the lab and then returning home in time for dinner.

Now Mrs. Sabin asked, "Frozen daiquiri?"

Dorothy took a cocktail from Mrs. Sabin's tray. "Thanks." She put the glass to her mouth. Just the scent of the rum in it sent her back to her youth, and to the sight of her mother pouring a drink for a customer while her gentle pop dwarfed the jingling crate of beer that he was carrying into the bar.

A young couple stepped over. "May I?"

A dirty cotton smell trailed from the husband's rumpled seersucker suit as the young man took a glass. He had the look of many of the research fellows Dorothy knew: baby-faced, half-starved, eager. This one seemed to have a few too many teeth for his mouth, despite the wideness of his grin. He had a pretty wife, though, sleek and elegant and almost a head taller than he was (instantly endearing her to Dorothy) and as alert as he was giddy. The pair looked to be in their mid-twenties, at most. Sabin was probably the only person at this dinner party over thirty, though Dorothy would get there next week.

"Goodness, these are delicious!" The husband sipped his drink as his wife took one, wafting perfume—the source of the Tabu. "What did you say it was called?"

Beneath her smile, Mrs. Sabin clenched her jaw as if determined not to look at her husband, still over by the phonograph with Barbara. "A frozen daiquiri. You blend them in a Waring. I had one at the Stork Club in New York and was determined to recreate it."

"The Stork Club!" the husband whistled. "That's some place!"

From the way the wife fixed her gaze on him over her cocktail glass, it was apparent that he'd never been there.

"I've just been there the once," Mrs. Sabin said. "Joan Crawford walked by our table."

"Joan Crawford!" The wife laughed. "I've always wanted to know—are her eyebrows drawn on or are they real?"

"I don't know. I wasn't able to get a good enough look. At that moment, Albert was pointing out the many flaws in our hosts' latest publication." She started to say more, then stopped.

"Sylvia, are you talking about your bad boy again?" His wife on his arm, Robbie Ward sauntered up, all charming smile, his spit of hair freshly combed back from the surrounding scalp. Robbie was a nice man. A real get-along guy, Dorothy could see after spending the day with him. No wonder Sabin hired him. Even if Robbie would ever make a discovery, Dr. Sabin could push him aside and take credit. It was done all the time—senior scientists claiming the work of their juniors, putting their name on something simply because it came from their lab.

"Dr. and Mrs. Ward, and Dr. Horstmann, have you met Dr.

Salk?" Mrs. Sabin asked as Robbie helped himself to a drink. "And this is his wife, Donna."

"I've been an admirer of your boss for years," Dr. Salk told Robbie. "I met him at Woods Hole, at the marine biological lab."

Mrs. Ward asked Mrs. Salk, "What brings you this way?"

"Jonas is considering a fellowship at the University of Michigan after he finishes his internship at Mount Sinai."

Dorothy gazed at the glass shepherdess figurine on the mantelpiece. The University of Michigan had turned her down for both a fellowship and a staff position, another reminder of her folly in not accepting Dr. Sabin's offer.

"They paid for us to take a scenic trip across the country for his interview," said Mrs. Salk. "Can you believe that Jonas had never seen a cow?"

Dr. Salk's toothy grin was apologetic. "I'm a city boy. First generation New Yorker."

"Oh, you'll have your fill of cows by the time you leave Ohio," said Mrs. Ward.

The young doctor and Robbie launched into a discussion about the internal medicine program at Michigan, both trying to outdo the other in their praise of the director who had rejected Dorothy. Across the room, Barbara Johnson turned away from Dr. Sabin. He took her by the shoulder to turn her back to him.

Mrs. Sabin saw them, too. She lifted her tray to Mrs. Ward. "Drink?"

"No, thanks, Sylvia. I guess Robbie hasn't shared the news." Mrs. Ward's face went red. "I'm expecting again."

There was a ringing pause.

Mrs. Sabin was the first to break it. "Again? Why, that's wonderful! When?"

Dorothy recognized the brittle brightness in her hostess's voice, and Mrs. Ward's blush. It must be common knowledge that Mrs. Sabin couldn't have children.

AT DINNER, ROBBIE HANDED THE ROLL BASKET TO DONNA Salk. "Where'd you say that you met old man Sabin?" he asked her husband.

Dr. Salk took a roll, then swiped at his face, a relief to Dorothy, who'd been watching a noodle scrap dangle from his chin. "Woods Hole." The noodle survived. "On Cape Cod. The marine biological lab."

"Yes, yes," said Dr. Sabin. "Back in—when was that?"

"1938." The noodle jiggled. "I was just entering my last year of medical school—twenty-three."

"You started your last year of medical school at twenty-three?" Robbie exclaimed. "When did you enter high school?"

"At thirteen. I skipped three grades." Dr. Salk's wife pointed to her own chin. He wiped at the noodle successfully. "Dr. Sabin was at the Rockefeller Institute, I remember. I could tell that he was a genius." He giggled. "I wanted to be you," he told Dr. Sabin.

Robbie took another helping of stroganoff. "You sure about that?"

Everyone except Mrs. Sabin and Barbara Johnson chuckled. Her blond wing obscuring her face, Barbara was pushing a forkful of stroganoff toward her broccoli. She had been distracted throughout the meal, not speaking when spoken to, mindlessly passing serving dishes, laughing too late at a joke. Something was up with her.

"What were you doing at sixteen, Dorothy?" asked Mrs. Ward.

Dorothy paused in her chase of cucumber slices around the salad bowl with some teakwood paddles. "Giving piano lessons."

Nobody spoke. After a moment, Mrs. Ward said, "That's sweet."

"Jonas and I met at Woods Hole in 1938, too," said Mrs. Salk.

"Yes," her husband said with his goofy grin, "but I didn't want to be *you*!"

Mrs. Salk smiled tolerantly as the men laughed. "You certainly fought my father hard to get me."

"True." Dr. Salk took a gulp of water. "Her father didn't want a poor guy like me marrying his pride and joy. He's a big dentist in New York, and I was just a schmuck who was the first in my family to get a college degree. Her father only agreed to our marriage after I finished medical school—it was 'Dr. Salk' on our wedding invitations or no deal. He also insisted that I come up with a middle name for myself for the invitation."

"'Edward,'" said his wife.

"Like an English king." Dr. Salk laughed good-naturedly.

Robbie dug into his food. "You didn't have a middle name?"

"Not an English one." He shrugged. "I didn't sound American enough to my father-in-law. I guess no goyish middle name marks you as a Jewish immigrant. I don't mind being considered a 'new man'—I'm kind of proud of it—but evidently my father-in-law does."

Dr. Sabin leveled a hostile stare at him from the head of the table.

Mrs. Ward said, "Sylvia told me this house was on the Underground Railroad."

Mrs. Salk exclaimed favorably. Barbara looked up.

"That's what they say." Dr. Sabin pushed a chunk of meat into his noodles. "Runaways would travel from the river to the stream at the bottom of our back woods. We're only a mile from the Ohio."

Mrs. Ward shook her head. "Just think of the terror and the bravery that played out right here on this spot!"

"Sometimes, when I'm alone at night, I can feel the trauma in the air. I believe it leaves its mark on a place." Mrs. Sabin glanced at her husband. "But maybe it's not from that."

Her shining hair swaying, Barbara Johnson scraped her chair against the carpet and stood. "Excuse me."

Everyone watched as she hurried from the room. Dorothy had the uncomfortable thought that the woman was pregnant.

In a firm voice, Mrs. Sabin asked, "Do you have any scholarly papers on the horizon, Dr. Salk?"

Startlement, then pleasure, then chagrin flipped across the young man's eager face. "I have one. I know, I know—Dr. Sabin already had a slew of papers under his belt at my age."

"Four," Dr. Sabin said, "if you are twenty-six."

"I'm twenty-eight and I have two under mine," said Robbie. "Well, one and a half." He looked at Dorothy. "You?"

"I just want a job," she said.

Dr. Salk and Robbie laughed. They couldn't imagine that she wasn't joking.

Dr. Salk stabbed a chunk of meat. "What do you think of the work that Drs. Paul and Trask are doing on polio?"

"Albert," said Mrs. Sabin, "weren't they the men from Yale who went with us to the Stork Club?'

Robbie reached for the basket of dinner rolls. "Trask and Paul have quite the dog and pony show, going around the country collecting sewage and dead flies wherever there's a polio outbreak. Got a bunch of kids falling ill? Call the men from Yale!"

Dorothy made a mental note: get her CV ready, and call the men from Yale.

"I understand that both are independently wealthy," Dr. Salk said over the scratching of knives on china. "They wander the alleyways with their specimen bottles as if they were still lads on their family estates, netting butterflies and gathering songbird eggs. Me, I'm trying to get as far away from sewage and flies as possible. I had my share growing up."

The Wards laughed uneasily.

Oh, what did she have to lose? Sabin already hated her. "We did that today," Dorothy said. "In Cleveland."

There was a startled pause.

"Collected sewage?" Dr. Salk grinned as if he thought she were kidding.

"As a matter of fact, yes. And flies. Will you be sharing your results with Drs. Trask and Paul?" she asked Dr. Sabin.

The ticking of the grandfather clock in the corner swelled. Robbie glanced at his boss. He burst out: "Albert and I are working on a paper about the occurrence of poliovirus in sewage."

"Very early stages," Dr. Sabin said quickly. "Earliest stages."

Robbie frowned in disagreement. "We're going to do more with the data than Trask and Paul ever dreamed of. They're just recording whether they find poliovirus in their specimens to track outbreaks. We use it to show—"

"Have you heard of Sister Kenny?" Dr. Sabin asked no one in particular. "A doctor at the Mayo Clinic, a Dr. Anderson, called today, to tell me about her."

Robbie blinked at him, frowned, then shifted gears. "'Sister'?" He slathered butter onto a roll. "Is she a nun?"

"She's a nurse from the Australian medical corps," said Dr. Sabin. "They call them sisters there. Apparently, she has come to our shores to tell us that we're treating our polio patients all wrong. She has a new method."

"Say, I've heard of her!" Dr. Salk flashed his teeth. "She was in New York recently, at my hospital. A woman, telling us doctors what to do! I'm proud to tell you that they ran her right out."

"What's her treatment?" Robbie asked.

Dr. Salk waved his fork. "No more casting patients. No more splints or casts to keep limbs or the spine from twisting. Instead, she applies hot wet wool packs to the paralyzed areas. She thinks that loosening the paralyzed muscles will cure them—can you believe that?" He looked for Dr. Sabin to second his righteous outrage before shoveling up more noodles.

"This *nurse* really thinks she can fly in the face of years of experience and upend standard treatment?" Robbie exclaimed.

The damage had already been done. "You should like that," Dorothy told Dr. Sabin. "Aren't you doing your special autopsies for that very reason?"

"What autopsies?" Dr. Salk asked.

"Dr. Sabin is testing a theory about how polio enters the body," Dorothy said.

"Oh?" Dr. Salk looked between her and Dr. Sabin. "Where does it enter? Not the nose?"

Dr. Sabin stared at her.

These men. You'd think that beating polio would be more important to them than staking out turf.

Barbara returned to the table, her face wan. Had she been vomiting?

"Jonas," Dr. Sabin asked, "who's making a splash at the Rockefeller Institute these days?"

The men played a competitive round of Who-Knows-Who before the wives turned the conversation to which sights the Salks should see between Cincinnati and Ann Arbor. Not fitting into either group, Dorothy ate another helping of stroganoff, listening as Barbara Johnson left through the kitchen without saying goodbye.

"What's wrong with Barbara?" Mrs. Ward asked.

Dr. Sabin interrupted Dr. Salk mid-sentence. "Apparently, she touched some contaminated tissue earlier this evening."

Everyone stopped talking.

"She had direct contact."

Robbie's hairline jumped. "With which type?"

"The one from Cleveland."

The two men locked stares across the table. Dorothy could feel Dr. Salk looking to her for an explanation.

In a small voice, Mrs. Ward asked, “Can you catch polio that way?”

After a long moment, Mrs. Salk folded her napkin, then put her elbows on the table to lean toward Mrs. Sabin. “Tell me more about the Underground Railroad. Do you think anyone escaped through these very rooms?”

6

NEW HAVEN, CONNECTICUT, 1941

Music from the carillon tower across campus seeped through the panes of the mullioned window—Christmas music, although it was only December 4. Sixty-six minutes ago, a frowning middle-aged woman in a tweed skirt and pearls had ushered Dorothy into this richly paneled den that smelled of cherry pipe-tobacco and books, then left her to stew.

Not yet acclimated to Easterners' custom of keeping their rooms at the temperature of the surface of Mercury when it was cold outside, Dorothy sweated within her man's camelhair topcoat (the only coat long enough to fit her). In the space of an hour, she'd gone from relief at getting this chance to interview at Yale in the nick of time, to pride (Yale!), to worry that her interviewer's late arrival signaled a poor outcome, to shame for even applying. Of course they had second thoughts. She'd been foolish to think otherwise. She knew who she was.

The typing in the antechamber stopped. She heard voices, and then a gentleman strode into the office. He dropped into the leather chair behind the desk, his professorial robe billowing. "Sorry to keep you waiting."

Dorothy sprang to her feet and offered her hand like a man would do when his superior entered the room.

The gentleman returned slowly to his feet, tipping back his head as if he'd been unblindfolded at the base of the Empire State Building. He scowled as he shook her hand. "James Blake. Sit."

She did. *Smile. Smile as if you are not Henry Horstmann's daughter.*

He sat again with a grunt. Sunlight poured through the leaded panes along with the Christmas carols, casting a shine upon black hair so flatly oiled to his narrow head that it seemed painted on. "You were expecting Dr. Paul."

"Yes."

It had been at Dr. Paul's invitation that she'd come. She'd written to him the minute she'd returned home from Cincinnati. To her amazement, he'd written back.

He'd wanted to know about her pediatric training and, specifically, her experience in treating polio patients. Her response prompted another letter in which he wanted to know her thoughts about the use of antibody serums and nasal sprays. When she'd written that she found neither to be of much value, he'd called. He explained that he felt that instead of trying to *cure* this pestilence, the wiser course was to figure out how to *control* it, and this, he said, should be done by clinicians who knew the disease best. Would she like to interview for a fellowship?

She'd leaped.

Meeting with him hadn't been easy. The members of the Yale Polio Study Unit were constantly chasing outbreaks around the country. Only after months of cancellations due to his emergency travel did they fix a date, and not a moment too soon. Her residency at Vanderbilt, already miraculously extended for six months, ran out in three weeks. Although he'd begrudgingly acknowledged that she wasn't a total disaster, Dr. Morgan had his limits.

Now Dr. Blake said, "Dr. Paul is not here."

Dorothy waited for a further explanation. *Just be quiet. Give them time, and people will tell you what you need to know, if you just keep silent. Humans don't like silence.*

Dr. Blake crossed his arms and frowned. “You are tall.”

She nodded.

“How tall are you?”

“Six foot one. May I offer you my CV?” She retrieved it from her briefcase and held it out to him.

He signaled for her to put it on the desk, then picked up an ivory-handled letter opener. “Dr. Paul was called to an influenza outbreak in New Jersey. Trask went with him. We don’t just investigate polio, you know.”

“Should I come back?”

“No.” He manipulated the letter opener between his fingers like a baton. “He said I should make the decision.”

She felt her hopes crumbling. She smiled harder.

“I hired a woman once. Three years ago.” The letter opener clattered on the polished wood. He picked it up again. “She fell in love with a student and embarrassed my department. I’m not inclined to take a chance on a woman again.”

Dorothy’s coat got hotter. She saw her chances slipping away for this job, for any job. “What if a man made a similar mistake? Would you not hire men again?”

“Pardon me?”

“Wouldn’t you just figure that the issue was with that particular man and carry on? Yet if a woman makes a mistake, it’s not forgotten for fifty years. Every other woman is suspect.”

He stopped twirling the letter opener. “I can’t say that I appreciate your attitude.”

She surely did not appreciate his. She rose. “Thank you for your time, Dr. Blake.” She remembered to add a smile.

“Sorry to waste your time. Good day.” He busied himself with some papers.

She stood over his desk. Whether he liked her or not, this was her last chance. She had no more prospects, at this late date not even San Francisco City and County, with its limited focus on research. All her training, all her self-deprivation, all her hopes of supporting her family and her promises to the children who suffered or—she winced—died, would be for nothing.

"I am sorry, too. Dr. Paul had told me about the Polio Unit's focus on prevention. I thought it an intriguing strategy, as opposed to concentrating on treatment. Your program might lend itself well in the development of a vaccine—or perhaps I've been unduly influenced by my association with Albert Sabin. Another way to prevent poliomyelitis would be to go that route."

He looked up. "You've worked with Dr. Sabin?" He retrieved her curriculum vitae and flipped through it. "I don't see it on here."

"I assisted him with one of his remarkable autopsies in Cleveland this summer."

"You know Dr. Sabin."

"Yes. Actually, I've had the pleasure of having dinner with him and other colleagues at his home and have spent some time in his lab. I'm considering Cincinnati Children's at his request." All of which was marginally true.

Dr. Blake pulled a paper from the rack on his desk, then flopped it in front of her. "This goes to print on the first of the year. Read."

> TIME Magazine. For January 4, 1942 issue.
>
> One means by which infantile paralysis is spread far & wide has been discovered. The common housefly, according to topflight poliomyelitis researcher Albert Bruce Sabin and Robert Ward of the University of Cincinnati, is a carrier of the disease. In their report on polio made last fortnight in *Science*, they told how they and Yale experts John Rodman Paul and James Bowling Trask spent the summer catching flies, a summer job that may eventually help to bring poliomyelitis under control.

> Last July and August, during polio outbreaks in rural Connecticut and Alabama, and in Cleveland and Atlanta, the doctors trapped thousands of flies in those parts. They mashed up the flies in sterile water or ether, gave it to monkeys in feedings, injections, or nose drops. Down came the monkeys with polio.

She could feel Dr. Blake's annoyance as he shifted in his chair. She dropped to the last paragraph.

> Dr. Sabin suggested that these findings may clear up the old mystery of why polio comes in the summer. And they further substantiate earlier theories that the disease comes from eating infected food.

"'Topflight polio researcher,'" Dr. Blake sneered. "As if Sabin is the spokesperson for the polio control effort. Dr. Paul and Dr. Trask have been working on the possibility of houseflies carrying polio for four years now. They've published papers on their findings in *JAMA* and *Science*, and now here Sabin swoops in and gets the national headlines. As if he's trapped a single fly."

"Actually, he has. I helped him and Dr. Ward to collect specimens this summer."

"What was he up to?" Dr. Blake's gaze sharpened behind his glasses. She'd seen that gleam before, on the faces of men at the bar when discussing schemes while Pop had washed dishes and Dorothy sat reading comics.

"I think that Dr. Sabin's interest in houseflies has to do with his study on poliovirus in digestive system tissue."

"Yes. And?"

Dr. Sabin obviously wanted to keep his work secret, but she'd figured out where he was going with it. Was it her responsibility to keep quiet about it? In fact, was keeping quiet even right? Shouldn't everyone be pooling their knowledge to work toward the same goal—beating polio? She plunged on.

"Flies carry the disease from feces harboring poliovirus, humans ingest food tainted by polio-carrying flies, and then the disease replicates in the gut. What this suggests is that poliovirus enters the body through the mouth." Suddenly, she was melting in her monstrous coat.

"I saw his paper," said Dr. Blake. "If that's the case, how does polio get from the gut to the nervous system to paralyze patients? How does it make the jump to the nerves? What's the missing link?"

"That would be the million-dollar question."

She had to get out of there and out of her terrible coat. "Thank you for your time." She turned to go.

"No. Wait."

She paused, resisting the urge to dig under her collar.

"Maybe you can bring some attention to our work in the Polio Unit. Trask and Paul may not be interested in making headlines in popular publications, but donors are. Are you interested in headlines, Miss, excuse me, Dr. Horstmann?"

"I'm interested in conquering polio, Dr. Blake. I'm interested in making a breakthrough, whatever that takes. And breakthroughs often prove to be newsworthy."

"You're right." His slick cap of hair moved as he frowned. "Perhaps you might be a fit for the Polio Unit after all."

"I should like very much to work with Dr. Paul and Dr. Trask, but if that's not possible—"

"It might be possible. Dr. Paul did recommend you highly."

It did not do to look too eager and spook him. She waited for him to make an offer.

"Would you be willing to travel?" asked Dr. Blake. "Paul and Trask never know where they will be on a given day. They go where polio goes. It's not the kind of job for a wife or a mother."

"I'm neither of those things." She pushed down a tiny pang. "Nor do I plan to be." Her heart beat harder at the thought of boarding a train rumbling at its platform or climbing stairs into the mouth of a waiting airplane. "I have always wanted to travel."

"Then I think we might have a deal. How does being a Commonwealth Fund Fellow in the Section of Preventive Medicine of the School of Medicine sound?"

"Very good, sir."

"The position starts in four weeks. January third."

She wished to fall to the ground and weep. Saved in the nick of time! She kept her voice level. "I should like that."

He offered his hand. She surreptitiously wiped her sweating hand on her coat before she took it. His hand was so soft that it seemed to dissolve into hers. It had never wrung a mop or washed glasses in its life.

Even as she shook with Dr. Blake, the urge to tell Pop *right now* broke over her. She'd be traveling, Pop! She'd be fighting polio! She was at Yale, Pop, Yale! Oh, Mutter would have to repeat it to him, over and over and over, but how Dorothy longed to see every inch of his face crinkle with glee.

"Say," Dr. Blake said, "there's a conference on poliomyelitis in progress in New York this weekend. Starts Friday—tomorrow. Would you care to go? You can be our department's ears and eyes. It's at the Waldorf."

The Waldorf Astoria? That was the lair of royalty and celebrities.

"Sabin will be there."

She would not blink. "I'm interested."

"Good. I'll have Mrs. Beasley make arrangements." He got on the phone and called her in.

"Bring us recognition, Dr. Horstmann," he said as they waited for the secretary. "But of the right kind." He picked up the letter opener again. "I fear that Sabin will get a bit of the bad kind if word ever gets out about that girl."

"That girl?"

"His lab technician. They're trying to keep it hush-hush, but things like this get out." He saw her expression. "You don't know? The poor thing contracted polio in his lab after coming in contact with the live virus. She was completely paralyzed. Put her in a wheelchair for life."

7

NEW YORK, NEW YORK, 1941

What a difference three days made! On Thursday morning, Dorothy was a reject melting in a man's wool coat. On Sunday afternoon, her recapped heels were scraping the plush maroon carpet of the stairs from the Bull & Bear restaurant in the Waldorf. True, she'd eaten the cheapest thing on the luncheon menu, Welsh rarebit, which sounded exotic but was just a kind of grilled cheese sandwich. Now her footsteps rang from the colorful mosaics on the Waldorf lobby floor as the smell of roses, courtesy of a bouquet large enough to fill a bathtub, followed her from its urn on a marble pedestal to the bank of elevator doors. She pushed the button.

Ladies glided by wearing hats that cost more than her annual income. In the past three days of the virus conference, she'd seen more furs on women than on creatures in the San Francisco Zoo. *Remain calm*, she told herself. *Act like you are used to this. This is America, where you can be whoever you say you are, if you are crazy enough and willing to work hard enough and tough enough to not look back.*

The Art Deco ladies embossed on the brass doors parted. "Floor, please," the operator asked.

Dorothy stepped into the elevator car. "Twenty-ninth" froze in her mouth. Next to the Christmas wreath on the thick polished wood paneling of the rear wall stood the real Laurence Olivier.

She was acutely aware that she'd had on her good wool dress for four days in a row now, which was fine when conferring with a group of scientists, who were oblivious to a crumpled collar or a dabbed-at catsup stain but who howled if you mistook a cross section of pancreatic tissue for gall bladder tissue on a slide. It was not fine for meeting the King of the Stage and Movie House. People claimed that the Waldorf Astoria, the tallest hotel in the world, was a vertical Beverly Hills, and it was true. Here she was in one of its elevators with Laurence Olivier.

Was he wearing mascara?

A single dark lock fell onto his famous brow. "Good evening." His voice was every bit as richly melodious as it had been when he had played a tormented Heathcliff in *Wuthering Heights*. It went right through her bones. He smiled. "You are certainly tall."

"Yes, I am."

"Hold the door, please!" a woman cried.

She was stunned to see Sylvia Sabin hurry aboard, shapely and creamy-skinned in a red wool coat.

Heat flooded Dorothy's face. Dr. Sabin had singled her out at the conference, keeping her by his side, introducing her around as if she were his protégé and they'd not had a falling out. She'd seen his type before. There would be a price.

"Twenty-ninth," Mrs. Sabin told the operator. She squinted at Dorothy. "It's Dr. Horstmann, right?"

"Floor, please," the operator asked her again.

Before Dorothy could answer, someone else breezed into the elevator car, wafting the scent of Tabu.

"Twenty-eight, please." Donna Salk, hatless, breathless, and brimming with energy uncontained by her tight peplum suit, drew back. "Sylvia? Dr.—"

"Horstmann," said Mrs. Sabin.

"—Dr. Horstmann!" Mrs. Salk patted her throat. "Why, this is old home week!"

Dorothy told the operator her floor. The car lifted in its shaft.

Mrs. Salk ignored He of the Cleft Chin, just four feet behind her. "How wonderful to see you both! Of course *you're* here, Sylvia—Albert is the star of the virus conference! And Dr.—"

"Horstmann," Mrs. Sabin said.

"Dr. Horstmann . . . well! Is everyone finding a lot to do in town?"

"I've lived here before," Mrs. Sabin said coolly.

"Oh, that's right," said Mrs. Salk. "Your husband was at the Rockefeller Institute. My father's practice was in Manhattan. Growing up, whenever we came into town to shop, Mother insisted on staying here." She sighed. "I thought I'd had my fill of the place. There's so much noise—food carts rattling in the halls, people laughing outside your door, taxis honking down on the streets at all hours. You'd think for the money, they'd put in thicker windows so you could sleep at night. Sorry," she said to the elevator operator, "I didn't mean to insult your employer." She swung back to Mrs. Sabin. "But now that we're moving to Michigan, suddenly I can't bear to leave it all."

"Your husband got the fellowship," Mrs. Sabin said.

"Yes. Jonas is thrilled. He adores Tom Francis. They're determined to develop a vaccine for influenza." Mrs. Salk addressed Dorothy with an encouraging smile. "And you're here because—?"

Behind her, Laurence Olivier cleared his throat. Even that was mellifluous.

Mrs. Salk turned to him. "You should meet this woman, Mr. Olivier."

Dorothy braced herself. How was her hair?

"Her husband is Albert Sabin."

Dorothy stifled a laugh. She'd actually thought . . . *Oh, dear, you have let this new job go to your head.*

"He's the famous polio researcher," Mrs. Salk continued. "You might have read about him in *Time* or in the newspapers."

The spotlight properly upon him, Laurence Olivier seemed to inflate. "Albert Sabin. I have met him. We both spoke at a March of Dimes fundraiser in Washington."

The elevator stopped. "Twenty-eight," said the operator.

"'Bye, Sylvia!" Mrs. Salk waved as she got off. "'Bye, Mr. Olivier! 'Bye, Dr.—"

"Horstmann," intoned Lawrence Olivier.

The door closed. Up the car rumbled.

"Is he close to getting the vaccine for polio?" asked Laurence Olivier. God's voice. He had God's voice.

"They have a ways to go," said Mrs. Sabin.

A ways? No one was giving it a lot of thought, nor could they even get started, until they figured out how poliovirus got from the gut to the nerves. But he wasn't asking Dorothy. He was asking the famous Dr. Sabin's wife.

The elevator door opened. "Twenty-ninth."

"Vivien and I wish to have a child," Laurence Olivier told Mrs. Sabin. "I could not bear to lose it to polio. We are counting on your husband, madame."

Dorothy stepped out after Mrs. Sabin. The door closed, leaving them on thick carpet woven in a medallion pattern.

Mrs. Sabin hiked her purse up her forearm. "Say, would you care to come to my room for a drink?" When Dorothy paused, she looked at her watch and laughed. "Two oh eight. I know it's early for booze, but"—her purse swayed as she spread her gloved hand—"we're in New York. It's actually late."

"I have a train to catch back to Nashville."

"Please. *Please*. Just one, if you like."

"I'LL ONLY STAY A MINUTE." DOROTHY TOOK THE CUT-GLASS tumbler from Mrs. Sabin. "I've got to finish packing. And I don't want to be in the way when Dr. Sabin returns."

"Oh, he won't be back anytime soon." Mrs. Sabin poured herself a whiskey from the bar console in her room. "Arguing with his peers is far too exciting." She came over and kicked off her shoes before dropping into the club chair next to Dorothy's. "He excelled on his debate team in high school. His teachers told him he should be a lawyer."

"I can see that."

Mrs. Sabin sipped her drink. "If he were a lawyer, he'd be one of those prosecutors who tears his foes to shreds. He takes his energy from winning. Sometimes I wonder if winning is more important to him than what he is actually fighting for."

Dorothy gazed at her over her glass. She realized now that Mrs. Sabin had enjoyed a wet lunch.

"I don't know if Albert told you I'm a photographer."

"No. He hasn't." Did the woman imagine that he talked of anything but science—and himself?

"Although Albert likes to think that I'm a singer. I was singing when we met."

"Oh."

Mrs. Sabin lifted her drink. "I remember it like it was yesterday. I was straining to hit my notes, when I noticed an intense, wavy-haired young man staring at me from the front row." She paused, her glass against her lip. "Thinking about it, he rather did look like Laurence Olivier." She drank.

"I can see that."

"Without the mascara." She drank again, then wiped her mouth with her knuckle. "He would not take his eyes from me throughout all my numbers, as if he were a hungry lion and I an innocently grazing gazelle. He made the hair stand up on my arms, yet, even as he did, something stirred in me." She lifted a shoulder. "I liked being hunted."

Dorothy rubbed her untouched drink between her hands. She really needed to get out of there.

"My husband is a hunter, Dr. Horstmann."

Dorothy looked up.

"Surely you can see that." Mrs. Sabin hoisted herself onto her stocking feet, then padded over to the window. She waved Dorothy over.

Dorothy came, thinking of gracious exit lines. She did not want to be there when Dr. Sabin arrived.

"Aren't they beautiful?"

Far below, tiny women and men streamed down the sidewalk glittering in the winter afternoon sun. New York sophisticates, all of them—what exciting lives they must lead!

"I went to the Met yesterday. To see the photography." Mrs. Sabin put her drink on the windowsill. "I was walking by the Stieglitzes, when it dawned upon me: Where are the works by women? I started looking for them, but all I saw was more stuff by Alfred Stieglitz, or by his disciples, or his enemies." She patted the pocket of her skirt until she came up with a pack of cigarettes. "They call him the 'Godfather of Modern Photography,' as if one man had invented it, when dozens of men—and *women*, I'll have you know—had brought the art along. Why does history have a way of singling out one man for all the glory?"

She flipped open a slim silver lighter and touched her cigarette to its flame. "He photographed Georgia O'Keeffe naked—did you know that?"

"Who?"

Mrs. Sabin blew out smoke. "Stieglitz. O'Keeffe is his wife. That's how she got started. People flocked to see his nude photographs of her, so when he showed her paintings in his gallery, she already had an audience of people curious about the work by the famous naked lady. She kept their interest by making her paintings as erotic in their way as Stieglitz's nude photos were of her." She drew on her cigarette. "She says her close-up paintings of flowers aren't actually vaginas, but have you seen them?" She exhaled smoke. "Those are vaginas."

Dorothy watched the miniatures down on the street. It always came back to striving and procreating. Humans weren't so very different than bacteria in that way.

A key scraped in the door. Dr. Sabin came in, face bright. He threw his key on the bureau, then his almost empty pack of Old Golds. He was undoing his tie when he saw them.

"Dr. Horstmann? What a surprise! Sylvia—were you ever going to tell me she was here?"

He strolled over to the window and kissed the back of his wife's head. She inhaled deeply, as if happy to see him, or to detect perfume.

"So, did Dorothy tell you that she took a job with Trask and Paul?"

"No. You did, Albert. Three times."

"Well, she should have gone with me," he said amicably. "You're going to wish you did when I vanquish polio," he told Dorothy.

"I just hope one of us does." Dorothy could feel Mrs. Sabin watching them as she smoked.

He tugged off his tie. "Well, may the best man win."

Mrs. Sabin picked up her drink. "You know you got the job because Albert pushed for you, don't you? He called Dr. Paul the night you had dinner at our house. How he sang your praises! He made you sound like the most indispensable thing in medicine since ether."

Dorothy couldn't move her mouth to thank him. She had gotten the fellowship on her own merit. Hadn't she?

Dr. Sabin went over and put his arm around his wife. "It sounds like Sylvia has been having a little too much fun. You'll have to excuse her."

"There's nothing to excuse," Dorothy said.

"Thank you!" Mrs. Sabin cried.

"I should be going. Thank you for the lovely conversation." Dorothy started toward the door.

"You've got to be careful what you wish for," Mrs. Sabin called after her.

She stopped, her hand on the doorknob.

"Albert championed Barbara Johnson, and look what happened to her. She's in a wheelchair now."

"Sylvia, that's enough." *Sorry*, he mouthed to Dorothy.

Dorothy's hand was still on the doorknob. "Is Miss Johnson going to be all right?"

"You tell me!" exclaimed Mrs. Sabin. "He sent her to Warm Springs." She turned on her husband. "Why did you do that? I went to see her in the hospital when I heard she got polio. But the second time I went, she was gone. The nurse said you'd sent her to Warm Springs."

"Warm Springs has the best rehabilitation care in the country," he said.

"But she was in an iron lung! She wasn't ready for rehabilitation. She was getting the care she needed in Cincinnati."

Dr. Sabin paused. "What you don't know, Sylvia, was that she was doing well. She was on a cuirass ventilator. She was ready to move on."

"Was she? Or was it that were you ready for her to move on?"

Voices sounded in the hall. A woman seemed to be upset.

"Albert, go see what it is."

"Excuse me."

Dorothy stood back as he stepped outside, leaving the door open.

"What is happening?" he asked someone.

A male voice cried, “They broke into the Giants game on the radio! The Japanese attacked Pearl Harbor!”

“Attacked?”

“Bombed! Hawaii! By air! They say our men fought back but—”

“Frank!” the woman exclaimed. “Please, I just want to go! I just want to be home with the kids.”

“Excuse my wife.”

“What if we’re next?” she cried.

“Pardon us.”

Dorothy glimpsed the pair rushing by the door with their suitcases. Sabin pulled back into the room. “Did you hear?”

Sylvia was already at the radio.

Uneasiness wormed through Dorothy’s gut as the radio warmed up and then Albert dialed through a babble of frequencies. He came to tersely delivered words.

It was true. The United States was under attack.

The announcer finished his report; symphonic music resumed. Mrs. Sabin leaned against her husband, who kissed her hair.

“I have to call my family.” Dorothy let herself out. Even as she walked down the hall, it felt like a trap door had opened beneath her. She didn’t know when or how she would feel its movement, but as surely as the bouquets in the lobby smelled of roses, the world had just changed course.

1942

A GRANDMOTHER

A mother is always a mother. It is a role that changes but gets no easier over time. No, Mrs. Horstmann did not have the same troubles as her widowed eldest daughter, Catherine, who was across the table, begging her sullen fifteen-year-old to eat his sauerkraut. Catherine worried that her Paul would sicken on a diet of meat alone, but Mrs. Horstmann knew that he would not. The boy would eat what he needed—he knew what he liked, and it was not fermented cabbage.

On the other hand, Mrs. Horstmann had a genuine worry that his mother might indeed sicken. Catherine had scarcely eaten in the three weeks since her eighteen-year-old son, Peter, had run out the door to join the Navy after Pearl Harbor was bombed and war had been declared. He was to ship off to the Pacific soon. Getting her daughter to eat was not as easy as serving something that she liked.

Mrs. Horstmann told herself to stay calm. She was successfully caring for her grown son, Bernard, Catherine's younger brother, who had been born too emotionally fragile to fit into the world without help. She had successfully brought Catherine herself to adulthood, although the girl had gotten every childhood disease and had gotten it hard, unlike Dorothy, the youngest, who came out of the womb as sturdy as a bull. Dorothy was like her father in that way. Yet look what happened to him.

Mrs. Horstmann took a breath.

She frowned at her glistening heap of sauerkraut, reminding herself that she'd successfully delivered Catherine to a husband in marriage and taken her in when her husband had died. She was helping her to raise her kids now, even if it did mean taking on more hours at the Cole Valley Bar and Grill. Whatever it took, she'd do it.

Her hand in her lap went to the letter in her apron pocket. And then there was Dorothy.

Mrs. Horstmann forced a forkful of beef, spaetzle, and her good sauerkraut into her own mouth. She let it mingle on her tongue, as if it might be choked down more easily that way. Across the table, her husband tucked into a mouthful, the sleeves of his brown sweater pushed up to reveal the grizzled curls that crept down his arms to his knuckles. She could always count on Henry to take pleasure in his food, even in these times. Sometimes she thought a weakness in the mind might be a mercy.

To look at him now, you would not know what a specimen of a man he had once been. She had taken Catherine to the picture show to see *Tarzan's Secret Treasure* last week, and the leading man, Johnny Weissmuller—bah!—was a puny creature compared to Henry Horstmann in his youth. Every girl in their village had her eye on him. He was her brother's age, four years older than she.

One day, when she was twelve and he was sixteen, she had been sent to the field by her mother with bread and cheese for the men who were mowing their wheatfield. Henry was among them, his blond hair glinting in the sun as he wielded his scythe like a god. When she handed him the basket, she saw that his beautiful face was striped with welts, a reaction to the bits of chaff needling his skin.

Seeing her expression at his temporary disfigurement, he'd pulled his shirt over his head and galumphed over to her in a hunch. "I am a monster! I'm going to catch you, little girl!"

Both of them laughing, he chased her through the mown field, where the wheat stubbles jabbed her bare feet. "Come here, Little Sister!"

She fell. When he picked her up, he saw that her feet, dangling over his arms, were bloodied.

He shrugged his shirt back onto his shoulders, his swollen face crestfallen. "Little Sister! I am sorry. What a stupid game—I did not mean to hurt you."

His long, hooded eyes were such a clear, brilliant blue, his regret so genuine, that she almost gasped with love for him.

After that, she angled to be near him whenever possible, at market, after church, though not at school—he had left at fourteen to work his family farm. He was kind to her, but only as one would be to a friend's younger sister.

At twenty, he was conscripted into the army, as was every German boy his age. When he marched out of town, singing "Muss i denn" with the boys, she'd thought that she would never see him again. So many of them did not return.

Two years later, when she was eighteen, she got a letter. He was in America, in a town called Spokane. He was working for his uncle who had a restaurant. After all this time, he could not forget her. Did she still like him?

He knew that she liked him?

If she did like him, he wrote, as soon as he found better work, he would send for her.

She did not wait.

How happy his uncle had been when she arrived unannounced at the restaurant! His delight to see her made her forget her weariness, though the voyage from Hamburg to the Great Lakes, and then the journey by train across wild lands to Spokane, had been alternately thrilling and terrifying. Henry's uncle seemed more impressed that she had all her teeth than that she'd learned some English during her travels—asking to see her teeth seemed a strange custom, but this was America. Henry's uncle called over a woman to come "show her the ropes," and Anna Horstmann was wondering why he would be so proud of ropes, when Henry appeared, carrying a barrel.

His brilliant blue eyes lit with such happiness under their long hoods that her blood rushed to her head.

They were soon married.

A baby came quickly.

The restaurant was not a restaurant.

She had another child in short order, the way you do when you cannot keep out of bed. She loved being pregnant. She loved to think how the baby got in her belly, and how the babies looked like their beautiful papa.

She was pregnant with her fifth child—let us not think now about the two babies that she'd lost in between—when Henry became ill.

One day, she'd come home from the market to find him sitting in the middle of the parlor on a footstool. They had a nice parlor, then, and a nice little house dripping with gingerbread trim. He had left Uncle Henry's restaurant and gotten a job on the railroad. He was working his way up to conductor.

He'd been on that footstool when she'd left to go to the market, which was odd enough. A big man like him perched on a little footstool? In the middle of the room? He looked like a circus bear balancing on a tiny ball. But for him to be there, doing nothing, an hour later? A chill went over her.

She asked him why he was sitting there.

He growled, "Leave me alone."

Henry never spoke to her that way.

She didn't know why the question popped in her mind: "Henry, what is my name?"

He stared at her, fear darkening those eyes as blue as the sky above the Rhine in June.

She drew back in horror as he jumped up, then galumphed through their pretty little house much like when he had played monster those many years ago. He scrambled into bed and fell unconscious. He was still out when the doctor's buggy jingled up.

"Brain fever," said the doctor. "Encephalitis. There's nothing I can give him."

"Will he live?"

"If he does, you may not know him when he wakes."

But would he know *her*? That was what mattered to her.

After three days, he woke. But his English was gone, along with the ability to concentrate long enough to do anything but the simplest tasks. He lost his job on the railroad. He went back to work in Uncle Henry's restaurant that was not a restaurant, where he shambled about the place like a grizzly without teeth.

But he did know her. And the children. And delighted in his food. And music. And in her. Oh, especially, he delighted in her.

People pitied her. They thought that "Poor Henry" caused her grief. But he didn't. His illness burned away all the layers accumulated by the rough business of living and left his core of pure love. Her darling Henry did not leave her. No, her grief came from not having the time to properly show baby Dorothy a mother's love. Busy with helping Henry to renegotiate his life while she fought to keep the household together, she'd had little chance to cuddle the child. She gave her to Henry to hold instead.

The bond took.

As soon as Dorothy could walk, she tottered after her father. While Mrs. Horstmann served beer and fried frankfurters at Uncle Henry's restaurant that was not a restaurant, Dorothy helped her papa to burn the garbage, scrape chewing gum from the sidewalk, or wash cigar smoke film from the mirror over the bar. Dorothy was right there as Henry hoisted barrels, mopped floors, and threw out the occasional smart aleck.

At first it pained Mrs. Horstmann to see her daughter skipping after her father as he did such lowly labor. But seeing how happy the two were together, she swallowed her pride and sorrow for not providing for them better, as well as—she didn't want to admit this—her jealousy of Henry for holding her youngest child's heart, and let them be. Before long, Mrs. Horstmann made it her business to think of ways the two could have fun together. She took no small pleasure in that.

As soon as she had squirreled away enough money, Mrs. Horstmann moved the family away from Uncle Henry's grip. She took them to San Francisco, "the Paris of the West," which sounded promising, then found a sliver of a house tucked in a modest row near the university, thinking rubbing shoulders with scholars would be good for the children. Perhaps she could even fix up the attic and take on a college student as a boarder; only potential husband material for Dorothy need apply. But the sole place of work that would take her, Henry, and Dorothy was another bar. And then Prohibition came.

There was a time when only Dorothy could work. Imagine that, a thirteen-year-old girl keeping her parents and mentally frail big brother afloat! Thank goodness Catherine was married, as to not burden Dorothy further. After school, Dorothy gave lessons on the piano, an instrument she'd learned to play as a little one at Uncle Henry's. She'd never complained one minute about having to miss dances or other kinds of entertainments for young people. That had grieved Mrs. Horstmann, too.

Now the Yale people wanted Dorothy. Of course they did. Who else could they get to willingly run into the fire? Going to polio outbreaks all over the country—what would keep her from getting it? She said she was safe, but Mrs. Horstmann knew better. Even their own president had gotten polio.

Mrs. Horstmann pushed her noodles with her fork, her own appetite gone. A mother is always a mother, although a child isn't always a child.

8

NEW HAVEN, CONNECTICUT, 1942

While the rest of the country prepared for war, Dorothy had prepared for January in Connecticut. She failed. She had thought it might snow but hadn't pictured a foot of it falling overnight. She had thought it would be cold but hadn't imagined a chill so deep that it seared her toes and fingers. Now she curled her aching appendages within their woolen coverings as she tramped single file between her two new colleagues, their rubber galoshes crunching on the shoveled sidewalk.

Dr. Paul's words trailed in the bitter wind like the fringe of his orange-and-black-striped scarf—Princeton's colors, she would find out later. Kids didn't learn Ivy League lore while soaping the day's special at the grill onto the barroom window.

"The typical epidemiologist deals dispassionately with large groups of people," he was saying in a plummy voice that was outsized for his small stature. "It is the multiplication of observations which give him his results. He deals with numbers and statistics. Now the *clinical* epidemiologist—"

Dr. Trask, long, taciturn, and bony within layers of scratchy tweed, projected his baritone voice from behind her. "That is Dr. Paul's term. You'll only find clinical epidemiologists here with us at Yale."

"Then that makes me one," Dorothy said as cheerfully as her frozen face would allow.

Dr. Paul, a winsome man in an elfin way, turned to look up at her past the earflaps of his winterized fedora. His cornflower-blue eyes were watering from the cold. "That's correct. Even our fellows in epidemiology are of the clinical variety."

She felt the sting of being reminded that she was only a temporary hire, though she knew he had no idea how that hurt her. She told herself that one needed to have more experience to be hired onto the faculty at Yale. She was lucky to have any job at all, let alone here.

"As I was saying," Dr. Paul continued, "we *clinical* epidemiologists start with one sick individual. We then cautiously branch out into the setting where that individual became sick—the home, the family, the workshop, the community. We aim to place the patient in the pattern in which he belongs."

Dorothy thought of her father—when he'd come down with encephalitis, had anyone tried to figure out where he'd gotten it? "The lone sick man never pops up out of nowhere," she said.

She felt a pat through the back of her coat. Behind her, Dr. Trask boomed, "Precisely."

"It's not a new concept, obviously." Dr. Paul led them up the shoveled sidewalk toward a large, nondescript building on the otherwise stately campus. "This approach was the heart and soul of traditional family practice, when the local doctor had his finger on the pulse of the community. But now that treatment has shifted away from the home and into the hospital, clinical epidemiology is only practiced by those of us who deliberately do so."

"We're old-fashioned," Dr. Trask rumbled, "in a new way."

Dorothy curled her fingers more tightly within her gloves. Being old-fashioned in whatever way rarely got headlines. When she had arrived at Dr. Paul's office that morning, the *Time* magazine with the article that had so inflamed Dr. Blake was on his desk, under the saucer of his coffee cup. Her new boss seemed to care little that alongside the "topflight" Dr. Sabin, his own name was mentioned, too.

Dr. Paul held the door for her to pass through it. Including his hat with its earflaps and small yellow feather, he was a full head shorter than she was, putting his sights at eye level with her brassiere. She was glad for her heavy coat.

"I've never liked the term 'preventive medicine,'" he said, seemingly oblivious to his view. "Dr. Blake has pinned that title to our department, but to my taste it's too boastful, too suggestive that great things might be just around the corner."

She whisked herself past him and through the door. "But don't we want to suggest that great things are just around the corner?"

He uncoiled his orange-and black scarf as Dr. Trask entered. "Even when they are, it's unseemly to brag." He smiled when he saw her raised brows. "My nanny devoted her life to passing on the tenet that members of my family must never draw attention to themselves. Attention-grabbing is for the arriviste. I suppose she succeeded."

The men kicked off their galoshes inside the foyer. Dr. Blake had granted her the fellowship in order to make a splash, but it was going to be hard to do so in this turgid pond. "Shouldn't we be proud that we are the nation's leading disease sleuths?"

"'Disease sleuths'?" Dr. Paul laughed. "Heavens, you have been around Albert Sabin too much. He's been talking nonsense about 'disease detectives' since I've met him. We are scientists. That should be good enough."

"We can't all be Albert Sabins," boomed Dr. Trask. He assembled his craggy face into a smile. "Thank goodness."

"But we are sleuths," she said, "are we not?"

"We're scientists, Dr. Horstmann," said Dr. Paul, "not vaudevillians. We're not here to capture the popular imagination or to entertain. We're here to learn."

"So that we can save people," she said.

"If you insist on putting it in a splashy manner, yes."

He led the way down the hall, the gassy laboratory smell of Bunsen burners and the acrid bite of chemicals seeping from behind frosted glass doors. The tap of shoe leather on tile accompanied them downstairs, to the underground level of the building.

"Now for our most precious learning tools." When he opened the door, a sharp latrine odor burned her nasal passages.

She put her hand to her nose and stepped into the dim room. Rows not unlike that of a library spread out before her, but unlike a library, the stacks held not books but banks of galvanized metal cages. As her eyes adjusted, she saw small black hands gripping the wire of some of the cages, and small humanoid shoulders, furred and gray, huddled within the cells. Coming from the clinical side of medicine, she hadn't worked much with lab animals. Conducting research would require it. She had not fully considered this when signing on to the study group.

A man emerged from the gloom, an infant macaque clinging to his neck. The man was short and thick, like a mighty tree still living though hewn halfway down, and so muscular that the bib of his overalls strained over his chest.

Dr. Paul patted the man's powerful chambray-bound arm. "Hello, Eugene. Did you have a good Christmas?"

"Very good, thank you. And you?" He was Black, as were the few lab animal handlers whom Dorothy had met, and radiated calm, which seemed rather a miracle for someone who spent so much time underground with doomed animals.

"Dr. Horstmann, this is Eugene, our animal handler *suprême*. We lose very few specimens in his care, which we very much appreciate, given how valuable these animals are. What is the price of a cynomolgus monkey like this one?" he asked Dr. Trask.

Trask's bellow seemed to rattle the cages. "Eight dollars apiece."

Dorothy made four dollars a day as a fellow. Lest she be jealous because of her relative value, she reminded herself that she did not give her life to research, as did these beings.

"Nice to meet you, Mr.—" She offered her hand to shake.

"Oakley." He moved to respond, which the infant monkey took as an invitation to scramble onto his head. With a hand broader than the creature itself, he eased the frightened young animal back down onto his neck as he shook hands with her.

"Careful, Eugene," said Dr. Paul. "That juvenile will get too attached to you, and then you'll have to take it home to nurse it along."

The set of the man's jaw as he glanced at Dorothy, and the protective hand cradling the monkey, told of his guilt on that count. She guessed that he had taken that baby monkey and many other baby monkeys home many other times. She wondered if her colleagues had any idea.

She thought she might like this man very much.

When the other doctors moved down the row, Dorothy reached up to touch the frightened animal. "May I?"

The baby burrowed into Eugene for protection. The infant's glossy tuft of hair, the tiny buttons of its spine ridging down its back, its twiggy leg and arm bones, swamped Dorothy with the urge to hold it. She lifted her fingers toward the creature.

It squeaked, setting off others, who set off others. Suddenly hundreds of screeches ricocheted from the cinderblock walls.

Dr. Trask's smile for her was kind. His voice carried easily over the din. "It's best not to have any contact with them beyond the business at hand."

"Let Eugene manage them," Dr. Paul said as the handler drifted away from them, soothing the animal. "You can get in trouble otherwise. Remember what happened to Bill Brebner."

"Yes, I've heard," she said.

"Sabin managed to capitalize on it. The B virus, indeed." Dr. Trask snuffled. "I'm surprised that he didn't call it the S virus."

Dr. Paul peered into a cage, then read the tag on the door. "Oh, Sabin will make advances before too long—you can be sure of it."

"Not without us, he won't." Dr. Trask looked into the cage as if to see what had gotten his colleague's attention. "He can't move forward without our studies. No matter what he thinks, he cannot solve the riddle of polio alone."

In the rear of the room, Eugene leaned against a desk, stroking the animal's small back with thumb and forefinger. This man loved the very creatures that he readied for pain. How did he settle that with himself?

She pulled herself together. "At least Dr. Sabin is asking questions. Ultimately, we all want the best, for the children, for everyone."

"Sometimes I wonder," said Dr. Paul.

THEY TRAMPED BACK TO THE SCIENCE BUILDING, WHERE they re-shucked their winter armor in the vestibule. Mrs. Beasley stopped typing and stood as they entered Dr. Paul's outer office. "Your visitor arrived early," she said briskly. She glanced at Dorothy, then lowered her eyes with a frown.

"Oh, I think you'll like this visitor," Dr. Paul said to Dorothy. "Come see."

Robbie Ward rose from his chair in Dr. Paul's mahogany-paneled sanctum.

After greetings all around, Dr. Paul said, "Dr. Ward said you two met last summer while he doing his fellowship with Dr. Sabin."

Robbie grinned at Dorothy. "Yes. We bonded over a cadaver."

"Are there chairs enough for everyone?" Dr. Paul asked. A chair short, he instructed Mrs. Beasley to bring one. She threw Dorothy a troubled look before she left.

"Sit, sit." Dr. Paul motioned to Dorothy.

She sat, reluctantly, as the men stood over her. "What is Dr. Sabin up to these days?" she asked Robbie.

"He's closing down his program in Cincinnati to take a commission in the Army, but already he's been sent to the Pacific to look into a mosquito-borne encephalitis. First thing he asked the local docs was, how do the livestock in the area do with this encephalitis? Do they get it? When the docs said no, even though mosquitoes prefer the blood of cattle over humans, what does Sabin do? Tells them to send in cows to sleep among our soldiers! Let the cows get bitten so the boys stay well."

The men laughed.

"Poor cows," Mrs. Beasley murmured as she struggled in with the extra chair.

"My wife is hoping to see you," Robbie told Dorothy as they got situated.

"There should be plenty of chance for that." Dr. Paul signaled for Mrs. Beasley to bring them coffee. "Dr. Ward will be joining the Polio Study Unit."

"You're a fellow, too?" she asked him.

Robbie glanced at Dr. Paul, who was brushing something off his bow tie.

"We need Dr. Ward more than ever. With the war"—Dr. Paul straightened his tie and looked up—"I'm afraid Uncle Sam will make demands on Dr. Trask and I, taking us away from the study unit more than ever."

"I've been called to go to Chicago in the morning," said Dr. Trask. "Some kind of unidentified fever is sweeping the training camp there."

Dr. Paul sighed, gazing toward the door for his coffee. "Polio doesn't stop for war. Next outbreak, somebody will need to answer when the call goes out for epidemiologists if James and I aren't available."

"A call that *clinical* epidemiologists will best fill," said Robbie. He shot Dorothy a playful frown.

How well Robbie knew the party line. She wondered how many interviews he'd had.

"You'll train together," said Dr. Paul, "and then, Dr. Horstmann, you can assist him. Meet our new associate professor!"

It was as if all sound had drained from the room. Dorothy could hear only the thumping of her heart.

They discussed which aspects of the poliovirus might be best studied during the winter months, before fresh epidemics were upon them in the spring. Dorothy could not fully focus. Robbie Ward was no more qualified in epidemiology than she was. And now he was her boss.

Mrs. Beasley came in with the coffee service. She poured them cups and handed them out, her yellow cashmere cardigan draping from the clasp at her neck. When she left with a swish of tweed skirt, Dr. Paul said, "Do you know she has a PhD in mathematics? A remarkable woman. Quite smart."

9

WARM SPRINGS, GEORGIA, 1942

So this was what a heat wave in late May in Middle Georgia felt like: hot, junglelike, and still, as if the steamy air took away the will to move. That afternoon, she'd seen a squirrel stretched out on a limb, belly to branch. Now, in the sticky evening, Dorothy would have liked to have stretched out, too, and not just from the heat. She'd been up since sunrise, swabbing the throats of paralyzed polio patients and their grieving families, drawing blood from terrified children, setting fly traps, collecting sewage—a typical day's work for a clinical epidemiologist. Out in the parking lot, the trunk of her university car was full of specimen vials that had clinked in metal chests of dry ice as she'd driven south from Atlanta. Now that she'd chased pockets of polio all the way down to Meriwether County, they would clink again for the ninety minutes it would take her to drive back up to Atlanta and to her blessed hotel bed. But not just yet.

Her eyes adjusted to the falling daylight as a record platter dropped onto a turntable and the dreamy purr of Glenn Miller's trumpet rose with the winking fireflies into the pines. Waiters circulated among the candlelit tables with drinks. Laughter spouted from behind her—a young woman was enjoying the attention of suitors. The scene was like that of any other country club dance,

Dorothy imagined—she'd never been to one—if a person overlooked the wheelchairs, crutches, and limb-traction apparatuses bristling from among the revelers. Here, it was as if sons on aircraft carriers weren't strafing bombers in the Pacific and brothers weren't being trained to use bayonets and grenades in Europe. Here, a different kind of war was going on.

At Dorothy's side, the director of the facility, a friendly woman whose pearl earrings, perfect chignon, and silk cowl-neck dress spoke of sophistication, shook her head with fondness as she looked out over the dance. "Isn't it something?"

"Oh, yes. Thank you for the tour. Once I realized how close I was to Warm Springs, I had to come see."

"Finest polio rehabilitation center in the world."

A tuxedoed master of ceremonies bounded onto the dance floor and grabbed the microphone from its stand. "Don't be SHY!" he puffed into it. "Grab a partner and DANCE!"

Sweating push-boys, their white shirts and trousers reminiscent of soda jerk uniforms, careened wheelchairs from the tables. Little kids on crutches hopped onto the parquet. Young couples stomped out, leg braces jingling. Dorothy thought of the March of Dimes Birthday Balls that she had attended every January the past few years, celebrations on FDR's birthday at which people across the country were encouraged to come "Dance So That Others Can Walk." Who among those foxtrotting to big band music at the birthday balls imagined this parallel world in which every dance step was a victory?

"Would you like to join us?" the director asked.

"Oh, I wish. But no, thanks. I have to get back—" Dorothy stopped. Jolting against her restraining straps as her push-boy jostled her wheelchair toward the dancers was . . . Barbara Johnson?

Dorothy had forgotten Sabin's lab technician had been sent here, although it had only been, what, not even six months since Mrs. Sabin's outburst about Barbara at the Waldorf? It seemed so long ago. Barbara looked older than Dorothy remembered, her face thinner, the creamy skin around her mouth hardened into parentheses. It was her blond hair, with its luxurious peekaboo wave, that gave her away. A glance at her hands, oddly placed in her lap, made it apparent that she hadn't been the one to brush it.

"Actually, I see someone that I know. Will you excuse me, please?"

She sidestepped two lovers in wheelchairs holding hands. "Miss Johnson?"

Barbara's blank look lowered into a squint of recognition. "Dr.—?"

"Horstmann. Call me Dorothy. It's wonderful to see you." She indicated the handles of Barbara's chair. "May I, please?"

A slight pause and then: "I guess so. Thanks, Milton," she told the push-boy.

Dorothy took over. "Where to?"

"Away from here."

Dorothy wheeled her around and pushed her down a paved walkway, the music trailing behind them. They didn't speak as they passed through a patch of woods and then by a glassed-in pavilion, nor when they came upon what looked like a long white frame garage—the changing booths for a row of connected swimming pools.

Dorothy stopped at a bench close enough to a pool that she could smell the sulfur of the hot spring that fed it. "Here okay?"

"I guess."

Dorothy parked the wheelchair and sat down next to her. What did you say to someone who had lost so much?

In the distance, the MC shouted into his microphone: "Who's ready for some Andrews Sisters?"

A disembodied shout rose up: "Boogie-woogie!"

Barbara said, "Did you know I'm a celebrity here? I'm 'the Researcher Who Got Paralyzed While Trying to Find the Cure.'

That puts me somewhere between being polio royalty and an item out of Ripley's *Believe It or Not.*"

"How do you feel about that?"

"Not good."

A pair of bats flitted in the deepening twilight; spring peepers screamed from their hiding places. "I'm really sorry, Barbara."

"That's not what I need from you."

Dorothy nodded. "What do you need from me?"

She could feel Barbara thinking. She waited as Venus glimmered into life, then the Little Dipper. More and more stars pricked the darkness, until the Milky Way had cast its gossamer veil.

Barbara asked, "Did you see Dr. Sabin's paper?"

"Which one?"

"The one I prepared the tissues for. Last summer." She smiled. "It gave the polio boys something to talk about, didn't it? Now that we have disproved once and for all that the virus enters through the nose and have pinned its entry to the mouth, maybe we can get somewhere."

Barbara said "we," as if it were her paper. But she had done her part, hadn't she? Although her name would never appear on the article, she had given her body to it.

"Have you made any advances lately?" Barbara asked.

Dorothy fought off the tears needling her nasal passages. She shouldn't have come here when so tired. "Everyone is interested in houseflies these days. Who knew that flies would be the rage? Much of my work centers on them, catching them, studying them, harvesting live virus from them. My group's trying to dial in how long the virus is shed by polio patients in their stools and how long the flies can carry it in their bodies. Not very attractive stuff."

"None of it is. I suppose you know of Dr. Sabin and Robbie Ward's other paper from last fall, the one on poliovirus and flies? I was putting together the statistics for that one when I had my accident."

Dorothy drew in a breath. "They must have really missed you."

Silence mushroomed into the night.

She lightened her tone. "I've heard that other researchers are trying to chase down leads that poliovirus is found in well water. The Swedish are particularly bent on proving it's in fruit, like apples that have fallen to the ground. A group here is even looking into it being in chickens' spinal cords."

"Good luck with those." Barbara's laugh was genuine. "We used to get some ridiculous letters, full of wacky suggestions. One lady had a dream that polio was carried either in beetles or groundhogs, she wasn't sure which, but we must pursue it. A man wrote that we could cure it with dog manure."

"How?" Dorothy exclaimed.

"I don't know, but at least there would be no shortage of supply." When they were done laughing, she said, "Speaking of materials at hand, a doctor in Berlin told us he'd found success with injecting patients with their own urine. Just never mind the infection, the joint pain, the mental depression, the sore throat, and the fever that resulted."

"Good grief!"

"Unbelievably, as busy as he was, Dr. Sabin always took the time to dictate letters to all of these 'helpers.' He was amazingly kind to civilians. But if you were in the medical community and made a dumb suggestion, heaven help you. In more than one letter to doctors with offbeat suggestions, he called the writer 'moronic.'"

"Somehow, I can picture that."

An owl hooted for its mate. The women looked up into the pines toward the sound.

Dorothy grew serious. "What bothers me is that we still don't know how polio leaps from the stomach to the nervous system to paralyze people. It should show up in the blood if that's the case, but it doesn't. But how does it get to the nervous system, if not through the blood?"

Barbara caught on immediately. “There can be no stopping the infection until you know that. Who’s working on that problem?”

“No one. Almost all our resources have been directed to the war. Most researchers have either enlisted or been sent to work on infections affecting the troops. Dr. Trask is at a training camp in Chicago. Dr. Paul is over in Europe. You’ve probably heard that Dr. Sabin is closing down his laboratory. The Army wants him. Robbie Ward had to come to us.”

“Robbie? Ward? At Yale? I didn’t know that.”

“Yes.”

“But he’s not interested in epidemiology, is he?”

“He’s interested enough. The study unit has managed to hire on a couple of other MDs, but we can hardly contain outbreaks, let alone make advances in understanding them. Meanwhile, polio doesn’t give a hoot about the war. It’s paralyzing the young at its same grim clip.”

A push-boy bounded up. “You ladies care to—”

“No,” they said together.

He looked to Barbara. “You sure you don’t want to—”

“No, thank you, Wilbur.”

As he trotted off, Barbara said, “At least you can go to outbreaks.”

Dorothy grimaced. “I know. I’m lucky.”

A rustle came from the pine woods on the other side of the pools. A doe stepped into the moonlight, slender and exquisite.

Barbara sighed. “I did hear that Dr. Sabin was going to join the Army. The higher-ups here delight in reporting his whereabouts to me. They think that we must be great friends and colleagues. He did get me admitted here, after all.”

Weren’t they—great friends and colleagues? Maybe even more?

The doe, deciding that they were a threat, leaped away with a flash of white tail.

Barbara stared at the woods into which it had disappeared. "The last I saw Albert Sabin was when we appeared before the university panel making an inquiry into my injury. He told the panel that I should be commended for my part in helping with his research and honored for my fine spirit. 'Fine spirit'! You realize, those stuffed shirts thought that I was in love with him. They thought that he was defending my honor, as if I'd dropped the toxic tissue onto myself when I'd swooned over him. I made a moment's slip, that's all. It had nothing to do with him. But they could not imagine a woman being passionately in love with the work and not with the man."

Sweat broke out, soaking Dorothy's already damp scalp.

Barbara looked at her, the moonlight reflected from the swimming pool shimmering on her face. "Just find a vaccine, would you? It's the only way we'll stop this thing. With Sabin or not—will you do that for me?"

Dorothy swallowed. "Yes. I'll try."

"And don't make stupid mistakes and end up like me. This is a monster we're fighting, a real bastard of a virus. Do not end up like me, Dorothy. I'm counting on you."

She leaned down to brush Barbara's hair out of her face. "Okay."

Barbara breathed in deeply. "All right, then."

AN HOUR LATER, THE HEADLIGHTS OF DOROTHY'S CAR CUT a pale swath through the dark, exposing a flurry of winged insects flitting above the road. The gentle ascent and descent of the two-lane highway through hills, the hum of the engine, the warmth blowing through her open window, and her own exhaustion sent a melody looping through her mind. *DA da da da, DA da da da, DA da da da, DUM da dum.*

Beethoven's "Moonlight Sonata."

Once, when Dorothy was eight and newish to San Francisco, she and her father went to see a music program at a theater around the corner, on Haight Street. Someone at the bar had given Mutter the tickets.

"You two enjoy yourselves!" her mother had said as they left the bar. But Dorothy was already in heaven just being on a lark with Pop. He was a big, handsome man—she had his same long-lidded blue eyes, but they looked better on him. As they walked down Haight, Dorothy watched for women to turn their heads his way, which they often did, although Pop himself never seemed to notice. Back in Spokane, the ladies who worked upstairs at Uncle Henry's restaurant fussed over him and tried to get him to speak English, which only made him laugh at his own hopelessness and then use the opportunity to convince any of them who could play piano to teach Dorothy, once he'd seen her plinking the chipped keys of the restaurant's old upright.

Oh, Dorothy was madly in love with him. And now to be with him in such a grand place, a genuine palace with red velvet seats, curtains, and walls, all of it dripping with gold? When the music began, she gasped. The melody seemed to strum her very bones.

One-two-three, one-two-three, one-two-three, the bass notes rowed determinedly on, like oarsmen along the shore. How she'd thrilled when the higher notes the pianist played with his right hand broke away from the striving bass of his left and began to go their own way. The treble cried out pitifully, only to grow quiet; it scaled emotional heights only to fall low, with the bass always there to catch it, rowing on and on and on.

Dorothy was trembling from the beauty of it when her father had leaned toward her, smelling as he always did of someone else's spilled beer and his own peppery sweet scent of sweat and soap.

"I like that lower hand," he'd whispered. "It does not mind if the upper hand steals the show. It knows it is strong."

She had looked over at her father, smiling with proud joy, as if the music were his to give. When he saw her watching, he leaned over and kissed her on top of her head.

—A deer and her fawn leaped from the woods.

Dorothy rammed on the brakes. The chests thumped inside the trunk with a chittering of glass.

IT WAS NEAR MIDNIGHT WHEN SHE'D ARRIVED AT THE HOtel. When she checked on the vials for damage, only four containing sewage water from Atlanta had broken. She mopped the mess with the rags that she kept in her trunk for spills, then doused everything with the bleach she carried for the same reason. She was dragging herself through the lobby, thinking that in the morning, she could go back out to the filtration plant and get more samples, when the clerk at the front desk called her over.

She aimed herself toward him.

The clerk was a wiry young man with an eyepatch that bisected his bristly blond hair and whose left sleeve was folded and pinned at the shoulder. He'd told her he'd been at Pearl Harbor. She hated what war did to young men. "Telegram, ma'am."

She thanked him and opened it as she walked away.

May 24, 1942

Dr. Dorothy Horstmann
Winecoff Hotel, Atlanta

TRASK INFECTED W/ HEMOLYTIC STREP AT ARMY CAMP CHICAGO. DIED IN 48 HRS. HEARTBROKEN.

Beryl Beasley

1944

A NURSE

1944

Two and a half years into the war with Germany, in the woods outside of the sleepy town of Hickory, North Carolina, a plank fell with a mighty twang. A prison guard bellowed at men up to their chests in the trench that they were digging for a water line. The din of hammering, sawing, and profane shouts filled the piney forest as an Army jeep whined by. Building a polio hospital so quickly that the crew seemed to be pulling it up from the hard red clay was loud work. They'd been at it for only fifty-four hours, and already the roof was on the main building and patients were being admitted.

It wasn't fast enough.

Ambulances, automobiles, and horse-drawn wagons idled nose-to-tail along the dirt road. From the checkpoint at the gatehouse to the Army tent outside of which Margaret O'Shea now stood, anxiety floated from the vehicles as palpably as smoke from a stovepipe.

Will Little Johnny be able to walk again?

Can you stop our Bobby's pain?

Is Mary going to die?

"Margaret?" Dr. Farragut's voice came from inside the admissions tent. "Margaret, are you there?"

"Yes. Sorry." She held open the screened wooden door for a teenaged boy carrying a little girl whose legs flopped beneath her pink chenille robe. Behind him trudged a man with his hat pulled down, though not quite low enough to hide the tears watering his leathery face.

Dr. Farragut followed them to the door. "Get her home," he said after them. "We will telephone you. Do you have his number?" he asked Margaret.

"Yes, sir."

Above the cloth of his mask, he softened his gaze at Margaret. And here, in the sticky heat, among despairing parents, terrified children, and the threat of death and permanent harm, warmth unfurled in her chest. Were they monsters to be in love in the time of polio?

She'd slept on the backseat of the car and eaten nothing but tomato-and-Miracle-Whip sandwiches since they'd left Chicago a day and a half ago. She'd cleaned up in the grubby bathrooms of filling stations along the way. Now she was seeing patients in a hot musty tent in buggy woods. Anything to be with him. They'd had to send away this poor family because beds had to be saved for the paralyzed, not the merely very ill and feverish like this little girl, and all Margaret could think about was if Dr. Farragut—Ted—would take her in his arms again tonight. That's how crazy love made her. It made everything else a blur, even hardship, even polio, even the thought of her brother, Sim, flying over a forest somewhere in Europe now, two weeks after the D-Day landing in Normandy.

A tall woman, no, a beautiful giantess with messy yellow hair, a long narrow torso, and broad hips, loped up with a crate clinking with glass. She had long hooded eyes and a large mouth, which widened, as she got closer, into an apologetic smile that seemed to say that she was sorry about this madness, but if one had to be in it, she was glad to be in it with you.

"I'm Dorothy Horstmann, from the Yale Polio Study Unit."

Ted—Dr. Farragut—looked her up and down with a frown. "This is admissions. You want the hospital."

Dorothy Horstmann turned her head toward the teenaged brother now loading his sister into the family truck. Margaret watched, too, as the boy laid a blanket over the sprung seat and tenderly put the little girl down before smoothing her robe over her. The child looked up at her brother, adoring.

Distant drums of panic beat in Margaret's ears. *Don't think. Shut it down.*

"You couldn't take that child?" Dorothy Horstmann asked.

Dr. Farragut peeled off his surgical cap and swiped his arm over his sandy waves of hair. "You think I should take her?" He clapped back on his cap. "See that, Yale?" He pointed to a low-slung black station wagon crawling between a Ford and a mule-drawn wagon, its chrome trim blazing in the sun.

"The hearse?"

A voice with a thick Boston accent rose from within the tent. "In some places they've run out of ambulances, so they've pressed hearses into service. It's to be expected."

Dorothy Horstmann squinted through the screen at the man sitting on a camp chair next to an oscillating fan.

"Come in! Take a load off. Open the door for her, honey," he told Margaret.

The wooden door squawked on its hinges as she held it for the newcomer, who exclaimed her pleasure at seeing the square-headed, pixie-eared, jovial man. Everyone in the polio world knew Basil O'Connor, the president of the National Foundation for Infantile Paralysis.

Margaret followed her into the tent to prepare for the next patient. It was ninety-some degrees in there, hot enough for the top of Margaret's uniform to be translucent with sweat, yet Mr. O'Connor's shirtsleeves were rolled down and pinned with diamond cufflinks. His only nod to the heat was that the coat of his signature pin-striped suit was arranged over the back of his folding chair. He dressed with the flamboyance of a waif who had struck it rich, which was exactly what he was.

Everybody knew his story. A tinsmith's scrappy son, who as a newsboy eventually took over all the routes in town, he'd talked his way into Dartmouth and Harvard, then had hit it big by partnering with Franklin Roosevelt in FDR's New York law firm back before Roosevelt was president. Roosevelt, familiar with O'Connor's Midas touch, put him in charge of his new investment—a dump of an inn at some hot springs in Georgia. O'Connor turned it into a world-class poliomyelitis rehabilitation center, then spun from it the NFIP, or "the March of Dimes," as the singer Eddie Cantor dubbed it, the most successful philanthropy of the age. They said there was a reason the poor boy from Taunton, Massachusetts, could wrought such a miracle: he could smell a clever angle from a mile away. Margaret wondered why he was here.

Mr. O'Connor unhooked wire-rimmed glasses from his elfin ears. "We get hearses because hospitals ask their local funeral homes for help when they run out of ambulances to transport the kids. This outbreak only started two weeks ago, and the hospitals in Charlotte and Gastonia have already run out of beds. They were pitching tents on the hospital lawns." He pulled a handkerchief from his back pocket. "I said to hell with that. We're building a three-hundred-bed state-of-the-art polio hospital from the ground up, and housing for the staff and a rehabilitation center. In five days." He started polishing. "Or less."

"I've got to get back out there," said Dr. Farragut. "I don't have time to chat. Margaret, you ready?"

"Actually, Ted," Mr. O'Connor said, dabbing at his nose, "I sent for Dr. Horstmann. At least, I sent for the Yale Polio Study Unit. Where's everyone else, Dot?"

"It's just Joe Melnick and Robbie Ward, up at the hospital. I'm here to take blood samples from those who aren't admitted."

"Blood samples?" said Mr. O'Connor. "Is that typical?"

"It is for me." Dr. Horstmann gazed toward the truck. "In fact, I need to catch that family before they drive off." She riffled through the box, grabbed three glass syringes, pulled up her mask, and strode out into the sunlight.

"You going to call her off?" Ted exclaimed. "There's no room for her here. She's holding up the line."

"Oh, I think you might want to rethink things, Ted." Mr. O'Connor shifted in his canvas chair. "You might find her useful. She's an MD. An internal medicine doc, as well as an epidemiologist."

"Great. Margaret, get me some more tongue depressors."

Margaret reached into the supply cabinet and grabbed a handful of the flat wooden sticks. She couldn't look at them without thinking of Popsicles, and of Sim. Even in that musty tent, she saw herself with him, when he was eight and she was six, on the sidewalk outside their house. He was licking a cherry Popsicle that he'd bought with his newspaper route money. One glimpse at her wistful face, and, his red-stained lips pursed with concentration, he broke the treat down its length. They then sat knee to knee on the curb and licked their melting portions, racing with the sun for every red drop. She had loved him so hard that it hurt.

"Margaret?" Ted raised his eyebrows.

"Sorry." She gave him the tongue depressors.

Mr. O'Connor hooked his glasses back on, then sat back in his camp chair, as comfortable as a general on the battlefield. "You ought to get Dr. Horstmann to give you a hand when she's not playing vampire. Sabin says she's a rising star in polio research."

Ted stuffed the flat sticks into the breast pocket of his gown. "Sabin? Albert Sabin?"

"Yep."

"What a prick."

"Ted!" Mr. O'Connor exclaimed mildly. "There is a lady present."

"Sorry, Margaret. I heard that pr— I heard *Sabin* speak at a conference right before the war. He had the nerve to stand up at the podium and announce that Claus Jungeblut's vitamin C therapy for polio was complete hogwash, and proceeded to outline why—with Claus Jungeblut sitting right there in the front row! The way he tore apart that poor gentleman before his peers was unconscionable."

Mr. O'Connor smiled with half of his mouth. "But was Sabin right?"

"Yes. Damn him." Ted scribbled on his clipboard. "No ink. Margaret, get me another pen."

She was retrieving it when Dr. Horstmann came back in. "Got that group. Thanks. Your next patient is out there. Listen, do you mind if I take samples when you examine each of your patients?"

"Dr. Horstmann," said Mr. O'Connor, "wait. I haven't seen you to tell you in person—the war has gotten time all bunged up for me. These past two years don't seem to have existed. Or I don't seem to have existed. Both! Anyhow, I've meant to tell you, I'm sorry about Dr. Trask."

She hesitated, then took a vial out of her box. "Thank you. We miss him."

"I'm sorry about Dr. Trask, too," Ted said. "I'm from Chicago and heard all about it."

All of the Chicago public health community had heard. It was the talk of the department office the day, two years ago, that Margaret had applied for the nursing position, the same day that her brother had gone into training at Chanute Field to serve as a pilot. She was filling out papers when she heard that an epidemiologist had died two days after contracting streptococcus at an outbreak that he was investigating. Lots of soldiers were dying from it—at Chanute Field.

The chipped yellow-and-green linoleum floor had seemed to rise up: Sim was already in danger and he hadn't even left home.

"Dr. Trask was a good man," Dr. Horstmann said. "He thought nothing of his own risk when he had to run into the fire."

"Say." Mr. O'Connor leaned forward. "That's a good line. 'Our doctors run into the fire.' We have to use that somehow."

Margaret held on to the rickety card table that served as Ted's desk. She saw an airplane flying into a wall of fire, its body engulfed with flames. She saw Sim's determined face in the cockpit, his mouth pursed in concentration, even as a wing broke from his plane like a halved Popsicle.

A man in overalls put his face to the screen. "Anyone in there? I've got a boy out here who's having trouble breathing."

Ted cocked his head quizzically. "Margaret? My pen?"

She laid the utensil in his hand.

"My, you are dreamy today. Thinking of something special?" He flashed her a knowing look over his mask.

He couldn't save her brother, nor could a single one of his kisses. But at least he could make her body sing. And when it sang, for that moment, nothing could hurt Sim.

She followed Ted out into the hot sun, before another life could be lost.

10

HICKORY, NORTH CAROLINA, 1944

Dorothy told herself she was just worn out from two years of whacking down outbreaks across the country when they were short-staffed, overwhelmed, and underfunded during the war. She shouldn't let this guy bother her. Maybe under normal conditions, back in his hospital in Chicago, where cheerful teams of nurses, technicians, and orderlies could make things right, Dr. Ted was pleasant. It was another thing, she knew, to stay sweet when you were racing to get kids out of cars and into ventilators before they stopped breathing.

Now Ted was jabbing his thumb toward a faded green Ford behind the hearse at the front of the line. "Hey. Yale. You get that one. I'm getting this one." He didn't wait for Dorothy to answer before ducking into the hearse.

Her face mask was sodden with breath and sweat, and her wretched girdle was strangulating the tops of her thighs, and she couldn't even begin to think about her bladder. But there was a reason driving her to put up with her own discomfort and Ted's bitterness while she admitted patients and gathered blood samples.

She'd found poliovirus in a patient's blood.

Last summer, a nine-year-old girl from New Haven had been admitted to the hospital with a temperature of 101, muscle pain, and stiffness in her back, neck, and left hamstring, but, as in 95 percent of poliomyelitis infections, her illness never advanced. She was back home and symptom-free within a week. Dorothy would have never guessed, while routinely studying specimens forty-eight days later, that it would be a blood sample from this child, who'd had such a mild case, that would cause a mouse injected with it to develop paralysis. Now she was determined to find a second positive sample.

With a pluck to her girdle, she approached the faded green Ford, her ears ringing with the din of hammers banging, saws rending wood, and shovels slicing through dirt.

The woman in the passenger seat cranked down her window. She was young, with her hair pulled back with a pink ribbon.

"Good afternoon. I'm Dr. Horstmann."

"Shhh. She's getting her rest. This is the most she's slept in two days." The blue veins wandering under the tender skin of the young mother's temple were visible when she turned to gaze at her child. "Don't she look like an angel?"

Dorothy peered over the seatback. A bedspread obscured the patient's face.

Over in the driver's seat, the father gripped the wheel as if he were steering his car through the mountains in a blizzard.

"Sir," Dorothy asked him, "could you please carry her into the tent?"

He turned, slow as an automaton. His pupils shone.

Dorothy drew back. Had he been drinking?

She took a breath, then asked the mother, "Tell me about your little one."

"Her name is Shirley. Shirley Blanche Reese. She is five years old. She loves to sing, and she's good at it, too."

"When did she become ill?"

A frown puckered the mother's pretty face. "Yesterday morning. She woke up with a fever. Gracious, she was on fire! Then she started throwing up. She said her neck hurt, her back hurt, and her legs did, too. When she tried to stand and couldn't, we rushed her straight to the doctor in town. He said we'd better get to the hospital in Charlotte quick, but they were full up there, so they sent us way out here."

"Is she able to walk now?"

"I don't know. I haven't woken her up to see. She's been asleep since we left Charlotte. She needed her rest." She cringed as Dorothy opened the back door. "Shhh! You say you're a doctor? Pardon me, but you don't look like one."

"Yes, ma'am." Dorothy peeled back the blanket. Her pulse whooshed in her ears.

She glanced at the mother then, swallowing, rested two fingers against the child's still neck.

Her heart pounding, she gathered herself before reaching into the front seat.

She placed her hand on the mother's shoulder.

A SMALL MAN IN A BIG FEDORA WAS PERCHED ON ONE OF the camp chairs inside the tent when Dorothy went back in to telephone the coroner. He waited until the call was placed, then rose and took off his hat, revealing a shiny dome hugged by a roll of dark hair. A camera hung from his neck.

"I'm Alfred Eisenstaedt for *Life* magazine. Basil O'Connor sent me up here to find you. Say, I'm sorry about that child."

She nodded, then went back out to the patient's mother.

He was still there after the body had been removed and the mother, still wailing, was escorted to the hospital building by that quiet nurse, Margaret.

"Could I help you?" Dorothy looked longingly toward the restrooms by the canteen.

"Basil O'Connor wanted me to shadow one of you docs for an

article about the opening of the hospital. But if you want me to vamoose—"

Ted came in. "Sorry you pulled that one, Yale. That was rough." He frowned at the *Life* photographer. "Who's this?"

The photographer introduced himself and explained why he was there.

The Chicago doctor pointed at Dorothy. "Go with him, Yale."

"No. You need the help."

He shook his head. "Uh-uh. Go. Go do what you were going to do before I got you tangled up in this. Don't you guys usually collect flies and feces?"

Dorothy peered out the tent at the string of waiting vehicles stretching past the checkpoint and into the woods. Every one contained a family hoping for a miracle. "I've got to get out there."

"Look, Yale, if people like you don't figure out how this disease ticks, then people like me are never going to see the end of lines like this. Got it?" The doc flashed her a look of gratitude before hardening his face. "Get out of here. I don't want you around. You're bad luck." He stalked to the next car with his clipboard.

The photographer spread his hands. "I'll be like a fly on the wall. You won't even know I'm there."

THE MOTHER'S SCREAM WAS STILL ECHOING IN DOROTHY'S ears as she swayed in the backseat of an Army jeep sixty-five minutes later. The driver, all helmet and determination, was following a farmer's truck down a road so narrow that mountain laurels whacked the vehicles from both sides.

The jeep hit a rock in the dirt, popping her from her bench. In the front seat, the *Life* photographer grabbed for his hat as it flew off. She snagged it midair and handed it back to him.

"Good catch!" He plunked it on his muff of hair. "If I may

ask"—he raised his voice over the rumble of the jeep—"what do you hope to find when we get to this patient's home?"

"*Scheiße* and bugs," she muttered.

"What?"

She drew in a breath. "Feces and flies. I'll be collecting feces and flies." She nudged the fly trap at her feet. "We're still trying to figure out how polio spreads from person to person."

His brows disappeared into his hat. "You don't know?"

"We don't even know how polio operates in the body."

"Still?" he shouted. They hit another bump. "It's been what, thirty years?"

She tried to control her fury. "Questions keep coming up that we can't answer, because we're too busy just trying to keep people alive."

The jeep burst into a clearing. Chickens flapped for cover as the vehicles pulled into a hard-packed dirt yard. The jeep stopped, as did the rattling of her bones.

Children were pouring out of the unpainted house as the driver, tipping back his helmet to take in her full height, helped her from her vehicle. The smell of pine, horse manure, and baking bread hung in the bright sweet air.

The mother came out onto the porch, drying her hands on her apron. Dorothy introduced herself, then told her she had admitted her daughter to the hospital that morning with bulbar poliomyelitis.

The mother covered her mouth. "How bad is she?"

"She can't breathe on her own right now, I'm sorry to say. She's in a ventilator."

The mother blinked.

"An iron lung," Dorothy said.

The mother's eyes filled with tears. "Is she a vegetable?"

"No. Not at all. Most kids get back enough muscle strength to do their own breathing. And physiotherapists will do everything they can to get her walking again."

"She can't walk?"

"Not just yet. But we won't give up on her."

The mother jerked, then, swallowing loudly, wiped her eyes on her apron. She straightened. "Will the other kids get it?"

Dorothy's blood boiled up. The virus sneaked into the body, took its nefarious journey to the nerve cells, then zapped a child who'd just been jumping rope or roller-skating or feeding the dog. She was doing everything she could to trap, corner, and then shine a light on the evil thing, but it wasn't enough. All she could tell this mother was "Only about eight per one hundred thousand children are severely affected."

"But my Louise was."

"Yes, ma'am. I'm sorry."

"How do I keep the others from getting it?"

"We don't know, ma'am. That's why I am here."

THE *LIFE* PHOTOGRAPHER SNAPPED AWAY WITH HIS LEICA all afternoon. While Dorothy was setting up fly traps—to the immense interest of the kids, who would not be shaken even when she baited the traps with rotten fish—Mr. Eisenstaedt kept snapping. He was at it when she put on yellow rubber gloves to draw water from the well. His camera was clicking as she waded into the creek with a specimen jar, curious children in tow. Even when she came staggering out of the outhouse with a bucket, he didn't back off, although she warned him that poliovirus was found in feces and a child who'd been paralyzed with it lived there.

"You realize," she said, trying not to slosh the pail, "that we still are not sure how polio is transmitted."

"You've made me aware of that."

She put it down as far from him as possible. "What I'm saying is that until we know, you should limit contact with others, and for heaven's sakes, don't get near this stuff."

He wound his film, then took another shot. "Okay."

"Adults are not immune from the disease, I'm saying."

"Oh, I know." He raised thick brows as arched as an owl's. "What about you? Aren't you afraid that you will get it?"

"This is my job. It's you I'm concerned about."

"Don't be." He held up his light meter, took a reading, and then focused his camera. "When this is in my hand"—he took a picture of her filling a vial—"I have no fear."

"Viruses don't care if we're afraid or not."

He advanced his film. "So why aren't you afraid? You epidemiologists know more than anybody how bad it is, yet, as Basil O'Connor told me, you folks routinely 'run into the fire.' One of your colleagues even died doing so not long ago. Dr. Trask. You should be hiding under your bed, but here you are, dishing up live poliovirus. Where do you get the courage?"

"Is it courage? I am *sick* of being beaten by something so tiny that you can't even see it with a microscope." She took a breath, then filled another vial. "Where do you get your courage, Mr. Eisenstaedt?"

He lowered his camera. "I watched out my window as my best friend and his family were taken to a Nazi prison camp. My whole neighborhood, little kids following fathers carrying suitcases, mothers hushing their babies, grandparents holding hands—" He looked away, then drew a breath. "My parents got us out." He smiled at her grimly. "It's not so much courage in my case, either. Just good old-fashioned fury."

One of the little girls skipped out into the yard, a grubby doll staring from the crook of her arm. "Mama says come eat supper!" The child peered toward the bucket. "Ewww!"

Dorothy waited until she was sure Mr. Eisenstaedt saw that she understood him before she turned to the child.

AFTER MR. EISENSTAEDT AND SHE WASHED UP, THE MOTHER fed them a meal of buttered cornbread and fresh peas doused with milk brought in from the springhouse. Dorothy capped off the day by drawing blood from the children, who were now self-proclaimed "deemeologists" like Dorothy. She was on the porch, recovering from a battle with the youngest girl, a wiry three-year-old who'd fought like a badger against the needle, while Mr. Eisenstaedt packed up his equipment.

"Why are you testing the children's blood?" He put a camera in the velvet cradle of its case. "According to their mother, none of them have been sick, just the one who was hospitalized."

Dorothy straightened from charting her notes and rubbed the right side of her lower back, always a trouble spot when she got tired. "Actually, we very rarely find poliovirus in the blood, even in those who are paralyzed with it. I've only seen it once."

"Then why do you do it? Seems like a lot of trouble, wrangling kids to take samples of blood that won't have the virus in it."

She swallowed. "What if the virus *is* in the blood, and we're missing it somehow? It was there, that one time."

He reached for his pad of paper.

She held up her hand for him to stop. "Don't print that. Please. That's not the current thought in the field. The scientific community will think I'm nuts."

He watched her with his bright brown eyes. "All right. I won't. But you'll let me know if you ever find out otherwise?"

The troop of children redescended with a chorus of chattering. One of the little boys picked up a flash unit. "Mister, what's the best picture you ever made?"

Mr. Eisenstaedt folded up his tripod. "That's easy: the one of Joseph Goebbels glaring at me when he found out that I was a Jew, after I'd photographed him all morning."

"What?"

He relieved the boy of the flash device, then ruffled his hair. "I think the one of you getting your blood drawn by Dr. Horstmann is going to be pretty good. If they use it, I'll send you a copy of the magazine."

"Put me in the magazine!" said another child.

"Put me!"

"Put me!"

"You're all going in there, if I have any say about it."

The kids cheered.

The girls gathered around Dorothy and played with the combs in her hair and ran their fingers through the ruffled neck of her dress as he put the last of his equipment in their cases. When he was done, he pulled Dorothy to a stand.

"It has been a pleasure to run into the fire with you, Dr. Horstmann."

She gazed down into his alert owlish face. "More than you know, Mr. Eisenstaedt."

He patted her arm. "Oh, I think I do."

11

NEW HAVEN, CONNECTICUT, 1944

Four weeks later, a Waring blender was roaring in Dorothy's ears when Robbie strolled into the lab waving a *Life* magazine. Dorothy let the machine scream for fifteen more seconds, until the blood was thoroughly mixed with the sterile distilled water, then she switched it off. "What'd you say?"

"I said, a star is born!"

She glanced at the *Life* cover. A stern foreign general dripping with medals rose like a monolith above the date: July 31, 1944.

"Just a sec."

Robbie flipped through the magazine as she poured the mixture into vials, put them into an angle centrifuge, and then turned it on. Maybe this would be the batch of serum to reveal poliovirus in the bloodstream. It was in there, somewhere—she knew it.

She had fifteen minutes for the mixture to spin. She took off her rubber gloves. "Now what?"

Robbie shook the open *Life* with both hands. "How does this happen? You're in here. The nurses trooping to their tents are in here. That god-awful admissions hut and that grump from Chicago and his good-looking nurse are in here. Even the convicts digging a trench made it in here. But not little old me."

She raised her voice over the whine of the centrifuge. "I can't help if Al didn't find you and Melnick to be photogenic."

"'Al.' Huh. Mr. Eisenstaedt is 'Al' now. Is there something I should know about you two?"

She slapped his arm as she looked over his shoulder. The magazine spread was like a photo album of that first exhausting day in Hickory. Here was the distressed teenaged boy carrying his little sister out of the admissions tent. There was Ted-from-Chicago, checking in a patient from the interior of a hearse. In the middle of the page, the farm kids surrounded their mother and Dorothy as she showed how to set up a fly trap. Good heavens, she was an Amazon in a ruffled plaid dress!

Next to that photo was one of Dorothy drawing blood from the youngest brother. Even as she cringed to see herself, she marveled at the details Al had captured in a single shot: The boy turning his face away in pain. The worry pinching the siblings' brows. The stare of the dirty doll in the littlest girl's arms. Dorothy's own frown of concerned concentration. All told of the gravity of the moment. Strange how you don't fully feel the tragedy of a situation when you're in it. Only afterward do you see what you survived. And then you marvel.

Dr. Paul pushed into the lab, his chin buried in his bow tie in a frown. He glanced up at Dorothy, then down again.

"Have you seen this?" Robbie was still grinning. "Dorothy's the only doctor mentioned by name. Looks like we've got ourselves a celebrity."

"Yale is mentioned, too," Dorothy said quickly.

Dr. Paul's frown deepened.

Robbie didn't seem to notice. "So is that overbearing Australian woman, Sister What's-her-name—"

"Kenny," said Dorothy.

"—Sister Kenny with her method of scalding, I mean healing, children. But no one gets the air time that you do. I'm just surprised that Sabin isn't in here, even from the Pacific, seven thousand miles away. A polio miracle is not a miracle without our buddy."

"I've seen the article. Dorothy, do you have a few minutes?"

"Of course. But the centrifuge has eleven more minutes."

"Robbie, watch it for her, please."

He led Dorothy down the hall, his small figure as upright as a tack. Why wasn't he using the time while they walked to explain something to her, wringing value from every moment, as was his habit? She glanced at the wartime poster above the drinking fountain as they passed, her heels tapping on the tile. It was of an arm bursting through the surface of water, grasping for help, with a sailor hat floating next to it. In the background, a ship was going under, smokestack and all. LOOSE LIPS SINK SHIPS, it read.

By the time they'd reached his office, her gut was aching. Something was wrong. He indicated a chair. "Please, sit down."

Had she bungled her study? She froze with another thought: Had someone else found poliovirus in the blood first?

Behind the mahogany desk built for a man twice his size, Dr. Paul leaned onto his forearms. "I will make this quick, Dorothy, out of respect. We've been called to cut costs due to the war. I'm not going to be able to keep you on."

She felt a punch to her lungs.

"The men in our unit have families, children—you understand. I couldn't let one of them go. I know you want what's best for them. I know you want what's best for the program."

Her work, her apartment, her life—what was she to do? Where was she to go? Who had the money to harbor a unicorn during the penny-pinching of wartime, let alone to fund her research? She was so close to proving that the presence of poliovirus in the blood wasn't a fluke. Why she wasn't seeing it there with every infection, she didn't know, but damned if she wasn't going to figure it out. It just made sense that the virus was traveling through the blood—how else was it getting to the nervous system? If only they'd just let her prove it, they'd have a place in which to nail polio in its tracks. How could they stop her now?

"You do understand, don't you, Dorothy?"

She was the drowning sailor in the poster, hand up, clutching for help that would never come.

"Yes. Of course." She even smiled.

12

SAN FRANCISCO, CALIFORNIA, 1944

Christmas had come to the polio ward in San Francisco. Someone had placed a wispy redwood sapling on one of the metal supply cabinets and draped it with tinsel and red and green paper links. A green cellophane wreath stuck with a lightbulb candle—not to be turned on, due to the wartime dim-out—hung on each papered-over window. Bing Crosby crooned "White Christmas" from the crackly record that a nurse had brought in, great for setting the holiday mood as long as you didn't look at the government poster recruiting nurses for the war.

It didn't smell like Christmas, however. No amount of peppermint from the candy canes, donated by a church group and now lying partially eaten on nightstands, could mask the sheepy odor of boiling wool. It canceled out the nip of rubbing alcohol and disinfectant, and other sickroom smells. Ever since American hospitals had adopted the Kenny Method, you could find your way blindfolded to the polio ward simply by following the stink of hot wet ewe.

Dorothy checked the gauges of her patient's whooshing ventilator. Good pressure. She made a notation. On a nearby bed, five-year-old Mikey, dressed only in a cotton loincloth, as were most of the other polio patients, male or female, toddler or adolescent, watched as a nurse lifted a steaming strip of army blanket from a pressure cooker with tongs. The masked nurse, her eyes equally as troubled as her awaiting patient's, slung it, dripping like spaghetti noodles from the pot, onto his thigh.

Tears wet Mikey's lashes but he did not cry. In her four months at the university hospital here in San Francisco, Dorothy had never failed to be astounded by the courage of her young polio patients, nor by that of the nurses, who suffered along with the children. They were the real heroes of this pandemic. Now that her eyes had been newly opened to the resilience of children—not just her polio patients, but all of them, in the other wards—and to the strength of the nurses caring for them, she saw that she'd been given a chance to see something wondrous. She was grateful. She really was. She was also furious. These kids should never have to battle for their lives like this.

The nurse, a tiny girl named Evelyn, wrapped the hot strip around Mikey's leg and followed it with a length of rubber sheeting before safety-pinning both into place with a piece of cotton blanketing. This pack would stay on for an hour, as would the ones that were to be placed on his other thigh, his calves, his feet, his belly, and his arms. And then the process would start again.

Dorothy felt a gaze upon her. Four-year-old Janice was studying her from the mirror angled over the end of the ventilator that she'd been checking. The child's soft young face was as solemn as an undertaker's.

"Hi, Janice. May I take a peep inside your little house to see how you are doing?"

Oh, those trusting, innocent eyes.

Dorothy was unlatching Janice's tank when a disturbance arose in the hall. The cries of nurses and the booming of a hearty voice accompanied the scuffle of footsteps.

"Do you think Santa is coming to visit?" Dorothy whispered.

Little Janice was scowling her disbelief when a large white-haired woman plowed into the ward. She bulldozed through the beds, the plume on her Puss-in-Boots hat lofting to the beat of the jouncing of her jowls. The satchel on her arm banged against her green cape.

"HELLO, CHILDREN!"

Nurse Evelyn lowered tongs long as her own forearms. "Ma'am! Please! You'll upset the patients."

"Upset them?" The woman flung back her cape. "I'm curing them!" She pointed to the steaming rag dripping from Evelyn's utensil. "Did you get that good and hot?"

"You were right," Dorothy whispered to Janice. "Not Santa. I'll be right back."

She confronted the woman. "Sister Kenny—"

She beamed at Dorothy. "*She* knows who I am!"

It was hard not to. The Australian nurse's wide, flat face, not unlike that of a gingerbread man, was in countless magazine and newspaper articles. The world was begging for a cure for polio, and Sister Kenny was the closest now to delivering it.

"Sister Kenny—"

"Merry Christmas to you, Nurse—"

"Dr. Horstmann."

"*Dr.* Horstmann! Well!" Sister Kenny gave Dorothy's surgical gown a quick up and down in confirmation. "You are certainly tall. Taller than me, and that's saying something!"

"To what do we owe this—surprise?"

Sister Kenny's cheeks expanded with a smile. "They're filming my story in Hollywood. Rosalind Russell is playing me—a fair likeness, I might say. I just had to pay her a visit on set. Imagine her delight! After I was done advising everyone, I insisted on a drive up the Californian coast. I saw whales! It was such a treat for a girl from the Australian Outback like me."

She turned to the stunned children on their beds. "Boys and girls, I'd like you to meet the person who thought up the method that is going to make you walk again." She raised her arms, her satchel thudding against her upholstered chest. "Me!"

Mikey burst into tears.

"Tears of joy, tears of joy!" Sister Kenny exclaimed.

Dorothy reached over to comfort him. Children dreaded the Kenny Method. Nurses dreaded applying it. The science behind it was unprovable. But it was better than encasing kids in full-body casts and often seemed to work. The sad fact was, the treatment for polio was no more advanced than its prevention.

The nurse who'd followed Sister Kenny from the hall pulled a piece of paper from her pocket. "May I have your autograph?"

Sister Kenny glowed. "Certainly!" She mined a fountain pen from her satchel, then uncapped it. "Wait until you see my film! It tells the harrowing story of my struggle to bring the Kenny Method to America. Oh, the trouble doctors gave me, rebuking me, reviling me, when all I wanted to do was to bring salvation! I'm sure you know what I mean," she said to Dorothy. "I bet the boys have given you the dickens!"

The record hit a scratch. Bing sang, "*I'll be— I'll be— I'll be—*"

Dorothy found that her heart was thumping. "We all want what is best for the patients."

Sister Kenny shoved her autograph at the nurse and took a piece of paper from another as the record kept skipping. "Really? I've met plenty of doctors who just want to maintain the status quo. Be honest, Dr.—"

"Horstmann."

"*I'll be— I'll be—*"

"Be honest, Dr. Horstmann. People are in this for different reasons. Me, I just want to be the one who gave deliverance to the suffering. You? What do you want? For yourself, I mean. Would someone PLEASE stop that record!"

A nurse went over and raised the arm from the platter. The room quieted, save for the groaning of the iron lungs.

"Oh, come now, there's nothing wrong with wanting something. One has to know what to ask for, to know what one *wants*, and then to go after it, everyone and everything else be blasted." The nib of Sister Kenny's pen scratched against the paper. "That applies to everything in life."

Nurse Evelyn finished pinning the pack on Mikey's other leg. "You mean," said Dorothy, "that the only thing standing between wanting and getting is knowing what to ask for?"

"Yes."

Dorothy felt a jolt of anger. This hardly seemed fair to her little patients, paralyzed through no fault of their own. "If that were true," she said, keeping it light, "wouldn't we all be millionaires?"

"The only reason we aren't all millionaires"—Sister Kenny capped her pen—"is because we don't all want to do what it takes to be millionaires. Same for traffic cops, clergy, or Nobel Prize winners. We are what we have willed ourselves to be, whether we realize it or not."

Dorothy opened her mouth to protest, then stopped. What if there was something to this?

"I'll remember you. The girl who was taller than me! First I've met." Sister Kenny dug into her satchel. "Who wants my book? It's a beauty!"

LONG AFTER COPIES OF *AND THEY SHALL WALK* HAD BEEN laid next to sticky candy canes on the nightstands and Sister Kenny and her plume had strutted out, and after Dorothy had worked through the night, snatching a few hours of sleep in her office, she was catching up on paperwork before leading students on her morning rounds when a colleague popped inside the door.

Martin, pale and given to moles, was twenty-eight but looked eighteen, although he had three kids. With so many men at war, at thirty-three, Dorothy was the dowager of the pediatrics floor.

"From your friends at Yale." He dropped the journal on her desk and pushed up his glasses with a sniff. "You're in it. Page 284."

"Thanks." She wasn't aware of any of her work being published in Yale's *Preventive Medicine*. She'd had to leave the study group with her findings uncompleted.

She waited until he was gone to find the page.

The Isolation of Poliomyelitis Virus from Human Extra-Neural Sources.

IV. SEARCH FOR VIRUS IN THE BLOOD OF PATIENTS

By **Robert Ward, Dorothy M. Horstmann,** and **Joseph L. Melnick**

She scanned the article, her heart pumping. In the four months that she'd been out here, she'd heard little from Robbie and the others. Had they found more evidence? Was this proof that she had been onto something? They must have used some of her findings—why hadn't they told her?

She flipped to the conclusion. The final paragraph seemed to radiate from the page.

> Virus was detected in the blood of 1 patient . . . The results of this study suggest that the presence of poliomyelitis virus in the human blood stream is not a common event.

She could almost hear a door thudding closed. All her work, debunked.

Even if she ever found a research lab to employ her, she'd never be allowed the funds to follow something considered to be a dead end. She was relegated now to treatment, sopping up the damage caused by poliovirus instead of fighting to destroy it in the lab.

She scraped up her empty coffee cup and swung out into the hall.

An expanse of sweater swelled into view. Before she could react, she collided with a wall of knitted wool smelling pleasantly of man.

Large hands clasped her arms. "Pardon."

She looked up, and up again, a good six inches above her head. Under a silky cap of brown hair, the ends of green-gray eyes crinkled in a smile.

She caught the words before they burst from her own mouth: *You're tall.*

She laughed out loud.

His smile faltered.

"No— Oh, no." He thought she was making fun of him. And he looked so nice. Why was she such an idiot? Without warning, tears blurred her eyes.

His expression flattened into alarm. He reached into his trouser pocket, then handed her a handkerchief.

She took it. "Thank you." After a quick swipe, she gave it back. "I'm sorry. I don't know what's wrong with me."

"No need to apologize. We are in a hospital. You have plenty of company."

"It's not that. It's just— Oh, I don't know what I'm saying. I'm sorry."

"Please." He spoke with what sounded like a British accent, only less clipped. "No more 'sorries.' Might I refill that for you?"

Her gaze trailed to the mug she'd forgotten she was holding. "I didn't sleep last night."

He gave a staunch nod, as if she'd given a reasonable explanation for her ridiculousness.

That alone made her fall in love with him.

13

His name was Arne Holm. He was Danish, from a town called Kongens Lyngby, on the outskirts of Copenhagen. He was in San Francisco, he told Dorothy, to talk to the people at Abbott Laboratories about securing a supply of penicillin for a hospital in Denmark, now that enough of the drug had been made for the US war effort. He'd come to Dorothy's hospital to talk to doctors about their experiences with the new drug and been seeking the attending physician on the pediatrics floor when they'd collided. He laughed about it again as they ate doughnuts in the hospital cafeteria, a spartan place that smelled of scorched coffee.

"I was eager to, as you say, 'run into' the attending pediatrician, but I did not mean to crush her."

"Don't worry—I'm still standing."

His eyes were the most singular smoky green. The irises seemed to be made of velvet. She couldn't stop staring into them—when she wasn't scanning the long, smooth planes of his face. Even the small mole on the fine skin of his cheek was beautiful. All this on a man a full head taller than she was.

A trace of powdered sugar rode the knob of his other cheek as he grinned. "I suspect it would take more than me to bowl you over."

Oh, you've done a pretty good job of it, she thought, stirring her coffee. When she looked up, delight zinged back and forth across the little red-Formica-topped table that the two of them dwarfed. What was it about some people that made you adore them on sight and made them adore you back, for no apparent reason? It was rare and it was magical.

She took a sip of the tarry stuff in her mug to balance herself. "Have you had interesting reports on penicillin from the physicians on the other floors?"

"One of the doctors told me of curing a patient in septic shock with it. The patient would have had no chance otherwise. His infection was resistant to the sulfa drugs."

"That's too often the case with sulfa."

He nodded. "Another doctor told me of his luck with pneumonia, just the kind of reports that I hoped to hear."

"We've had our successes in pediatrics, too. Just two weeks ago, a five-year-old girl came in literally choking to death with diphtheria. She was unresponsive to diphtheria serum, but after a ten-day course of penicillin, she is well and back home with her parents. Miraculous." She drew in a breath, absorbing the importance of this to her personally.

Her mug clicked against the Formica when she set it down. "I'm also absolutely thrilled about penicillin's effectiveness against Group A streptococcus."

"Yes?"

"Imagine parents no longer fearing that their child's sore throat is going to lead to scarlet or rheumatic fever. Strep throat will no longer mean possible permanent heart damage or death. I think pediatrics is going to look very different in the future. I, for one, will be thrilled to not be the bearer of tragic news so often."

"That is very good." He drew a breath and smiled with her. "Very good, indeed. How close to one hundred percent effective would you say penicillin is against streptococcus?"

She held up a napkin and made as if to wipe his face. "May I? There's some powdered sugar."

"Please." He held still for her.

She brushed the powdered sugar from his cheek. Buzzing from touching him, she said, "All of the studies aren't yet in on the efficacy of penicillin, but it's still fair to take a page from the newspapers and magazines and call it the 'wonder drug.'"

"*Vidunder middel.* Wonder drug."

She tried and failed to repeat his words in Danish.

"Not to worry, Dr. Horstmann. I like the English. WON-der. That is a good word. It is like a breeze."

They repeated the word with that concept in mind and laughed.

"I suppose streptococcus bacteria don't think penicillin is such a WON-der," she said. "I've seen too many on petri dishes to not imagine them eating, reproducing, and thriving at their hosts' expense, the awful little gluttons. Now they face a plague of their own."

"It is the end of the world for them." He lifted his coffee. "To that I say, *skål.*"

She tried to clink his cup.

"No!" He pulled back, then saw that she felt chastised. "I am sorry. Sometimes my words cannot keep up with my mouth. I only mean to say that to do it as we do in Denmark, you must first look the person in the eye." He fixed her with those velvety sage-colored eyes.

When their gazes were connected, he said, "Once your eyes meet, you speak as if you mean it: *skål.*"

Her pulse accelerated. "*Skål.*"

When they broke apart, the color of the rest of his face matched the apples of his cheeks. He seemed surprised to find his coffee in his hand, then took a drink.

At last, he asked, "Where are you from, Dr. Horstmann?"

"Here." Surely, he could hear her heart thump.

"You are lucky. San Francisco is a magical town."

"I guess I know it too well to think of it that way."

"That is a shame. I have only been here for three days, but I love it. Would you like me to show you around?" He laughed when he saw her expression. "I am serious. May I be your guide? You can tell me if I have not got it right."

They made a plan for the next day that she had off.

He would be going back home the following week.

14

The living room smelled of hair and the well-used oven heating up in the kitchen. Bearlike in a pilled brown cardigan, Pop reached from his chair for Dorothy. "*Schatzi!*" The blue of his eyes nearly disappeared under the swags of his lids as he crowed. "You've come home!"

Dorothy hung up her coat, then stepped around the card table at which her forty-three-year-old brother, Bernard, was too engrossed in making another modeling clay map of the state of California to look up. With a pat to his shoulder, she moved on, past the bushy Christmas tree strung with tinsel and bubbling lights, to Pop in his sagging throne.

"*Schatzi! Mein Schatzi!*" He thumped her back like a drum and then deafened her with kisses to her ear. She'd lived at home since she returned to San Francisco four months ago, but to Pop, every day was homecoming day.

He let her go, then rubbed hands as big as porterhouses. "*Schatzi*, put on our favorite record."

He sat back and folded his huge paws, laying his ridged nails over his knuckles.

She took the heavy platter from its browning paper sleeve, then placed it on the record player of the polished walnut radio cabinet, a recent purchase courtesy of her employment at the hospital.

"No, no, no, no, no, no, no. Not that silly machine. Put it on *our* machine. The one we like." He gestured to the old crank-up Victrola on the scuffed table next to him, then sat back and closed his eyes, trusting that she would do as he asked.

She came over and wound the handle, then set the weighty puck with its needle upon the record. "Moonlight Sonata" strummed through the phonograph's fluted horn.

"Thank you, Dorothy," he said in German, his only language. It was just as well that he rarely left his chair now. In these paranoid times of war, people were just looking for spies, and a German accent alone was suspect. She'd noticed a new poster of a grotesque German on a telephone pole between here and the hospital, warning citizens to be suspicious of their neighbors.

Their song rowing in the background, Pop humming and nodding along with it, she gazed out the window by his chair. A bank of morning fog, unusual for winter, was sliding over the pointed gables of the rowhouses across the street. A Red Cross worker, her navy cape and red headdress flapping in the mist, strode down the sidewalk, as typical a sight in wartime San Francisco as had been a pack of girls jumping rope out front when Dorothy was a child. She could still hear her girlhood self joining in when she wasn't helping Pop, to sing to the *thunk* of the rope:

I had a little bird,
Its name was Enza.
I opened the window
And in-flew-enza.

She'd been seven when the Spanish flu had first raked across the city. All of a sudden, it seemed like to her, everyone in town had to wear masks for what felt like forever to a seven-year-old but was actually closer to a month. When few people fell ill, it was decided that San Francisco was spared, and the whole town was invited to take off their masks.

Church bells pealed and sirens wailed on the designated day. People poured onto the street. All at once, everyone ripped off their covering, then turned their face up to the sky, as if the whole town were newly hatching.

Through dancing neighbors and shouting shoppers she ran, her shoes kicking up the gauze squares trailing cotton strings that littered the streets. Pop was in the emptied bar, mopping the floor.

"Papa! Pop! We're free!"

"What?"

He'd dropped his mop and lumbered behind her as she dragged him by the hand out onto Cole Street, where revelers were throwing their masks in the air and laughing.

Peering into each other's eyes, Pop and she slowly untied their own masks, then—ta-da!—plucked them off.

She pointed to his mustache, askew under his wedge of nose.

"Thank you, *Schatzi*." He combed it with his finger. "Now my scrub-brush is free, too."

How long did it take for the pandemic to come roaring in after that? It was hard for a child to tell. All she knew was that for the next good while, as she and her friends sang about "in-flew-enza," Mary Kiess's mother and Milly Strasser's father and Esther Heller's sister and the grocer on Stanyan Street and their priest and the mailman all died. Schools closed and funeral bells bonged, but still her rope thwacked the ground, the foghorn in the bay bellowing its mournful *bee-OH*.

And then it got the father of her best friend, Rosie.

The singing stopped.

The rope went silent.

It is a frightening thing to see the living room next door in which you played with dolls and drew crayon horses on butcher paper now filled with people in black. It was even scarier to see your best friend sobbing.

Dorothy had crept along the edges of the living room, past

murmuring masked neighbors, past the sofa crowded with masked relatives, past the framed photograph of Rosie's father flanked by little American flags, to get to her friend, who crouched behind the rocker, tear-stained and red-faced. Dorothy was nearly suffocating from the smell coming from the heavily perfumed women gathered around Rosie's mother when she caught the glance of one of the neighbor ladies.

Mrs. Kaiser, a short, sharped-eyed woman who looked just like her biting dachshund, turned to Mrs. Aldacruz. "Isn't that Henry Horstmann's daughter?"

Dorothy twisted away from their unapproving frowns like a worm being put on a hook.

"Why does God take the good ones," Mrs. Kaiser demanded of her neighbor, "and spare the useless, like that retarded Henry Horstmann?"

The ugliness of the word struck like a pistol shot in the back: "retarded."

"He should be in a home. What is Anna thinking?"

Pop had a home. And what did "retarded" mean? Dorothy knew that Pop was different than the other fathers. He was sweeter and better. Much more fun. But even as she knelt next to her crying friend, it was falling together with sickening clarity: why he couldn't learn English, or read and write, or hold more than the lowest job. She'd always thought that he was just easygoing, that he didn't mind cleaning up vomit at the bar, that he enjoyed letting Mutter rule their household and Dorothy lead him around. The chill of understanding sank into her bones: Pop had no choice. There was something wrong with him. He was lesser than other men.

Now Pop opened one eye as the music flowed through the phonograph. "Aren't you listening?"

"Pop, I have to go."

Both eyes flew open. "Where? *Schatzi!* No. Stay with me. The good part of the song is coming." He spread his bear's paw toward the music.

She said the only words that would make him let her go: "I've got to get ready. I'm going to meet a fellow."

"A fellow?"

Bernard looked up from pinching clay into the peaks of the Sierra Nevada.

Pop's droopy lids raised in a smile. "Will I like this fellow? Does he like Beethoven?"

"Yes, Pop. But you can't tell Mutter."

He grinned. "Our secret. I won't."

She knew he wouldn't. He wouldn't be able to remember long enough.

MUTTER WAS OUT IN THE KITCHEN AT THE WORK TABLE, rolling out dough to the thud and squeak of her rolling pin. Dorothy kissed her white-streaked auburn hair smelling of cooking and sebum, then took an envelope from her purse. She laid it next to the electric mixer on the counter.

"Why don't you use the mixer?" Dorothy had given the appliance to her mother two Christmases ago. Dust blanketed its chrome body.

"I will." Mutter thumped and rubbed her rolling pin into the dough. "Stay for dinner. I am making your favorite—*bayrischer Gulasch*."

Dorothy lifted the lid of the pot on the stove. The sweet meaty smell of beef, onions, and carrots cooking in wine swarmed out. She clamped the iron lid back down. "I can't. I'm going out." She ate a pinch from the noodle dough balled in a bowl.

"Out?"

"Back to the hospital." That wasn't a total lie. She was to meet Arne there.

Her mother kept thumping her rolling pin. "I do not understand why you do not come home. I make it nice for you. I cook, I clean for you. I give the best bed to you."

"I didn't want it, Mutter."

"I want you to have it! I was so happy when you came back home to us. I could not believe—a gift! But you are never here." She spoke in heavily accented English. Dorothy wondered if she'd been bothered on the streets for it. Her mother wouldn't say if she had. In all of her life, Dorothy could not recall her mother ever confiding in her.

"I would wake everyone up with the hours I keep."

"Dorothy." Mutter stopped her rolling and turned to look up at her, her eyes big behind thick lenses. "Your father is not doing so well."

Dorothy's heart clenched. She knew this. She knew that over time, his forgetfulness was frequently tipping into confusion, and she could not bear it.

"Stay for him. He asks about you all day. Won't you stay for him?"

"Yes, Mutter. I will. But not today."

"When?"

"Soon."

"Why not today?"

"Soon, I promise." The way it usually went with men, it wouldn't be long before this one was gone, and this one was guaranteed not to last—he was to return to Denmark next week.

"'Bye, Mutter. Love you." She took another pinch of dough and loped through the living room, where Pop gasped and shouted, "*Schatzi*, you're home!"

THAT AFTERNOON, MR. HOLM, IN A GREEN WOOL SCARF AND navy peacoat that would have skimmed the ankles of the average man, towered above the Christmas tree still standing in the hospital lobby although it was December 27. The overhead light shone on his fine brown hair, which gleamed like a sheet of taffeta. When he spied her striding across the speckled tile, his face crinkled into a smile.

"You look beautiful!" His smile wavered. "Is that okay for me to say?"

"Yes. Thank you." *Quit your insane smiling.* "I'm ready for your tour of my native town."

"I am prepared to give it, but only on the condition that you call me Arne."

"Fair enough. And I am Dorothy."

"May I call you Dorte? 'Dorothy' is 'Dorte' in Danish. I fear I will slip into it. It suits you."

"I'll take it as a compliment." Was she going to grin like this the whole time they were together?

A nurse walked by, the white wings of her cap turning toward them until she could twist her head no further.

"We seem to be of interest."

They must look like visitors from a planet of titans. "I think so."

"Should we go?" He crooked his arm for Dorothy to take.

Outside, the fog had lifted, leaving blue skies as a backdrop to the white stone buildings of the campus. They strolled along, eliciting either stares or gazes intently pointed away. "Here we have your typical December day in San Francisco," he said, oblivious to them. "I am proclaiming it to be typical because it has been thus since I arrived a week ago."

"That seems reasonable."

"Back home in Denmark, we have clouds in December, and constant wind and rain. In addition, we only have seven hours of daylight. The sun rises mid-morning and sets in the mid-afternoon."

"That sounds . . . dark."

He grinned. "You would think so, but it is not. We compensate by lighting candles—entire banks of them. In truth, we cannot wait for the days to shorten so that we can get out our candles."

"How smart to make lemonade out of lemons."

"'Making lemonade out of lemons.' A good expression—I will keep it. I collect American sayings. Correct me if I get them wrong."

They strolled uphill, then stopped in front of an ornate Victorian building. In front of it stood a Pacific Indian totem pole, as out of place as one of her crazy tufts of hair.

"Here we have the anthropology museum." He tapped the totem pole with his umbrella.

She pretended to inspect the carvings when, in fact, the crouching eagles stacked up the pole were familiar old friends. Having grown up just down the street, she often came to visit them. "I see."

"I have always been interested in anthropology. In Denmark, we have our Vikings. Here, you have your California Indians. Both are long gone. Well, the California Indian not so long—1916, I believe. A man named Ishi was the last."

"You know of Ishi?" Every Northern Californian schoolchild heard the story of Ishi, the "wild" Indian who walked out of the woods, starving and alone, the last of his kind on the earth.

"I have been told that Ishi lived right here in this building. He was put on live display in a museum exhibit. People would stroll by as he made arrowheads or skinned rabbits."

"You do know a lot about him." When she was a girl, she went into the museum just to see Ishi's photograph and the arrowheads he'd made. How her young heart had ached for him.

"One of the university doctors befriended him," said Arne, "and got him to show him how to hunt with a bow and arrow. The doctor picked his head to learn all the secrets of bow hunting—"

"Picked his brain, I think you mean."

He thought about the difference, then laughed. "That might be worse! He picked Ishi's *brain* to learn all his secrets, and so himself became the world's leading expert on hunting with a bow. They were great friends, he and Ishi, best of friends, but when Ishi died of tuberculosis, who autopsied Ishi? His doctor friend—against Ishi's religion, I might add. He sent Ishi's heart to one laboratory, his brain to another, and so on, distributing pieces as if his friend were a scientific curiosity and not a man."

She thought fleetingly of Dr. Sabin and his confession years ago about his friend's autopsy. How easily the line could be crossed between pursuing knowledge and human decency.

Arne tilted his head. "I see I am troubling you. I am sorry. That is not what I wished to do." He held out his elbow to usher her again. "We shall only speak of happy things the rest of the day," he said firmly. "Today will be a day of light. I shall no longer be your guide of San Francisco—"

"But you were doing so well!"

"No. I made you sad. But I can be a good guide in the Danish art of hygge."

"Hooga?"

"That is it—hygge. I think you'll like this new tour better."

"What is hooga?"

"Hygge? Well, we shall start with this first example." He unwound his scarf, then wrapped it, still bearing his warmth, around her neck. "You will rarely catch a Dane without his scarf. A soft one is best." He hesitated, then cheerily tied it. "Knitted by a loved one is even better."

She wondered who had knitted this one. "But now you've lost your hygge."

He looked down at her with those velvety sage eyes. "Once you have achieved hygge, it is not as easy to lose as that."

They walked along, her drawing in his scent on the scarf, him stealing glances at her and smiling.

"Tell me about yourself," she said.

"Oh, there is not much to tell. I teach—well, I taught—English in the state high school."

She paused. "You're a teacher? I assumed that you were a doctor, or hospital administrator, since you are here to get penicillin for your hospital—not that it matters."

"Yes."

She waited for more of an explanation.

They kept walking, her new dress shoes rubbing sore spots on her heels and toe-tops as the silence widened between them. Denmark was occupied by Germany now. Would a teacher be allowed out of the country? Would *anyone* be allowed out of the country? How had he gotten here? There were no civilian transatlantic crossings during time of war. She thought of the spy poster she'd seen that morning. Perhaps she should not have scoffed.

"It must have been difficult to get here," she said.

Twin brushy Monterey pines stood sentinel to the entrance to Golden Gate Park. "A park!" he proclaimed. "This will be very good for our hygge, especially if there are ponds and wildlife and such. Nature is a friend to hygge, as are companions, human and otherwise."

As a doctor, you learned to be direct, even though you feared the answer. "Mr. Holm, how did you get to the US?"

He winced.

The heels of her awful shoes tapped against the sidewalk in syncopation with his footsteps. Her heart sank lower with each second that he didn't answer.

He indicated the concessions stand ahead. "Ah, drinks for sale. A hot drink could help our achievement of hygge." He looked at her directly. "Please, allow me to buy you a cocoa."

She was sick of hygge already. She was sick of disappointments, and of this hideous war, which tainted everything, including what had been a lovely walk in the park save for the blisters rising on her feet. "I should be getting back."

He stopped and faced her. "I am not a German spy, if that is what you believe. Think about it—who would choose a man my size to do their secret bidding? I cannot exactly sneak about."

She laughed in spite of herself. But who was he, then?

"One moment." He veered over to the vendor.

The man inside the booth had the pitted face of someone scarred with acne. When Dorothy and Arne ambled up, his jaw hung like a potato in the bottom of a sack at the sight of them. "Wow. Are you two tall! What are you, some kind of twins?"

"You should see our mother," said Arne.

Dorothy's gaze fell on the poster taped to the window of the stand. It featured a close-up of a hand lying open next to the smoldering remains of a rifle stock. Strands of barbed wire in the background suggested a battlefield. SOMEBODY BLABBED, it read. BUTTON YOUR LIP.

Arne bore two steaming paper cups from the counter. "Now, let us try again."

The Dixie cup warm on her hands, she sipped cocoa that tasted slightly of wax as they ventured on through a grove of shaggy eucalyptus trees. "Tell me about you," he said. "You grew up in San Francisco . . ."

She sucked in a breath. "Then I trained here, did my residency in Nashville, then was at Yale."

"Yale. Impressive."

She did not tell him that she had been let go.

"And before that—you grew up here?"

"Yes." Now it was her turn to keep quiet. To talk about Pop seemed to dishonor him. He was so much more than a man with a brain injury.

The park grounds grew more wooded; the bamboo walls of the Japanese Tea Garden came into view. Soon they were picking their way down a path that meandered over a murmuring stony brook and through stands of twisted pines. Grasses, mosses, and ferns grew so lushly here that even the air smelled green. No one was in sight.

They stopped at the tea house, where she went to the window. The room seem to vibrate with abandonment.

How often had she peered in here as a little girl, watching as well-dressed San Franciscan mothers and daughters were served tea. How precise and proper the Japanese ladies serving them were, how very honorable. Their every movement was controlled, graceful, powerful in their silence. They seemed to be of a different species than her own mother, slinging drinks and washing dishes at the bar that also employed Pop.

Arne ducked to look into the tea house window. "This cozy house looks particularly well suited for hygge." He stepped around to the front. "'Oriental Tea House.'"

"'Oriental Tea House'? It's not called the Japanese Tea House?"

He pointed to the hastily made sign bound to the original.

"We're not even supposed to say 'Japanese' now? What kind of people are we becoming, suspicious of everyone?"

He gazed at her long enough to acknowledge her own suspicion of him. "This is why we must always look for good," he said gently.

"Frankly, I don't even know what good is anymore. We're the good guys, yet did you know that all Japanese Americans have been taken from their homes here in San Francisco, the home of our hygge tour?"

He shook his head.

"Old folks, children, entire families, anyone who is one-sixteenth Japanese or more were put in camps in the desert. Relocation camps. Why don't we just call them what they are—concentration camps, here in America."

He waited with a gentle smile. "Dorte, you can find bad everywhere, if you look, and look you must do, if you are to battle it. But you also must look for the good, to remind you what you are fighting for." He grimaced. "I know this from experience."

When he saw her watching him, he smiled, though sadness lingered behind his gray-green eyes. "This is a hygge tour, so today we are looking for the good. To that end, I know of a delicatessen near here that serves the perfect corned beef sandwich." He reached out and took her elbow. "You start where you can start."

15

A cloud sharp with the aroma of spices and roasting meat steamed the windows of the deli on Haight Street. At their little table, she repositioned her hands around the bread as if that might somehow make the sandwich fit better into her mouth. Arne was not having the same trouble.

He finished chewing a huge bite, then took another and gulped it before he spoke. "The food here is always strictly kosher. It is quite delicious, yes?"

"Oh, yes." She attempted another bite. He must be Jewish. Was he a refugee? Then why would he want to go back to Nazi-occupied territory?

"You said that you taught English in high school." She wiped her lips. "Did you mean the language or literature?"

He tipped his glossy hair. "Both!"

His story made no sense, but couldn't she let it go, just for today? "I got a degree in English literature in college, before I could apply to medical school."

"Ah, then, what books do you love?"

"Jane Austen, for starters."

He munched, then swallowed. "Oh, now that is a given."

She pointed to where mustard had dribbled onto his chin. "Though *Wuthering Heights* is my favorite. You hate Heathcliff for his cruelty, yet you also pity him, understanding that he has only known heartbreak."

"I marvel that Brontë wrote the book though tucked away on the moors of Yorkshire," he said, wiping. "How well she knew the human animal, even in her isolation."

From behind a black curtain at the back of the restaurant emerged a short man with a halo of silver around his gleaming head. "Mr. Holm!" he cried, wiping his hands on his apron. "David told me that you were here."

Arne jumped up, exclaiming, then bent down for them to thump each other on the back, and then the man's wife came out, and there was exclaiming and kissing anew. After Dorothy had been introduced to the Levys, Mr. Levy told Arne, "I'm making something special in the kitchen. Come back and try it."

Mrs. Levy, the top of whose fluffy black hair came up to Dorothy's ribs, took Dorothy's hands as the men trooped back to the kitchen. "I'm glad to see Arne with a nice woman. And a doctor! He deserves all the happiness in the world after what he has done."

They released hands. "And what is that?"

"You know, his mission to evacuate the Jews."

Dorothy shook her head.

"You don't know? Oh, he should have told you! Arne is a hero!"

"He is?"

"If you count helping to save seven thousand Danish Jews, he is. He and a band of schoolteachers put together the plan."

"My goodness!"

"They organized regular fishermen, holiday cottagers, anyone with a little boat. He himself hid a family in his home."

He wasn't Jewish?

"Then, in a single night, a year ago October, the flotilla of little boats ferried them all to neutral Sweden. His group got out almost every Jew in Denmark, my aunt and uncle among them. But the authorities found out who is responsible for this miracle. He cannot go back to Denmark, not that he'd want to."

He couldn't go back? He'd told her he was getting penicillin for his hospital in Denmark.

"Why wouldn't he want to?"

Mrs. Levy flashed a worried glance toward the kitchen. "Perhaps you need to ask him that."

THEY WERE HEADED PAST THE TURRETED ROWHOUSES AND storefronts of Haight Street after dinner. Misgivings about Arne's secrecy overruled the pain screaming from her blistered heels and toes, reminders that vanity never paid. Who was this man ambling by her side? He had claimed to be rounding up penicillin for a hospital in Denmark, yet Mrs. Levy just told her that he'd been kicked out of that country. He'd chatted up the doctors at her hospital as if he were a colleague, though he himself admitted that he was a schoolteacher by trade. He was here in the United States at a time when travel overseas was impossible and entry into the country forbidden—who'd gotten him in? And the story he'd told Mrs. Levy about helping seven thousand Jews to escape Nazi occupation! Was he even Danish?

She kept her voice friendly. "I didn't know that you were a hero."

Arne glanced at her. "Who told you that?"

"Mrs. Levy."

She rolled her gaze up at him. He scowled.

Shouldn't he be bragging? If she'd rescued seven thousand people, she'd at least be dropping broad hints. "You should be proud. You saved all those people."

"They saved themselves. I just helped to find boats for them to get away in."

"But Mrs. Levy said that you organized the escape."

"I was one of many." He looked down at her feet. "Are you okay? You are limping."

"Yes."

He raised his brows with doubt.

"Bad shoes. I think I have blisters."

She was glancing at a passing car when her feet flew off the ground. Suddenly, her back was against one of his arms, and her knees were hooked over the other. She was being carried down the street like a very large toddler.

"What are you doing?"

"The good that I can do."

"But—I must be breaking your back!"

"Allow me this privilege, please."

A young couple walked by, their heads turning in unison. A woman pushing a baby buggy gaped, then pushed her buggy faster. Had they never seen Zeus toting Hera down the street before?

She laughed in spite of herself. "People are staring."

"Let them! Maybe we will be the one good thing that they see today."

She liked that idea until it occurred to her: Did he plan to stagger like this all the way back to the hospital?

"A street car will be coming along soon. You can put me on one."

"I cannot do that. I would feel like a cud."

"You mean a cad."

"*Cad*," he voiced to himself. Louder, he said, "I do not wish to be a cad. Where is your home? I could take you there."

"No!" She had never taken a man home. Mutter and Pop would never let him out of the house. She cleared her throat. "No, thank you."

His face, close enough that she could smell his aftershave, was troubled. "I cannot send you off in an injured state. Do not think me forward, but I am staying at the Stadium Hotel."

They both looked toward the Victorian hotel building, just up the block.

"May I take you there? I keep sticking plasters in my travel kit. I can patch you up, then accompany you wherever you wish to go."

If this man was a spy, he was lousy at blending in. His goodness made him stand out like a beacon in the darkness. And his back had to be breaking.

"You are very generous. Thank you."

When he carried her into the hotel, the man at the front desk froze before his wall of keys. A bill floated from his hands.

"My sister is in trouble," Arne called to him. "Sorry," he whispered.

Once up the elevator and at his room, he put her down long enough to put his key in the door. Doubts about the propriety, if not the safety, of her being here were tumbling through her mind when she felt her legs being swept up from under her again.

"Carrying me across the threshold, are you?"

"What do you mean?"

She blushed. "I can walk."

He carried her to his bed and ceremoniously put her down. Now he was blushing. "I will just pop in here and get the bandages." He hurried to the bathroom, snatching up discarded socks along the way.

"No candles in here?" She called after him. "That's not very hygge."

She heard the sink running, and some rummaging through a bag. He came back carrying a damp washcloth and a tin of Band-Aids. "I made up for the candles by having a little Christmas tree. But I took it to the hospital on Christmas Day."

"You had a Christmas tree? In here?"

"A small one. I will admit that I am a bit homesick. I thought that having a tree would bring me a little cheer. But no, having a tree without family on Christmas Eve is the opposite of hygge." He opened the Band-Aid tin. "It is a very bad idea to dance alone."

"You danced on Christmas Eve?"

"Around the Christmas tree. You do not?"

She shook her head.

"I cannot believe! It is a favorite Danish tradition. The whole family joins hands and sings as we dance around the tree."

"You dance *and* sing? Really? Everyone? Even grown-ups?"

He chuckled. "I think the grown-ups like it best. Even if there are just two of you."

It was as if some plug had been pulled in him. He sagged with a loss of energy. His gaze trailed to her legs, which seemed to sadden him further. "You are wearing hosiery."

"Yes." She pulled her dress over her knees self consciously.

"Forgive me. You must truly think me a cad." He shook his head. "I pictured myself as the hero, doctoring the doctor's wounds. I had forgotten about hosiery." He made a show of placing the box of Band-Aids next to her on the bed, then backed away. "Perhaps you would like to use my WC?"

"Thank you." She took the tin and washcloth and hobbled into the bathroom, where she sat on the toilet, took off her shoes, then unfastened her garters.

She raised her voice through the closed door, as if that might cover their awkwardness. "Now that you mention it, I seem to remember a scene describing the dancing around the tree in the Hans Christian Andersen story 'The Fir Tree.'"

His voice carried through the door: "Yes."

"I love that story. Poor little fellow." She rolled her hose down over her leg, peeling it from the bloody spots on her heel and toes, then quickly repeated the operation on the other leg. "He just wanted to be a Christmas tree." She clenched her teeth as she dabbed an open blister with the dampened washcloth. "How proud he was, getting chosen out of all the trees in the forest to be chopped down. Little did he know that he was cheering for his own death." Her wounds were stinging as she flipped open the tin of Band-Aids. "Maybe that is not the most hygge of stories," she called, her voice echoing from the tiling.

It was quiet on the other side.

At last he said through the door, "But maybe it is the most true of his tales. Maybe we all are just striving for our own end."

Whoever this man was, in her bones, she knew he was a good one. She closed the tin resolutely, then came out. "Then one should make the striving glorious."

When he raised his eyes, she held out the tin of Band-Aids. "Could you help me, please?"

He hesitated, then took the tin from her. He opened it with a scrape of its white metal lid, drew out a bandage, unwrapped it, then, as gently as would a father tending his child, applied it to the wounded heel that she turned to him.

They repeated the process, her presenting her wounds to him, him covering them, his warm fingers brushing her feet and toes. When he was done, he shut the lid, then eased down on the bed next to her.

He crossed his little finger over hers. They sat like that with their fingers intertwined, tension crackling across the space between them, until suddenly he inhaled, and, the wool of his sleeve sighing across her dress, pulled her into him.

She turned her face up to his. He touched his lips to hers.

She thought she might melt with pleasure, when suddenly, he removed himself and stood.

"It is my hotel room and not proper. I must not be a cad."

"A cud? You're not!"

He sighed, then drew her up from the bed. "Ready to go?"

"No. I'm really not." She rested her palms on the wall of his chest. Even the feel of his inhalations undid her. "We may never have this moment again."

"That is guaranteed. There is no moment that we ever have again. Every moment is a beginning and an end."

Must he always philosophize? "Oh, Arne. Can't we just—" She brought her lips to his. And for a timeless, dazzling, glorious moment that neither of them would forget for the rest of their lives, Arne Holm was wordless.

DOROTHY DID NOT KNOW THAT SHE COULD TALK—OR KISS—so much. It was night when they left the hotel, leaning their heads together as they walked, as if their minds were physically connected.

After a warm stretch of silence, he said, "I think you would like Denmark."

"I would? Isn't it dreary?" she joked. "It needs all that hygge. And weren't you kicked out?"

He pulled away, then stopped. His face was serious. "Dorte, will you come to Denmark? Not now—not while it is occupied by hate-filled men. But it will not always be occupied, I promise you. There is too much resistance."

"Stay here," she pleaded.

"I cannot. I have one last matter of business."

"With the penicillin?"

He hesitated. "Yes."

She gave him one more chance to explain himself. "You're taking it to a hospital? In Denmark?"

"I am taking it where it is needed." When he saw her expression, he said, "I promise I am not delivering it to Nazis, if that is what you think. But do you remember that sign we saw in the park, the one that said someone blubbed?"

She thought a second. "You mean blabbed. And that means you don't trust me."

He kissed her. "I do trust you. Believe me, *elskede*, I do. And I will tell you everything when we see each other again."

She felt ill. "But how do you know we will see each other?"

"It does not take me months to know that there is something good, and right, about us together. And something as good and right as we are must be fought for. And so, I will fight to be with you again. And so, Dorte, I will win." He tucked a wing of her hair behind her ear. "You will see."

1945

A SECRETARY

Beryl was rolling a piece of stationery onto the platen of her typewriter when Dr. Paul came breezing in, his grin as wide as his red bow tie.

"She took the job!"

Beryl didn't have to ask who. In her eleven years as his secretary, she'd seen Dr. Paul as excited as a child with a Christmas puppy about a new hire only once, and it was the person he was thrilled about now. "Congratulations."

He rubbed neatly groomed hands, as delicate as a child's. "I didn't think she'd come back. I had to offer an associate professorship to get her to budge. A fellowship just wasn't going to cut it."

Beryl dialed down the paper to type in the address as he went into his office. Dr. Horstmann would have come no matter what he offered. The woman burned to wipe out polio. She would have scaled the Empire State Building and beat her chest like King Kong from the dirigible mooring mast if she thought it would help the cause. Didn't he see that? If Dorothy hadn't immediately leaped when he said that he wanted her to return to the study group, something else would have been holding her back, and not the insulting offer of another fellowship. Hadn't he seen the insult in that the first time, when he'd passed her over for an associate professorship for Robbie Ward?

Dr. Paul was pleasant but he was blind. Sometimes Beryl got

weary dealing with it. Only knowing that she was unlikely to ever find a less blind boss, and that the Yale Study Group was the most likely place on earth to find a way to prevent, if not cure, polio, kept her here.

Just because she typed up statistics didn't mean she couldn't interpret raw data. After a slight dip in polio cases during the first two war years, they were climbing again. They were sure to worsen. With the promise of soldiers coming home soon from Europe now that the war had been won there, and with the war in Japan accelerating in hopes of bringing it to an end, this summer families were loosening up and going to lakes, swimming pools, and parks. The upcoming homecomings would only fuel the greedy monster, providing a bumper crop of babies to devour.

Her gaze went to the framed photo on her desk. She was prepared to say that the child was her niece, though none of her employers had ever thought to ask her about it. In truth, Emily was a daughter to her. Beryl loved her with a fierce maternal fervor that had taken her as off guard as had the friendship that had blossomed into more with her mother, Paula. It stabbed Beryl in the heart every time she saw the child limp after her friends on her withered leg. No child should have to endure that. It was tough enough negotiating your own differences without having another one tacked on.

She rolled the paper down to type the salutation line. In his office, Dr. Paul was rummaging through his desk. It was going to be a bad summer for polio, yet the study group was hung up on measuring the efficiency of DDT against flies. Did the men not read their own statistics? Public health officials could refit Army trucks that had rumbled through Normandy to make them spew tons of the chemical on US streets. They could strafe rural America with the nasty stuff from former bombers by air. But even Beryl could see that DDT was killing flies but it wasn't killing polio. How many ways did they have to measure this to see it? So many nights Paula had her work cut out, comforting Beryl as she lamented their blindness.

Come back, Dorothy. Come back. We need you to cut through the nonsense.

Dr. Paul appeared in his doorway. "Mrs. Beasley, do we have any pencils with new erasers? I wore my last one out mapping where to spray when we go to Paterson. Oh, and would you mind picking up some sandwiches for lunch? For the usual crew."

When she reached into her desk and produced a pencil, he shook his head with appreciation. "You're a life-saver."

16

PATERSON, NEW JERSEY, 1945

The August heat brought them out in droves, the little girls in puffy-sleeved dresses, windmilling their arms in the spray, the bony little boys high-stepping into it like drum majors. The most daring of them dashed up to the truck, took a blast of DDT to the face, then slapped the fat bumper and ran back to their friends.

The vials in the specimen chests strapped over each of Dorothy's shoulders jingled as she waved her arms. "HEY!"

One look at her and the pack of truck-chasers ran away screaming. Already they chanted "Fee-Fi-Fo-Fum" whenever she entered their buildings. Poking them with needles hadn't exactly recommended her to them, and she'd had to stick most of the kids in this housing project for her study. But if having kids think she was a monster kept them out of this poison, so be it.

"Dorothy? Dorothy Horstmann?"

She turned around. Albert Sabin, elegant in his khaki officer's uniform, approached with a grin.

She found that she was glad to see him, any past misgivings about him dimmed by the relief one felt when a soldier returned safely to the States. "What are you doing here? You're supposed to be in the Pacific."

"I could ask the same of you." He was aiming to peck her cheek when she stepped in a puddle iridescent with DDT.

Scheiße!

He reached for the bigger of her specimen chests. "Let me take that. I've seen donkeys in the marketplace at Cairo less loaded down than this." He shouldered the chest with its jingling cargo. They tussled briefly for the other before he gave up and settled for the one. "Our orders, sir?"

"To the car," she said. "But I'm taking you out of your way."

"I was just going to the train station."

She paused. "The train station's the other way."

He set out in the direction she'd been going. "Lead on."

"I don't want to make you miss your train."

He didn't answer, only kept walking.

Frowning, she caught up with him, her specimen chest thumping her hip. "When did you get back? I just read that you found a vaccine for sand fly fever"—she caught up—"and are close to one for Japanese encephalitis."

"I am." He hiked up the strap of the chest. "What am I carrying here?"

"The usual. I'm back at Yale."

"I didn't know you'd left."

"For about a year." Of which five months had been torture. She'd not heard from Arne. She only recently found out why she wouldn't.

"What's your study on?"

She brought herself back to the conversation. "The effect of exterminating flies with DDT on polio case numbers."

He nodded, pleased. It was his paper suggesting that houseflies might be responsible for the spread of polio that had started the public health stampede to spray the dickens out of them. Her study for the Polio Unit was a direct result of it.

"And how is that going?" he asked.

"Not all that promising. In areas that we hand-sprayed to monitor closely, plenty of flies are being killed but cases are hardly dropping." If it had been her decision, she would have studied the effects of DDT on children before the wholesale spraying had begun. She looked at him expectantly. "What brings you to Paterson?"

He hiked up the bag on his shoulder. "I just returned from Okinawa."

That wasn't really an answer but—"Okinawa!"

The news this summer was full of reports of suicide bombers and hand-to-hand combat there. The Japanese soldiers fought like they didn't care whether they lived, and most didn't. Only five percent of them were said to survive. The Americans, though victorious, had been shattered by the carnage they'd seen. "Okinawa" had come to be shorthand for "slaughter."

"I was there collecting encephalitis tissue," he said.

"In the middle of Armageddon?"

"I set up my assays in a cave and was quite safe."

"In a cave!"

He shrugged. "I'm just grateful that I wasn't in Nagasaki."

A chill descended over them. Last week, the second atomic bomb had been dropped on that town, three days after the first A-bomb fell on Hiroshima. A new kind of war had begun, one in which entire cities were obliterated by a single blow. Although no pictures from the bombings were allowed in American papers, hundreds of thousands of children, women, and men had to have died, the scale of suffering unimaginable. Overnight, the rules of humanity had changed.

"You should be home in bed with a bottle of whiskey." She stopped at her university car, a brown Chevrolet the shape and color of a June bug. "Seriously, why *are* you here?"

He looked at his watch. "I could talk all day, but I have to catch a train."

"Where are you going?"

"New York."

"Get in the car." When he raised his brows, she added, "You might as well. I'm going through town on my way back to New Haven."

"Thank you. But I have my train ticket."

She peeled the specimen chest strap from his shoulder. "Get in. I'm shanghaiing you to New York and getting you a meal. No man who just got home from a cave in Okinawa is going unfed as long as I have something to say about it."

HOT GRIMY AIR SMELLING OF EXHAUST BLASTED THROUGH the rolled-down window of the university-owned June Bug. Over in the passenger seat, his head thrown back, the khaki tie of his uniform loosened, his mouth hanging open, Dr. Sabin slept like the dead. He'd fallen asleep within fifteen minutes of leaving Paterson. Dorothy supposed that conducting experiments under stalactites while men were trying to butcher each other just outside had been exhausting.

In Fort Lee, she drove by an empty Howard Johnson's. Every window of the restaurant had been boarded up, even in the dormers and cupola, with this sign taped to the door:

CLOSED FOR THE DURATION

DUE TO SHORTAGE OF GASOLINE AND MANPOWER

Where plate glass through which one could see people eating fried clam strips had once been was a government-issued poster depicting a beautiful woman putting amorous moves on a very pleased sailor. **He volunteered for SUBMARINE SERVICE**, it read.

Would life ever be the same? The war was nearly at an end, but the dread of getting news that a friend or relative had died or was missing still hung like a noxious vapor in the air. The fear of a stateside sub attack or air raid still lurked just below consciousness, a fear revived every time sirens went off for an air raid drill. And while no attacks had happened so far, just last month an unarmed US Army bomber, lost in the rain, crashed into the darkened Empire State Building between the seventy-eighth and seventy-ninth floors. Three crew members and eleven people from a Catholic war relief agency had been killed.

Yet, somehow, in the face of all this heartbreak and strangeness, everyone carried on. They read the paper, went to work, shopped for Sunbeam bread and margarine at the Piggly Wiggly, cooked dinner, and, after listening to the radio, put themselves to bed after brushing their teeth with tooth powder, just like they had always done. Dorothy had always wondered how people survived the horrors of the American Civil War. Now she knew. No matter how many shortages and restrictions nor how much fear floated in the air, unless the war was actually being fought on your doorstep or your loved one was hurt or lost or killed, everyday life trudged on. Even when you knew that the man with whom you'd fallen in love was never coming back, on life slogged.

Ahead, above the trees, the George Washington Bridge came into view, its girders resembling a squared-off Eiffel Tower. Next to her, Dr. Sabin twitched in his slumber.

When she had not heard from Arne right away, she wasn't surprised. International communications were limited due to the war. Yearning to talk to someone who knew him if she could not have the man himself, she'd gone to have a heart-to-heart with the Levys. A heart-to-heart. Arne would have liked that expression.

She'd had to learn from the Levys that Arne Holm had been married.

He lost his wife the year before Dorothy met him. A tragic death, they'd said in troubled voices. She'd been caught taking a Jewish family to safety. She'd been executed outside a police station near Copenhagen.

Dorothy had taken the news in shocked silence. No wonder he'd not told her. How he must have loved his wife, so much so that he couldn't bear the pain of talking about her. His time with Dorothy must have been an attempt to forget his beloved wife—a failed one, judging by his silence these past long months. *You're a fool to think you'll ever hear from him again*, she scolded herself as the June Bug whined to a stop at the tollbooth. *You've got to scrub that man from your mind.*

Ahead, above the gaping chasm of the Hudson River, a ribbon of highway dangled. Dorothy looked at her watch. Just before five. They'd be over the bridge in ten minutes. Not quickly enough.

She rolled up her window as she started the car forward. She hated bridges over water in general, and suspension bridges with their flimsy cables in particular. Having had to fetch her pop on the brand-new Golden Gate back when she was in medical school, her mother frantically finding her in anatomy class after being tipped off at the bar that "friends" were dumping him there as a "funny" prank, might have had something to do with it.

Now, as she approached the first Erector Set tower, she tightened her grip on the steering wheel. She imagined the great cables snapping, the bridge swinging free, and the car sailing into the abyss.

They'd almost made it to the middle when the honking started. First it was a panel truck coming from the New York side. Then another vehicle joined in, and another, until all the cars and trucks around them were blasting. Was someone going to jump? She felt sick.

Dr. Sabin sat up. "What's going on?"

"I don't know."

People were beginning to hang out of their car windows, shouting, waving, as if they weren't dozens of stories in the air and only a few feet of concrete and some guardrails weren't the only things between them and the atmosphere.

Dr. Sabin buttoned his collar, then called out the window to the truck driver gleefully laying on his horn next to him. "Say, what's going on?"

The truck driver's thick chin dropped to his bow tie. "You don't know? Have you been living in a cave?"

"As a matter of fact," Dr. Sabin called, "yes."

"Japan's going to surrender! Truman's going to announce it any moment!"

The traffic stopped. Two cars ahead, a sailor and a young woman sprang from a car and began jitterbugging in their lane, the wind whipping his baggy trousers and her polka-dotted skirt. The image of Pop, clinging to red metal rails, his shirt billowing in the blast, flashed through her mind. It turned out that her brave giant of a pop was afraid of heights.

"Are you all right?" said Dr. Sabin.

"I don't like bridges."

She felt his hand close around her biceps. He squeezed gently. "Don't worry. I've got you."

Sweat soaked her scalp. She saw herself with her arm around Pop, inching toward land.

"Hey. Hey—you're going to be okay." Dr. Sabin released her. Suddenly he burst out, "Step right up and see the amazing lady scientist!"

She glanced his way.

"Got you to look!" He laughed. "Guess I haven't lost my touch. That's from my carnival barker days."

"You were a carnival barker?"

"In high school. And a good one, I daresay. My exhibits got the most traffic, even when they weren't girly shows. My favorite was"—he lifted his voice—"BABIES IN INCUBATORS! Don't forget to see the BABIES IN INCUBATORS! Come and see the WORLD'S SMALLEST LIVING INFANTS!"

She tried not to feel the wind on her face. "Are you serious?"

"Completely. I worked the baby incubator exhibit at Coney Island. The building had a row of what looked like small iceboxes with a glass door, each one with a premature baby in it. The nurse would take out a baby and display it next to a milk bottle, to show the crowd how small it was in comparison. A Dr. Martin Couney presided, with his daughter, who'd been a premature infant herself, as his nurse. He didn't lose any of the babies the summer I was there."

More people were joining the bridge dancers. Why didn't they just stay in their cars?

"The only difference between Dr. Couney and every other doctor with a premature patient was that he decided the impossible was possible. He made me want to be a hero, just like him."

She glanced at him again.

He laughed. "Even carnies have dreams."

"For a rich boy, you certainly were adventuresome."

"Rich boy? Where'd you get that idea?"

"Isn't almost everyone well-to-do in the medical boys' club?"

Another pair had alit from the car just ahead and was foxtrotting around its bulbous fenders.

Dr. Sabin glanced at her, then away. "I remember marching with the German troops as a boy."

Please, people, just get back in your cars.

"Like little boys everywhere, my brothers and I marched down the main street of our town with them."

"When was this?" she asked in spite of herself. "In the First World War?"

"Oh, no. Before that. Almost ten years before, back when the Germans fought the Russians for the corner of what is now Poland in which my family lived. Poor little Bialystok. The town has changed more hands than a snowsuit in a family of six sons."

"You're from . . . Poland?"

"When the Germans came marching in, the Russians had

already fled, taking all our livestock—the only thing of value, really—with them. There was a church along one of the main streets, with a big area around it that was empty, so the Germans broke their march and settled there for a rest."

He smiled when she glanced at him. "I sat down against the church wall, next to a young German soldier—young, I say, because when he took off his helmet, I saw that he had a boy's plump pink face, white eyebrows, and pale hair. For days I'd had nothing to eat, so with big eyes, I followed each trip to his mouth of his big black slab of pumpernickel spread with butter as thick as the bread itself. When he saw me watching his every bite, he stopped, picked up his other slice, and gave it to me. Nothing has ever tasted so delicious since."

He sighed before continuing. "I had to pilfer the countryside for food for my family with my older brother, who was four years older than I. We went on long hikes, trying to get something to eat from this farmer, that farmer, a little bread, a few potatoes, a few greens. The German armies were on the march, as well, accompanied by horses and wagons, but we didn't dare to hitchhike. Yet when they saw these two scrawny kids on the road, they would pick us up and give us a ride. We weren't used to such kindness from our occupiers. It was very different when the Russians were in charge."

More people had gotten out of their cars and were smoking cigarettes and chatting. Dr. Sabin got out his own pack and offered her one. She shook her head.

"It was not good to be a Jew during the Russian occupation. The pogroms were often started in the churches, by a sermon preaching that the Jews had killed their god. Fired up by the accusations from the pulpit, mobs of soldiers and local hooligans would get drunk and break into homes or start fires or even kill any Jew who happened to be passing by." He put a cigarette between his lips. "And the police would just stand there."

He lit his cigarette, then snapped his lighter closed. "Therefore, it was of no consequence"—he blew out smoke—"certainly not an item recorded in the newspaper nor lamented by anyone other than his parents, who were just poor Jewish weavers, when their five-year-old son, walking by a church, was attacked by a mob. The Russians threw bricks at him, stones, whatever they could get their hands on. One of the bricks caught the top of his cheekbone." He pointed to the corner of his eye, to a scar the size of a thumbprint, nearly faded from sight. "His parents feared he would be blinded. But he wasn't. Not completely." He opened his eyes wide. "He can still see from it."

"Oh, Albert, I'm so sorry." She kept her hands on the steering wheel. "All this time I thought you were a son of wealth and privilege."

He piled on his Lower East Side accent. "Fourteen, I was, when we escaped to America. English, I knew not a word of. I was going to follow my parents into the silk mills and be a warper on the looms."

"You were?"

He assumed his educated voice. "But there was no room in our new place for me, so they sent me to live with my "rich" uncle in New York City, where I shared a bedroom with my cousin in their little apartment. My cousin aspired to be an actress, so she made me read her lines to her—an excellent way of learning English, I might add. Her name is Sylvia Sidney. You might have heard of her."

"Sylvia Sidney! *The* Sylvia Sidney? She's worked with every leading man in Hollywood."

"Which would make her a leading lady—yes, she is my cousin. She is who made me realize that in America, you can make yourself into whoever you want. I watched Sophia Kosow become Sylvia Sidney. It was Sophia who made Abram Saperstein decide to make himself into Albert Sabin. Albert *Bruce* Sabin, I should say.

Do you like the sound of it? I gave myself that middle name at fourteen. I thought Bruce had an elegant ring to it."

When she turned to him, she saw the scorned and dismissed and now defiant fourteen-year-old in his face. Something pinched in her heart. How could she, Henry Horstmann's daughter, not have recognized this fellow dreamer?

"Should I call you Abram?"

He laughed. "Absolutely not. Sweet little Abram has been dead a long time. Long live tough old Albert."

"Long live tough old Albert!"

He blew smoke out the window. "My parents settled in Paterson, New Jersey, where they still live. They were doing well when I saw them today."

"So that's why you were there."

He ground his cigarette in the ashtray. "I probably shouldn't be telling you this."

"You can. I won't talk."

"Because believe me, I tell this to no one."

"Oh, I believe you." She drew a breath. "I have a few secrets of my own."

"I know."

"You know? What do you know?"

He smiled as he tapped his forehead. "You keep it all locked up in here."

Their eyes met. The arrogance that had been so irritating when she'd thought he was the son of bluebloods was taking on a whole new meaning. How well she knew the need to prove oneself.

When they chuckled together, it was as comrades.

The traffic jolted to a start as mysteriously as it had stopped. People made a dive for their cars. Automobile horns continued to punctuate the music floating from up and down the lanes of the bridge, along with snatches of conversation, as if everyone were attending a great cocktail party in the sky.

He took her arm again. She put the car in gear. It took twenty tense minutes of focusing on the pavement to get within striking distance of the New York side of the bridge.

"I promised you a meal, Dr. Sabin," she said when she could speak again, though suddenly she was exhausted.

He released her arm. "Albert."

Her skin felt oddly bereft for a moment, a normal physiological response to the release of prolonged pressure. That was all. Honestly. "Where do Okinawan troglodytes such as yourself like to eat?"

"I know just the place."

17

NEW YORK, NEW YORK, 1945

Heat radiated from the street at the base of the bridge as she turned the June Bug toward the city. A car radio wasn't necessary to confirm whether President Truman had officially announced the surrender of Japan. There were plenty of New Yorkers out on the hot sidewalks upon which to gauge it. As the Bug crept down side streets that Dorothy mistakenly thought would be quicker, mothers with diapered babies gathered on the steps of brownstones. Boys in striped shirts and canvas-belt-cinched khaki shorts darted in front of apartment buildings. Gaggles of teenaged girls sashayed down the pavement, huddled padded shoulder to padded shoulder. Old couples crept forward, hand to arm. It seemed like everyone had turned up outside.

The car crawled to the top of Central Park. Albert pointed out the windshield. "Head down Lexington."

A traffic cop waved them down the street. Soon skyscrapers and blocks of high-rise apartment buildings shadowed the thoroughfare, the sidewalks ever filling with ladies in high heels, men in suits, workmen in coveralls. The bubbling river of humanity flowed south and eastward, toward the middle of Manhattan, everyone in a holiday mood. When would Truman speak? When would the four grim years of war finally stop, years during which you kept your head down and took it, years in which you made do, you sacrificed, you dared not to dream, years during which you held your breath as you lived your daily life, waiting for the bully's reign to end?

She was nudging the car past the Waldorf Astoria when a Duesenberg pulled from the curb, the first parking space for miles.

"I believe this is a sign that we are to get out and take the subway down to Gramercy Park from here." She pulled in.

"Maybe this meal was not meant to be."

"Now I'm determined," she said, turning off the car.

But once on the sidewalk, it was apparent that going uptown to the nearest subway station would be going against the tide and impossible. "Where's everyone going?" she shouted to a mob of servicemen, mostly sailors in dress blues.

A seaman, whose soft pink face and smudgy features pegged him as a teenager, gaped at her. "Lady, you are tall!"

"That is true. Where are you going?"

"Times Square!" his red-haired buddy answered.

"Why?" Albert asked.

"To see the zipper sign on the Times Tower when it announces the end of the war!"

"Everyone's going!" said Babyface.

Without consulting her, Albert joined the flow, turning with it westward between skyscrapers onto Forty-Ninth. He expected her to follow.

Shaking her head, she did.

Others were crowding onto the sidewalk. Groups of secretaries, WACs in khaki jackets and skirts, businessmen with their hats pushed back on their sweating heads in the August heat, people of every color and shape squeezed together on the pavement, their sheer numbers crushing everyone close. The air smelled of bodies, cigarettes, garbage, and excitement.

They were part of the sailors' pack now. When the baby-faced sailor slowed to say he was looking for the RCA Building at the new Rockefeller Center, the red-haired one yanked him away.

"Say!" Babyface exclaimed. "I was trying to see! The Hall of Motion's in here."

"You want to get flattened?"

"I hear they stick you in a room and play the sounds of bombs bursting, to see how you'd do during an air raid. You press a handle with an electric current running through it, and the gauge shows how jumpy you'd be."

"You need a machine for that?" Red exclaimed. "I can tell you what *you'd* be doing. *You'd* be shitting your pants!"

"There are ladies here," Albert said.

The sailors peered at the oak cluster of his Medical Corps insignia on his sleeve. "Oh, right, Doc. Pardon."

"Hey." Their handsome buddy, whose rows of wavy hair springing from his tipped-back sailor's cap rivaled Albert's in dark lushness, looked closer. "Hey, you're that famous polio doc, aren't you? Dr.—Dr.—"

Dorothy righted a sailor who'd stumbled. "Boys, meet Dr. Sabin."

The handsome one snapped his fingers. "That's right. I'm from Cincinnati—you spoke at the Rotary Club there. My dad took me before the war."

The other sailors craned their necks to see him as they all kept walking.

"So, Doc," said Handsome, "when you going to lick polio?"

Albert scowled at the pleasure of being recognized. "I am working at it." He glanced at Dorothy, watching him. "As is this fine scientist, Dr. Horstmann."

"A lady scientist?" Red exclaimed. "I never met one."

"We're sort of like unicorns," Dorothy said wryly.

"They're just like other scientists," Albert said firmly, as if that were a compliment.

She was pushed against him by the crowd. Charges shot through her where their bodies made contact.

The crowd carried them into Times Square. The racket of thousands of partiers echoing off the office buildings made her woozy. A man with a camera in his hand pushed his way through the crowd. It took Dorothy a moment to switch gears and recognize him. "Mr. Eisenstaedt! Over here!"

They hugged each other when they met. "How are you?" she cried.

Rounded eyebrows thick as Groucho Marx's mustache disappeared into his hat. "Overwhelmed! What a crowd!"

"Getting any good pictures?" she shouted.

"I won't know until I get in my darkroom!" he shouted back.

Albert shouted, "That's what my wife says!"

Mr. Eisenstaedt scanned the heaving crowd. "She a photographer?"

"Wants to be." He stuck out his hand. "Albert Sabin."

"Dr. Sabin," said Dorothy, "this is Alfred Eisenstaedt. He's the photographer who made Hickory miraculous."

Mr. Eisenstaedt laughed, then looked around as he spoke. "Basil O'Connor made sure I mentioned 'the Miracle of Hickory' several times. The article got more miraculous by the page." He stood on the toes of his wingtips to peer over the crowd. When he came down, he grinned at Dorothy. "Run into any fires lately?"

"Every day. You?"

"Always."

At that moment, the handsome sailor from her earlier pack swerved free of his pals and loped up to a lone nurse who was watching the zipper sign. The sailor grabbed her and tipped her back.

Mr. Eisenstaedt looked through his viewfinder. "Oh my God. It's the Miracle of Hickory!" He dropped into a crouch. *Snap, wind. Snap, wind.*

The nurse raised her fist against the sailor, but he grabbed it, held it down, and bent her deeper. Everyone cheered.

Snap, wind. Snap, wind.

"Poor girl," Dorothy said.

"'Poor girl'?" Albert said. "She must feel complimented that the sailor wanted to kiss her."

"It's not a compliment if she didn't agree to it. It's an attack."

The nurse broke free, then wiped her mouth to the roar of onlookers. She looked ready to cry.

The roiling crowd around her remixed and reconfigured like the pieces in a kaleidoscope. Mr. Eisenstaedt waved at Dorothy and trotted toward the zipper sign.

Albert was watching her. "You see things that other people don't."

They faced one another, stillness within pandemonium.

"What do you see in me?" he asked. "I'm curious."

She met his unblinking look. She saw pride. She saw loneliness. She saw herself.

A deafening roar went up. They turned to see the zipper flashing its message around the Times Building.

*** OFFICIAL *** TRUMAN ANNOUNCES
JAPANESE SURRENDER *** OFFICIAL ***

Confetti, ticker tape, fluttered from office windows, dusting the wild crowd. It was like being inside a pan of popping corn.

He touched the wing of her shoulder. They faced each other, still as figures in a snow globe, while all around them confetti fell. Everyone was kissing as if it were New Year's Eve.

His voice was quiet within the tumult. "I should like to kiss you. But—only if you thought it was a compliment." He picked confetti from her hair. "Would you, Dr. Horstmann, take it as a compliment?"

Would she? For a moment, she was a fourteen-year-old, too-tall girl on the way to give piano lessons, looking at an anxious boy who'd just named himself "Albert Bruce." Her eyes must have told him what he needed to know.

His lips were softer than she had imagined.

Mr. Eisenstaedt trotted up with a bottle of champagne.

"Where'd you get that?" Albert said lightly.

"You'd be surprised what people will give me when they find out that I work for *Life*."

"Let's have that bottle." Dorothy took a slug, started to pass it back, then stopped and took another drink. She wiped her mouth with her hand as she handed it to Albert. He drank some, then gave it back to Mr. Eisenstaedt, who wandered off chuckling.

Albert rubbed her arm. "If only—"

She pulled away from him, afraid of what he was going to say. "Please. Don't use those words. It's the most destructive phrase in the English language. Whole lives can be wasted just thinking it."

"Fair enough." He took her by the elbow and steered her out of the melee.

She glanced over her shoulder, half expecting to see the visible disturbance that they'd left in the air.

1948

A WIFE

Soon after they'd bought the house in Cincinnati, Sylvia had built the darkroom—literally, sawing the wood and nailing up the walls herself. She built it in the basement, the only part of the house that Albert had no use for. It was perfect for developing photos with its cool constant temperature of sixty-five degrees. Like a cave, Sylvia thought, as she rocked the photo she was developing in its bath of fixer.

Caves made her think of Mammoth Cave, where she'd gone on one of her family's educational vacations as a girl. All of her childhood vacations were educational. Her father, a civil engineer who had worked with the architect Frank Lloyd Wright, insisted that every waking moment of his children's lives was to be filled with enrichment. They were steeped in lessons on science and history, in trips to natural wonders, museums, and historical sites, in concerts, exhibitions, lectures. Forget lullabies—their mother, a brilliant soprano, sang them arias from Mozart. Tregilluses were raised to become geniuses or, if they were girls, to marry geniuses. The family's nickname for Sylvia was "Dodo." Legend was that she got it because her brother couldn't say "Sylvia." Whatever the reason, the other little Tregillus geniuses took much pleasure in calling her that.

Sylvia transferred the wet print to the rinse bath. Little Dodo had not liked Mammoth Cave, as she recalled. It was not yet a national park when her family visited, so they were given a tour by a local man who had the neck of a lizard. Sylvia's father had asked him if they might see the famous hieroglyphics made by the Indians who once lived there.

As they were shown some scratchings on the cave wall, Sylvia had not been able to stop thinking about the person who had drawn them. What if it was a girl, and she'd gotten lost in the cave? She could hear the girl's heart deafening her as the flame of her rush torch dwindled. The girl had featured in her nightmares for years after, as had the pale cave fish with no eyes because they long ago forgot how to use them.

Now Sylvia's chest burned with affection for her girlhood self as she held up the dripping photo of a child. It was of a little girl stomping in a puddle as her mother peered longingly into the window of a dress shop, two separate worlds captured in one frame. Sylvia hung it next to a photo of a toddler trying to escape her stroller. With one dimpled leg flung over the side of her torture chamber, the child had all the determined ferociousness on her baby face of a prisoner on jailbreak. Sylvia took photos all over Cincinnati with the Rolleiflex that she'd bought with the first money she'd made on the Chautauqua circuit with her family. Most of the photos were of children.

She hung the photo to dry, then went back to her enlarger. When she held up a negative to the light, her hand was so close to the red bulb that she could just make out her bones. It intrigued her to think that there was a whole other creature hiding within her, living its lonely life.

Albert and she were trying to have children. She thought they might step up their efforts when the war ended. But Albert re-upped with the Medical Corps for a year, and when that ended, he traveled all the time anyway. Polio case numbers had grown like wildfire after the war. All of a sudden everyone in polio was talking about finding a vaccine. When Albert was home, they often had visiting researchers over, either at dinner or, just as frequently, staying in one or more of their other six bedrooms. Scientists, it appeared, did not believe in hotels.

But that was what she'd signed up for when she'd married her genius. He worked; she supported his work. If he looked good, Dodo looked good. That was the deal.

She'd just put another print in the developing bath when Albert entered the darkroom.

"Close the door!" she cried. After years of her explaining that when he barged in without warning, he was letting in the light and possibly ruining a day's work, he still came charging in, the cliché of the absentminded scientist.

Drawing in a sigh, she kissed him. They stood side by side, peering at the drying images hanging before them, her arms crossed, him taking off his tie.

She looked over at him. "We look like a couple of devils in the red light," she said affectionately.

He said nothing, his mind elsewhere.

"How was work?" she asked.

"Fine." He started unbuttoning his shirt. "These pictures are very good, Sylvia."

His praise flowed through her like wine. "Thank you."

"What are you going to do with all this?" he asked.

"I don't know." Although she did know. She dreamed of it, night and day.

"Are you going to sell them? Are you going to be another Ansel Adams and be famous?"

He said this playfully. Ansel Adams was the only photographer that Albert knew of.

"Maybe." She didn't aspire to be Ansel Adams. Margaret Bourke-White, now, was another story. Margaret Bourke-White, staff photographer of first *Fortune*, then *Life* magazine, chronicler of the Great Depression, illuminator of hidden lives, was who Sylvia wanted to be. Miss Bourke-White was married to a famous writer, Erskine Caldwell. Their book, *You Have Seen Their Faces*, documented the lives of the poor whom they'd met on a photo-journey through the South. Caldwell wrote the words; Bourke-White made the photos. Miss Bourke-White and her husband were equally famous. A team.

Sylvia'd been crushed when they got divorced.

Albert slid his arm around her waist. "Well, you are as good as Ansel Adams."

The happiness in his tone made her turn and look. Was he close to making a discovery, or getting in a new flush of funding? Something was going on with him.

He pecked her on the cheek. "I don't know how you can stand it down here. It's as damp as a cave." He unclasped a cufflink. "Don't worry about dinner. I have to get back to the lab."

"Anything new there?"

He paused. "I'm going to a conference in Washington tomorrow. I'll be gone two nights."

"You're leaving again? Who is going?"

He made a dismissive sound. "The usual. Basil O'Connor called it. It's a waste of my time, keeping me from my work."

"Then don't go."

"You go when you are the top man."

She could feel him flying away from her even as he stood next to her, undoing his other cufflink. She straightened a developing tray. "Is Dorothy Horstmann going to be there?"

"I don't know."

"You don't? Don't you correspond with her?"

The memory of the argument they'd had when Sylvia had found that letter last winter clanged between them. Dorothy's fond tone in the letter was unmistakable, deny it as he may.

He peered at a drying photo, rattling his cufflinks in his hand. "I like this one best."

"Have you seen her lately?"

"Who? If you're talking about Dorothy, she's at Yale."

"Not London?"

"Not anymore." He drew a breath. "Sylvia, she's hardly likely to drop all of her work to drive cross-country to have a tryst with me, if that's what you think."

"You travel a lot. She travels, too. Don't try to make me sound crazy."

"You're not crazy, Sylvie. You just have too much time on your hands."

She stared at him. Between feeding and boarding cheap scientists, dazzling university and March of Dimes powers-that-be at fundraisers, and anticipating Albert's every need, she hardly had time for her photography, let alone to dream up wild schemes between him and Dorothy. What else was she to think when Albert had gone to a virology symposium in Sweden last year and had come home gushing praises for the fabulous Dorothy Horstmann?

"I haven't forgotten that letter, Albert."

"You're bringing that up again?"

She knew what she read. She had not conjured up Dorothy thanking him for *his* letter and then reminding him of "all of those splendid Scandinavian days" they'd had. Dorothy had asked when he was going to come see her in London, where, she wrote—too adorably, Sylvia thought—that she had to keep the Bunsen burners at full flame in her ex-machine-shop basement lab just to keep her face warm.

"Poor Dorothy, in her charming London cellar."

"What?" He turned his attention to the hanging photos. "How'd you get this woman to pose for you?" He indicated the photo of the mother gazing into the shopwindow.

"I didn't."

He left. She shut the door quickly after him, then checked the prints in the tray for light damage. A few minutes later she heard the rattling in the pipes of the water making its way down from his shower.

18

WASHINGTON, DISTRICT OF COLUMBIA, 1948

The National Foundation for Infantile Paralysis had taken the idea of a "roundtable meeting" for the first conference on developing the polio vaccine literally. In a room that smelled of mimeograph ink and men's much-worn suits, Dorothy was one of two women seated at the biggest circular table she'd ever seen. Basil O'Connor never did things by halves. He'd summoned every leading light on polio to this massive table, and he was putting them up at the best hotel in Washington. She was grateful to be among them, weary as she was from the move back to New Haven the previous week after living a year in London.

Now Albert Sabin, distinguishable from his rumpled peers by his perfectly tailored coat and vest, stood, raised his cleft chin, and smiled at the colleagues gathered around the acreage of polished wood. He was careful, Dorothy noticed, to skip over her.

So that was how it was going to be now. Fine. All the better.

"While I'm not in the habit of quoting non-professional journals, I'd like to read a passage from *Time* about the state of poliomyelitis research as of June 1947, back in the Dark Ages." He smiled again. "Just last year." He shook open a magazine.

"'Now keep the ash can covered, never drink out of a stream.
Take care that all the food you eat and kitchenware is clean.
Kill the rats and kill the mice and make the roaches go,
For that's the way to really whip that mean old polio.'"

Some of the gentlemen laughed. Others applauded.

He continued reading. "'In San Antonio last week "Red River Dave" McEnery was yodeling "The Polio Song" daily over station WOAI.'"

"You yodel it, why don't you?" someone cracked—one of the Johns Hopkins boys, Dorothy thought.

He smiled. "I will spare you that."

Cigarette holder clenched between his teeth, Basil O'Connor motioned for everyone to pipe down.

Albert read again. "'San Antonio, with 30 cases, had a bad case of polio jitters. Nationally, the incidence of infantile paralysis, 813 cases, was up almost 17 percent over last year. But the only state in which the disease had reached epidemic proportions (one case per 1,000 population) was Florida, where 126 were afflicted, and 6 had died.'" He looked around the table for emphasis before continuing. "'To Miami by plane the National Foundation for Infantile Paralysis packed off a special "polio team," headed by Dr. David Steven Grice of Harvard. With him were a Yale epidemiologist, Dr. Dorothy M. Horstmann'"—he paused to look into Dorothy's eyes, giving her an actual jolt—"'an orthopedic nurse, and four physiotherapists. Three other "flying squads" of polio experts have been recruited at Northwestern, Stanford, and the D. T. Watson School of Physiotherapy, to speed to the scene of any outbreak on two hours' notice.'"

He put down the magazine. "Nice mention, Dr. Grice." He found Dorothy's gaze again, prompting another shock. "Dr. Horstmann."

Next to her, Robbie Ward gave her a nudge as all eyes turned her way. She felt the smiles blooming around the table. They suspected that she and Dr. Sabin were having a fling.

Her fury ignited. Would they accuse other colleagues simply interested in the same subject of having an affair? Even as she seethed at the unfairness and wrongheadedness of their assumptions, thinking of Stockholm, she blushed.

IT WAS IN THE "DARK AGES," IN THE FALL OF LAST YEAR. Albert and she were motoring down the Söderström River in a speedboat, the blue-and-yellow Swedish flag flapping like a rooster tail behind them. The Swedish minister of health, a lanky man with a narrow face and long upper lip, looked between the two of them seated on the bench in the stern, within arm's length of the flag—and each other.

"What you are saying," he said in excellent English, "is the poliovirus *is* found in Stockholm's water system."

All gazes went to the green water rolling away from the boat. Albert nodded for Dorothy to answer.

"Yes." A damp breeze grabbed at the hat pinned to her messy tufts. When she held it down, Albert steadied her arm. "The virus has been found in your water," she said.

"But," the minister said hopefully, "you cannot catch the disease from it."

"No," said Dorothy. "You can't."

"I am not clear. Our great Dr. Kling states in his *théorie hydrique* that the poliovirus lives in the water. You, too, say that the virus lives in the water. We base many of our public health measures on that principle."

"And we have confirmed his theory," Dorothy said, "insofar that poliovirus is found in the water. My group did a study of the East River in New York City from 1940 to 1945 and confirmed that poliovirus was indeed found in the water there, particularly during epidemic years, but—"

"*But*," Albert said, bolstering her.

"—but it does not replicate there. The virus shed from infected humans gets into the water, but does not infect others from there. The Yale Study Group believes that poliomyelitis is not a water-borne disease."

The minister looked into the emerald water. "That is good, then." He leaned over and dipped his hand into the flow, then cupped it to his mouth.

"However," Albert said, "there might be other organisms in that, including typhus, giardia, various other dysenteric agents—"

The minister shook off his hand, then wiped it on his pantleg.

"Tell me, Dr. Sabin," he said, readjusting his hat with his clean hand—the other lay limp on his lap, a plaguey thing—"how are you coming along with a vaccine for infantile paralysis? We work very hard to keep our people safe, but you know as well as I that admonishing people to stay indoors and not to eat apples that have fallen on the ground only goes so far. We need real protection. Sweden suffers from some of the worst outbreaks in the world."

"There are various laboratories at work on one, including my own. And your Dr. Gard has made good progress." Albert put his arm around the back of Dorothy's seat. "But we still have so many questions to answer before any of us can make serious headway."

"We're not clear on transmission," said Dorothy, acutely aware of his arm. "It would help if we knew how it traveled, once in the body. We're sure poliovirus replicates in the intestines, but we are darned if we know how it gets there."

Albert's arm came to rest against her shoulders. "Not from eating dirty apples."

She felt its weight as all of them laughed.

The minister turned around to face the back of the driver of the boat. Albert and she sat in silence, he seemingly comfortably with his arm draped around her, she not so much so. Yes, they were friends, especially after V-J Day in Times Square, when they'd bonded over revealing their upbringings—well, at least after he had divulged his. They did have that kiss, but it was never to be repeated, an anomaly that happened in the swirl of a historic moment. They were just a couple of disease detectives, equally, maybe obsessively, dedicated to tracking down polio. Strong feelings between like minds should not be confused with anything else.

Ever.

The minister turned back to them. "*Could* polio travel through the blood?"

Dorothy sat up. Albert's arm fell away. "What?"

"I read a transcript from your speech in 1944," the minister said to Albert. "You stated that you found poliovirus in the blood of three different monkeys. Doesn't it follow—?"

"You were aware of that speech?" Albert exclaimed. "I thought no one noticed, with the war going on." He glanced at Dorothy, who was rounding her eyes at him in silent outrage. He knew that thesis was the hill on which she'd staked her reputation, and he didn't tell her that he'd written about it? "It didn't pan out."

She heard little else until the boat glided up to a pier.

The minister rubbed together his hands. "Now I should like to take you to a special place for dinner. The other scientists from the symposium await us."

The driver docked the boat, and the minister jumped out. Albert handed her up to him, rocking the boat in an awkward exchange of her gargantuan person, which further infuriated her. She leaned into following the minister from the pier.

Albert grabbed her arm. "May we have a moment?" he asked the minister.

She bit back anger as the minister looked between them. He bowed. "I shall go in to see to the arrangements."

Albert let her go when he was gone. "Dorothy."

She rubbed her arm pointedly.

"I should have told you about that finding."

"Why didn't you? You know I'd care. Why would you keep this from me?"

"There's nothing to keep from you." He raked his hair. "I didn't tell you because I was ashamed."

"Ashamed!"

"Ashamed of getting ahead of myself. It was based on shoddy work. I shouldn't have mentioned that particular finding in my lecture before I had evidence to back it up."

"You still could have told me about it. You know I'd be interested."

"There was nothing *to* tell. I had no idea what I was seeing. I didn't know at which point in their infection the monkeys were or even which monkeys were infected—the blood was pooled from a group of them. When I tried to reproduce the results so I could figure it out, I failed. I didn't want to disappoint you by telling you that I hit a dead end."

"It would have added to my knowledge."

"No, it wouldn't have. All it would have done was discourage you, and I wasn't about to do that. I know how much your theory means to you."

"'My theory' is not for me." She flung her arms wide. "It's for the world."

He pulled in his chin. "Well, that's grandiose." He smiled. "But I like it."

She clasped her mouth. That didn't keep in the laughter when it came. He joined her, and soon they were laughing only because they were laughing. He slipped his arm around her, as would one with a dear friend, or a lover, until their laughs melted into chuckles.

They grew quiet. The putter of boats on the river, the splash of the waves against the piers with their floating green beards of seaweed, the murmur of automobiles in the city all receded. His brown eyes, his fierce will drew her in, and for a moment they were back standing in the confetti of Times Square. He brushed a lock of hair from her temple.

Someone exclaimed, "There you are!"

They broke apart as Dr. Paul trotted up.

"Where were you?" Dorothy said, too heartily. "You missed the boat ride."

Dr. Paul's gaze darted between them. "My car wouldn't start when I was leaving Dr. Kling's house. The university sent a car and took me directly to the restaurant."

"Glad you made it." Albert clapped him on the back. "Shall we eat?"

It wasn't until after the dinner, when Dr. Paul and she had returned to the hotel and had gotten out of the elevator, that Dr. Paul looked up at her, his small, neatly groomed face troubled.

"Dorothy, it's not just your reputation you must consider. It's Yale's."

He said nothing more, nor did she.

When she'd returned home from the trip to an offer by the Lister Institute for a year-long fellowship in London, she'd taken it. She would put an ocean between her and Albert, and an end to any talk.

If only it had ended her loneliness.

"ARE WE THAT MUCH FURTHER IN OUR UNDERSTANDING OF polio than we were last year?" Standing at his place at the circular plane of mahogany, Albert stared down two colleagues who had been smirking between him and Dorothy. "Bob? Tom? How many different strains of the three types of poliovirus are there? Do you know? Do you even know for certain that there are just three types?"

Dorothy felt movement across the field of mimeographed pages. Many of the scientists were looking downward, like so many schoolchildren hoping to avoid being called upon by Teacher. Few of these cowboys wanted to be stuck with the grunt work of typing polio strains. They were here to save the world, not catalog infectious agents. She felt that way herself.

Basil O'Connor raised his hand. "All right, the first question in our hunt for the vaccine is how many types and strains are there? What's the second, Dr. Sabin?"

Albert waited until there were no smirking glances between him and Dorothy. Did he not realize that dueling the other scientists over her honor only made them look more like lovers?

"The second," he said, scowling, "is where do scientists get a safe, steady, abundant supply of each virus type to make the vaccine?"

Across the way, the Johns Hopkins group lowered their eyes. They needn't have been secretive. Everyone in polio knew that they were working on replicating the virus in tissue. The fact was, everyone in polio knew everything about everyone else's business. Or thought that they did.

"Third—"

She looked up to see Albert watching her. She glanced away as if forked by a demon. Those stupid letters she'd sent from London! Emboldened by their newfound comradery, she'd overplayed her hand. She'd pretended to be someone she wasn't, breezy and overly friendly, using the ocean between them to hide behind. He must have taken it the wrong way.

A scalpel flicked behind her breastbone. But had she meant for him to do so? Oh, the confused, self-sabotaging follies of the lonely!

"Third, what is the exact route of the virus to the central nervous system, so that we can fix the exact time and place for a vaccine to work?"

Eyes turned again in her direction. Would she always be known as the crackpot looking for the virus in the blood, where it stubbornly would not be found?

"Along with my colleagues Drs. Bodian and Francis," Albert continued, "I will oversee the first of these objectives, typing the strains. The four laboratories that have agreed to do the typing, the University of Kansas, the University of Pittsburgh, the University of Southern California, and the University of Utah, will report to us."

On her other side, one pencil-smudged shirtsleeve rolled up, the other fallen down, Jonas Salk raised his hand. "Send your strains to Pittsburgh! I welcome the challenge!"

Heads cranked in his direction. The scientists from the other laboratories frowned, even as Basil O'Connor plucked at his pinky ring and cocked his brilliantined head in interest.

Albert cleared his throat. "Thank you, ah, Dr. Salk. Perhaps I should aim my next remarks especially to you, then." He waited for the chuckles around the table to subside. "I would like to describe now the method for typing I found to be the most efficacious."

As he explained his painstaking process, Dorothy's attention wandered across the table, to where the sole other woman was bending her brown pageboy over her notes. Dorothy had met Isabel Morgan at other events—she couldn't have avoided it. Their colleagues threw them together at every opportunity, expecting them to be instant pals, they being two ladies and all. The truth was, the most she had in common with Isabel Morgan was the extra leg on their Y sex chromosomes.

Isabel Morgan had been brought up in New York City, with comfortable summers on Cape Cod, the coddled daughter of a Nobel Prize laureate and his esteemed biologist wife, a far cry from a girlhood spent helping her pop clean the toilet at the bar. Dr. Morgan had started out at the prestigious Rockefeller Institute, as had Albert, then had joined the world-renowned virologists at Johns

Hopkins as a full-fledged member of the team, not as some temporary staffer being strung along year-to-year on fellowships. They were the same age, thirty-six, which only ground more salt in Dorothy's open wound.

She was frowning at that perfect chestnut-brown pageboy when Dr. Morgan looked up and, catching Dorothy, smiled.

"I will now turn the floor over to my colleague, Isabel Morgan," Albert said. "As you know, Dr. Morgan has been using another method to discern the types of strains. From what she tells me, she takes a completely different approach than I do. That cannot be good!"

Male chuckles arose around the table. Dr. Morgan put down her pen with cool stare.

"Of course, you know that I am jesting," he told her.

Everyone knew he was not.

She rose with a swish of full skirts, then began to speak with the polish of the East Coast elite that she was. Her pretty words drifted past her male colleagues' ears like daisy petals on a breeze, judging from their vacantly smiling faces. Only Jonas Salk seemed to register the import of them, his mouth opening by the millimeter with every step of her explanation.

"Are there any questions?" she asked when she was done.

Jonas's hand shot up.

Dr. Morgan smiled at his enthusiasm. "Yes?"

"You say you used a *killed* poliovirus to test the strains on the monkeys?"

"Yes. I inactivated it with formaldehyde."

Albert didn't bother to raise his hand. "You killed it with formaldehyde, just like Brodie had . . ." He lifted his brows. There was no need to finish his sentence. This crowd knew the rest of it: . . . *in the vaccine used in the trial that maimed children.*

"Yes, Dr. Sabin. I did use Dr. Brodie's method." Dr. Morgan lifted her chin as if warding off an attack. Indeed, it was an attack. Aligning her work with Brodie's was career discrediting. "I found that formaldehyde works very well. None of the monkeys in my experiments contracted poliomyelitis from the killed virus that I introduced to them. I believe where Brodie went wrong is that he wasn't aware of the three different types of the poliovirus. All of them needed to be included in his formulation. His vaccine could have killed two of the types perfectly, but if a third had slipped through, the vaccine would have been worthless."

"There you go!" Jonas pushed up his smeared glasses in excitement. "If what you're saying is true, we don't have to waste time knowing how the virus travels through the body. We just need to know all the types and then get them in the vaccine. We can have a vaccine available to the public in a fraction of the time."

Albert's chair screeched as he stood. "Doc-tor Salk. I have never heard such irresponsibility."

The junior man's face reddened. "It's not irresponsible if you've got two small sons at home."

"You think that I'm not in a hurry because I don't have children?" Albert seemed to swell over the litter of pages separating him from his red-eared colleague. In other settings, a punch might have been thrown.

Basil O'Connor pushed himself to a stand. "Gentlemen, gentlemen. We all agree: we want a safe vaccine, and we want it as quickly as possible. Maybe that requires us to think in novel ways."

The colleagues sprang to life, voicing their opinions until the mahogany of the conference table rang with them.

Dr. Morgan raised her voice over the ruckus. "The issue is, I'm not ready to test my vaccine in children."

"Fellas!" Mr. O'Connor made tamping gestures. When the men had settled down, he said, "What did you say, dear?"

Dr. Morgan glanced at Dorothy. *Dear!*

"I said, I won't test my vaccine on children."

Mr. O'Connor toyed with his pinky ring. "You won't? Why not? Isn't that the point?"

"We have far too much work to do before we can even think of that. What if we missed a type? I couldn't live with myself if a single child contracted polio from the vaccine I'd had a hand in."

Jonas puffed out his chest, the Little Engine That Could. "We'll catch them, every single strain—you can be sure of it—if I'm in charge. I will not let any parents down. Their kids will be safe with me."

Dorothy could feel the other scientists restraining themselves from rolling their eyes. If identifying all the strains were that easy, it would have been done long ago. But Mr. O'Connor nodded like the benevolent king-maker that he was. "That's just what the public wants to hear. In fact, that's perfect. Can I quote you on that, Dr. Salk? I've got reporters outside."

Jonas's toothy grin widened. "Sure. Why not?"

19

At lunch, in a smoky restaurant loud with the argumentative scientists populating its booths, Robbie Ward sawed into a steak. "What do you think of Salk trying to take over the typing?"

"Let him." Dr. Paul gathered salad onto his fork with his knife. "We need someone who will not miss a single type. The vaccine has to cover them all."

Dorothy watched him eat with particular fascination. He did so in the European style, without switching his fork from hand to manicured hand, a style she had made herself unlearn while in high school. How different her parents looked while they employed it, hunched over, their plates inches from their mouths.

"Salk's obviously doing it to bring attention to himself," said Robbie. "Did you see him with those reporters after the meeting? He preened like a starlet posing for *Photoplay*."

"Good. Let him stake his reputation on it. Nothing motivates a scientist more than maintaining his good reputation." Dr. Paul tucked his lettuce into his small, neat mouth, then glanced over at the Johns Hopkins table. "I wonder if they are having such a philosophical discussion."

Robbie squeezed his baked potato until it puckered out of its foil. "I doubt it. They're consumed by replicating the virus in tissue, except for Isabel Morgan. Apparently, she's on her own quest, perfecting her method of cross-checking strains with Brodie's vaccine."

"She'll come to a bad end, I fear." Dr. Paul shook his head. "You can't say that no one tried to stop her. Bodian and Howe say she's ungovernable."

Dorothy laid her napkin on the table and got up. "Excuse me."

"Hey!" Robbie grabbed her wrist. "Where you going? Don't go over to the other side! We love you, Dottie!"

"I'll try to remember that."

As she crossed the dining room on the way to the powder room, a busboy halted in her path, his bin of smeared dishes clattering. "You are tall!"

"Am I? Still?"

She was applying lipstick before the mirror when Isabel Morgan pushed into the flowery-papered room. Dorothy's pulse blipped.

Dr. Morgan came to stand next to her. "That's a good color on you."

"Thanks." Until she'd seen their reflections together, Dorothy had not realized that she had only an inch or so on Dr. Morgan. They were two big girls, and science nuts at that, as rare and inscrutable as Sasquatches by *Ladies' Home Journal* standards. "Good work on your typing technique, by the way."

"Thank you. I can see that I will be the only one to use it, with Sabin pushing for his method."

"Dr. Salk seemed interested."

Dr. Morgan rolled her eyes. "Another strike against me."

"I don't know—Mr. O'Connor seems taken by him."

"You're right. Mr. O'Connor does seem pleased with him. When I passed them in the hall after the meeting, he was looking downright jolly when the reporters were having a feeding frenzy on Jonas."

Dorothy screwed down her lipstick. "People are desperate for good news."

"We all are. The man I'm seeing is begging me to bring home

my experimental vaccine for his son. He's so desperate for Jimmy not to get polio that he'll try anything. He can't understand why I'm reluctant to try an unproven vaccine on his boy. I get the shivers just thinking about it."

Dorothy dropped her lipstick in her purse and got out her comb. "We know too much. We've seen what happens when people get hasty. We can't afford to lose the public's trust—once you do, it's hard to get back."

"Would you please tell that to the man I'm seeing?"

Dorothy raked at a stubborn tussock in silence, monitoring the tender spot in her heart that she noticed only when prodded, like a bone broken in one's youth. Four years had passed, but her wound from Arne was far from closing over.

Dr. Morgan caught Dorothy's glance in the mirror. "We really should be friends, you know. For ourselves—not because the men throw us together."

Dorothy felt a weight slide off. "I'd really like that."

"I think they're hoping that we'll have a catfight."

"Ha!"

Dr. Morgan drew her comb through her pageboy. "Speaking of catfights, can you believe that spat between Sabin and Salk? Sabin was terribly rough on the poor guy." She hesitated. "I'm sorry. You and Albert are friends, aren't you?"

"No more than anyone else."

"I thought it was more than that."

Heat rushed to Dorothy's face.

Dr. Morgan studied Dorothy's reflection. "Wait. Maybe that sounded wrong. I only meant that you two have been focusing on the same problem, the pathway of the virus through the body. He talks about you, you know."

"Oh no!"

"Don't worry—he has nothing but praise." Dr. Morgan laughed. "That might be a first for Albert."

Dorothy started to object, then realized that would be true.

Dr. Morgan dropped her comb into her purse, then put out her hand. "Dr. Horstmann, it has been a pleasure. If I can ever help you with your research—"

They shook hands. "Same here, Dr. Morgan."

"Please, call me Ibby. At least, all the men do."

"Is that what you want to be called?"

Dr. Morgan paused. "Actually, no."

"What would you rather be called?"

"I have never minded Isabel."

"Let me know how I can help with your research, Isabel."

"Will do." Grinning, Isabel tucked her purse under her arm. "And enjoy Albert Sabin's sunshine while it lasts. Doesn't he turn on everyone eventually?"

1949

A MOTHER

If you wanted the best butter in town, you had better go to Rosner's, where it was scooped straight from a wooden tub and wrapped in butcher paper to your order. They said the secret to it was happy cows—you had to be mindful of what you were feeding them. Rosner's was down on State Street, and not frequented often by Viola's people, but that didn't bother her much. Viola was known for her good cooking, and good butter was at the heart of it. If you really want to shine at something, you've got to go that extra mile—in this case, literally.

Anyhow, she liked the walk. It took her along the outer edge of the Yale campus, an exciting place that usually brimmed with young folks with a future. She wanted her boys to be comfortable there. Her husband worked for Yale, and not as a custodian like his father and his cousin. His job was in the research laboratory, where he was instrumental in experiments designed to figure out poliomyelitis. One of his colleagues, Dr. Dorothy Horstmann, was coming to dinner that night. Thus, the need to get good butter.

It being June, the squirrels scrabbling up trees were about the only form of life on campus that day as Viola guided her boys, Eugene Jr. and Robert, under the gaze of stately buildings. She imagined the college kids were all at the beach—that's where Eugene said they went. Must be safer from polio than the swimming pools here in town. In truth, it was hard for her to picture college kids or anyone cavorting on the sand. Five years after the Normandy invasion, the word "beach" still made her stomach hurt. She still saw soldiers wading through the surf with their guns held over their heads, like in the newsreels. She'd lost her brother, James, on that "beach." The barrage balloon that he'd flown across the English Channel to secure the coast for the soldiers had been shot down before he could land it.

On she led Eugene Jr. and Robert, one to either hand. State Street was just ahead, with automobiles lurching by, belching exhaust, and the awnings of storefronts flapping in the wind. The minute they made the State Street sidewalk, mothers steered their children away from her and the boys, but she was avoiding them, too. It was June and polio season—everyone kept their children apart. Wasn't anything personal.

A pair of nuns sailed past, their habits billowing. A man in a fine business suit swerved away slightly. A skinny old lady with red-dyed hair came right up to them, smiling at the boys so long that Eugene Jr. looked up at Viola for direction. Viola's stare back down at the boy said, *You're going to see people going overboard like this. Just smile.*

Viola had stopped to tie Robert's shoe—the child just could not remember to double-knot—when she saw the little girl in the parked car.

The child was young to be all by herself in a car, younger than both Eugene Jr. and Robert, maybe four years old. She had a smudged look of a pencil drawing partially erased, with lilac circles etched in the tender skin under her eyes and straw-colored hair so thin that her ears parted it. She was sucking on the round collar of her dress like she was getting nutrition out of it.

"Mama," Robert said, "can we go look at the hardware store?"

Viola got up from tying his shoe, one creaky knee at a time. "Yes." She'd had bad knees since her teens. Heaven knew what kind of shape they'd be in if Eugene hadn't come along and rescued her from working for the Petermans by getting her pregnant on their wedding night. Mrs. Peterman had those four rambunctious boys and a girl who was just as bad, yet Mrs. P. thought she should have a floor you could eat off of.

Viola was standing sideways, half watching her boys ogle the display of pogo sticks and Radio Flyers behind the plate glass of the hardware store window and half watching the little girl gnawing at her collar, when a mother with two little boys stopped to look in the window of the neighboring fabric shop. The mother, a trim, pretty thing with a little pink bow in her hair, smiled at Viola, then Eugene Jr. and Robert.

"My boys would rather be over there."

Viola smiled, then her heart jerked. Did the woman mean for her to move? She'd grown up in Atlanta, and those lessons couldn't be unlearned.

The woman dug into her purse and took out a pencil and paper, then, as her boys shoved and elbowed each other (Viola's boys knew better than to act up like that in public), started drawing. Viola could feel her blood settle. The woman was taking notes to re-create the clothes on the display dummy, that was all. Viola had done the same before, too.

The woman glanced over again, then showed her pretty teeth in a smile. "How do you get your boys to behave so well? Such handsome little gentlemen, straight as little soldiers! Mine are a pack of hooligans."

Viola looked down at Eugene Jr. and Robert, who were looking up at her, waiting for a cue. Her heart got too hot for her chest. Above their clip-on maroon bow ties and crisply starched white shirts, which she took exquisite care to iron, their faces glowed like angels'. The corner of Eugene Jr.'s front tooth was chipped a little, and one of Robert's eyes was slightly smaller than the other if you looked at him closely, but, oh, they were beautiful boys. She didn't know why God would give her such perfect boys. Viola worried about them every single second of her life.

She was gathering herself to invite the rowdy boys to come look at the pogo sticks with Eugene Jr. and Robert, when a young woman came out of the fabric store. As thin and plain as watered-down milk, she had a shopping bag hanging on the crook of one bony arm and a little identical girl tottering from each hand. The twins were dolled up in frilly dresses and floppy yellow bows bigger than their heads, way overdressed, as if coming to downtown New Haven were a rare and great occasion. A glance at the mother's faded cotton dress, worn so thin that you could see her slip through it, confirmed the family's limited pocketbook. Something scraped in Viola's chest to see how much effort the woman had put into her children's appearance while expending so little on herself.

The twins pattered along in patent-leather shoes until they grew even with Robert and Eugene Jr. One twin stopped, her mouth ajar.

Her mother couldn't budge her. "Mary? Come now!"

But Mary wouldn't. And now the other twin had stopped, all round blue eyes beneath that outrageous bow.

Eugene Jr. and Robert looked up at Viola. She found that she was holding her breath.

Little Mary beamed. "Mama! Those boys are brown!"

The woman blushed. "Shhh! Don't say that." She grimaced at the other mother as if looking for an ally. "They've never seen a colored person before." To Viola, she said, "I'm real sorry."

She dragged her twins to the curb, to the car with the lone child inside, where the little girl stopped eating her collar and got up on her knees to peer into the shopping bag the woman had dropped on the front seat. The woman stuffed the twins into the rear, then hurried around to the driver's side. The girl fell back as the car jerked away from the curb.

"Some people!" The other mother's face went the pink of her hair bow. "What a hick." Her boys were staring at Eugene Jr. and Robert. She rapped one on the arm. "Stop picking your nose!" she exclaimed, then moved them along.

Viola wanted to drop to her bad knees to hug her boys to her chest—Eugene Jr., who was laughing with embarrassment, Robert, who gazed at his big brother in wonderment. If only she could spare them. But all she could do was to take them by their soft greenstick hands and go on to get that butter.

FOR THE LONGEST TIME, VIOLA HAD THOUGHT EUGENE'S boss's name was "Dr. Horseman," which struck her as funny, what with those teeth that she was now sinking into a dinner roll—long, like everything else about her. Dr. H. was a nice lady, though, and with that gold hair fluffed into peaks and those friendly eyes, she was pretty, even with being about a foot too tall.

"These are so delicious." Dr. Horstmann dabbed her mouth with her napkin. She ate neatly as a princess, Viola thought. She must have been brought up rich. "What is your secret, Mrs. Oakley?"

"Butter."

Dr. Horstmann laughed. "Yes, I did slather it on a bit thickly. This brand is particularly tasty. But the roll itself, why is it so—"

"Butter."

Across the table, Eugene was spackling his own roll with a golden glob. "Viola goes to some shop on State Street for it."

"Rosner's," said Viola. The very word made a shadow pass over her. She saw the little twins staring at her boys and her boys' discomfort.

"Well, it's certainly worth the trip." Dr. Horstmann crinkled the corners of her eyes. "Everything is just scrumptious. Thank you for preparing this delicious meal."

Viola squirmed under the praise. A lifetime of flying under the radar will do that. "How is that study coming along?"

"We're making progress, wouldn't you say, Eugene?"

"Yes."

Everyone ate. Viola listened for the boys: upstairs, quiet. "Eugene says you're looking for the poliovirus in the blood."

"Well, that's my goal. But first I have to demonstrate the correlation between the development of antibodies in the blood and the resistance to infection. I'm trying to show that the antibodies are protective only against the strain of which the subject was infected."

"How do you look for that? If you don't mind me asking."

"Eugene, you tell her."

Eugene cleared his throat. Already sturdy-built, he seemed to bulk up even more when he talked about something important to him. "First, we feed monkeys the poliovirus by mouth. Then, we take daily stool samples, and blood samples—"

"—with Eugene keeping the animals calm," Dr. H. added, "which is very, very important if one doesn't want to get bitten."

"They're scared," Eugene said.

Dr. H. shivered. "I'd gotten bitten once, before I worked with Eugene, and I must tell you, I fainted dead away." She pointed to a jagged white crescent on the web of skin between thumb and forefinger. "When monkeys bite, they bite hard."

"Comes from being scared," Eugene said.

"I'm sick to have to hurt them. The only way I can do what needs to be done is knowing that you're doing your best by them." Dr. H. ducked her head at him. "Thank you. Your work means so much to me."

Eugene got that fierce look he got when trying not to smile. "The monkeys help us to get rid of polio, I help them."

"Well, I don't know what I would do without you."

Seeing her husband so happy made it hard for Viola to swallow her mouthful of Chicken Divan, a recipe she had gotten from a Betty Crocker booklet. "That technician who got scratched in your lab by the infected monkey and died—" She swallowed again. "He refused Eugene's help. He insisted on handling the monkeys himself."

Just like that, the air stiffened. Viola could feel her husband bristle. She had said something wrong.

Dr. Horstmann put down her forkful of broccoli. "What was the story on that man? I never knew him. He was hired and passed away the year I was in San Francisco."

I'll tell you, Viola wanted to say. *The man was a fool. He treated Eugene like dirt. He insisted on handling the animal himself, and look where that got him. Dead.* But she just said, "You find anything interesting today?"

Eugene kept eating, one of his brows in that stubborn curl. She hadn't meant to put him on the spot.

Dr. H. drew in her breath, then let it out slowly. "Yes, in fact we did." She looked at Eugene. "The challenge feeding of the Lansing strain hasn't infected Becky so far."

Eugene nodded, his mouth going into a line. Becky was his favorite chimpanzee.

"We'll keep an eye on her," Dr. H. said. "I think the antibodies are doing their job."

Becky was one of the chimpanzees Eugene had brought home for extra care as a baby. He'd set his alarm and gotten up during the night to tend to her, then he'd taken her to and from work in his jacket. Viola warned him about getting attached to her, to any of the creatures in his charge, but he said that was the price he was willing to pay. His heart for their lives.

One of the boys called for Viola from upstairs. Probably Eugene Jr. He was prone to nightmares these days.

When she came back, Eugene and Dr. H. were off talking again.

"Tomorrow we'll try the strain that Isabel Morgan sent me," Dr. H. was saying. "She said it's a new one, a Type II."

"Hope it's not as virulent as the Mahoney," Eugene said. "So far none of the chimps have had paralysis, knock on wood."

Both he and Dr. H. rapped on the table.

Dr. H. ruffled the back of her hair. "I just wish I wasn't called out of town so much. We really need to concentrate on this."

Viola sat as still as the bread basket by her plate. When it was time to clear off the dishes, she wouldn't let Dr. Horstmann help, no matter how much she protested, and Dr. H. did make a fuss. But she and Eugene were in a discussion about their polio experiments, and Viola wasn't stopping that. Something good might come of it.

VIOLA CAME INTO THE BEDROOM AFTER CHECKING ON THE boys one last time.

Eugene was down to his T-shirt and shorts. "Why did you bring up that man who died?" He pulled back the bedspread, then climbed under, the coral tufts of chenille rippling. "That is a sore subject."

She put her glass of water on the nightstand.

He saw her face. "Look, I'm sorry. But if I'm ever going to get out of the basement and into the lab more, I can't be offending Dr. Horstmann."

"She didn't look offended. Anyway, she's not even a full professor. She can't help you! She can't even help herself."

Viola slipped under the covers next to him. It occurred to her that Dr. Horstmann was trying to find her way up, too. So many were trying to move up—Dr. Horstmann, Eugene, her, even that woman with the dolled-up twins. Everyone was so busy trying to pitch themselves up out of the soup, they couldn't see the person flailing next to them.

Eugene folded his hands on the chenille-tufted mountain of

his chest. "I'm glad I have *some* way of fighting polio. Whatever it takes to kill the beast that took our Linda." His head scraped across his pillow as he turned to look at her. "You know I can't rest until I do."

The old wound flared up so sharply that it took her breath. She saw Linda's terrified eyes—her little Linda, still so tender, so innocent. Oh, those eyes, those eyes. Even having two more children after she'd left them had done nothing to lessen the pain.

Eugene turned back to stare at the ceiling.

That man, thinking he could conquer polio by being an animal keeper! He might as well be bailing out a sinking ship with a teaspoon.

She studied his profile, its familiar contours so dear to her. Yet was he *so* outrageous, believing himself to be in the fight? At least he was doing *something*, something dangerous, something that few men ever would or could do, something that smashed his heart into pieces in the process, for their Linda. Eugene Oakley was the bravest man she knew.

She nestled up close to him. He looked down, then swung his arm around her. "What're you doing?"

"That Chicken Divan recipe was weak," she said. "Don't you think it lacked a pinch of cayenne?"

"Is that all you got to say?"

She put her hands to the prickly flesh on his jaw, then brought his face to hers. "You know it isn't."

20

ON BOARD THE RMS *QUEEN MARY*, 1949

Dorothy batted down the green skirt of Butterick Pattern Number 3789, billowing up like a parachute in the briny wind whipping through the promenade deck. The evening gown had turned out well enough for the first she'd ever made. (Associate professors sending most of their paychecks home couldn't afford to just pluck their eveningwear off the rack at Saks.) She'd stitched it up between trips to Kalamazoo and Dallas, and now she was standing three stories up at the rail of the *Queen Mary, the actual* Queen Mary *ocean liner*, beating the skirt into submission.

She was a little foggy-headed. She'd boarded the ship in New York, straight from a trip to Cairo. Before that, she'd been on outbreaks in Maine, Massachusetts, Michigan, and Texas, and that was just in July. It seemed that Henry Horstmann's kid had become the "It Girl" of polio response teams, known for her ability to swoop in and calm anxious authorities around the world—her, whose childhood idea of an exotic journey was the streetcar ride past Golden Gate Park to Playland with Pop.

She drew in a breath of ocean air, then pushed into the Main Lounge and into the swell of muted trumpets.

Out on the dance floor of the Main Lounge, a mass of dancers scuffed against the parquet. She watched them, evening bag clutched to her green-rayon-covered chest, until they sorted themselves out to be individuals, some of whom she knew. There was the elfin-eared Basil O'Connor dancing energetically with a young woman, his cigarette holder clenched in his teeth. There were Wife of and Mr. Harry Weaver himself, the tiny-mouthed fellow her age who'd been appointed by Basil O'Conner to head up the commission for the vaccine. And there was Albert Sabin with—Sylvia.

Blood rushed into Dorothy's face. She smoothed her dress, mentally clubbing herself for the way her heart hitched. *He is your colleague and only that, and this is his wife.*

"There you are, Dorothy!" Dr. Paul trotted up, tidy in his tux. "You look beautiful." He blushed furiously. "Join us at our table."

His hand placed lightly at her waist, he led her over to where the stag Johns Hopkins and University of Michigan crews were in a discussion that entailed much scribbling on the backs of business cards and gesticulating.

"Enders brought up gamma globulin, and all Hades broke loose," Dr. Paul explained to her. "They've been arguing for an hour." His fingertips trembled on her waist. "Gentlemen, here's Dorothy!"

"Oh, hi, Dottie."

"Hello, Dot."

"Hey, kid!"

"John!" Tommy Francis from the U of M cried to Dr. Paul, "Be the tie-breaker: Does the future of beating polio lie in therapeutics like gamma globulin or in the vaccine?"

Dorothy interceded. "Neither. It lies in clinical epidemiology."

Dr. Paul relinquished her to clasp his hands and shake them over his head like a prizefighting champion. The men groaned.

"Spoken like your creature," said one. "Did you pay her to say that, John?"

Dr. Paul grinned. "You give me too much credit."

Indeed, they did. Until someone figured out the path that the poliovirus took through the body, so that a *safe* and effective vaccine could be developed, their best bet was prevention. She didn't need Dr. Paul to come up with that.

"Well, good thing we're not depending on the vaccine to get us out of this mess," said one of the Johns Hopkins gang. "Because there's the person furthest along in the race." He nodded across the room. "And she seems a little, uh, preoccupied."

Everyone followed his gaze to where Isabel Morgan sat forehead to forehead with a man in an officer's formal uniform. Isabel was doing most of the leaning, Dorothy noticed.

"Too bad, buddy, looks like your Ibby's taken," someone said to another of the Johns Hopkins crew, who stuck out his lower lip in a mock sad face.

After drinks were ordered, her boss turned to her with a twitchy smile.

"Would you like to dance?"

The men at the table froze mid-argument. Grins grew on their faces.

Such asses. "I'd love to."

Out on the dance floor, she refused to acknowledge the table of snickering jackals. She and John must look absurd, like a Great Dane waltzing with a Pomeranian. But he had given her a job when no one else wanted to and had taught her everything he knew about clinical epidemiology—her scientific father, the sophisticated father she never had, though he would *never* come close to replacing Pop in her affection. Having a father like Pop was what had made her strong.

"You are a wonderful dancer," Dr. Paul said as they chugged past the bandstand. "Add that to your list of talents."

She laughed.

"I am serious. With your grace, your charm, your breadth of experience, and brains—Dorothy, you are the most sophisticated woman I know."

When she looked down at him, his eyes were filled with pleading. She didn't understand what he wanted. Maybe she needed to not understand. Oh, this crazy, mixed-up world of men and women. "That's a lovely thing to say."

"I mean it."

"Dorothy!" Sylvia Sabin broke away from her husband to sweep through the dancers, her diaphanous pink gown glimmering. "I was hoping to see you!"

Albert began to follow, then stopped by one of the three-story marble pillars at the edge of the dance floor to light a cigarette.

Dorothy smelled roses as she and Sylvia embraced. Up close, she could feel as much as see that Sylvia was glowing. Was everyone revved up on this ship?

"How are you?" she asked Sylvia. "Are you still photographing?"

"You remembered!"

"Of course. It's interesting."

"*I'm* interesting?" She laughed. "That's a first."

Albert came up behind Sylvia. "Good evening, Dr. Paul, Dr. Horstmann." He ground out his barely smoked cigarette in the crystal ashtray on Dorothy's table, then rested his hand on his wife's hip.

"What a pleasure to see your lovely wife," said Dr. Paul. "You shouldn't keep her hidden."

"Where is your wife, John?" Sylvia asked him.

"Oh, these conferences aren't for her."

"This is my first overseas one," said Sylvia. "I'm only here at the urging of Albert's boss, who insisted that if we are ever to have a child, I had better start coming along on Albert's trips. As if we don't know about the birds and the bees!" She looked over her shoulder and saw her husband scowling. "We're among friends here, Albert! Don't be such a stick."

"I'm glad that you could come!" Dorothy sounded too enthusiastic, even to her own ears.

The band struck up a new song.

"Oh, I adore the Andrews Sisters!" Sylvia exclaimed.

"Then we had better dance." Albert grimly led her off by the hand.

"Shall we, too?" Dr. Paul asked Dorothy.

She let herself be taken back onto the parquet, where the Sabins had disappeared among the dancers. Soon Dr. Paul was paddling by her side. If one were above them, looking down through the glass ceiling of the ship's salon, the swirl of humans below must appear like a school of fish, turning and shimmering, shimmering and turning, as if to some intangible signal. What sixth sense did humans use to respond to the movements of others, to keep them from colliding?

"Sylvia looked radiant, didn't she?" Dr. Paul said above the music.

"Yes! Really lovely!"

"Poor thing," he said. "Rumor is, she's recovering from a breakdown."

ISABEL MORGAN, IN A MINK STOLE AND SAPPHIRE SUNBURST earrings, was on the arm of her gentleman, laughing with the scientists at the stag table, when Dorothy and Dr. Paul came in for a landing. A conga line was forming on the dance floor, and Dr. Paul had begged off it.

Dorothy opened her arms. "Isabel, finally, in the flesh!"

"Finally!"

They embraced. They'd become long-distance chums over the past year, exchanging letters, lab specimens, theories, and gossip. When one finds a fellow unicorn, one clings to her.

Now her friend's thick cheekbones seemed to be lit from within. She was beautiful in her joy.

Dorothy smiled to see her like this. "How is your study coming along?"

One of the bachelors swished his highball. "Dot is the only woman on Earth whose first thought to ask another woman is about her study."

"Have you not met Ibby?" said Isabel's escort.

Everyone laughed, including Isabel. "Dorothy, John," she said, "please meet my fiancé, Colonel Joe Mountain."

Fiancé? Dorothy felt a twinge. Jealousy? Fear of losing her ally?

Dr. Paul stopped sponging his neck from their dance session long enough to shake hands. "Are you the Joe Mountin who set up the Communicable Disease Center in Atlanta? It is high time that we met. I want to talk to you about our latest study on flies."

Even if the medals encrusting his formal cutaway jacket hadn't marked Isabel's gentleman as a military man, his upright carriage and the chill in his pale eyes would have. "That's a different Joe Mountain, I'm afraid. He spells his name M-O-U-N-T-*I*-N. I'm just a computer programmer."

"Just!" Isabel put her arm around his waist. "You should see his computer. It takes up a whole room! The newspapers call it the 'Giant Brain.' Joe is the giant brain behind the Giant Brain."

"It is big," he said coolly.

"I saw one of those computers," said one of the stags, "at Westinghouse. The man operating it reminded me of the scene in *The Wizard of Oz* where the little snake-oil salesman is frantically working the levers of his room-filling machine. He's all machine and no wizard."

Gazes fled from the frowning colonel.

Dr. Paul dabbed his upper lip. "Do you have business in Europe, Colonel Mountain?"

Isabel squeezed her fiancé. "I'm going for the polio conference, but Joe is going for the tour of Denmark."

"Getting in some R and R, eh?"

"Well, I'm not going for the food," Joe said aridly. "Pickled herring is not at the top of my list."

"I have a family friend who promises to show us everything Danish," Isabel said.

Dorothy's hand went instinctively to her heart. She put it down. "You should ask your friend about hygge." *See? You can talk about Danish things without cracking.*

A Brylcreemed lock bounced over a stag's eye. "Hooga?"

The Sabins broke off from the conga line. Albert guided Sylvia over to the table, her breasts straining against her shimmery gown. This was not your typical dowdy beige sack-dress favored by scientists' wives.

"Hey, Al," said another stag. "What's hooga?

Albert tightened his hold on Sylvia's waist. "The Danish art of being comfortable. Why?"

The stags roared.

"What's so funny?" Sylvia asked.

"Is there anything that he doesn't know?" someone cried.

"Apparently," said Sylvia, "he doesn't know about the birds and bees, at least according to his boss." She smiled. "But he's learning." She grinned with the fresh round of laughter.

Albert's smile was not a smile.

A beautiful young couple sauntered up to the table. A threat tightened the air as surely as it would had a magnificent new buck confronted the head of a herd of elk.

"Hilary, man," said one of the stags. "Do you know what hooga is?"

Hilary Koprowski glanced at his darkly gorgeous wife, a famous physician herself. If his job at Lederle Laboratories developing the polio vaccine didn't pan out, with his blond good looks, Dr. Koprowski could always find work in Hollywood. As the highest-paid scientist in this group, being employed by the private sector, he was unlikely to ever need to.

He shrugged. "Hygge's the Danish way of being cozy, right?"

A groan went up over the cha-cha music.

"Know-it-all," someone said.

"Hey," another over-Brylcreemed stag said, "World's Most Expert Expert, meet the World's Most Expert Expert's Expert."

Koprowski flashed perfect teeth. "I assume I am the latter."

"Hardly," said Albert. "Unless your expertise comes from stealing ideas."

A couple stags moaned under their breath.

"How's the vaccine work coming, Hilary?" a Johns Hopkins man asked.

"Excellent," Koprowski said. "I'm testing it on volunteers."

His beautiful wife nudged him. "Hilary, stop. They'll believe you."

"No worries about that, Irena," said Albert. "I never believe a word he says."

The laughter was more uneasy now. Like most university men, Albert believed that those who worked in a commercial lab were puppets to the corporation for which they worked. The fact was, university men were just as subject to outside control, tied as they were to the purse strings of the March of Dimes. Researchers were nothing without funding, of which Dorothy was only too painfully aware.

The factions continued to parry jabs. Having returned so recently from calling her own shots for three weeks in Cairo, Dorothy hadn't grown back the shell needed to absorb all the nonsense. She moved to Isabel Morgan's side.

"The good times never end."

Isabel laughed as she clung to her officer, who was watching the boys thrust digs as would a spectator at a fencing match. "Never."

Dorothy fluffed the tufts at the back of her head. "When you aren't tramping around Denmark with your friends, I'd love to hear more about the nervous tissue that you are using to grow poliovirus."

"Come with us when we go," Isabel said, provoking her boyfriend's scowl, "and I'll tell you all about it. I'm having great luck with it, with all three strains, and just as much luck immunizing the monkeys that I've fed it."

"That's wonderful!"

Isabel nodded. "Just a few more trials—"

"Aw, she's ready now." Howard Howe, another of the Johns Hopkins boys, put down his drink. A wraithlike man with a lopsided face shaped like a footprint, he had the off-putting habit of looking at someone other than to whom he was speaking. "Don't be such a stickler, Ibby." He smiled at Dorothy although his words were clearly meant for Isabel. "Your vaccine is ready to go on humans."

"We can't go off half-cocked with a vaccine for kids, Howie," Isabel said.

"You've had brilliant success on monkeys!" he exclaimed to her, but with his eyes on Dorothy. "Dozens are fully immune now. But isn't the point of all this to save humans from polio?" He flashed a glance at Isabel before addressing Dorothy again. "Or do you just want Sabin to beat us?"

His words fell just as the bachelor table hushed.

All eyes cut toward Albert.

Dr. Paul tucked his handkerchief inside his tuxedo jacket. "Put away your sabers, gentlemen—and ladies. We all want the same thing: to save the world from polio."

"*Safely*," said Albert. "We are not in a race—"

Howie moved his stare to Sylvia. "Oh, yes, we are!"

Sylvia pointed to her décolletage. "Me?"

Albert glared at Howie. "We are not in a race against anything but polio."

Howie sputtered with laughter. "I'd say that was a pretty important race!"

"Howie. My friend." Koprowski shook his gorgeous head. "Don't you know that the most important part of being in the race is behaving as if you aren't in it?"

Sylvia shrank from Howie's stare. "You people! I don't understand you. Why are you all here on this ship arguing when you should be pulling together to save children's lives?"

Just then, the drummer put out an urgent tom-tom call: *DUMP-dump-dump-dump-dump. DUMP-dump-dump-dump-dump. DUMP-dump-dump-dump-dump.* A cry went up as couples spread over the parquet to the pulse of "Sing, Sing, Sing."

Sylvia raised her voice over the excitement. "Well, I know why *I'm* here!" She tucked into her husband. "I want to dance!"

Albert stiffened. "I think we're done with that."

The stags turned curious looks on him. Most of them had wives at home, many raising housefuls of kids, women who were giving up their own dreams so that their husbands could make discoveries and names for themselves. What happened to a wife who didn't toe the line?

"I'll dance with you," Dorothy said.

Albert handed over his wife. "I'll be in the smoking lounge." He strode out.

The floor was so crowded with ladies and gents Lindy Hopping in gowns and tuxes when Dorothy and Sylvia clattered onto it that they could only find room a few feet from their table. Dorothy's bones were shuddering from a hop in heels when one of the bachelors said, "I always thought Dottie was a lesbo, ever since she turned me down."

21

COPENHAGEN, DENMARK, 1949

"That one liked to dress as a man, you know."

Dorothy straightened from studying the life-size portrait of a woman in a powdered wig and a heap of skirts. Isabel Morgan's friend Bente Larsen was waiting for her, her eyes sparkling like half-hidden jewels under her thick crinkled lids. Papery skin cross-hatched by age stretched across her cheekbones when she smiled.

"You are looking at Queen Caroline Mathilde of Great Britain," she said, her excellent English accented with British. "Her brother was the English Mad King George."

Isabel's beau, Colonel Mountain, cast a gaze at the painting, his upright posture intact. "I see the family resemblance. The protruding jaw, those bulging eyes."

Rigid in his blue Air Force uniform, he clung to Isabel's hand like a teenager, although he had at least a decade on her, and Isabel was no bobby-soxer herself. They had invited Dorothy to join them on their tour the day before the conference was scheduled to end. She was glad that she went, and not just to catch up with Isabel. She was amazed to discover Copenhagen was rife with giants like her, both men and women. There were several of them milling past the artifacts here in the Rosenborg Castle. Although they stuck out in the crowd like giraffes among zebras, no one paid them the slightest attention, let alone stopped them to inform them of their height. Being tall in Denmark was . . . normal.

Isabel leaned past Dorothy to ask, "Bente, what's this queen's name again?"

"Caroline Mathilde."

"I think she's pretty, in a chipper sort of way."

Bente craned her mop of white floss toward the plaque on the wall. "She was only fifteen at the time of this painting."

"That explains it," Isabel told Joe. "Have you ever seen a fifteen-year-old girl who *wasn't* pretty?"

He frowned, his response to nearly everything.

"Although you can't convince them of that," she said to Dorothy. "At least I couldn't be convinced of it, when I was fifteen or sixteen."

"Well, I don't think she's pretty," Joe said. And that was that.

Bente examined a porcelain bust of a child. "Caroline Mathilde's husband, Christian VII, was quite mad. More mad than her brother, Mad George, if that's possible."

"Was every royal insane back then?" Joe asked.

Bente sucked in her breath as if preparing to dive into water, a habit that had startled Dorothy at first. She had looked about for an emergency each time Bente did it, until Dorothy came to understand that gasping was just something that many Danes did when considering or before making a point. "Caroline Mathilde wasn't insane," Bente said, "in spite of her habit of wearing men's clothes when she reviewed her troops. In fact, preferring pants might be proof of her sanity. Look at those panniers—they're the size of picnic baskets. And those skirts! They look like theater curtains. After being weighed down like that, who wouldn't want trousers?"

"I hate to see women in them," said Joe.

A man entered the room. Tall, silky-haired, and angular-faced, with arms and legs that poked from within his baggy clothes like Tinkertoys, he paused to inspect an elaborate clock. Dorothy felt a punch to her solar plexus. It took her seconds to believe he was not Arne, then seconds more to beat back memories of Arne's touch, his voice, his sweetness.

"Caroline Mathilde took her husband's physician as her lover," Bente was saying. "She and this doctor ran the country while her husband drank to excess or pounded his head against the wall."

Joe scowled. "Pounded his head against the wall?"

"Literally. Until he drew blood."

"He was jealous," Joe stated.

"Maybe, but he'd begun that habit long before she took a lover," said Bente. "He was unpredictable and violent, not just with himself, but with others."

The Not-Arne was inspecting a ship model carved of ivory. Dorothy sighed. "She must have been desperate."

"She had a child by this other man," said Bente, "and everyone knew who the father was."

Isabel pulled Joe's hand closer. "At least she found happiness."

Bente gasped in the Danish way. "Did she? She was run out of the country at bayonet's end by her mother-in-law's soldiers and locked up in a castle in Germany, where her brother, Mad King George, let her languish. She had taken the matter into her own hands and was laying plans to make her escape, when she came down with scarlet fever."

"Scarlet fever, huh," said Joe. "Like a kid."

"She was little more than one," said Bente. "She was twenty-six."

"Did she die?" Isabel asked.

Bente nodded her white floss.

Dorothy firmly placed Not-Arne out of her sight. "What a shame. She could have survived if they'd had penicillin then. I wonder what she would have done if she'd gotten back her throne?"

"Hmm," said Joe. "She could have turned out to be a despot. A female Hitler. Good riddance."

Bente inhaled. "Oh, we would never have had a Hitler here,

female or otherwise. That's not the Danish way. We're the peaceful sort."

Joe smiled as if he'd caught her in a mistake. "Weren't the Vikings from Denmark?"

Isabel tapped his arm. "Stop."

"Well?" he said, grinning.

Isabel shook her head indulgently. "If we're going to play 'What If,' what if there had never been you? What if you weren't here to lead air raids all over Germany, night after night that last year of the war? Your bombings took the stuffing out of Hitler. How much longer would the war have lasted without you?"

"Let's not play '*It's a Wonderful Life*' now," he scoffed, failing to keep the gratification out of his voice.

Isabel touched her head to his shoulder. "We're so lucky there's a you." They strolled to the other side of the room.

Bente pulled at the ends of the scarf tied around her neck, then noticed Dorothy watching. "My husband and I were like that, too, when we first married." She saw the question in Dorothy's eyes. "He's no longer with us. He died twenty-nine years ago, in a laboratory accident. He was a biologist, from Cambridge—that's where I learned your language. We were dear friends with Isabel's parents." She glanced at Isabel, then lowered her voice. "I can't say that my Carl wasn't jealous when Tom Morgan won the Nobel for his work in genetics. Carl had thought he'd make a few discoveries himself. Scientists are such competitive people, aren't they?"

"It seems so."

"I suppose they must have *something* to motivate them. *Something* must drive them to stay cooped up in their dreary labs when the skies are blue, the birds are singing, and their young wives await them in pretty new dresses."

Their gazes met, then broke to pore over another portrait.

The Not-Arne ducked under the door to enter the next salon. What would it hurt to ask?

"Would you happen to know an Arne Holm from Kongens Lyngby?"

"Arne Holm? *The* Arne Holm?"

"Is that a common name?"

Bente gasped in the Danish fashion. "It's a revered name, isn't it?"

"So you've heard of him?"

"What Dane hasn't? He, Aage Bertelsen, and some others hatched the plan that kept most of Denmark's Jews out of concentration camps. Did you know him?"

Did. Past tense. "Briefly."

"In the States? I thought I'd heard he'd gone there after—" She frowned, then cleared her throat.

"After his wife died?"

Bente nodded.

Dorothy kept her face neutral. "I met him in San Francisco."

"Did he tell you that he arranged for owners of even the smallest dinghies to row the Jewish families to their freedom in Sweden in October of '43?"

"He didn't tell me but someone else did. He wouldn't talk about it."

"It might not have been a particularly happy memory for him, what with his loss. No wonder he volunteered to go on the mission with the White Buses."

"What are White Buses?"

Bente released a sigh that meant regret in any language. "You don't know of them?"

"Bente!" Isabel called from across the room. "Bente, please come tell us about this fascinating clock!"

Bente grimaced at Dorothy, then went over to where the lovebirds stood before a golden apparatus the height of an eight-year-old child. She waited until Dorothy joined them to explain how, when the chimes struck, the glass waterfalls began to flow along the sides of the clock's case and a dozen miniature lords and ladies promenaded at its base.

"I heard it play once," said Bente. "In fact, I was with your father." She blinked. "And mother. It put up an awful din. It sounded like two carnival carousels playing at once."

"I wish we could get someone to play it for us," Isabel said. "Do you think there's someone here who could?"

Bente frowned. "I used to know one of the curators . . ."

"Oh, please go see!" Isabel exclaimed. "I'd really love to hear it. Please, Bente!"

"You might as well go," Joe told Bente. "She *will* have her way."

Bente smiled. "I knew Isabel when she was a child." She patted Isabel's arm. "I'll go."

She strode off on the sensible shoes favored by the Danish.

ONE TRIUMPHANT PRIVATE SHOWING OF THE QUEEN'S clock and tour of the castle gardens later, they were hiking to the famous statue of the Little Mermaid. Bente and Dorothy led the way through streets lined with tall buildings topped with steep tile roofs. A breeze smelling of the sea and frying fish tugged at their skirts and scarves.

Bente checked on Isabel and Joe, strolling directly behind. "Perhaps we should be strewing rose petals in their path," she told Dorothy.

"I think not. We'd make terrible cherubs."

Bente chuckled, then called to the lovebirds, "Almost there!"

"They didn't hear me," she said when she turned back to Dorothy. "As is the way of lovers, they have ears and eyes for no one else. The trouble begins when they think that no one sees them, either."

Dorothy looked at her questioningly, but Bente only directed the group to the harbor's edge and then down an earthen spit built into the stony gray wash. Just ahead, people had gathered around something at the shore. When a pair stepped aside for the man to examine his camera, a small bronze statue of a naked woman curled on a harbor rock came into view.

Their foursome came to a standstill before it.

"That's it?" said Joe.

"That's it," said Bente. "That's *The Little Mermaid*."

"It's not very big," said Isabel. "Why all the fuss?"

Bente inhaled in her Danish way. "We love our H. C. Andersen here. What can I say?"

Behind them, a man said, "We were at his house today."

The four of them turned to find Albert and Sylvia Sabin.

Dorothy stepped back to let some tourists photograph the *Little Mermaid* statue as Albert kissed Isabel's checks. The Sabins were looking very much the sophisticates, with him in a paneled knit sports shirt and her in a stiff skirt and wide belt, big sunglasses perched on her nose.

"What are you two doing here?" Isabel asked him good-naturedly. "Joe, you remember Albert Sabin and his wife—"

"Sylvia," said Sylvia.

"And this is Bente Larsen." Isabel laughed. "I needn't introduce you to Dorothy."

"You certainly don't." Sylvia brushed her lips past Dorothy's cheeks.

Albert kissed Dorothy, too, as would any American gentleman on holiday.

Sylvia removed her sunglasses. "Albert saw your group and was in a hot hurry to catch up." She claimed his arm to snuggle against him. "We had just left our hotel room," she said, hardly suppressing an impish smile.

Albert shifted slightly away. "We'd gone to Odense," he clarified.

Bente corrected his pronunciation of the city. "I know, it sounds nothing like how it appears. When it comes to speaking Danish, you cannot rely on your eyes."

"Rather like dealing with a virus," Albert said.

"Or husbands," said Sylvia. She laughed.

Bente's gaze darted between them. "Did you go to Hans Christian Andersen's birthplace while you were there?" she asked in a level voice.

"Yes! It's no better than a hut," said Sylvia. "How did people live like that?"

"Many people live like that," Albert said. "Or worse. Not everyone has had your comfortable Midwestern upbringing."

He said it jovially enough, but afterward a beat was dropped.

Bente picked it up. "Poor H. C. He did come from nothing."

"Maybe that inspired him," said Dorothy.

"More likely it was a hindrance," said Albert.

Sylvia glanced between them. "*I'm* feeling inspired to find a drink. Anyone else?"

They retreated to a nearby restaurant, where Albert seated his wife, then took a chair next to Dorothy, lit a cigarette, and sat back.

"Finally!" He blew smoke away from Dorothy. "We get to talk!" He leaned forward. "Is it me, or is Koprowski being cagey about his progress on his vaccine? Does he have one or not? If he does, how good can it be? We haven't even identified all the strains of the virus yet."

Sylvia watched them with an unlit cigarette between her fingers. She gave Joe a surprised smile when he clinked open his lighter and started talking to her.

Dorothy turned to Albert. "You're right. Koprowski is up to something. But what bothers me is that all the Pitt boys, other than Jonas, are fixated on developing gamma globulin treatments. Doesn't that seem like a colossal waste of time? They can never produce enough to meet demand."

Albert made a chiding sound. "Not when the demand is greater than ever, with both kids and young adults getting ill. We can't call it 'infantile paralysis' anymore, now that young adults are the fastest-growing group of polio patients. We're losing this battle, Dorothy."

She paused to drink a glass of water, absentmindedly glancing at the others in their party. "John Paul told me something that has been sitting in the back of my mind. While working among the Eskimos just below the Arctic Circle at Chesterfield Inlet this summer, he found that only children under three were escaping paralysis from an outbreak that was affecting twenty percent of the entire population."

Albert ground out his cigarette. "Yes?"

"Only *nursing* babies were spared. But as soon as they were weaned, around the age of three in that culture, they were susceptible to paralysis. It's as if there were something in mother's milk that protected them."

Something switched behind his eyes. His gaze took on a different intensity. "Mother's milk?"

Their waiter, a narrow older gentleman, came with a tray of small chilled flutes filled with a tawny liquid.

"*Snaps!*" Bente announced as the waiter placed them around the table. "A drink for special occasions."

"Looks interesting." Joe grasped his glass and was about to sip it.

"Oh, no. Stop!"

Joe scowled.

"There is a process to this." Bente pinched her flute between thumb and forefinger. "Raise your glass." Her sleeve rasped against her sweater as she did so. "Prepare to swallow it all in one gulp, but first, look your partner most intently in the eye." She leveled her gaze at Joe, who was still frowning from being reprimanded. "Now say, '*Skål*.'"

Arne's presence came swooping in. Dorothy fumbled for her glass. When she'd clenched herself back into stability, Albert was waiting for her with his lifted glass.

Behind him, Sylvia offered her drink to his back. "*Skål*," she said to no one.

Dorothy leaned around Albert and raised her glass to Sylvia. "*Skål*."

"Now," said Bente, "look your partner in the eye once more, then repeat the process with everyone else at the table."

"How does people's food not get cold?" Joe groused as he raised his glass to Dorothy.

WISPS OF WATERCRESS REMAINED OF THE APPETIZER SERVED with the *snaps*. The flutes themselves were empty. Joe pushed himself up from the table. "Time for us to get back."

He assisted Isabel from her chair.

"Oh!" Isabel exclaimed. "Dorothy and I didn't get a chance to talk."

"We'll catch up later," Dorothy said.

"Us, too, Albert," said Sylvia. "We should go."

He opened his mouth, then closed it, before rising next to her.

Dorothy was left at the table with Bente, a cluttered ashtray stinking before them.

"Would you like to order dinner?" said Bente.

Dorothy had no other plans.

After their elderly waiter had come, and they'd given back their menus, Bente said, "It's easy to be attracted to the alpha male."

An icy finger traced Dorothy's spine. It was useless to pretend that she didn't know what Bente meant.

Bente folded her hands on the table, her knuckles as wrinkled as elephant knees, her fingers crooked at the last joint. Yet there was a grace to those hands. Dorothy could imagine those fingers when they were long and slender. They were beautiful, once. Bente, Dorothy realized, looking up into her face, was beautiful, once.

Dorothy was imagining the young woman as Bente spoke. "It's

genetics. My husband studied traits on a chromosomal level, but even I could tell you this: we're attracted to whom we're attracted. We haven't the least control over that attraction, yet we pretend that we do." Wrinkles wreathed the young Bente's face as she smiled. "Dr. Sabin must be terribly hard to resist."

"We're just colleagues."

Bente withdrew her hands to her lap. "I was in love with Isabel's father."

Dorothy glanced around the restaurant, now filling with couples groomed and dressed for dinner. She enjoyed Albert's company, that was true. The way their minds lit off the other was intoxicating. Oh, be honest—she wallowed in their comradery, she provoked him for it, and then she gulped it down with the thirst of a woman in love with a man who loved his dead wife. Because the fact was, it was Arne she was still in love with. In their brief time together, she'd connected to him in a way that still made her want to howl like a speared beast at the loss of him. Feeling like this could cause her to make mistakes, if she did not keep her head.

"I wasted a lot of years," said Bente, "pining for what I couldn't have."

The waiter brought their salads. Bente smiled at him. "*Tak.*"

They picked through their lettuce, each of them retreating to another place and time. At last Dorothy said, "Tell me about the White Buses."

Bente looked troubled. "Perhaps this isn't the best time."

"Please."

In any language, Bente's inhalation was one of misgiving. "Very well." She laid her fork among her scattered greens.

"By the end of 1944, the war was going badly for Germany, as you know. Allied planes—Americans, Brits, Canadians—had won the war in the air and were bombing cities all across the Third Reich. At this time, we were hearing in Scandinavia that our prisoners in German concentration camps were dying by the hundreds from disease. The idea went up that a team of doctors and nurses in a caravan of buses from neutral Sweden should be allowed to remove the sickest Danes, Finns, and Norwegians from the camps. The Germans agreed to it."

Dorothy raised her brows. "They did?"

Bente gave her white fluff a shake. "Not out of altruism. As I said, the Allies were destroying Germany from the sky. Not just factories, but railroads and bridges were targeted. Roads. The Nazis realized that anyone traveling on them would be going to their deaths at the hands of the Allies. They said, 'Let the Scandinavian rescuers come. Why waste bullets on them when the Yanks can do it for us?'"

A young couple was being seated at the table next to them, their faces giddy with love. Bente waited until Dorothy returned her attention.

"When the Swedes understood what the Germans had in store for them, they painted the buses bright white, in hopes that the bombers would see them and know that they were hospital buses. They outfitted the buses with beds and medicine, then stockpiled them with penicillin. Word was that many of the prisoners were in precarious shape and would need treatment on the spot."

"Arne was buying penicillin in the States—for hospitals, I understood."

"So that's where they got it. I hadn't heard. That bit wasn't in the papers. All I know is that the men and women on the White Buses saved many lives with it. At least the ones who got out of Germany did." She sucked in her breath. "They were very brave, going on this suicide mission. Arne, I could understand, what with his wife's—" She sighed, then dabbed her withered lips with her napkin. "Well, he's with her now."

"What do you mean?"

"Oh, dear. Don't you know? Arne Holm is dead. He died on a White Bus mission."

The waiter came. Dorothy stared through tears at the plate he set before her.

When Bente finally spoke, it was in a singsong manner, as would a mother to a little child who had fallen. "Here we go! Look at this! *Stjerneskud*—that's 'shooting star' in English. It's considered to be *smørrebrød*, a type of open-faced sandwich which we typically eat for lunch, but I think it's too special for that."

Dorothy stared at the fried fish fillet piled with orange curls of smoked salmon, tiny shrimps, and asparagus chunks laced with mayonnaise and dill.

She looked up. "Joe flew air raids over Germany."

Bente paused with her salt shaker. "I know, dear."

"It could have been his bomb that killed Arne."

"Yes. I suppose that's possible." Bente put down the salt, then reached across the table, knocking her knife into her plate with a clink. Her hand was warm upon Dorothy's. "You cannot dwell on that."

She wanted to free herself of Bente's hold. How could she ever speak to Joe again, to Isabel?

Bente squeezed her fingers, then withdrew. "One advantage of advanced age is the realization of how intricately we all are bound up together." She laughed. "At least, it took *me* this long to learn it."

The young beauty that was Bente seemed to recede, until all that remained were her clear blue eyes, glimmering beneath crinkled lids. "If only we knew how deeply we are all connected, perhaps we'd work harder on being kinder."

She picked up her knife and fork. "Now eat the fish, dear. It's good."

22

Someone was playing Gershwin when Dorothy stepped into the hotel lobby after dinner with Bente. Although it was not yet dusk—daylight didn't fall until close to nine o'clock in Denmark in August—lamps had been turned on throughout, revealing every slung-back modern chair to have a researcher perched on its edge. They were all there: the University of Michigan men plotting with the Johns Hopkins boys; the Rockefeller Instituters scheming with the National Institutes of Healthers; the Pitt fellas huddling with the Baylors. Only the Yalies were missing from the arena, being an early-to-bed tribe like their chieftain, John Paul. The rest were kicking back before their final day at the conference, honing the rivalries that had heated up over the week.

In the center of this buzzing assemblage, Hilary Koprowski was pummeling "Rhapsody in Blue" into the keys of a baby grand. His dark-haired wife sat next to him on his bench, sipping a glass of wine, detached, bored, gorgeous. Dorothy had heard that Irena Koproska was working with Dr. Georgios Papanicolaou on a test to detect cervical cancer in women. She and Dr. Papanicolaou, "Dr. Pap" for short, claimed that they could find cancer in a tiny sample of cervix smeared on a slide. They had the knowledge, right now, to save thousands of women a year by catching the cancer in the early stages, unlike the polio crowd, who were still puzzling over the route of the virus through the body after thirty-some years. Irena must have thought they were a dull lot. Her lithe figure slumped within her black gown, her languid gloved hand from which a cigarette smoldered, and her heavy-lidded gaze all said so.

Someone waved: Sylvia, alone, and dazzling in a strapless dress the scarlet of well-oxygenated blood. She was flagging Dorothy from a settee behind the piano.

Dorothy started over. Halfway there, she saw Albert moving toward his wife, a drink in each hand.

She paused.

"Hi, Dot!" Howie Howe beckoned her over from his seat by a potted plant.

Dorothy kept going.

Sylvia was taking her drink from Albert when Dorothy arrived. Sylvia smiled up at her. "Hello, you. Come join us in Social Siberia. Apparently, one doesn't bring wives to these things. I'm afraid I've made a pariah out of Albert."

Dorothy wouldn't tell her that Albert did a good enough job of that on his own. "That can't be true. Irena is here."

"Oh, she's not a wife," said Sylvia. "She's—"

Albert sipped his drink. "A goddess?"

Sylvia nudged him. "Hey!"

"I meant the goddess Athena—brainy."

"That's worse! I know how you lust for a beautiful mind. He'd rather have a woman in his lab than in his bed."

"You two!" Dorothy sighed, weary of being stuck in a mire of innuendos. She'd brought it on herself, hadn't she? She'd let her loneliness make a fool of her.

Koprowski banged to a finish. The air rang with the final note.

"Hey, Albert," one of the Pitt boys called over the whistles and applause flooding the room, "can you top that?"

Albert waited until everyone had calmed. "I don't need to top that. While Hilary was laboring over the keyboard this evening, I got a cable from *Time* magazine." He tapped the folded bit of paper peeking from the breast pocket of his suit jacket. "They're interested in doing a story with me."

Irena spoke up from the piano bench, her husky voice rich with her native Polish. "When you talk to them, please tell them that my husband has a little tale he would like to share."

Koprowski leaned into his wife. "Irena!"

"What tale would that be?" asked a Johns Hopkins boy.

She raised eyes that were pools of allure. "A story about a rat."

"Don't go talking about Sabin that way," quipped a Baylorite.

"Very funny," muttered Albert.

Koprowski rubbed shoulders with his wife. "Darling, they don't want to hear it."

"Tell them!"

"Yes, tell us," Howie Howe said to him, though looking at Sylvia, who shrank back.

Koprowski shrugged. "All right. If I must."

He swung around on the bench to face the crowd. "It was last year. The boys in the lab and I had been injecting Type II poliovirus into the brains of cotton rats. We then pulverized their brains with saline solution to make a sort of soup, which we then injected into more rats, whose brains we pulverized to inject into more rats—"

"Got it," Albert snapped. "You were weakening the virus until you had it in attenuated form."

Koprowski bowed. "Correct. When we felt it was weak enough, we fed it to chimpanzees. To our gratification, they remained symptom-free, even when exposed to the most virulent Type II virus known to us, the Mahoney."

"The Mahoney strain," someone said. "Wow!"

Albert snapped open his lighter and lit a cigarette. "Congratulations." He blew out smoke. "Your chimps didn't get polio."

"They didn't. I thought that rather significant, but if I follow your drift, yes, that didn't mean my vaccine would work on humans.

But who dare I try? Who else?" He stroked the lapel of his tux, then flicked his wrist. "*Moi.*"

"I am glad you did not tell me of your plans then!" said Irena.

"You never have to worry about me, darling. My work is solid." He nuzzled her cheek and then continued. "My assistant, Thomas Norton, insisted on being a part of it. So Norton and I poured ourselves a beaker full of rat-brain cocktail—" He motioned for Irena's half-empty wineglass. "May I, darling?" He lifted her glass to the crowd. "We raised our beakers, clinked them, and then we drank them down." He drained Irena's wine, then smacked his lips. "Tasted like cod-liver oil."

The room erupted in groans or laughs or both.

He indicated for the men to settle. When they did, he glanced at his wife, then smiled. "Then Norton asked me, 'Have another, Boss?' I told him, 'No, thank you, Norton, I'm driving.'"

The men roared.

"Juvenile," Albert muttered to Dorothy.

Sylvia shrugged with a swish of satin. "I thought it was funny."

Basking in the delight of his peers, Koprowski swiveled around to the keyboard. The air soon sparkled with his spritely rendition of Mozart's "Alla Turca."

Howie Howe fixed Sylvia with his colorless eyes. He said to Albert, "You didn't tell us what are you talking to the *Time* reporters about."

The others quieted.

Albert knew to whom Howie was addressing his remark. He drew on his cigarette. "Oh, it was not nearly as interesting as relating how I drank rat-brain cocktails."

Koprowski broke off playing. "What was it, then?"

"Just about how mother's milk seems to confer immunity from polio."

Dorothy stared at him. This was John Paul's study; she'd just told him about it this afternoon. John hadn't even written it up yet.

Albert would give him credit, wouldn't he?

Dorothy felt a tap on her shoulder. She turned to find a man towering over her, his silky brown hair and the stubble on his angular cheeks glinting in the lamplight. His smile drew up the corners of his eyes and his mouth, crinkling them like blinds raised to let in the light of day.

"Hello, Dorothy," said Arne.

23

Dorothy blinked. It wasn't really Arne. Anxiety had produced this apparition grinning before her. She'd conjured it up—the jutting shoulders, the spread-collar shirt, the fedora held to a torso the length of a travel-trunk. She blinked again. No, this man was real. She could smell the scent of his aftershave.

"I hoped," he said, "that I would find you here."

He had to be another Arne look-alike. Another man like the one she'd seen in Rosenborg Castle or like the ones who'd startled her over the years, picking out apples at the grocery store or striding down a city street or entering a movie theater. A wincing closer look revealed that this man was thinner than Arne. Unlike Arne's smooth face, this man's was lightly pitted with scars, as if he'd had a bad case of chicken pox. His speech was different, too. There was a subtle halt to it, as if he were working to find his words. Her Arne, ever the philosopher, had never had trouble voicing his mind.

"I came," this man said in his careful way, "when I read the news . . . coming from the Poliomyelitis Congress . . . in Copenhagen."

Who was he? He obviously knew her. Had she met him at an outbreak? In a hospital somewhere? During her fellowship year in London, depressed and lonely, she'd kicked up her heels a few desperate evenings. Surely not from then.

She blushed. "How are you!"

He pursed his lips in an awkward smile. "The question is, how are you, Dorothy?"

Koprowski's galloping piano music and the laughter of the stags thumped through her ears. She blinked to clear her cloudy head. Was this how dementia started?

A hand thrust between her and the stranger. "Albert Sabin." Albert bared his teeth in his not-smile. "I don't believe that we have met."

The men clasped hands. The stranger said, "Arne Holm."

Her knees buckled. Both men grabbed an elbow.

"I'm all right!" Shock—relief—joy—nausea—spurted through her, until her nerves settled on fury, putting starch back into her legs. He shows up *now*? In nearly five years, he could have written.

"How do you two know each other?" Albert asked.

"I am—" Arne looked to Dorothy for help. She wouldn't give it. "—Dorothy's old friend."

Old *friend*! Anger flamed up anew. Tears scratched at her eyes, which made her even more furious.

Arne saw her expression. "Perhaps this is a bad time."

"I think it might be," Albert agreed. "Nice to meet you, chap." He moved to show him away.

Sylvia latched on to her husband. "Hello!" she said to Arne. "I'm the wife."

"Hello, Wife."

Her long gloves *shished* against her red bodice as she reached out to shake his hand. She renewed her hold on Albert's arm. "Tell us, where's a good place around here to have a little fun?"

"I am not . . . the man to know." Arne gave her a crumpled smile. "I have not been in Copenhagen . . . since the war."

Dorothy couldn't help it. "Where *have* you been?"

"In Odense." He looked at her as if begging her to understand.

Sylvia laughed. "You mean Oh-DENSE! I'm not even going to

try to pronounce it right. Albert and I were there today. What an adorable town!"

Why was he still looking at her like that? For four and a half years, he'd left her hanging.

"For such an adorable town," Dorothy said, "it has terrible mail service. Letters never seem to go out."

Arne hung his head. "The postmaster . . . is not to blame. The mail is not much good to you . . . when you are in hospital."

"You're a doctor?" Sylvia asked.

"No, a patient . . . in hospital for eight months . . . five days of them unconscious. Afterward, I spent twenty months . . . in a rehabilitation hospital in . . . that 'adorable' town. I have a great respect now . . . for physio, speech, and occupational therapists. I walk, speak . . ." He glanced at Dorothy. ". . . and now write, thanks to them."

"My goodness," said Sylvia. "Did you have polio?"

"No." Arne drew in a breath. "White knight syndrome."

Dorothy's ears filled with a hissing not unlike that of a television set left on after midnight. "You were on a White Bus."

He nodded.

"You were bombed."

He nodded, slower now.

"But you survived."

His eyes watered. "Pardon. Foolish of me." He swiped at them with his knuckle. "I did not think . . . I would ever see this moment."

Sylvia looked between them. "Oh, dear, what is a 'white bus'?"

Dorothy fought back a howl for his suffering; for the cruelty, the stupidity, the sheer baseness of which humans were capable; for the lives taken; for the lives wasted; for the theft of her prime, and his. How did you get those years back? How did you put the pieces together again? Could you, ever?

"You knew about me," he marveled.

"I was told about the White Buses only today, but I heard that you were—" Their eyes met. *You're alive. Oh, Arne.*

Albert crossed his arms, Sylvia still attached to one of them. "How did you say you two knew one another?"

Dorothy pored over Arne's face, his scars, his suffering, now clear to her. How she yearned to cradle his face between her hands.

Sylvia laid two gloved fingers against Dorothy's back and pushed. "Go, you. Get out of here! You don't need us old marrieds."

"Perhaps they don't want to go," Albert said.

Sylvia's scarlet bodice heaved. "Oh, Albert. For a man who can spot the slightest abnormality in heart tissue under a microscope, you can be so terribly blind."

24

The air held the mucky smell of seaweed. Waves lapped against stone walls. Over the gritty crunch of two pairs of footsteps on brick, Dorothy could hear boats bucking at their moorings, the spindly forest of their masts lit by streetlamps. To her other side, tall wooden houses, dark save for a few windows glowing yellow, overshadowed the harbor. She closed her eyes and tried to believe.

"As shabby as Nyhavn is now," Arne was saying, "the area was even more disreputable . . . then. A place for brothels and hard drinking."

She brought herself back to the moment. "The red light district?"

"Is that . . . what you would call it? The red district?"

"The red *light* district."

"I see. Yes. H. C. Andersen lived here . . . for much of his adult life."

She asked him questions just to hear his voice. "What is the Danish people's preoccupation with this man?"

He laughed. "You Americans have your American dream. I suppose we have ours, too. The poor cobbler's son became . . . the consort of kings. He is our own rags-and-riches tale—"

"Rags-*to*-riches."

He nodded. "—his riches being stories that took his work . . ."

into most homes in the Western world. That is quite an achievement, if you think about it."

She was not mistaken—the more he spoke, the more his voice was strengthening. Joy fizzed inside her like champagne. "And Hans Christian Andersen lived here in Nyhavn?"

"We usually call him 'H. C. Andersen' in Denmark. And yes. In that building." He pointed to a five-story house with banks of crowded windows that made lacework of the facade. "Second floor. Right there."

They peered at one of the windows, a yellow rectangle shining in the night.

"H. C., born into poverty, was a guest of royal courts around the world. He even lived with Charles Dickens's family for five weeks . . . until Dickens asked him to leave. It was recorded . . . to have been an uncomfortable visit. H. C. could not speak a word of English."

The light in the window went out.

"By all accounts, Dickens wanted him gone. But his youngest children did not. H. C. entertained them with his paper cuttings. You have heard of them?"

She shook her head.

"Andersen was famous for folding paper then snipping away with his scissors . . . until, at the end of his tale, he had an intricate silhouette or paper doll or puppet to present to his little listeners. Dickens's children did not care if his words sounded like gibberish. They adored him."

"Words aren't the only way to communicate."

She could feel Arne gazing down at her. "Perhaps they are the clumsiest method," he said. "Or the least reliable, when conveying the truth."

"Yet we humans depend on them most."

"Maybe that is where we as a species have gone wrong." Even as they stood together quietly, she could feel her body—no, that unfathomable being inside her—straining for and then clasping onto his hidden self until the two whirled with joy together. She could hardly breathe from the sheer impossible wonder of it all.

An owl swooped soundlessly through the cool sea air just inches over their heads. She cowered, then laughed. "Did you see that?"

"A friendly spirit." He put his arm around her. Together they scanned the sky, her head resting against his shoulder. Above the rooftops, silvered clouds slid through the darkness.

He kept his hold on her when they walked on. "H. C. craved admiration from the rich and powerful, but he always came back here. For the longest time, disreputable Nyhavn was the place he chose in which to live and work."

"It's what he knew."

"Yes, people often revert back to what they know. They think they deserve no better. Cold?" he said when she shivered.

She laid her cheek against his shoulder. "Not now."

In time, as they walked along, he told her about his injury. He told her that he heard doctors say that he'd be a "vegetable," and how once he'd understood that he might always be that broken, he wanted to die. Only the thought of her had kept him going.

"But what if you did not wait for me?" he said. "And if by some miracle that you did wait, what if once you saw the state I was in, you did not want me?"

Tears salted the back of her throat. "I thought you didn't love me. I thought you were grieving for your wife, and that was why you'd abandoned me. Why didn't you tell me about her?"

They stopped. He brought her before him.

"Dorte, it hurt too much to talk about her. I did love her, with all my being. That is how I love."

She looked down.

"After she died, I thought I would never love again. I did not want to." He raised her chin. "Then I met you."

She rested her forehead against his throat.

"Imagine my terror of losing you," he said, his voice rumbling in her head. "For the longest time, my brains were too scrambled to know how to search for you, even if one of the nurses could have done my writing for me." Her forehead rode the wave as he swallowed. "As my mind came together, I was ashamed for you to see my body in its ugly state. And then once I was well enough to leave the hospital, I was ashamed of how much time had passed."

"No more wasting time." She lifted her face. "No more shame. For either of us."

He drew a deep breath. "I cannot say if that is possible. I have not tried . . . I do not know . . . if I am a whole man."

She brought his hand to her mouth and kissed it. "There's only one way to find out, isn't there?"

She led him back to the hotel.

THEY LAY IN HER BED, FROM WHICH THE COVERINGS HAD fallen to the floor. Her body still glowing, she clung to him like a shipwreck victim to a raft. It was the first she had fully given herself to a man. It would not be the last.

"Are you ever going to stop grinning?" she asked.

"Apparently not."

Happiness flowed in and around and between them as they savored their own recollection of their lovemaking.

Shuddering with a sigh, she rolled onto her back, then she put her head on his chest. She chuckled. "For the rest of my life, I am going to cherish the look on Howie Howe's face when we walked through the lobby to the elevator."

"The place did get rather quiet."

She chuckled again, then put her nose to the skin of his chest and breathed.

"Maybe we should have gone up separately," he said.

She rocked her head on his ribs. "I wasn't wasting another moment with you on *them*. Anyhow, what was the use? Someone would have figured it out. It's impossible for two giants to flit around unnoticed."

"Then maybe I should make a respectable woman out of you."

"I don't care about them," she said, a little hurt. Did he think her disrespectable?

He rolled onto his side to look at her. "I do not care about them, either. And I do not much care whether or not our love is certified by a court. But I do not joke about wanting to be with you always. I have known it since we met. Our souls are old friends. Old lovers. You know this, too. Now that they have found each other, let us not keep them apart."

She remained still even as the being that was within her danced.

"I know there is much to work out"—he grimaced—"like the small matter of upon which continent we should live. But the big matter is that we belong together."

He got up on his elbow and scanned the room.

"What?" she said.

"I seem to be caught without a ring to offer you to pledge my troth."

"Oh, I don't need—"

"I do not mean to legally bind you. I do not mean to own you, Dorte, even in the eventuality of our marriage."

"Oh, Arne."

"I just mean to give you a sign of my devotion. A ring would do better but—" He reached for the bedside table, then rolled back to her. On his palm, he offered a blue-and-white china dish. "Dorothy Horstmann, will you accept this as a token of my love, now and forever?"

"An ashtray?"

He sighed. "At least it is Royal Copenhagen."

She laughed. "Yes. Yes, Arne Holm, I will accept your ashtray." She brought his face to hers. "Yes, I will love you, now and forever. Yes." She kissed him with every word. "Yes. Yes. Yes."

He pulled her on top of him; she savored the solidity of his body beneath hers. His eyes dark with wonder, he reached up and touched her face.

1950–1951

A SCIENTIST

1950

A bluebottle fly, shiny as a hubcap, buzzed against the screen of the kitchen window, furious that it was being kept from the roses blooming just outside. In the yard, Jimmy, the stepson of Isabel Mountain, née Morgan, was hitting a baseball with a neighbor boy. He looked her way—Isabel lifted her hand to wave—and then he shouted to his friend. She lowered her hand, strangely heavy, then returned to the Betty Crocker cookbook opened on the table and to the task before her.

"CHEESE SOUFFLÉ—*Flavorful and Tempting*" sounded easy enough. She could figure out how to make the sauce and separate the eggs, just like she'd mastered sewing on buttons, laundering, and mopping the floor, chores the housekeeper used to do when she was growing up, but that she was taking a certain satisfaction in doing now that she was married to Joe. Making a soufflé was nothing compared to whipping up a vaccine for polio. That had been a bit like using a recipe, too—Maurice Brodie's recipe, to be specific, may he rest in peace. You just took one part polio-victim stool (its viral strain identified) to three parts saline solution, centrifuged it, poured the virus mixture into specially cultivated kidney tissue, grew it, whipped it in a Waring blender, killed it with formaldehyde, strained it, and voilà! Vaccine! At least for that strain of the virus.

Twenty-seven minutes and one dish of cheesy goo firmly wrestled into the oven later, she sank down at the kitchen table with a *Time* magazine. She had thirty minutes to recover, after which she would have to rouse herself to wage war on the brown mushroom sauce. Thank goodness the Waldorf salad, her post-lunch project, was already in the fridge.

Still bearing whipped egg white on her left cheek and her frilly apron-front, she flipped through the pages. She was in search of her favorite section, Medicine, to see which of her friends had made it in that week. Her own name had appeared in the column three years ago, when she'd first developed her vaccine. Since then, she'd had to put off reporters' inquiries with facile claims of "I'm refining it," or "It needs more testing," or "Almost ready!" A *New York Times* reporter had called the lab for an update on the day she'd been packing her things, leaving to marry Joe. Howie Howe had been only too eager to take the call for her. Howie hadn't anything new to tell them then, but with her gone, he would soon. He definitely would soon. She'd been the only obstacle in his way.

She paused on an advertisement for American Airlines in which the lady of the house was imagining a trip. The woman, pictured in pearls and an apron, seemed to be dreaming not of her own vacation, but of her menfolk's, with her husband happily casting a fishing line and her son catching things with a net. Evidently, the missus was to spend her holiday making sandwiches for them.

The medical column was on the next page. "In Mother's Milk," the headline read.

The title jolted her eyes out of commission; her brain went its own way. A routine scan for pregnancy commenced: Nausea—no. Fatigue—no, unless you counted the weariness that came with the boredom of pushing a Hoover over the carpet and dusting the stereo console. Sore breasts—no.

Please, do not let it be too late for her to have children.

She reengaged her eyes with the page as an ache radiated through her chest cavity.

> Because polio is usually a warm-weather disease of temperate zones, doctors jumped at the chance to study a polio outbreak two winters ago among Eskimos at deep-frozen Chesterfield Inlet, in Canada's Northwest Territories just below the Arctic Circle. One striking fact was soon evident: though infants under three got polio just as older children and adults did, none of the infants suffered the devastating paralytic stage of the disease. And the infants up to three years old, following local Eskimo custom, were still being nursed at their mothers' breasts.
>
> The coincidence was so striking that Dr. Albert B. Sabin of the Children's Hospital Research Foundation in Cincinnati—

Isabel broke off. The boys at the lab had said Sabin bragged about something along these lines at the polio conference last August in Copenhagen, but she'd been too caught up with Joe to give it notice. Now that she thought about it, she remembered Dorothy Horstmann telling her even before then about John Paul's study among the Eskimos. John must have been the doctor "jumping at the chance" that the reporter had referred to. How did he feel about Sabin getting the write-up for his discovery?

She needed to call Dorothy. Surely the polio boys would be sniping about this. How on edge they must be these days, with no recent breakthroughs in vaccine development to report until Salk and the others finished typing, though polio was claiming more lives than ever. The fellow who won the Nobel in medicine last year got it for inventing the frontal lobe lobotomy. Whoever made an advance in polio would surely kick someone like that out of the way. The public, staring down the barrel of another polio summer, would lionize its deliverer. No wonder Howie was ready to move on it.

Her gaze trailed to the air conditioner advertisement opposite the article, in which a woman, dressed only in a slip, sat within a frosty block of ice. **ICEBERG weather in your bedroom!** the copy promised. The woman contently brushed her hair while looking in a mirror, as beautifully preserved in her slab of ice as a fly trapped in a chunk of amber.

Isabel jumped up and ran to Joe's study.

She found her address book and dialed the university. Yes, the secretary said, Dr. Horstmann was there. Yes, she would go see if she could find her.

Isabel watched her stepson throw a dirt clod at his friend out in the yard while she waited for Dorothy to answer. She almost cried when she heard Dorothy's voice.

"Hello? Isabel? Isabel, are you there?"

"Sorry. Got something in my throat." She pulled herself together. "I was just looking through the most recent *Time* and had to call you. Did you see Sabin's piece?"

A pause lingered over the phone line. "I saw it."

"Did John Paul? What did he say about Sabin making off with his work?"

"John is John—he's happy about it. He's pleased that someone took his fieldwork and did something with it."

"John Paul is not normal."

"No."

They both laughed.

"You should have seen him at the bacteriologists' meeting in the spring," Dorothy said over the line. "He was beaming like a dad at a talent show when Albert presented his paper on mother's milk and polio. Afterward, Albert entertained the group with responses he got from the public after his local paper caught wind of his study. Not only had mothers offered to send in their own milk, which was all very kind and generous—"

"People will do anything to help," Isabel said.

"—but others suggested some, well, interesting alternatives. One man offered the milk of his sheep. Another woman wanted to send her goat's milk AND its blood. Sabin looked at all of us and said, 'I worry about that goat.'"

It felt good to laugh. Isabel realized that she had not done so in days.

"There actually might be a therapeutic component in mother's milk," Dorothy said, "as wild as it sounds. Not a single mouse given it developed symptoms when subjected to poliovirus. Now Albert just has to figure out what that magic substance is."

Isabel wondered if Dorothy and Albert were still so chummy. There was a time when she could have sworn that they were more than just colleagues. "Are you still seeing him a lot?"

"Our paths cross." Dorothy didn't elaborate.

Outside the study window, Jimmy and his friend were shoving each other. "Sabin wouldn't dare test his—I mean, John's—theory on mother's milk on humans, would he?" Isabel asked.

"It would be ideal. How else are we to know for sure if it works? But I don't know how he could engineer a challenge. How could he purposely expose human children to polio?"

"No one would ever do that."

"No one who is ethical, that is."

Jimmy pushed his friend to the ground. "Maybe we will have to come to testing on children," Isabel said. "Outbreaks worsen every year. Parents might demand that we take risks."

Dorothy was silent for a moment. "Are you still talking about mother's milk?"

Isabel had given up everything because she could take her trials no further. She could not be responsible for even one child's death.

She would not have a single child clamped inside an iron lung because of her creation. But maybe she'd been wrong to be so cautious. Somewhere around the world, a child was dying this very moment from polio.

"Isabel? Hello?"

"Have you heard any news from my lab?"

"Your lab?"

"From Howie, maybe."

"No. Should I?"

Outside, the boys were rolling in the grass. "No. I just— Oh, nothing. What are you working on?"

"Same old thing. I'm desperate to prove that poliovirus travels through the bloodstream. I'm afraid that I've made rather a joke of myself by now. Old 'Virus in the Blood' Dorothy. I've devised an experiment to track it, but it's very cost- and time-intensive. John wants me to focus on other things. But—" Dorothy blew out a breath. "I *know* it's important. It kills me to be taken away from it."

"You should stick by your guns. Insist that they fund you. Make a big noise with Basil O'Connor— Oh, no. Dorothy, I have to go. My stepson is pummeling the neighbor boy."

Isabel hung up. Neither boy appeared to be bleeding. She picked up the receiver and dialed.

Dave Bodian's secretary answered. Yes, he was there in his office. She'd put him through.

"Ibby?"

She was cheered just hearing her colleague's voice, which was as round and rubbery as his face and the bulbous features upon it.

"Ibby, what a surprise! How is our little Madonna these days? Married life agreeing with you?"

"It's lovely, thanks. Say, what did you think about Sabin's article in *Time* this week?"

He hesitated as if surprised that she should call about such a trivial thing. But soon they were chatting like old times. Yes, he was still interested in polio reinfection rates in monkeys. He could not seem to draw a bead on how long antibodies fought off the virus after infection. He didn't even know how antibodies were being produced, since poliovirus wasn't found in the blood.

"What is Howie up to?" she asked.

"I'm not exactly sure. He has been gone a lot recently."

"Gone?"

"You know Howie. He likes to slink around in the background like some sort of scientific Jack the Ripper. He never tells our secretary where he's going. But I don't have time to worry about it—he always turns up when I need him. You know Howie."

She did know Howie. "Have you checked the supply of my vaccine?"

"Your vaccine?" He sounded truly bowled over. "Why?"

Outside, a boy was bawling, although the notion of why his crying mattered couldn't quite find footing in her mind.

"I talked to Dorothy Horstmann today," she said.

Bodian was silent, not ready to drop the subject of her vaccine.

It wasn't her business if Howie was testing her vaccine or not. "She's working on finding poliovirus in the bloodstream," she said.

"Dottie? Still? She is persistent, isn't she?"

"She says she is certain it is there."

"Dorothy has good instincts—according to Sabin, she's a genius. What is it between those two?" He didn't wait for Isabel to answer. "Maybe we ought to listen to her. It has never made sense to me that the virus goes straight from the intestines to the nervous system, and now that I'm finding antibodies in the blood, I'm doubly doubtful. You say she has evidence?"

"Isabel!" Joe bellowed from the kitchen. "Where are you? Something's burning!

"Oh, no! I have to go."

"Trouble in paradise?"

"'Bye, Dave!"

She ran out to the kitchen, where smoke snaked from the edges of the oven door like wraiths escaping from hell.

"What is going on?" Joe, his hat still on, yanked his son through the door by the forearm. A thick runnel of blood connected Jimmy's nose to his mouth. "I come home and find this guy wallowing in the dirt and our house burning down. Where were you?"

"Here!" Howie was in too big of a rush. Someone had to stop him from giving her vaccine to children before it was ready. If a child died, if even a single one was paralyzed, her vaccine would rightly be scuttled. This tool for the good, and all her sweat and tears and the best years of her life given, freely, to find it, would be lost. "Nowhere!"

25

HERSHEY, PENNSYLVANIA, 1951

All the big guns were there at the roundtable meeting. Paul. Bodian. Enders. Sabin. There were the lesser lights too: Hilary Koprowski of the golden good looks, Howie Howe of the disturbing ones, eager Salk. Even Isabel Morgan Mountain had come out of retirement and was perched next to Dave Bodian, the eyes of the mink head on her stole glittering in the projector light. And then there was Dorothy, manning the humming slide projector, its smell of hot machine competing with the fumes of aftershave, cigarettes, and damp wool. Outside the window of the Hotel Hershey, light rain sifted down.

"Dottie," John Paul said, "could you see if you could sharpen the focus? I'll close the blinds."

Dorothy dialed the lens until at the far end of the smoky blade of light, the photo clarified of Dr. Paul looking Admiral Peary–like in a fur-lined parka. He appeared to be in a shack, listening to the heart of a small child, her worried elders watching from the foot of her cot.

The real-life Dr. Paul, now in his usual bow tie and heavy tweed (it being March—his summer-weight wool wouldn't come out until after Memorial Day), turned to the screen. His body encroached into the light of the picture, imprinting his fur-clad self onto his suitcoat. "It was this patient and her extended family who led me to my discovery. When their blood serum was tested for antibodies . . ."

Around the table, shoe leather scuffed on the tile as he went on. Caps clicked onto fountain pens. Everyone in the room was well acquainted with John's study. If they hadn't heard about it before Albert purloined parts of it for *Time*, they'd certainly heard of it afterward. With the novelty worn off, any interest they now had in it would be in Albert's response. Even in the smoky dim, Dorothy could feel eyes turning in Albert's direction. Would he apologize to John? Would John demand it? Why did Albert always insist on casting himself as such a villain?

John's sleeve cut through the photo as he gestured for Dorothy to switch the slide. She slid the armature into the projector. A graph flashed onto the screen.

"Now," he cried, "for the moment of truth!"

The only movement in the room was that of smoke wafting through the shaft of projector light. If there was anyone who craved drama, it was these cowboys who spent vast bleak swaths of their lives glued to the end of a microscope. Now they waited: Was Paul going to give Sabin the lambasting he deserved?

A paper clip pinged onto the tabletop.

John cleared his throat. "When I saw these results, it all became clear: a single exposure to a poliovirus type can convey *lifelong* immunity. I am convinced that the way to provide *permanent* immunity against poliomyelitis is to induce mild, symptom-free infection with weakened *live* virus strains, mimicking what we see here in nature. Thereby, I now align myself with Dr. Sabin"—he turned to Albert—"in your quest for a live polio vaccine."

There was a stunned silence. He was *teaming up with* Sabin, not challenging him to a duel? If the shoe had been on the other foot, Sabin would have skinned him alive.

"I'm sorry, Howie," John said to Dr. Howe. "I cannot in good conscience support the killed-virus vaccine that you were telling me about."

The polio boys glanced at one another in the dark. At last, a showdown!

Howie needed a moment to clear his throat of phlegm. "Dr. Sabin, how far along are you in the development of your vaccine? Is it ready for use?"

Albert's voice was thick with scorn. "You know that I can't proceed until the results of the strain-typing committee are in."

Jonas Salk waved to the crowd like Princess Elizabeth in her carriage.

"Howie," Albert said, "you do not have the typing information. All you have is Ibby Morgan's work on the recipe that Brodie cooked up in the thirties."

John indicated to Dorothy to switch on the room lights. She ground her jaw. She needed to be in her lab, working. It would be time better spent than watching this wrestling match. When it came to the race against polio, time was like quicksand: the harder she tried to escape being swallowed by it, the deeper she got mired.

At John's urging, she was doing some good work proving that chimpanzees who were fed poliovirus of one of the three types could not be infected again with that same type, but how she burned to take it just a step further. If only she had the permission, the funding, and the time to set up an experiment that methodically searched for the virus in the blood. But beside her latest study, she had epidemiology classes to teach, hospital rounds to make, and outbreaks to which to fly for the Polio Study Group. She'd hardly been home to see her family in three years, which would have broken her heart even if Mutter's cheerful letters hadn't failed to hide her despair over Pop's growing mental slippages.

And then there were the letters she owed to Arne. She was behind, four of his romantic letters planning their life together to her hurried one. How much longer would he settle for such an unreliable long-distance lover? There was going to be a lot of damage to repair when she went back to Copenhagen for the Second International Polio Congress in August.

She switched on the lights.

Isabel Morgan stood, the mink head on her shoulder staring in perpetual shock.

"Oh, hello, Dr. Morgan." Albert bowed. "Or should I say Dr. Mountain now?"

"You know our Ibby." Howie aimed his gaze at Tom Francis from U of Michigan, although he was speaking to Albert. Dr. Francis pointed to himself in confusion. "Staying home, collecting for the Mothers March is not enough for our gal!"

Basil O'Connor leaned forward, his carnation boutonniere brushing the table. "Do not knock the Mothers March, Howie. It's the biggest money-maker there is. Insistent mamas knocking on doors and collecting dollars every January equals the funding for whatever your little hearts desire, boys, and don't you forget it. Thank you, Mother," he told Isabel.

She stared at him before continuing. "I'm very glad that there will be plenty of funding, Mr. O'Connor, because my vaccine will need it for further development. So far it has only been found to be effective in monkeys."

"That's not true!" Howie exclaimed. "I've tested it on chimpanzees since you've gone."

"But," Isabel continued, "there's still a lot of work to be done before we test it on—"

"I've tested it on children, too."

Everyone stopped breathing. A notebook slithered to the floor.

"Howie, you didn't," Isabel said.

A smile bisected Howie's narrow face. "I did. I gave it to six mentally retarded individuals at the Rosewood Training School in Owings Mills, Maryland. And within twenty-one days, I was able to measure elevated antibodies in each."

"But that vaccine isn't ready for humans! I made it from monkey nervous tissue. It could destroy a human brain. You know that."

The boys shifted in their seats. Jonas Salk whispered to Dr. Francis.

"The director of the school begged me to use it on these kids," Howie said. "They have a bad habit of throwing feces at each other, and there was an outbreak in the area. He said he'd rather take his chances with the polio vaccine than to leave the children unprotected, and I agreed with him."

"But were the kids given a chance to make that choice?" she cried. "Were their parents?"

"You know the kids couldn't. And there were no parents to ask—these were all kids who'd been abandoned. The director had their well-being at heart. They were sure to get polio without it."

"Whoever you offered it to," Albert snapped, "it was a lousy choice. With a killed-virus vaccine, you're only offering partial protection—if you don't maim them first with that formulation."

Mr. O'Connor sat back and plucked at his carnation. "Parents are demanding help *now*, Albert. They don't have time to wait for you to devise the perfect live-virus vaccine."

"What if one is ready now?" someone said from the far side of the table.

Heads pivoted to where Hilary Koprowski, golden, gorgeous, and good-natured, had tipped back onto two legs of his chair.

"What if a live-virus vaccine were ready to be tried?" he said. "On humans."

Albert's mouth dropped open. "What are you saying?"

"I'm not the only one who has drunk a rat-brain cocktail." Koprowski rocked his chair forward onto all four legs with a bang. "Twenty volunteers at the Letchworth Village home had my vaccine with live Type II poliovirus. All the nonimmune children had developed Type II polio antibodies. None showed signs of the disease."

A stunned silence fell. Tom Francis looked up from his notes, then leaned toward Jonas. "What's this—monkeys?"

Jonas shook his head. "Children."

Albert threw his pen as if it were a tomahawk. "How *dare* you!"

Koprowski dodged it.

"Why did you do it?" Albert shouted. "Why?"

Koprowski folded his arms with a tilt of his golden head. "Someone had to."

"Why are you so cool? You may have caused an epidemic."

Koprowski spread his hands. "When Louis Pasteur saved that nine-year-old boy from rabies, it was an experiment. When Edward Jenner tested his smallpox vaccine on his infant son, it was an experiment. We must start somewhere, Albert."

"We don't have all of the types in yet. We don't even know how antibodies are made."

Dorothy said, "If I could take up my work on—"

"I'll have the typing done in weeks," Jonas blurted. "And do we *have* to know how antibodies come to be found in the blood? Does it matter, as long as a vaccine manages to produce them?"

Albert's shirtfront seemed to swell. The words burst from his mouth: "You know better than to ask a question like that! You have no business being in this room if you don't know the answer."

Jonas's teeth kept smiling even as the rest of his face fell.

Mr. O'Connor pushed himself onto his feet. "Fellas, fellas, we're all friends here. Everyone, take a fifteen-minute break. There's coffee in the back, isn't there, Dorothy?"

Would he ask Sabin if there was coffee? Or any of the other cowboys?

"I believe so, yes."

THE AIR REALLY DID SMELL LIKE CHOCOLATE IN HERSHEY, Pennsylvania. Now that the arguments had been momentarily upstaged by coffee and crullers, Dorothy had stepped away from her position at the coffee urn to the parking lot of the hotel, where the air was sweet with the aroma of cocoa, as if every housewife in town were melting one of the famous candy bars on her stove.

Dorothy ignored the rumbles beneath the strata of coat, dress, slip, and girdle that the scent produced in her gut. She was blind to the bell hops loading luggage into a Cadillac and to what her eyes told her about the imminent arrival of spring, informed by the sight of the robins hopping across the asphalt, dipping into puddles to produce worms the color of root beer. Across the way, a mother was pushing a baby buggy, her white gloves gripping the handle, her crinoline skirt flouncing under her coat.

The mother could have been in an advertisement for life insurance, baby food, aluminum siding, cars—the very picture of modern female beauty and fulfillment. Dorothy could have that. Well, maybe not the beauty part, but with any luck, the baby. She wouldn't be forty until July. There was still time.

Why was she fighting the natural order of things by staying on at Yale? She could be with Arne, if not having a baby, at least trying to make one, a lovely proposition in itself. She could be living the hygge life in Denmark, lighting candles, wearing fuzzy sweaters, spooning with her husband. Why was she clinging to her job at Yale, where, after all these years, after all her work, she was still just an associate professor? She would never rise above her role of hostess to a bunch of head-butting rams, even though she was *sure* she could prove how the poliovirus traveled through the body, if just given the chance. She could be saving lives, if only they'd let her. She could see why Isabel had gotten out.

The hotel exit door clanked open.

"There you are!" Dr. Paul exclaimed. "Goodness! You can really smell the chocolate factory out here." He looked at her more closely. "Are you all right?"

"Is break time over?"

"Not quite. Listen, Dottie, I have to tell you—Bodian's in there talking about doing a study on the occurrence of poliovirus in the bloodstream."

Every vessel in her body contracted. She felt the sensation of draining.

Dr. Paul grimaced. "I thought you'd scream."

This was it. Her sign to let it go. They had sucked all that was good from her, her pride, her enthusiasm, her ambition, even her best idea. There was nothing left of her but a hand on the coffee urn spigot.

"I don't care."

He squinted at her. "What? You don't? I was hoping you would." He frowned. "I was sure you would."

She should tell him about her plans with Arne. His commitment pledged with a little blue ashtray was more solid than anything John had ever offered.

"Is there something funny?" he asked.

"No. Yes. Well, not really. John, there's something I need to tell you."

"Don't say that you've accepted an offer at another university. Please don't go! Oh, Dottie, not now." He tugged at his bow tie. "I'll tell you what, I'll match the offer, at least I'll get Blake to do his best. This should sweeten the pot: Dottie, I promise that I will get you the funding."

"For what?"

"For the study you've been mooning about doing for the past decade. I'll find you the money. I'll put it up from my personal account if I have to, though I bet I can shake some loose from O'Connor."

"My study on poliovirus in the bloodstream?"

His grin sent his chin into his neck. "That's the one."

"I don't know what to say."

"You say yes! You say yes, you want to help prevent children and adults from getting paralyzed! Yes, you want to save lives! Yes, you want to unlock the mystery of the life history of the poliovirus."

"I do want to do those things." Who was she kidding? She lived to do those things.

"I could be wrong," she said.

"Bodian thinks not."

"I had other plans."

"You did?" He could look no more surprised than if she'd announced that she'd won the bathing suit portion of the Miss America contest. "Surely you want to beat Bodian to the punch. It's your idea, Dot. Now is the time to run with it."

Pieces of the puzzle began to fit themselves together. She knew just what strains of the virus she wanted to use, exactly how she wanted to prepare the serum. She'd get Eugene on board; set up a system for checking for symptoms; tolerate no more starts and stops, just go, go, go. She could finish the work before she left for Copenhagen this fall, where she could stay on to start a new life with Arne. She could find a job at the university there, and then make discoveries *and* babies. Sabin had a family; Robbie Ward did, too. Even Jonas Salk had it all. Why shouldn't she?

Dr. Paul clasped her hand. "Well, Dottie, what do you say?"

26

NEW HAVEN, CONNECTICUT, 1951

Twenty days later, six thirty in the morning. There were no windows in the polio ward, yet even with fluorescent lights buzzing overhead, somehow it still felt dark outside, windy and winter-edged, as spring mornings in Connecticut tended to be. Inside the ward, with its characteristic stink of wet sheep, the nurses' spongy soles squished on the floor as they retrieved bedpans or responded to plaintive bleats for water or Mom. Five toddlers in wrap-shirts and diapers clung to the rails of their cribs, one hysterical, three wailing in sympathy, one shuddering in aftershock. Dorothy lifted out the most frantic of them, a little girl trailing the smell of baby pee and Desitin.

Through her mask, Dorothy pressed her lips to the roaring child's damp fluff. The baby was as slick as a seal from screaming.

"Hey. Shhhhh. I've got you now."

The child was too deep in her misery to hear.

Taking care of the baby's withered leg, she held the child close and began humming Beethoven's "Moonlight Sonata."

"Ma'am!" A nurse plopped a wash basin on a bedside stand with a splash. "You have to put that baby down! Visitors aren't allowed."

Another nurse, a sweet, doe-like woman named Jeanne, looked up from where she was pressing her cheek against the tank of a ventilator, fishing inside a porthole. "Peggy, no!" Her sleeve scraped against the elasticized gasket as she withdrew her arm. "That's a doctor. Sorry, Dr. Horstmann."

The six-year-old girl inside the ventilator watched everything in her mirror.

Dorothy kept her voice down so as not to frighten the baby in her arms more than she already was. "Honest mistake. I should be wearing my lab coat."

The nurse must be new. They all knew Dorothy here in the polio ward because (a) a colossal female doctor was memorable, and (b) when she was in town, she came by the floor a lot, if not when leading students, just to make her unofficial morning rounds. This week she had stopped by every morning before going to the lab. She wanted to be reminded of the reason for the suffering she was about to cause.

Once the crying toddler had settled down to sniffing spasms, Dorothy unstuck a wisp from her cheek and handed her to Nurse Peggy.

She washed up and went over to the droning machine of the child who'd been watching. "Hello, Buffy. How are you today?"

Buffy's smile, with its bloody hole where a front tooth had recently been, was her answer.

"You lost another tooth!"

"I puthed it out with my tongue."

"Congratulations. Do you know where it is?"

"Yeth. There." Buffy pointed with her eyes to her bedside stand, to a sliver of enamel with a browning stump. "Doctor, how will the tooth fairy find me?"

Dorothy reached inside one of the elasticized openings and found the child's hand. "Oh, she will."

"But how?"

"She will, I promise."

Dorothy could feel a gaze burning into her—Nurse Jeanne, on

the other side of the ventilator. Children this young had someone assigned to their care at all times. If they panicked, the machine's artificial respirations would steamroll them. Dorothy knew only too well that they had to stay relaxed or get crushed.

"I told her that sometimes the tooth fairy gets tired," Jeanne said, already making excuses to protect the child. "Sometimes she forgets."

"Well, she's not forgetting you," Dorothy told little Buffy. "You just have to believe."

IT HAD BEEN 7:13 BY DOROTHY'S TIMEX BEFORE BUFFY HAD been ready to let go of her hand. Now Dorothy was winding her way down the service stairs, to the system of tunnels in the bowels of the hospital. She rubbed her arms against the chill as she ducked through a passage. It was cold in there year-round, and poorly lit, not unlike the sewers of Paris in *Les Misérables*, Dorothy liked to pretend, although it did not stink (excluding the smell of sweating pipes and dampness), nor had she encountered a rat. More often she felt like a rat, one in a concrete maze.

She seldom met another soul down there. Few medical staffers knew the system of unmarked passages even existed, or if they did, they rightly avoided it for fear of getting lost. Dorothy perversely enjoyed the challenge of maneuvering her way through, and the frisson of terror that came along with the real possibility of getting lost. She didn't know what that said about her.

Finally, she came to her exit, where she bounded up the stairs, as one might leap into bed in the dark to avoid the monster lurking underneath. Down a basement corridor and into the animal lab she went, where Eugene was in the back, feeding some baby rhesus monkeys.

"Anything yet?" Dorothy pulled on a rubber apron hanging by the door.

"Nothing."

Dorothy sighed with relief as she went to the first cage. A rhesus monkey Eugene had named Yvonne was huddled in a corner. She put a finger through the wire.

Eugene came up beside her. "She'll bite."

"I know. She'd be justified." Her glance went inadvertently to the scar in the meat of her hand. She didn't blame that monkey, a twenty-pound male, and she wouldn't blame this one. That one she'd handled without proper help, and this one she had given reason to distrust her. Why did people have the urge to stick their fingers into the cages of animals? *She'd* bite if some jerk pushed into the little private space she had.

Eleven days ago, with Eugene's help, Dorothy had injected Yvonne with the blood serum of one of thirteen cynomolgus monkeys who'd been fed banana mashed with live poliovirus and then had their blood drawn every day. The study called for rhesus monkeys to receive serum from one of the thirteen cynomolgus monkeys, a rhesus monkey for each day. Yvonne was the rhesus who'd been given blood from Day Five.

If only there had been a more humane way of actually seeing the virus in the blood! But the two electron microscopes in the country were not available for this kind of work, and so the monkeys paid the price. Now her heart tightened like it always did as Eugene drew the monkey from her corner.

He held the creature for Dorothy to examine her. As she did so, he made a series of whimpering grunts under his breath.

He saw Dorothy glance at him. He twitched a shoulder as if caught out.

"In all this time," she said, "I've never asked. Why do you do that?"

"Their mothers talk to them like that."

"How do you know?"

"I listen."

There were scientists who teased Eugene. They thought they were cute by calling him Dr. Dolittle. In a world where animal handlers tended to use brute strength and straps to subdue the subjects, his method of soothing animals, of respecting their fear and their sacrifice, was an anomaly. Dorothy found that his methods allowed her to do her work more quickly and efficiently. When the animals didn't panic, when they resigned themselves to their fate like children in iron lungs, they didn't suffer as greatly, for which Dorothy was grateful. She thought Eugene was brilliant, but he worried her. A heart with that much weight on it was sure to break.

The exam was done: Yvonne had no symptoms. Dorothy was torn between relief and despair. She would have made these animals suffer for nothing, and children would keep dying of polio.

BY 9:26, DOROTHY HAD SPELUNKED HER WAY THROUGH THE service tunnels to the medical school, and then up to her lab. No one was there. She turned on the record player. The armature jerked up and over to the first groove of the platter as she donned her mask and rubber gloves.

Bing Crosby's croon floated past beakers, bottles, and stainless-steel gadgets.

"Be careful, it's my heart."

She took a sample of centrifuged blood from the freezer and prepared to cut the middle out of the frozen piece. Fail or succeed, she had to wrap up the study by August, when she was going to the Polio Congress in Copenhagen and beginning a new life with Arne. Already he'd written about having gotten a flat on the outskirts of Copenhagen, where he'd found a job as an editor on a magazine.

She sliced carefully with her scalpel, even though a portion of her mind had shifted to thoughts of Arne. His clean smell, the feel of his sweater over the solidity of his chest, the delighted sound in his laugh came to her in a flurry. Funny how you experienced even those closest to you as memories of things they said or did, or as flashes of parts of them, or merely sensations, but never as a complete person, or even an entire face.

On Bing sang. "*It's not the note I sent you that you quickly burned, it's not the book I lent you that you never returned, remember it's—*"

Eugene burst into the lab. "Dorothy, it's Yvonne!"

Dr. Paul pushed the lab door behind him. "Oh, hello, Eugene. Say, Dottie—"

Dorothy held up her hand to John. "What, Eugene?"

His face wavered between a scowl and a smile. "Yvonne. She's limping."

"But I examined her less than an hour ago."

"I know. But when I checked her again just now—it's her left rear leg."

"Yvonne?" Dorothy stood. Her blood rushed from her head. "She has polio?"

John looked between them. "Who's Yvonne?"

Dorothy forced herself to respond. "My rhesus monkey. She got polio from blood serum—from which day after the cynomolgus was fed?"

"Day Five," Eugene said.

"Day Five!" She threw her arms around him, holding her gloved hands away from him like flippers.

"But the incubation period is longer than that," John said. "We don't see symptoms for twelve to fourteen days."

She let go of Eugene with a thump with the back of her gloves. "That's the point. We've been looking too late. Poliovirus is in the blood, John, soon after infection—enough to infect another subject with it—as early as Day Five."

"Are you sure?"

"Absolutely!" She waved jollily to Eugene as he backed out of the lab.

John shook his head. "Well, I'll be."

She took off her gloves and pushed down her mask. "I knew it was in there." She plunked down on her stool. "I knew it."

John rubbed his jaw. "Dorothy, one positive monkey does not a study make."

"Oh, I know! I'll start all over again, with more subjects, more strains, to make sure this isn't some kind of fluke. It will be several more months' work but—John, can you believe it? It's there! Oh, I just can't believe it! It's there!" She threw her arms around him in a hug, then pulled up her mask and started to put on her gloves.

"Before you get started on what you're doing there, I need to tell you something."

She snapped her glove around her wrist. "What?" she said, grinning behind her mask.

"Tahiti is experiencing its first ever outbreak," John said. "It's quite a puzzle. Why now? Why there? They've never had it before."

"Hmm." She sat down at the lab table, not really listening.

"Dottie, the World Health Organization has asked for you to go investigate."

"The WHO? Me? When?"

"As soon as you can get yourself together."

"But—I have this study! It's a long way from done. You didn't tell them I'd go, did you?"

"It's an honor, Dottie. A privilege. They asked for you specifically. You're getting quite the reputation for your investigative prowess and your way with foreign officials. Best in the world, some say."

"That's nice but—"

"A paper will come from it."

"A paper will come from *this* study! An important one."

"They asked me to go, too, Dot. I thought, well, I thought you and I could go together. We're a team." The gooseflesh above his bow tie went bright red.

"I can't go, John. Not now."

"I understand you wanting to work on your study. Bodian might be making headway now, too."

"I don't care about Dave Bodian. I care about this. Think what this means for vaccine development. Now we know where to stop polio—in the blood." She felt a jolt. "I've got to tell Albert!"

"Isn't that premature? Salk hasn't even announced the results of his strain typing—that's not due until Copenhagen. A vaccine can't be developed until we have every strain. There's time, Dorothy. This would be the perfect opportunity to represent yourself on the world stage, then you can get right back to it without missing a beat. Basil O'Connor will be sure to shower you with funding. The WHO will never forget this favor. At least think about it."

SHE WAS WALKING PAST THE BIG HOUSES ON ST. RONAN Street, halfway home though still a bit tipsy from the cheap champagne she'd popped open in the lab with Eugene, when she remembered. The wind cut through the wool of her gloves as she gathered her collar and turned around.

It was 8:50 according to the clock on the wall in the polio ward. The lights had been dimmed, but the ventilators groaned and flushed as loudly as ever. The nurse on duty at Buffy's bedside, a sturdy woman named Eileen, looked up from her knitting. The mirror over the end of the iron lung revealed the young patient to be deep in the open-mouthed sleep of the exhausted.

Dorothy pressed her finger to her lips at Nurse Eileen, who was putting down her knitting to rise, then laid a fifty-cent piece on the nightstand, took the tiny tooth, and put it in her pocketbook.

"She still believes." She eased her purse closed so as not to wake the child. "I'm not going to be the one to stop her."

27

COPENHAGEN, DENMARK, 1951

Out on the lake on the outskirts of Copenhagen, a rowing team sliced through the reflection of tall white clouds in the water. A late summer breeze ruffled the chiffon flounces at Dorothy's neck and swayed the fragrant boughs of the pine trees beyond the terrace on which her party sat. She sighed. Three nights of reuniting with Arne had turned her into a great oozy ball of lust. As he and the others talked, all she wanted to do was to gaze into his velvety gray-green eyes and stroke the tender skin of his wrist while recalling their thrilling moments together. But she couldn't.

From across the white cloth of the table, through the litter of plates smelling of dill and salmon, past the centerpiece of cut roses and next to Albert, who was leaning away from Jonas Salk as Jonas was edging his wooden folding chair closer, came an almost tangible tug. Ah, there it was—John Paul was watching her. Oh, dear, he was expecting some kind of response. She hadn't heard a word he'd said.

"What was that, John?"

"I said, only mad dogs and Englishmen and you, my dear, go out in the midday sun." He smiled stiffly at Arne, next to her, who was looking pretty glazed himself. "I was telling your . . . friend . . . about our time in Tahiti."

Now the others at the table listened in—Albert with a scowl.

"I'm afraid that's true," she said with a laugh. "You couldn't get me indoors. The sun felt incredibly good, coming from Connecticut in early April."

"Hence your tan," said Arne. Last night he had traced the straplines of her sundress with his finger. They exchanged a smile.

John noticed their exchange, as did Albert. She'd not elaborated on her relationship with Arne since they'd met him last year in Copenhagen. He was her "old friend" as far as they knew, although it seemed clear that they weren't buying it.

"You were quite fond of the ocean," John said firmly.

She remembered herself wading into clear turquoise water, the wet hem of her dress sticking against her calves. John and their hosts were on shore under a grass-roofed shelter, waving for her to come back. But she had been enjoying the moment too much. Who ever pictured *her* in the surf in Tahiti? She'd come a long way from sitting with Pop on the steps out back of the bar, eating the liverwurst sandwiches Mutter had made them.

John was still watching them. "Remember how you hot-footed it across the beach?"

"No one told me that black sand gets *hot*."

"Actually"—John cleared his throat—"I did."

"But it was so beautiful. It glitters like crushed black diamonds," she told Arne. "It's made from volcanic glass."

"You should have seen her in a grass skirt," John said, "belly-dancing with the local women. She jumped right in and shook her hips with them." His face reddened.

Albert put down his flute of champagne. "I was in the Pacific entirely too much during the war to ever enjoy Asia again. You couldn't get me there—"

"Didn't you just go to a conference in Singapore?" said Jonas.

"—*willingly*," Albert said.

"Well—" Jonas took a gulp of champagne, clearly still reveling in having delivered the results of the poliovirus typing project yesterday. "I'm delighted to be here. It's my first overseas conference." To Dorothy, he said, "Thank you for inviting me to this little party."

She smiled. Jonas had invited himself when he'd overheard her tell Albert that Arne's boss was having a reception for some of the international scientists at his home, but she was glad for Jonas to see this astonishing place. The "home" of Arne's boss, a publisher, turned out to be a modernized palace set within a forest and overlooking a lake. It was fun to see a place like this with someone who seemed as awed by it as she was.

"Tell me," John asked Arne, "what is the history of this place?"

Albert sipped his wine, his gaze upon Dorothy.

"It was built in the 1700s, I understand," Arne said, "by a fellow with the same surname as me."

"Holm?" Dorothy asked.

"Yes. He changed his name to 'Holmskiold' when he became a privy counselor to the queen. He got rich by serving her."

"The 1700s?" Dorothy straightened. "Was it the queen who liked to dress up like a man?"

"You know about our Caroline Mathilde?" Arne's grin radiated affection. "Is there anything you do not know?"

Dorothy glanced away, then watched the bubbles in her glass rise like the happiness in her chest.

"Dottie *is* rather a miracle," John said staunchly.

"She is," said Arne, beaming, "is she not?"

John and Albert frowned at one another, then at Arne.

"As it turns out, Dorte," Arne said, "this Holm was your Caroline Mathilde's enemy. He helped her stepmother-in-law to overthrow her, and for that, the dowager queen generously rewarded him." His eyes crinkled. "But maybe not generously enough for his liking. He ended up embezzling from the dowager queen and from all of the government offices to which she appointed him."

Albert eyed Arne. "Some people just can't help themselves."

"Greedy," said Jonas, taking another flute from a passing waiter.

"Strange how the universe seems to require balance," said Arne. "The dowager queen stole from Caroline Mathilde; Holm stole from her." He signaled to a different waiter.

"You don't really believe that," Albert scoffed.

"In symmetry?" said Arne. "Should I not? A man with my name built this place with proceeds from his queen, and now I sit here enjoying the fruits of his labor with mine."

Jonas lifted his champagne. "Hail, Queen Dot!"

John twisted his mouth into a smile.

Albert only scowled.

The other waiter brought a tray of canapés. "Here we go!" Arne said. "Everyone's favorite, *smørrebrød*. You'll have to learn to like this if you are to live here," he told Dorothy as the waiter placed a plate before her. "There's no escaping pickled herring in Denmark."

John's bitter smile flattened. "Live here?"

"You work for the magazine?" Jonas asked Arne. He picked up a triangle of the open-faced sandwich with his fingers.

Arne showed Dorothy how to pile capers and thin red onion slices on top of the herring, then he gathered a bite onto his fork. "Yes. As an editor." He fed Dorothy a mouthful. "Do you like?" He sat back with an expectant smile.

"Mmm." She dabbed her lips with her napkin as she swallowed.

Jonas gulped down his own big bite. "Will you be doing an article on the Polio Congress? I'd be glad to bring you up to speed, if you'd like."

"Is that how you got the interview with Maxine Davis at *Good Housekeeping*, Jonas?" Albert said, not kindly. "You asked her nicely?"

"You heard about that article?" Dr. Salk's toothy grin waxed and waned between proud and sheepish.

"I saw it."

Dorothy had seen it, too, after Albert had called her about it in a rage when it had come out.

"Did you call *Good Housekeeping*?" Albert demanded of Jonas.

"No. Mr. O'Connor put me in touch. He wanted me to get to know some people in the press."

"Basil did?" Albert stared. "*You?*"

Dr. Salk laughed. "That's exactly what I thought! May I?" He indicated Albert's untouched portion. "If you're not going to eat it . . ."

Albert slid the plate to him.

Jonas popped in another bite. "I think I was supposed to talk about the typing project," he said through the bread.

Albert's face darkened. "But you didn't, did you? You had to say that any vaccine using a live virus is dangerous, even lethal. That it's not the most up-to-date science. You know that I am working toward a live-virus vaccine. Now the public will be wary of it."

"I just—"

"Do you realize how much harder I'm going to have to work to get people to trust it, how many more trials and studies it will take to convince them of its safety compared to the killed-virus vaccine, now that you created a demand for it? If I didn't know better, I'd think that you were working on one of those 'superior' killed-virus vaccines yourself."

Jonas shrugged. "Parents want a vaccine."

Albert blinked with anger. "I knew it! I knew it when the article mentioned the advantage of using adjuvants. No layperson knows nor cares about buffering the vaccine with adjuvants. I knew you were up to something when you planted such an obscure recommendation. You must be using an adjuvant in yours."

"I was just trying to give people hope." Jonas took a slug of champagne.

"You haven't cornered the market on being a concerned parent, Jonas. I'm a father now, too. But I'm not in such a hurry that I'd deliver an inferior product."

Jonas dabbed his mouth with his napkin, then got up. "If you could point me toward the little boys' room?" he asked Arne.

When he'd gone, John said, "You're a bit rough on him, don't you think?"

"He's doing damage."

John frowned. "Perhaps you'd be better served concentrating on your own vaccine. What do you think about Dot's new study? It plays right into your hands." He glanced at Arne. "Dottie *must* speed home from Copenhagen and get right back to work on it. It'll keep her busy until the end of the year."

Arne turned to her, waiting for her to speak. But a gentleman from the next table came over and got Arne to introduce him to everyone in their group, then asked John and Arne to return with him to his table for a moment.

"I still cannot believe that guy," Albert said to Dorothy when they were gone.

"Which guy?"

"That idiot Salk."

"Albert. Jonas is all right."

"No, Jonas is not. He's ambition personified in the form of a giggling bumbler."

"Albert."

"There's no one who that guy wouldn't step on to climb up the ladder to his success."

She could not help but smile. He was describing himself. "I agree, he's very . . . motivated. But if he has the means to do some good—"

"He's an idiot."

"I wonder how far along he is with a vaccine."

Albert glared at her. "His science is bound to be shit."

"Really, Albert."

"Sorry. Excuse me." He made an exasperated sound. "You're right. No need to panic. Guys like him never end up going anywhere. They just make a big noise and then they implode." He tightened his mouth. "What is it with you and that Arne fellow?"

She put down her champagne. "Albert, I have to tell you about my study. Like John said, it does impact your work. I wanted to be further along with it before I came here, but I was stuck in Tahiti."

His pause acknowledged that she had not answered his question. "How does it impact my work? And where have you been this whole conference? I see you across the room and then, poof, you're gone. I'd think you were avoiding me if I didn't know better."

She reached through plates and glasses, past the bowl of roses, to clasp his fingers. "Albert, I found poliovirus in the bloodstream."

His eyes lit. "What? Why didn't you tell me?"

"I'm telling you now. The study isn't nearly done, but the evidence is beyond doubt: the virus appeared early in the subject's infection. Five days after oral exposure."

"Five days!" He whistled. "That's a week before it hits the nervous system."

"I know! Albert, the reason we didn't see it in the blood in the past was we weren't looking early enough. Antibodies must be wiping it out in the blood, before it gets to the nervous system."

"Dorothy!" He shook her fingers. "That's *huge*!"

Arne came back to the table, smoothing his tie over his white shirt. He paused when he saw their grinning faces and linked hands. "What'd I miss?"

"Everything!" Albert said.

A petite young woman, the daughter of the publisher, it turned out, came over and seized Arne by the wrist. After a brief introduction, he let himself be led away, looking over his shoulder at Dorothy.

"I'm confused," Albert said. "What is he to you?"

"Arne?"

"Yes. Arne."

Her "future husband"? Her "lover"? Her "betrothed-by-ashtray"? At that moment, all sounded weak or tawdry or ludicrous, which Arne was not.

John trotted back from the neighboring table, along with Jonas. "Dottie, look! They're racing."

Everyone peered toward the lake, where three teams of rowers skimmed the water in their needle-thin crafts. First one boat nosed out the other, then the other took its place. Prow to prow they raced, bringing the spectators on the terrace to their feet. All eyes were on the leaders when the third boat shot out and glided to the win. The diners cheered.

Albert turned to her with a smile that said he was not letting her off the hook. "Everyone likes a winner."

Why didn't she just tell him the truth about Arne and her? "Yes, they do, don't they?"

THAT EVENING, A SEA BREEZE LIFTED CURLS FROM DOROthy's cropped crown as she looked out into the rosy evening sky. Over the jumble of orange tiles and roof ridges, here and there a pile of sticks marked the ruins of a stork's nest on a chimney. On the house next door, the decorative iron ball topping its gable seemed close enough to touch. She found herself humming "Moonlight Sonata" as she gazed out over the tiled rooftops.

Arne came up from behind and kissed her on the side of her neck. "Do you like what you see?"

"Yes."

He craned around to see her face. "Are you okay?"

"Oh, yes. Just enjoying the view."

"It could all be yours, you know."

"Why do I feel like Christ being tempted by Satan?"

"Oh, I am not that bad." He kissed the nape of her neck. "Tell me, how do you deal with Dr. Paul's infatuation?"

"Honestly, Arne!"

"You cannot deny it. It is obvious that he is in love with you."

"He's married!"

"Marriage does not neuter a man, *elskede*."

"John is always a gentleman."

He rested his cheek against her hair. "Of him, I can believe. Is Dr. Sabin?"

"Of course."

"That I do not so much believe."

A dog barking in the distance broke the hush of nightfall. "Arne, every man is not in love with me."

"Men do not know how to feel about a woman who is also their peer. They can confuse excitement over their work with attraction. Especially when the woman is as compelling as you."

She turned around to face him. "I'm not compelling."

He laughed softly. "Let me be the judge." He tucked a lock of hair behind her ear, then re-tucked it when the wind blew it free. "Tell me, *elskede*, what is Dr. Sabin to you?"

"A colleague."

He waited.

"He's married." She laughed.

He frowned at her limp attempt at humor. He deserved an honest explanation. But what *was* Albert to her?

She put her hand to Arne's cheek as an offering.

He kissed it. "What do you say to joining your very married friends in the state of marital bliss?"

"I say yes, you know I do, when the time comes."

"I mean now."

"Now?"

"Well, tomorrow."

"Tomorrow!"

He kissed her hand again. "You sound surprised."

"I—I am." They'd discussed it all week—she would finish her study and come back at Christmas. She had to finish her work. Her whole life had led up to this.

"I do not mean to scare you up."

"Off. Scare me off. And you haven't."

"I am not trying to trap you. We Danes do not insist on marriage to show our love. But if not being married is what is keeping you from staying—" He clasped both her hands. "I want you to stay, *elskede*. Now that we have had these days together, I cannot bear being without you."

"But—I'm coming back. In four months. My study . . ."

"My boss has friends at the university. You can finish your study there."

"I know people at the university, too."

"You see? They will make you a full professor—universities here are not so unappreciative of women. Between my boss and your connections, we will get you the funding for the study. I have already asked him. He was impressed with you."

"You did? He is?"

If she were to get pregnant, would they fire her? They would in the US. If she were to be so lucky as to conceive, to protect her work she would have to finish her study on viremia before her pregnancy showed. She had to find a laboratory, funding, and a staff, quickly.

Bodian did not have these concerns.

He put his arms around her. "We can go to the registry tomorrow."

"I have meetings tomorrow."

He was silent.

Jonas had already announced the results of his typing program. The other speakers had already argued with each other ad nauseum on various topics. She and Albert were planning to get together to discuss her study but—

"I suppose I could skip them."

He made a Danish *I'm thinking* gasp. "What if we went to the registry when it opened? You could still get to your meetings." He smiled. "As a married woman."

"Oh, Arne."

"I do not have rings. Perhaps I can buy some while you are at the meetings. We can exchange them in private."

"I was pretty fond of my engagement ashtray."

"Yes, I saw that you brought it."

"I take it with me everywhere. Even Tahiti." She shook her head and laughed. "This is all so crazy."

"Is it?" He gathered her to his warm body. "Is it really?"

28

Dorothy had awakened beside Arne the next morning with the feeling that a roll of quarters had spilled inside her chest. Even now, as she waited behind Jonas Salk at a buffet set up in a university hallway smelling of floor wax and books, coins seemed to be pattering against the tender tissue of her lungs, leaving her slightly breathless. Her situation had not been improved by being told at the marriage registry to come back at eleven o'clock. While Arne used the delay to buy rings, she'd dropped into the Polio Congress meetings, where currently, inside the lecture room just beyond the buffet, a doctor from Pittsburgh was wrapping up his remarks about the effect of gamma globulin on polio. She pressed her hands against her solar plexus.

Breathe.

Dr. Salk hovered over the row of coffee pots. "Which one is the Sanka?

Dorothy pointed to the pot marked SANKA.

He flashed all those teeth. "Thanks."

Grinning as if amused by what a sport he was for serving himself, he hoisted the pot. A brown stream twirled from spout to cup with only a little splashing onto the white linen of the table.

He scanned the buffet up and down.

"Sugar?" Dorothy asked.

He nodded.

She indicated the bowl in front of him.

"Thanks." He picked up a cube with his fingers, dropped it in his cup with a splat, then sipped. She thought of his elegant, capable wife.

He looked at Dorothy over the rim of his cup. "Say, you're all dressed up. You look nice."

The netting on her half hat catching in her curls, Dorothy glanced down at her brown linen traveling suit with its tight waist, flared peplum, and rank of self-fabric buttons up the front—something to give Arne to work on after the ceremony this afternoon. The commotion accelerated in her chest.

He gazed around as she got her coffee. "I thought there might be little sandwiches."

"Maybe some are coming." She pushed away her nerves. "What do you think about Dr. Hammon's work on gamma globulin?"

Dr. Salk peered down the hall hopefully, then brought his attention back to her. "What?"

"You must be familiar with Dr. Hammon's work, coming from the same university and department there."

"Not so very much." He heaved a sigh. "I guess we aren't getting sandwiches."

"Hammon takes an interesting approach, injecting blood fractions with antibodies directly into his patients," she said, stirring. "He must have to inject a lot of gamma globulin into the children for them to get any protection, though."

"Four to eleven milliliters, he does, right smack in their buttocks."

She drew a breath across her teeth. "Ouch. A teaspoon of that thick stuff going in must hurt. Those poor kids."

"That's not the worst part. Did you hear? His trial was a mess. Parents of kids in the study insisted that their children get the real thing and not the placebo, so they took matters in their own hands and made sure they got it, bribing doctors or even stealing the plasma. The records were all skewed."

"That's too bad."

"I don't even think it works, not long enough to matter. Gamma globulin is a waste of effort, yet the March of Dimes gave Hammon close to a million bucks. That's just money down the drain." He glanced around furtively. "Don't tell anyone, but you know who else they've spent the big bucks on?"

"Who?"

"Me."

"That's great, Jonas."

"I have perfected a killed-virus vaccine that is both safe and effective—it's a beautiful thing." He grinned. "I've had success with a limited trial—but you can't tell anyone!"

She did not mean to gasp. "On children?"

His gaze darted to the lecture room and back. "Shhh. All I have to do is to scale it up and—"

The doors of the auditorium opened. Scientists poured into the hall.

"Dottie!" John Paul dodged through the crowd. "Dottie! My, you're looking nice," he said when he caught up to her.

"That's what I told her," Jonas said.

Dr. Paul flashed him a polite smile. "Excuse us. Dot, may I have a word?"

He led her down the hall, out the door, into a courtyard cushioned with mounds of yellow mums.

"I've been looking for you. Where have you been?"

The quarters ramped up their tumbling in her lungs.

He didn't allow her a chance to answer. "Some of the men on Bodian's team are talking. Dot, he found poliovirus in the bloodstream. Just like you."

The thudding in her chest stopped. Everything stopped.

"I understand that he just made his breakthrough recently and is moving into the next phase of his study. From what I could gather, there's still time for you to complete your work. You can still beat him."

Her heartbeat resumed and was throbbing in her ears.

"I know what you're thinking, Dot, and I don't blame you."

"Do you?"

"I suppose you'd like to kill me."

"I wouldn't mind."

He pulled back his chin when he saw that she wasn't kidding. "Well, I think we can salvage the situation."

She looked at her watch. Nine forty-five. In an hour, she would meet Arne, and her married life would soon begin. She thought she could have both her career and a family in America, but maybe Isabel Morgan was right. The boys were never going to give her a chance, even though it now was all hands on deck to beat polio. Just not her hands. Or Isabel's. Or any woman's, especially not after that woman was someone else's wife—or worse, a mother.

"I don't think that's possible."

"Please, Dot, hear me out. Forget the long voyage home. I can get you a spot on an Army plane due to take off at noon for Washington. Let's get you on that flight and back to the lab tonight. Let's beat Bodian at his game."

"It's not a game, John. It's people's lives. We could have had this knowledge years ago—" She didn't need to add, *if you would have let me.*

"I'm sorry, Dot."

Sorry? "We could have been this much further along in our understanding of polio, this much further along in the development of a vaccine. Instead, people are playing around with gamma globulin. Gamma globulin, for heaven's sake! You know that they could never make enough of that to be a real solution."

He held his forehead and then dropped his hand. "Men are weak, foolish, shortsighted, and selfish. Or maybe I'm just talking about me." His Adam's apple rose and fell. "But sometimes we have a chance to do the right thing. This is my chance now. Will you take the flight, Dottie?"

SHE HEARD THE THUMP OF ARNE'S STEPS AS HE TOOK THE stairs two at a time. He burst into the bedroom, a bouquet of yellow chrysanthemums in his hand.

"John Paul said you had left the conference. I ran to the registry, in case you went without me, and then ran back! Why are you here? Dorte, we will be late."

His gaze dropped to the bed and to the open suitcase into which she was fitting a folded blouse. His ears seemed to lower on his head. "What are you doing?"

She had to keep packing. "Arne, I have to leave."

He shook his head, uncomprehending.

"They are sending me home to finish my study." She glanced at him. *No, don't look.* "Bodian has made the same findings as I did and is finishing up his study. I have to beat him. John has cabled Eugene and my lab to set things up and got me a flight to Washington at noon."

"A flight? And you are going on it?" His voice broke in disbelief.

"I have to."

"You have to," he said flatly.

She drew in a breath and turned to face him. "Yes. I really do."

"I can see what is most important to you now."

"You are the most important to me. You are! And you always will be. But this is bigger than me." She grasped his arm as he tried to turn away. "I can have the work finished in a few months. Then I will come back permanently. It's only a small bump in the scheme of things."

A car honked outside.

He pulled away from her, then dropped the flowers on the chair with a lush thud. At the window, he said, "There is a taxi."

She followed him to the window. "Arne, please. I will be back very soon. Then I will be yours completely, I promise."

"Will you be?"

"Oh, I will. I promise I will! I will be the best wife and the best mother, if we are so lucky, and a darn good scientist, too. It's been done before—Marie Curie had her work and family. She had a full life."

"She died young of radiation poisoning, *elskede*."

Madame Curie also took up with a younger man after her husband died, and was called a homewrecker in the newspapers, but maybe that did not bolster her case here. She waved her hand. "My point is, she won the Nobel and still had a family. Arne, I can, too."

The taxi honked again.

"Just give me this moment and I will make it up to you, you'll see."

He picked up the little blue ashtray from the bedside table. "You had better take this."

Reluctantly, she took it, then held it to her chest. "Does this mean goodbye?"

"I do not know. Does it?"

"Arne, I have to do this. It'll save lives."

"Save lives or your reputation? Has not this other man, Bodian, made the same discovery? Can he not further your work just as well?"

Her heart stopped. He was right. She sat down on the bed.

He groaned, then pulled her up to him.

She laid her cheek against the brushed wool of his jacket; he pressed his chin to her hair.

The taxi blared its horn.

She looked up into his beautiful, wounded face. "What do I do?"

He kissed her forehead, then gently held her away. "You do what you think is right."

1952

A WIFE

A nurse swooped up with a wheelchair. "Mommy, you shouldn't be standing."

Sylvia kept her grip on the registration desk, her belly thrust out of her heavy winter coat as if it were trying to escape. She threw a look over her shoulder and saw stiff white wings perched above white cat-eye glasses. Behind them blinked the blue eyes of a woman a good decade younger than she was.

"It's cold out there." The nurse was peering through the plate-glass double doors. "Is your husband parking the car?"

Sylvia turned back around and drew in a breath. A contraction was coming on. Terror screwed down on her along with the pain. This was her second child. She knew what she was in for.

The registrar, an older stalwart woman with cavernous nostrils, spun around the clipboard with the form that Sylvia had just completed. She glanced at it, then blanched, something Sylvia suspected she did not do often, considering all the panicked men and women she must have seen here over the years.

"Help her get into that chair!" the registrar yelled at the nurse. "Now! Sorry, Mrs. Sabin."

The nurse pushed Sylvia toward the seat of the wheelchair, but Sylvia kept her stranglehold on the desk. Her whole body was clenching along with the excruciating charley horse in her womb. She couldn't move.

She should have come to the hospital sooner. She had been waiting for Albert.

"Mrs. Sabin, where is your husband?"

Sylvia shook her head.

The registrar got up from behind her desk and, trailed by the nurse, went over to the doors. The nurse went outside. The registrar asked Sylvia, "Did he come in another way?"

The contraction was losing its force now. When Sylvia could talk, she said, "He's not out there. I drove myself."

"Is he already in the hospital?"

"You tell me."

She'd phoned his secretary, left a message with her. Lately, he'd only been home just long enough to change his shirt and shower. Their little girl hardly knew him. He'd come back from the most recent polio roundtable meeting, a few weeks ago in December, a different man, more driven, if that were possible. Last time she'd talked to him was two days ago.

THEIR LITTLE GIRL HAD BEEN TAKING A NAP. SYLVIA WAS standing outside the shower, holding her belly with both hands. These past couple weeks, the baby's head had been grinding against her pubic bone. She tried lifting her belly up off of it, but she couldn't get any relief.

"Where have you been?" she asked him.

Albert's disembodied voice rose with the steam above the curtain. "The lab."

"All night?"

"I slept on the cot in my office." She heard the thump of the bar of soap hitting the floor, then his grunt as he bent to get it.

"The baby is due tomorrow, Albert."

"Babies don't care about due dates."

"I do!" The baby jabbed her in the rib as if in agreement.

"You don't understand," he said. "That damn Salk is testing on kids. Dorothy told me."

"Dorothy," she said.

"Salk won't admit it, though. I've got to beat him before he gets his inferior vaccine to the market. I'm doing everything I can to speed up mine." Something scraped the bathtub rim as he picked it up. She heard the splat of Prell on his hand. "I've got a bunch of boys around the country figuring out the best strains to use. I've got another bunch working on weakening live virus. Still another bunch is gearing up to feed live virus to volunteers."

She placed her hand where the baby was kicking. "Which of those things are you doing?"

"All of them." Water pelted the shower curtain as he rinsed.

The curtain zinged on its rings; he grabbed a towel and got out. She looked at his nakedness. It was her prerogative as his wife. All she saw was legally hers. "Stay home, Albert. I want you home."

He dried himself as if she weren't looking. "Don't worry, I'll be there."

"You're hard to find. Even if you don't care about me having your baby, what if there's a nuclear attack? The children and I will be burnt to powder before I could ever locate you."

"Now you're being extreme."

"Am I?"

"I'm sorry, Sylvia. The threat of Stalin bombing us is entirely more remote than our children getting polio. I'm closer than ever to delivering a safe and effective vaccine, but I have to get to it fast, before Salk hogs all of the funding. His vaccine, I promise you, is not as good."

He put his arms around her. She drank in his smell of damp flesh and soap.

"You do want me to protect our little boy from polio, don't you?" He patted her belly, then trotted to the bedroom.

She followed him. "It might be a girl."

"We already have a girl. It will be a boy."

"How do you know?"

"I know everything." He laughed.

THE YOUNG NURSE WITH THE WHITE CAT-EYE GLASSES shook the wheelchair. "Sit, Mommy."

If being treated like a child got Sylvia back to the delivery room and this baby safely out of her, so be it. She lowered herself toward the wheelchair until she and the twenty-five-pound bowling ball in her lap could drop the rest of the way down.

The registrar went back to her desk. "Let me call Dr. Sabin."

Good luck with that. Sylvia placed her hands below her breasts as Nurse Cat-Eye pushed her through heavy swinging doors. She could lay her palms flat against her ribs now, with plenty of space between her breasts and her belly. There was even room a few inches below her ribs. This was new. Her baby was being subsumed by her body.

Disoriented, she looked up. They were passing the leather-upholstered enclave of the Stork Club. One expectant father was smoking a cigar and paging through *Man's Life*, as comfortable as a man in his own living room. Another held his head in his hands. A third man, crushing out his cigarette, saw her and raised his thumb.

"Piece of cake," he said.

If she could have moved, she would have struck him.

A push through another set of doors brought her into the maternity area. She heard the cigarette-toasted voice of a doctor, the laughter of nurses. The topic was who'd done what at the Christmas party a few weeks back. She'd expected to hear laboring women crying out, the wail of newborn babies, but there was only this.

Her nurse said, "Let's get you in a gown, Mommy."

IT WAS COLD THROUGH HER ROUGH COTTON GOWN. SYLVIA shifted under the pressure of the baby forcing its way through her pelvis. Her bones ground against the hard steel of the table.

A woman's distant scream punctured the quiet. It escalated into a single heart-stopping shriek, then was subsumed by the tinkling of the surgical instruments that a nurse was arranging on the tray at Sylvia's side.

She looked up at the nurse, a different one, her eyes gray buttons on a face as pink as Pepto-Bismol. She was rolling thick padded gauze around Sylvia's head.

"Is that woman okay?"

"Who?"

"The screaming one."

The nurse paused her rolling to listen. "Oh, her? She's fine, sugar."

She did not sound fine to Sylvia, but Sylvia had other fish to fry. The vise in her belly was cranking down.

Panic flocked into her throat. The contractions were so close now that she had little time to catch her breath between them. She couldn't escape the searing pain. To think that for every person who walked the earth, a woman went through this agony. What a stupid plan!

"Lift your head," the nurse said.

"Why are you doing that?"

The nurse kept the gauze rolling. "To keep you comfortable."

Did they do this last time? She wouldn't know—they'd knocked her out as soon as they'd gotten her in her gown.

She winced at the light beaming down into her eyes. "So bright!"

The doctor came over. "It won't bother you soon, Mommy. Everything will be peachy."

Sylvia rose up in one last burst of strength, knocking a leather restraining cuff with her elbow. She squinted at it. It was lined . . . with fluffy wool?

"Dr. Aiken, I requested to be awake."

"Why?" he asked incredulously.

"To see the baby. I missed everything the last time."

"Well, there's nothing to see. Wait until we whisk him out, clean him up, and make him presentable."

"I'd like—" She grasped at breath. The pain was coming on strong. "—to bond with her."

"Bond?" He laughed. "You're going to wish you had an escape like this every day, soon enough. Lay back and enjoy it while you can."

Sylvia eyed the restraining cuff. If this "escape" was so enjoyable, why did they have to tie people down for it?

The nurse secured the padded gauze around her head. "Ready, Dr. Aiken."

"Be a good girl, Sylvia." The doctor raised a syringe to the light to check the dosage. "When you wake, a lovely little present will be waiting for you."

She snatched his arm. The pain was reaming into her core. She may have dug in her nails too hard.

"Betty! Doreen!" he yelled. "Get over here!"

Her arms were wrestled to the table.

She could only push out a single word. "Please!"

He came at her with the syringe. "Believe me, you will thank me later."

She felt the pinch and burn of the shot. Her bones were melting.

SHE WAS LITERALLY BESIDE HERSELF, WATCHING HER POOR strapped and padded self writhe as the floor of her trunk was cut open and the doctor delved deep with thick metal tongs. There was nothing, nothing, she could do but scream.

SHE OPENED HER EYES.

Her husband bent over her. "Well, hello, beautiful."

She was in a bed in a beige space with beige curtains. Snow flurries danced outside the window. The room smelled of rubbing alcohol and the dense bouquet of roses on her bedside stand.

He wiped the tears from her cheek. "Women always come out of Twilight Sleep crying. I believe there's something in either the morphine or scopolamine that triggers the tear ducts."

"Where's the baby?" Her throat was so sore—had she been screaming?—it was hard to speak. "Is it all right?"

"Yes, yes," he said fondly. He patted her wrist. She winced from the pain of his touch but, upon inspecting her wrist, found no bruise, no mark. The feel of fuzzy lambswool darted through a crevice in her mind, then other troubling sensations arose to the surface en masse. They vanished, quickly as a school of minnows, leaving her with only a bleak sense of dread.

"It's a girl, Sylvia."

She raised heavy eyes.

"She's perfect"—he chuckled—"if you don't mind her looking like me."

"I want to see her."

She fell back to sleep until he returned with the baby. He fitted the soft wrapped pupae into her arms.

The baby gazed at her with eyes the gray of the inside of an oyster shell. Sylvia's heart rose to life within her leaden body. She could actually feel the gaze from those wide gray eyes tug her organs, as if they were connected by a fishing line. Love gushed violently through her.

A nurse called Albert to the door. When he came back, he said, "Dorothy Horstmann is on the phone. She says it's important."

He left.

It didn't matter so much now that he did.

The child was waiting for her, staring at Sylvia as if she might explain just what the baby had gotten herself into.

Sylvia's voice was thick from the lump effervescing in her throat. "You're just who I wanted."

29

NEW YORK, NEW YORK, 1952

The water of Flushing Bay was brown in late April, as Dorothy could see only too well from the window of the little airplane as it lowered for a landing. The wings seemed to skim the murky chop, causing Dorothy to imagine herself underwater, banging on the ceiling of the submerged cabin as hats, briefcases, and seat cushions floated in a stew around her.

Papa! Pop!

She saw Pop's large face crumpling with determination as he plucked her from the water.

Wheels hit pavement. Dorothy was thrown from her imaginings and against her seatbelt. Her guts rattled like ice in a cocktail shaker as the craft bounced down the runway. That suited her. She couldn't feel herself trembling over what lay ahead.

"Well, that was a rough ride." The sunlight pouring through the airplane window spotlighted the six-hair cowlick rebelling from John Paul's neatly combed taupe hair. "How are you holding up?"

"Fine."

"Not deaf yet from the engine?"

"Not yet." Her eardrums felt thick from the roar, but she wouldn't complain. She knew what an honor it was for the president of the university to insist that she fly to the conference in his little airplane. She imagined that she was the first lowly associate professor to have ever set foot inside it—certainly the first daughter of the likes of Henry Horstmann.

"Ready to give your paper and change medical history?"

She had hand-carried her paper on board, apart from her briefcase, cradling it as if it were a child for the entire hop from New Haven. "I should practice."

"Practice what? You've read papers before."

"But not this paper. Not at the American Association of Immunologists."

"Oh, they're just a bunch of old fuddy-duddies."

"Very argumentative, critical, unforgiving old fuddy-duddies." She fetched her briefcase from beside her feet. "Who are not particularly old."

"Thank you." He smiled. "The men will be gentle with you. Just be glad you aren't Salk."

They popped along the runway like hard corn kernels in a skillet. "Why does everyone pick on poor old Jonas?"

"'Poor old Jonas' intimates that he has valuable information, but then he won't tell us what he is doing. He plays his hand too close to the vest for my liking. We're working for the common good."

"He tried to tell me about his work on a vaccine last fall but didn't finish." She snapped open the latches of her briefcase. "I think he'd be more open about it if he hadn't been shamed into secrecy."

"Oh, I don't think shame is what is keeping him quiet. I've heard that the March of Dimes has been funneling most of their funding to him, and they're being secretive about it. I suppose they don't want the scientific community to tell them what to do. Well, I hope O'Connor isn't disappointed. We'll see if he's still their darling"—he waited until she looked at him—"after the reporters meet the new star today."

"John, no! Tell me that you didn't!"

"Oh, I did." His grin was as boyish as his cowlick, as if the kid in him were bursting to get out of his buttoned-up middle-aged body. "I called all the press people. They need to know about our Dottie. One doesn't present Nobel Prize–worthy work every day."

"You're going to jinx me!"

"Get used to the spotlight, dear. You're not only the lead author of a groundbreaking paper, but its sole author."

She winced. He'd hit on a sore spot. If she'd had her way, she would have listed Eugene as an author on the paper, but lab technicians, and certainly animal handlers, weren't allowed. But Eugene had been her rock, always there to support her as she threw herself into difficult work.

She almost laughed now, imagining how bedraggled and insane she must have looked these past few months, a regular mad scientist complete with frazzled hair, pushing herself to the limit under the load of her study and teaching combined. One night in October, she'd been so bleary-eyed from observing and recording the condition of the monkeys with Eugene that she'd been startled on the drive home by the crowds of kids dressed up in costumes—she'd had no idea it was Halloween. Her celebration of Thanksgiving had been to write up statistics in the lab as she mindlessly shoveled in the cold leftovers that Eugene's wife, Viola, had thoughtfully sent. Christmas Eve had been like any other night of the year, except when she wearily drove Eugene home, the streets were decorated with silver bells and garlands that she was surprised to notice were there.

IT HAD BEEN STARTING TO SNOW WHEN THEY GOT TO EUgene's house on Christmas Eve. Juicy pats lumbered through the rays of the headlights and furred the orange glow of the electric candles on the wreaths hanging at the windows.

"Got to go play Santa," he said. "Thanks for the ride, Dr. Horstmann."

"Dorothy! When are you ever going to call me that? Merry Christmas."

He grabbed the door handle but didn't pull. "You okay? You've been quiet."

The snow slid down the windshield as quickly as it hit. At her insistence, she and Arne were writing to each other again, but lately his letters had dwindled. How could she complain? Most nights she'd been too tired to put pen to airmail onion skin. If he could just hang on until she got this work behind her, she could give him all the attention he deserved and more. But she was so very close, so achingly close, to flushing the monster from its secret den.

Eugene waited for an answer.

She wiped the condensation off the inside of the windshield with the back of her wool glove. "What if the reviewers at the journal turn down the article for publication? What if they find holes in my science?"

"They won't. You did the work."

"*We've* done the work." She leaned over and squeezed his solid arm. "I don't know how to thank you for all you've done."

She thought at first that he was pulling away from her, but he was only shifting in his seat to take his billfold from his pants pocket. He opened it, took out a photo, then dropped open the glove box. The lightbulb shone on the photo of a toddler girl dressed in patent leather shoes and a frilly bonnet.

"My little girl. Linda."

"She's adorable!"

"It's been twelve years. She was eighteen months old." He kept his eyes trained on the picture. "Polio got her."

"Oh, Eugene, I'm so very sorry. I didn't know."

"I read once that the ancient Egyptians believed that a person remained alive as long as someone thought of them. Only when people stopped thinking about him, or her"—his broad chest expanded and contracted—"did the person die."

The snow came more heavily now, first clinging to the windshield before gliding down in clumps. "All day, every day, that we have worked on this project, I have thought of Linda and all the little children like her who we're trying to save. By working with you on the battle in the blood, you gave me a way to keep my Linda alive." He nestled the photo back in his billfold. "And, *Dorothy*"—she could see his smile in the light from the glovebox—"to me, that is thanks enough."

THE AIRPLANE WAS RUMBLING TO A STOP OUTSIDE THE TERminal. Dr. Paul patted her knee. "Don't worry. You'll be wonderful."

A little ill, she opened her briefcase. She felt a jolt: there, on top of the pile of peers' manuscripts she was to review in her spare time, was the photo of Eugene's little girl.

Her scalp prickled. Why had he put this here? The picture was precious to him. What if she lost it? Why had he put this responsibility on her?

"Who's that?" Dr. Paul looked over her arm as he lifted his own briefcase into his lap. Under her bonnet, the child was all liquid dark eyes.

"Eugene's daughter. Linda."

"I didn't know that he had one."

"Yes. She di—" She caught herself.

She opened her folder, laid the photo on top of her paper, then put them in the briefcase and closed it tight.

All right, Eugene.

30

Ninety minutes later, after a taxi ride to Manhattan with all its skyscrapers and honking cars, and then after a run through the gauntlet of colleagues in the lobby of the Commodore Hotel, Dorothy gripped both sides of the podium. Her bowels felt scoured by the breaks she'd taken in the gilt-fixtured hotel bathroom. Nerves seemed to have liquified her intestines.

"Thank you." The microphone screeched. She pulled back from it a bit. "Thank you for the introduction, Joe," she told her colleague, Joe Melnick, still finding his seat. "It shows real generosity of spirit to say such nice words about me after you took on my polio outbreak duty since last fall. Please tell your wife and children thank you for lending their dad."

Comfortably ensconced in their seats in the cavernous ballroom, the audience chuckled. Joe's dark widow's peak dipped as he winked and nodded.

"And I must thank Dr. Paul." She sheltered her eyes and looked for him—there he was, presiding over the first row like a papa at a recital. "Without you, I wouldn't even be at Yale, let alone have been given interesting work and encouraged to pursue my hunches. Oh, those troublesome, nagging hunches! How lucky the person who is allowed to relieve themselves of them, egged on by her mentor. The fact is, one is only as good as one's mentor. And I am thankful to have the best. Thank you, Dr. Paul."

"That makes me feel so old!" he exclaimed over the applause.

The crowd laughed.

"Johnny," said Basil O'Connor, "you are evergreen."

As the laughter quieted, she looked down from the podium. All the legends were out there, Enders, Francis, Rivers. Albert. Should she do this? Nobody did what she was about to do, but that didn't make it not right.

"I also—" The microphone squealed from feedback. She pulled back from the mouthpiece. "Also, I want to thank someone who couldn't be here, my colleague Eugene Oakley. Mr. Oakley was instrumental in the sensitive care of my animal subjects, and a great help to me in their handling, which, if you have ever been bitten by a full-grown cynomolgus monkey, you will know is quite the blessing."

The boys chuckled. Some even pointed to scars on their hands and arms.

She waited until they settled down. "I want to thank, too, the monkeys and chimpanzees in my study themselves. Without their sacrifice, I would not have been able to prove my hunch. I hope from the knowledge gained through my work their lives will not be in vain."

The men glanced at one another. A doctor from Michigan smirked. She moved on quickly before she lost them.

"Finally, most importantly, I wish to dedicate my work to this child." She held up the photo. "This is Linda Oakley, my colleague Eugene Oakley's daughter." She turned to face the picture. "Linda, I want to thank you and all the children who inspire me to keep working, keep dreaming, and keep doing whatever it takes to snuff the daylights out of the poliovirus. Linda Oakley, I am thinking about you."

The boys went quiet. They stayed that way as she put on her reading glasses—her eyes had gone bad the day she'd turned forty. Time would be acknowledged whether you liked it or not.

Glasses on, she picked up her paper. "Now, gentlemen. Let me tell you about what Linda's father calls 'the battle in the blood.'"

SHE GATHERED HER PAPER, A WEIGHT LIFTING FROM HER chest, as her colleagues got to their feet and clapped. They understood her work. They appreciated her—*her*, Dorothy Horstmann.

The crowd was still up applauding as Dave Bodian trotted to the microphone. His rubbery features stretching into a smile, he made a show of adjusting the microphone mouthpiece to a lower height, then, pointedly looking at her, moved it even lower, setting off a round of laughter. The boys had simmered down by the time Dorothy had settled, glowing, into her seat between John and Albert.

Good work, Albert mouthed.

Up on stage, Bodian cleared his throat. "My friends, sorry to say, I am not going to thank my monkeys. But I would like to thank my wife."

The boys roared with laughter. Albert looked over at her and shook his head.

She wanted to tell Albert that it was all right. She was used to it. She expected it. What counted was that her work had been well received by this group. This was the group that would take her findings and run with them. Now they knew that if they made a vaccine that tricked the body into producing antibodies, it could kill the poliovirus while in the early stages in the blood. They could stop polio from robbing parents of their Lindas. Imagine!

Albert was scowling at her.

What? she mouthed.

He nodded toward Bodian. She made herself listen. Familiar phrases penetrated her rosy glow: "in the blood," "four to six days," "we were looking too early." She knew that he'd been pursuing the same possibilities as her, but now it was clear that his experiments were nearly identical to hers, only done with more subjects, over a longer period of time, and with the added intriguing suggestion that because of it, gamma globulin might actually be a viable treatment.

After he'd finished to applause as enthusiastic as it was for her, the meeting adjourned to the hall outside the ballroom. The reporters John Paul had called were there. They ran to Dave Bodian with pencils and notebooks in hand.

"How many years until we have a vaccine, Dr. Bodian?"

"Does this mean gamma globulin works?"

"Do you think you'll win the Nobel Prize?"

"If I did"—Dave reached for Dorothy, who was turning away—"I'd have to share it with Dr. Horstmann. We have been simultaneously mining the same vein." He grasped her hand and pulled her over while shaking it. "Congratulations."

Flashbulbs exploded as they shook.

"Edison meets Tesla," one of the reporters said.

"Jenner meets Pasteur," said another.

"Goliath meets David," Dorothy joked, even as her heart was sinking.

"Say," someone shouted, "Dr. H.! Show us the picture of the little girl."

Something lifted in her chest. Photographers stepped closer, cameras ready, as she opened her briefcase and took out the photo. When she held it up, they leaned in.

As a group, they paused.

One of the photographers stepped back.

Someone whispered, "Is she a Negro?"

Two quick flashes went off. Another photographer busied himself with checking his equipment.

A reporter turned to Dave and shook his hand. "I'm Stan Halberman for *Time* magazine. What do you think about having the same findings as Dr. Horstmann?"

"Well, it's excellent news, isn't it? I suppose this makes the work doubly accurate. There's no one I'm happier to have verify my work. Dr. Horstmann has one of the most respected minds in our field."

Dorothy removed her scowl from the photographers. People could be so disappointing.

Dave was grinning at her. "She also makes a mean gin rickey. Where'd you learn how to make them, Dot? You could work in a bar."

"Now that's a talent." Mr. Halberman pushed back his hat. "Say, can we get a picture of you two together?"

Someone was pulling them closer.

The *Time* photographer patted the small table at which the registrars had sat. "Dr. H., you sit here."

She did as she was told. Her knees bumped the underside of the table as if she were a grown-up sitting at a child's school desk.

"Now put your paper on the table. Here's a pen. Pretend that you're writing. Dr. Bodian, you come over here and look over her shoulder, as if you're telling her how to get it right."

Dorothy tried to laugh it off. "I'm afraid that I don't make a very good secretary. Why don't I stand and he sit?"

"That would be strange," said the reporter. "Miss Horstmann—smile!"

The flash went off. Dorothy's vision went blue.

THE REPORTERS WERE STILL OUT IN THE LOBBY OF THE Commodore, fawning over Dave Bodian and his amazing discovery (which happened to be hers first), when Albert had led her over to the Century Room and ordered her the Baked Half Lobster Egyptienne and a whiskey, stat. Now she sat in a plush leather booth and poked the white and red chunks of lobster with her fork as her joy bled out of her.

Albert stopped talking and watched her worry the lobster. "You shouldn't waste food like that."

"I'm sorry. I guess I'm not the best of company."

"No need to apologize. But you shouldn't waste that food." When she looked up at him, he said, "I'm sorry, it's my childhood coming out."

She nodded. Her mother would have fretted at the waste, too, or more likely, would have scooped up the dish and stretched it with noodles and potatoes to feed everyone in the family and any ailing neighbors to boot.

A waiter came over to the table with a basket and then, with tongs, held up a dinner roll like a priest with a host. Albert waved it onto his plate. Dorothy passed.

"I feel your pain." Albert buttered his bread. "I feel it keenly. Victory has been snatched from you by no fault of your own."

"I worked so hard!"

"I know. So we're going to make them all pay."

The waiter came to pour them water. When he had gone, she said, "Thank you, Albert. I appreciate that you are trying to comfort me. But I really am not out to make anyone pay."

"You're not?" He laughed. "Give yourself time, you will be." He cut into the meat weeping onto his white plate. "You were robbed of what you and I want most: respect."

"I don't know if you're making this better."

"I'm talking about coming out on top, Dorothy. I'm talking about getting credit. Don't you want to get credit?"

"Well. Yes. I suppose."

"You suppose?"

"Okay. I do want credit."

"Then you have to fight for it, because everyone else is fighting for it, too. Do you think anyone is going to give you a break? Do you think they'll coddle you because you're a woman?"

"Believe me, I don't."

"That's right. They won't. They'll steamroll right over you."

"You're not telling me anything new, Albert."

"Then get smart and get tough. Join with me to deliver the world from polio, you at Yale and me in Cincinnati. Together, we'll be unbeatable. All those jerks won't know what hit them."

"Don't you mean that polio won't know what hit it?"

He laughed. "Right."

1953

A STATISTICIAN

The phone rang while they were watching Edward Murrow on the television. Barbara's mother got up, tucked a pink foam curler farther under her hairnet, then rewrapped her robe around her middle. "Who could it be at this hour?"

Her mother left with a scuffing of slippers. *Who could it be at any hour?* Barbara thought as Mr. Murrow ground out his cigarette before asking his guest a question. Calls for her weren't exactly pouring in.

From the kitchen, her mother called in an odd voice, "Barbie!"

It was a short roll past the davenport and homemade bookcase to the kitchen. Clutching the collar of her robe, her mother held out the receiver as Barbara parked her wheelchair by the dinette table. *It's Dr. Sabin*, she mouthed with a scowl.

Barbara's pulse jumped. The bobby pins in her curls set for the night clicked against the receiver when she put it against her ear.

"Barbara?"

His voice threw her back into the lab, to the days when she'd been whole. She saw herself working side by side with him, needing neither food nor drink nor sleep. All she had needed was the work.

"Yes."

"Barbara, how are you?"

"Good. Better. I can use my hands quite well now." She was

proud that she'd set her own pin curls, but she wouldn't tell him that. The last time she'd seen him, once she'd returned to Cincinnati from her stay at Warm Springs, he'd taken her to lunch and had to feed her, a thought that made her steam now with embarrassment. She wouldn't see him after that.

"Excellent news." There was a silence. "Well, I shall not beat around the bush. I'm ramping up the work on my vaccine, and I could use you."

Her heart was pushing into her throat. "I'm afraid I'm . . . I'm still in my wheelchair. My legs don't work."

"Does your brain? Because I remember your skill with statistics, and I am in dire need of a top-rate statistician."

"I haven't worked in years."

"You'd be compiling the results of my experiments."

Had he not heard her? She had not worked.

"You'd also be working up the results of data that others send me, Dorothy Horstmann among them."

"Dorothy Horstmann?"

"I understand that you know her."

"I do. She's . . . quite special."

"She is. We—I—really need you, Barbara. I'm closing in on a safe live-virus vaccine to be given orally."

It was about time.

"Barbara?"

"Yes?"

"Now that Dorothy has proven that the virus enters through the digestive tract, from whence it's distributed in the blood, I know how to beat polio at its own game: send a weakened virus straight to the gut and trick the body into making its own antibodies. It will be much more effective than randomly peppering the body with killed virus that has been injected in an arm."

"Kids will like not getting shots, or that horrific gamma globulin."

"Exactly. We hope to take it to trial before too long. It's important that we get our stats in shape to convince O'Connor to promote our work."

Over by the refrigerator, her mother bunched behind her fists, blinking with hope.

She saw herself back in the lab with him, a tray of tissues before them. How she had loved how his eyes shone with intelligence, though his intensity slightly terrified her.

"Barbie, you look tired," he'd said. "You should go home, get some rest."

She'd started to protest.

"Put this tray back into the refrigerator. We'll get to it tomorrow."

Her head hurt, her midsection throbbed with cramps, and her tongue had gone to sawdust. Still, she had plucked up another glass slide between thumb and forefinger and raised her chin in defiance. "Who can rest while knowledge that might reduce suffering sits on the shelf?"

She cringed now. It had sounded overly dramatic then and it sounded just as corny as she recollected it, but she'd meant it. She had never imagined that she'd be the one sitting on the shelf.

Well, it was time to get off.

Her bobby pins caught on the receiver as she nodded. "When do I start?"

31

NEW HAVEN, CONNECTICUT, 1953

The phonograph needle crackled on the first groove of the record. The strains of Beethoven's "Moonlight Sonata" flowed into the room.

Dorothy padded across her living room rug, her stockinged feet buzzing from being on them all day. She collapsed into her armchair, too tired to rub them, too tired to take off her girdle, but not too tired to take off her bra. The twin funnels of the wretched thing lay out on the kitchen counter, flung there upon entering her little house. What a curious custom forcing one's breasts into the shape of cones was! Outside of the West, she hadn't encountered anything like it in her work around the world. She didn't understand the objective of it, but perhaps the Suri women she'd met in Ethiopia couldn't explain why they wore plates in their lips, either.

She heaved a sigh, laid back her head, and listened to the music.

She'd read once that Beethoven had written the piece when in his thirties, just for the fun of it. He'd composed it at a time in his life when patrons were swamping him with commissions, a masterpiece, just for himself. She closed her eyes now, trying to imagine the great composer reveling as he played his melody, rejoicing in his gift. But all she could see was Pop, his face angelic with ecstasy.

Dear Pop. Thank goodness she had a father like him and had

the balm of her childhood memories. On days like this, it helped to remember lying against his wet woolly back as he waded them into the heated water of the Sutro Baths, his chuckles reverberating through her belly, or to recall their fiercely competitive rounds of Drop the Clothespin in the Milk Bottle, a game Mutter devised for them for rainy days. She had just returned yesterday from a terrible outbreak in Australia, an ominous sign for the polio season ahead here. The fact was, polio was becoming more virulent by the year.

It broke all the records in the US last summer. The numbers were etched in her mind: 21,269 cases of paralytic polio, more than double the year before, and, at 3,145, double the deaths. There was still no sure weapon against it.

The telephone rang. Her heart blipped with hope like it always did, as if Arne would place an overseas call, let alone write to her after she'd stretched his patience to the limits. She hadn't received a letter in months. More likely it was Pop, whom Mutter had put on the phone. Their conversation would mostly be him asking if she liked Tony Bennett, to which she would answer yes. Courtesy of her sister Catherine, who still lived at home (along with Bernard and his clay maps), he was very fond of "Blue Velvet."

"Did I disturb you?" Albert said.

"Oh, hi, Albert. No." She inspected the bottom of her foot. She was annoyed to find that she'd snagged her nylon on a floorboard when going to the phone. "Are you all right?" Not an unreasonable question at 10:05 on a Monday night.

"I have a favor to ask." How like Albert to leap right into his demand without bothering to ask how she might be.

"Ask away."

"Do you have any of the Moroccan poliovirus strain that you can send me?"

"I believe I've got some in the deep freeze at the lab."

"Is anyone from Yale coming to Cincinnati this week who

could hand-deliver it? Anyone blond and over six foot tall?" A radio show was playing in the background on Albert's end, the overly dramatic voices of the actors echoing against tile and steel. He was still in his lab. Not surprising. He'd been even more relentless, if that were possible for Albert Sabin, since Basil O'Connor and the March of Dimes had recently formed a new committee on vaccines without consulting him or any of the old guard. The March of Dimes was throwing all of its might behind Jonas. "Why don't you come out here?" he said. "We can make beautiful music in the lab."

On her record player, the upper notes of Beethoven's sonata swelled, straining against the steadfast beat of the bass.

"I've got my own beautiful music here." That was how they were these days, jokey friends. "Besides, I have classes to teach. I've been gone for two weeks."

"Play hooky for a day. I'll pay for your flight."

"What will I do about my patients? Joe can't cover for me forever."

"You really have to stop practicing medicine, like I did."

"How am I to teach my residents, then?"

"I don't know, but I've been a much happier boy since new mothers can't call me at midnight."

Some head of pediatrics he was. But she'd met plenty of baby doctors who disdained mothers—and babies—although not him. She wondered why they went into it.

"Consider your coming here as a good deed for humanity," he said. "We can't let Salk's vaccine go unchallenged. We're working like Trojans here—Barbara is up to her elbows in stats."

"You need her."

"I do." She heard him click off his radio. His voice was more urgent now. "I can't believe that a bunch of non-medical men at the March of Dimes are calling the shots now. Any scientist worth his salt will tell you that Salk is totally irresponsible. He chose the most dangerous strains for his vaccine."

"I wouldn't call him totally irresponsible. I understand his logic. He wants to protect against the worst that polio can throw at victims."

"Then he should offer the best protection. His vaccine is only temporary at best. He told me himself he thought it was going to need frequent boosters."

She felt good that her discovery allowed Jonas to be able to know when and where to look for antibodies, to at least know if boosters were necessary. "Frequent boosters are better than nothing, which is what we have until your vaccine is ready, since gamma globulin has been proven to be a bust."

"Whose side are you on?" he exclaimed.

"The children's, Albert."

He huffed over the phone line. "Just come here, Dot. With your Moroccan strain. And all will be forgiven."

"I wasn't aware that I needed forgiveness."

"For not being here right now, yes."

The sonata's bass plowed stoically on as the treble wailed and dipped. "I wish I could come." She really did. This house seemed so very empty. There was a hole in its atmosphere, like the kind left in one's house after a pet cat or dog has died.

He sensed a chance. "Do, then! Come, now, before you win your Nobel Prize and I never have a chance at you."

"Cut it out. I don't even know that I've been nominated. It's secret."

"Not so secret that everyone doesn't know who's up for it. You've been nominated and you'll win. After I get my Nobel for my vaccine, we'll be Nobel Buddies."

She laughed.

"Dorothy. I'm serious. You ought to come here . . . permanently. We'd make a terrific team. Just think, we create our vaccine—"

"'Ours' now."

"—*our* vaccine, and they'll throw ticker tape for us. You and me, covered in confetti, riding in a convertible through Manhattan."

"You're not going to just tear up your own napkin this time?"

"You remember that?" She could hear the delight in his voice. "I'm not kidding, Dorothy. We're good together. I think you know that, too."

Where was he going with this? She was wondering how to let him down while appearing not to imply that he'd meant anything personal, when her doorbell rang.

"Is someone there? Don't tell me that it's John Paul. Does he come over much? You know that he's in love with you, don't you?"

"John is not in love with me."

Albert chuckled. "Right. Well, go get it, then. Tell John 'hi.' I'll wait."

She laid down the phone. It probably was John, though he usually called first, and this was late for him. Was there an emergency in the lab? Worry was gathering strength as she swung open the door.

The wind whipped Arne's silky hair over his forehead when he took off his hat. "If the mountain won't come to Muhammad, *elskede*, then Muhammad must come to the mountain."

32

She clapped her hand over her mouth just as "Ode to Joy" burst out of the phonograph. She laughed at the impossibility of it all.

Arne grinned. "I hoped that you would be happy."

"I am!" If she were a dog, she would be wagging herself sideways. She stepped into his arms.

It was a while before she could break with him long enough to lead him into the kitchen. "Let me get you something to drink. Are you hungry?"

She saw the phone receiver on the chair. "Oh, no!" She went over and put it to her ear. "Hello?"

"I suspect that isn't John Paul," said Albert.

"You're still there? I'm sorry! I forgot."

"Well, that makes me feel great."

"I really am sorry. I will send you your virus sample."

"Do that. Thanks." The phone clicked.

Arne was behind her when she put the receiver back onto the base. "Did I interrupt?"

"It was nothing." No, she should be open. She had nothing to hide. "It was Albert Sabin. He wanted a poliovirus sample. We— He and I—"

He nodded before she had to say anything more. "It is your

business. I know how hard you work. Come." They went back to the living room, where they sat down on the couch.

"I hope you are not angry at me for not consulting you before I came. Maybe I was afraid of the answer." He grimaced. "I had to see your face to know."

"And what is the verdict?"

He rubbed her shoulder. "I was right to come."

She laid her face on his hand. "Yes. You are." She almost laughed, thinking how tired she'd been. Not now!

She sat up. "But your work is important. How could you leave it?"

"Editing a magazine? No. I can find something like it here. In these times when people are so hungry for news, there is plenty of work. It is much harder for you to find the right team for your research. I understand this now. I am ashamed that I tried to take you from it."

"It wasn't your fault. Nothing was ever your fault."

His long face buckled in a grimace. "Perhaps you could help me find a place to stay . . ."

"Oh, Arne, I want you here with me."

"I can see that you might mean that."

"Of course I do!" She laughed. "I still cannot believe you are here!"

He let her lean on him. After a moment, he sat her upright. "Dorte, do not think I have forgotten my vow to marry you. I do not mean to cheat you of that, if that is important to you."

She lowered her face, embarrassed. She'd forgotten how forthright he was. "It is important to me, in due time. Is it important to you?"

"I thought it was important to you. In all the American movies, always it is about getting married."

She laughed. "My life is nothing like a movie."

"As for me, the Danish do not put such importance in marriage vows. When we love, we love."

She leaned into him again. "So do I."

WHEN SHE CAME HOME THE NEXT EVENING, SHE OPENED the door to the aroma of toasted bread and heated butter. Her exhaustion from her workday evaporated.

Arne strode forth and ushered her inside with a towel pinned around his waist and his sleeves rolled up. "You've been cooking," she said as he took off her coat. "Something smells wonderful."

"I went to the supermarket. There was so much of everything! Four kinds of bread, five kinds of margarine, I lost count of how many kinds of cereal—how do you choose?"

"We listen to the radio," she said as he hung her coat in the cloak closet. "Advertisers are only too glad to tell us what products to buy."

When he came back to her, she kissed his cheek (warm, smooth, perfumed with the spice of aftershave—lovely). "I worked in publishing," he said. "I know about advertising. We Danes are not above selling things. But in America, they specialize in making a person *crave*. I fear I shall become desirous of many things."

"As long as I am among them, so be it."

He laughed. "Now get comfortable. I will meet you in the dining room."

She tidied up in the bathroom, spritzing on some Evening in Paris, brushing her teeth, and with her hair—she did nothing. It marched to its own beat, as always. She was pushing it behind her ears when strains of the "Moonlight Sonata" floated upstairs.

Arne had returned to the kitchen when she got back down to the living room. She took off the Beethoven and put on Nat King Cole, then seated herself in the dining room glowing with lit candles.

She fingered the silverware at her place setting. “I could get used to this service,” she called out.

“What happened to the Beethoven?” he called back.

“I don’t need it.”

“You don’t need Beethoven?”

She smiled to herself as she raised her voice. “I have you.”

He brought out two plates with toast piled with tiny pink cooked shrimps. “I could not find good herring,” he said, sitting with her. “For my shopping tomorrow, I shall go further abroad to find a better store.”

“Tomorrow? I hate for you to have to spend all your time on housework. With everything under one roof at the supermarket, we Americans tend to do a week’s worth of shopping in one go.”

He lifted his glass. “*Skål.*”

She looked him in the eye. “*Skål.*”

She glued her gaze to his as they drank.

“You are a little frightening with your *skål*, *elskede*.”

They laughed. Her insides were warmed even before her first bite, and when she did take one: “Mm, Arne, this is really delicious. Thank you.”

“You are welcome.” He watched with pleasure as she ate, then he unfolded his napkin. “How do you have fresh food when you only shop once a week?”

“It wasn’t always this way here,” she said between bites. “I remember going to the grocer at the corner with my father, and then on to the butcher and the baker.”

“Did you never go with your mother? I was brought along by mine.”

“She sent me with Pop.”

They ate for a moment before he said, “You do not talk about your mother much.”

“Don’t I? She was always busy and hadn’t much time for me.” She paused with a forkful. “You know, I can honestly say that I’ve never had a real conversation with her.”

"Have you ever tried?"

He ate, watching her with a quizzical look in his sage-green eyes. She made a Danish gasp. "She was always too busy with the house, with my brother and sister, with working at the bar. It was always just Pop and me."

"Was that her choice, *elskede*?" He saw her expression, then reached across the table and took her hand. "I do not mean to tip the boat."

"Rock."

He frowned.

"The boat. And you are right. I never thought about how she felt about things. We all just went along with the arrangement. I thought that's how she wanted it." She saw her mother rolling out dough in the kitchen, washing glasses at the bar, putting patches on trouser knees—from the inside so that they wouldn't show—always shooing Pop and her out the door, freeing them to see the Ishi exhibit in the anthropology museum, to watch the trolley poles spark from the Carl Street streetcar, to throw stones into the pond in the Japanese Tea Garden. It had never occurred to her that Mutter would have liked to have come along.

"I mustn't trouble you now," Arne said. "You have enough worries on your dish."

"Plate."

He laughed at his mistake. "On your plate. Will I ever get it right?"

She took a breath, drawing in his grace. He was right. There weren't enough dishes, plates, or platters to hold all of her concerns at the moment. Polio season was coming.

33

Nurses were bustling about with paper pill cups and glass syringes on trays, their steps in syncopation with the draconian rhythm of the iron lungs. When Dorothy stopped to answer a question from one of the residents, an earnest young man from Indiana, she had to raise her voice above a new racket specific to the polio ward, that of the motor grinding beneath the rocking bed.

John Paul stepped forward when she was done. "Excellent lecture, Dottie," he said over the din. "I think you sold the residents on the benefits of the rocking bed." They gazed at the device upon which a prone patient rode as if on a mechanical seesaw. The bed worked on a simple principle: When the patient's head was up, gravity pulled the diaphragm downward and sucked air into the lungs. When the head was down, the air was forced out.

"Thanks. We've sorely needed an alternative to tank ventilators for our patients with less severe bulbar paralysis."

He nodded. "You were right to insist that we invest in the beds. I don't know why we did not jump on getting them sooner."

She knew why. A woman, Dr. Jessie Wright, had invented them, and much like Sister Kenny's method for rehabilitating polio patients, her idea was scorned until enough men embraced it. But Dorothy didn't feel like hashing this out now. She wanted to get home to Arne. Four days together had only fueled her need for him.

"We should order more of them before the polio season begins." John bobbed his head, trying to peer up into her eyes. "Say, you're certainly chipper today. Do we have a secret?" He grinned.

She wanted to tell him about Arne. But her happiness had been whisked away too often to risk it being jinxed. "I suppose I'm just glad for spring to be on its way."

"*Spring?*" He tugged at his bow tie and scowled. "Now I am suspicious. You are usually miserable in the spring, worrying, like the rest of us, about what fresh hell the next polio season will bring. This one promises to be monstrous. The Dottie I know would be tossing in her sleep at night."

"I have been sleepless." Which was perfectly true.

She had extricated herself from him with pleas of work to do and was in the office on the ward, writing up her notes so that she could leave, when Albert telephoned.

"Got the sample you sent. I would have rather had it hand-delivered," he grumbled, "but thanks."

"Glad to." Balancing the receiver between shoulder and chin, she added to a sentence in her notes.

"Say, who was that at your place the other night? The gentleman caller?" He'd made his tone uncharacteristically light.

When she didn't answer, he said, "You're right. It's not my business. But whoever this fellow is, he had better treat you well."

"I should let you go now, Albert, so that you can get home to your family."

He stayed on the line.

Out in the hall, a doctor was propositioning a nurse.

Albert said, "I called Salk today."

She wondered if she should intervene out there. Usually just the sight of her looming in her doorway like a Valkyrie in a Wagnerian opera was enough to shoo a creep away.

"I told him not to let O'Connor and those guys push him to make vats of his vaccine before he's ready. I was kidding. I expected him to reassure me that he would take the time to get it right, but instead, he tells me that nobody was pushing him except himself, and yes, by golly, he did have quite a lot of his stuff. He's got a technician named Elsie Ward who figured out how to grow poliovirus in tissue to make vaccine by the boatload."

She switched the receiver to her other ear. "Well, good for Jonas. What is the newest on your vaccine?" The hallway Casanova—Dorothy knew him, one of the hand surgeons—was being persistent. The nurse, a young mother of two boys, was trying to be nice but sounded scared.

"Good for Jonas?" Albert exclaimed. "He said he has another guy in his lab, Julius Youngner, who has developed a new titration test for antibodies. Evidently, if antibodies are present in blood serum, or even poliovirus in tissue, it causes a pH reaction. They're all set up now to rapidly see if their vaccine produces antibodies in their subjects."

"Say, I'd be interested in that test." It would cut down on the need for lab animals, if it worked. "Are they sharing it?"

"That's not the point. Dorothy, Salk's got a factory going there. Which means—"

"Just a minute." She put down the phone and then went to the door, where she positioned herself, Brünnhilde minus horns and braid, until the nurse got away.

"It's obvious that he's gearing up for a massive trial," Albert said when she returned.

"If he beats us out of the gate, at least we'd have a vaccine to use before yours is ready. Is that so bad?"

And was it so bad for her to feel proud that her discovery had opened the door for Jonas, and every other scientist in the race?

There was an angry pause. "I don't understand why you aren't helping me."

"I am helping you, Albert, in any way I can. Do you need any more strains for your vaccine? Do you want the results of the study on antibodies that I'm doing? I haven't written it up yet, but I can tell you—"

"Never mind. Have a good evening." He hung up on her for the second time that week.

THE BIG WOODEN CUBE WAS CROUCHING ON THE SIDE TAble when she got home. She unwrapped her headscarf and took off her cotton gloves as she stared at it.

"Arne?" she called.

"*Hej, elskede!*" he called back from the kitchen.

"Arne?" Its glass face shone in the light from the floor lamp. "What is this?"

He came out with a kitchen towel pinned around his waist. "A television."

"Yes, I know. But what's it doing here? Whose is it?"

"Ours!"

"Ours?"

He put his arm around her as they beheld the silent device. "When I was walking back from my interview today, I saw people gathered around a store window—men, women, children, all crowded around, laughing and exclaiming. I thought, was this a puppet show? Mummers? I did not know. I squeezed my way to the front. Inside the store window were rows of televisions, all of them playing the same program. *House Party*, someone told me. Then someone else said, 'Be quiet. "Kids Say the Darndest Things" is on.' Though who could hear it through the window?"

"I've never had a television."

"Me, neither. But when I saw all these people huddled close, I thought it was something that we could do together. When you are tired in the evenings. I see how tired that you get."

She kissed his cheek. "I do not deserve you."

They watched their first show that night. Giggling like children, they snuggled together on the couch and waited for the television set to warm up. A satin heart emblazoned with *I Love Lucy* in swirling script swelled into view.

It was a silly program, although Dorothy couldn't help but laugh. Lucy was desperate to get on her famous husband's nightclub show. She begged to join in when he was to perform in a barbershop quartet, but her husband, Ricky, wouldn't think of it. Banned from the show, Lucy sneaked into the act by pretending that she was the person being shaved by the quartet. Covered in hot towels, she tricked them all . . . until they unwrapped her face and she crowed.

Arne gasped as the others in the quartet, her friends Fred and Ethel, stoppered Lucy's mouth with shaving cream. "Why do they do that?"

"She wasn't supposed to be there."

"I know, but is that a reason to treat her like that? All she wanted was to be part of the show."

When the program was over, he said, "They are too cruel to Lucy."

She almost explained that it was slapstick humor, not to be taken seriously, when she thought, was it really funny to see Lucy roughly put in her place, which, as her husband implied, was at home awaiting the birth of their baby?

The telephone rang.

"People call at all hours here," Arne said.

"I'm afraid they do, in my line of work." She went to the hall and answered.

"Get on the radio!"

"Albert?"

"He's on. On CBS. They're billing the show as 'The Scientist Explains Himself.'"

"Who's on?"

"The damn boy wonder! Hurry!"

She turned on the radio in her kitchen and then listened, with Albert at the other end of the phone line.

When Salk's short address was done, she said, "Is he saying his vaccine is ready?"

"You can't tell, can you? He says he's got one, then no, he doesn't. Clear as mud. He called me this afternoon and read me his transcript, to ask me what I thought of it. He said he wanted to make a statement to get ahead of the headlines coming out of the AMA meeting announcing that he was going to have a vaccine ready for a nationwide trial soon. He's trying to tamp down the public's expectations, but all he's doing by talking about it is escalating them."

"A nationwide trial. Well, you suspected it was coming."

"I told him he would be crazy to go on the air with that statement. He'll have a stampede on his hands. And still he went ahead with it."

"My sense is that the March of Dimes people are putting pressure on him to deliver. They keep painting the picture that anybody who gives a dime to the cause is a stockholder in polio research, and as shareholders, they have a right to expect results."

"Yes, well, don't think Jonas doesn't love it."

She glanced out toward the living room. The television set was off. She saw Arne's corduroy-draped knees jutting out from the couch.

"Basil O'Connor isn't answering my calls," Albert said. "Evidently, he's answering Salk's."

"Let me talk with John, to see if he and the others can get through to Basil. He mustn't put all of his eggs in Jonas's basket."

"Thank you, Dot. I swear, you're my only friend."

"Oh, Albert, that's not true." Although she thought it likely that it was.

He kept her on the line to hear the latest about her own antibody study. She'd found some interesting subtleties that he would appreciate. She was stunned when she next looked at the kitchen clock and forty-five minutes had passed.

Arne was asleep in bed when she went upstairs. She wiped her face with cold cream, brushed her teeth, then slid under the covers next to him. She put her hand on his chest to feel his lungs rise and fall.

Please don't ever leave me. I need you so much.

34

DETROIT, MICHIGAN, 1953

The young physician conducted the tour of the Henry Ford Hospital's polio unit with the cheerfulness of a little boy playing doctor. He marched at the fore of the other docs in town for the polio vaccine roundtable, his crisp white lab coat and gung-ho spirit in stark contrast to the rumpled suits and acerbic skepticism of the visiting epidemiologists and virologists following behind him. From her tall-person's position at the back of the pack, Dorothy was sympathetic. She felt for those who had to try too hard.

"These are the latest word in ventilators." As if a salesman at a used car lot, the young doctor spread his arm toward the four rows, ten patients deep, of groaning and wheezing iron lungs out from which heads stuck. "We are the leading polio center in the region, offering the finest in poliomyelitis care."

Dorothy felt sick. She couldn't view this many polio patients as any kind of success. This October, the nation was just beginning to recover from one of the most deadly polio seasons of all time. Only last year was worse. Polio had left over thirty-five thousand children paralyzed. Nearly fifteen hundred American children who had been roller skating on the street, riding their bikes, or playing Monopoly were dead. It was just as bad in nearly every corner of the globe. Every scientist in this crowd was bitter. Polio had won again.

Next to her, John Paul saw her expression and grimaced. "The place is rather a factory, isn't it?" he whispered. "Makes one feel a bit bleak."

Her old pal Robbie Ward, working at another university now, leaned back toward them. "What do you expect? It's Detroit, home of the assembly line."

Their guide, overhearing, looked flustered.

"Be kind," Dorothy told her friends.

The group paraded between whooshing rows of machines. The young doc stopped to explain the features of the new devices.

Dr. Paul dawdled, falling behind the crowd with Dorothy. "You know that Henry Ford came to regret the success of his factories. He lamented the demise of the family farm, which his assembly lines and mass-produced cars knocked out in a one-two punch. When one of his factories threatened to overtake his childhood farm, he moved the old homestead and created a fairy-tale village around it."

"Greenfield Village," said Robbie, "where the bad old days are good."

Dorothy kept her voice down. "Who doesn't want to revise their past?"

John pulled in his chin. "Who does?"

The tour guide waved for them to catch up. "Gather 'round! Gather 'round! I want to show you our latest: rocking beds."

Dorothy's attention strayed to a little girl in a wheelchair. With her physician's eye, she noted that the muscles of both the child's legs had atrophied from the hips down and were thus likely to remain permanently paralyzed, though the child was using her upper body well as she played a board game with an occupant of an iron lung. Her opponent wasn't a child, Dorothy was surprised to see, but a grown woman, and a remarkably well-groomed one at that.

With her triple strands of pearls pooling against the rubber collar of her machine, her red lipstick, and her carefully curled poodle bob stuck with a pink velvet bow, she seemed to have been encapsulated while on her way to a cocktail party.

In the mirror mounted over her head, the woman caught sight of Dorothy watching her. "Don't worry! You can be next. I won't be long. Paula here has almost whipped me, and then she can whip you."

Dorothy went over to them. "What is this game?" she asked the child.

The girl ducked her head with shyness. "Candy Land."

"I've challenged every child in this ward and have yet to find one that I can beat. I'm rather a flop," the woman said cheerfully.

"My turn next," said the boy in the machine next to her.

The woman made an exaggerated eyeroll. "They *all* want to beat me."

The little girl chuckled. "Mrs. Konkle's own kids beat her when they come on Visiting Day." She wheeled up to the nightstand next to the woman, to point at the photos there. "That's Linette, Mary, Denise, Davey, Mikey, and Karen. Karen is only four and she whips her mommy all the time."

The woman pulled a face. "My own children. It's an outrage."

The little girl rolled back to the game board, picked up a color card, then moved her marker. When she landed on a spot that required her to go backward and lose her lead, her well-groomed opponent sang, "Do-over! You didn't pick up the card on top."

When the next card that was drawn advanced the child, Mrs. Konkle blinked in feigned annoyance. "You'd think that this game would be less cruel, created as it was by a fellow polio patient." She looked at Dorothy in her mirror. "I had my husband buy it when I heard that it was dreamed up by a Californian schoolteacher while she was in the hospital with polio. Little did I know this cruel game would become the bane of my existence."

The child drew a card for Mrs. Konkle, then moved her piece

on the board. "'Go to Candy Hearts!' That's at the beginning." She chortled as her opponent bugged her eyes in mock exasperation.

A nurse came over. "Losing again, eh?" To Dorothy, she said, "What do you think of Mrs. Konkle's hair? I did it today."

Mrs. Konkle fluttered her lashes. "You like? *I* think it's smashing, Esther. I've challenged the nurses to a competition," she told Dorothy. "Fanciest Hairdo." She pointed with her eyes down her row.

Dorothy peered down the line of tanks. Indeed, the hairdos of the young adults, the teenaged girls, and even the adolescents and little ones were as stylish as those of ladies just out from under hair dryers in a beauty salon. She realized that the bow in the fluffy hair of little Paula matched Mrs. Konkle's.

"My friend Paula here looks like Natalie Wood, don't you think?" said Mrs. Konkle. "When Natalie was in *Miracle on 34th Street*."

John Paul came over and touched Dorothy's elbow. "Dr. Horstmann, we're moving on."

"I hope you win a game soon, Mrs. Konkle," Dorothy said.

"It's JoAnne. And I won't," she sang. "Not with these little sharks around."

AFTER THE FIRST ROUND OF THE CONFERENCE MEETINGS starring an incandescent Jonas Salk, Dorothy had just enough time to go back to her room to freshen up. She was checking her hair in the bathroom mirror (hopeless, of course) when a knock came on her door. She and John Paul had agreed to meet in the hotel lobby in fifteen minutes, to walk across the street for lunch. Had there been a change in plans? She grabbed her hat.

When she opened the door, Albert held out a vase of pink carnations—the same one she'd noticed on the lobby desk when checking into the hotel that morning.

She took the vase. "When'd you get here?"

"Just now. Had a hard time leaving work. Do you know what today is?"

She plunked the stolen bouquet on the bureau by the door to pin on her hat. "October eighth."

"Yes. And—?"

"I don't know. It's your birthday?"

"No. That would be August twenty-sixth. Your present is late but there's still time."

"Did I get this on straight?" She turned her head left and right to show off her pillbox hat.

"Good enough. You really don't know what day it is?"

"Let me get my purse. No," she called behind her. She went over to her bed. It wasn't there.

He let himself into the room. "It's Nobel Prize Announcement Day!"

"How do you even know that?" she said, searching for her purse.

"How do you even *not* know that?" He looked around. "Where's all your luggage? My wife would need a trunk and a train case for a three-day conference, and maybe a hatbox or two."

He was by the bed when she'd retrieved her purse. Brushing off a twinge of awkwardness, she went over and stood by the door. "Traveling with the Polio Unit has broken me of any vanity. I keep a travel bag packed with the same two shirtdresses whether I'm going to India or Indianapolis."

They glanced at the unmade bed. She thought of Arne—for the first time that morning, she realized with a start.

"I told John that I'd meet him in the lobby," she said.

Albert remained by the bed. She went over and took him by the arm, but he pulled away from her and sat down.

She crossed her arms as she stood above him. "Albert, I haven't told you. I have a—"

He looked up. "I know you have a man. Why do you keep him hidden?"

She went red.

He sighed. "That's not what this is about." He put his head in his hands.

When he didn't move, she nudged his knee. "What is it?"

"Help me."

"Help you how?" she said gently.

"I can feel the tide turning against me. I'm not only going to lose the race, but I'm never going to have a polio vaccine."

"Then try harder. Come on." She offered a hand up.

OUT IN THE HALL, WAITING FOR THE ELEVATOR IN SILENCE, they watched the numbers above the door mark the car's slow progress to their floor. Albert really was blue. She tried to strike a light tone. "Have you seen anyone from the conference yet?"

He took a deep breath. "If you mean the boy wonder, yes, in the lobby, just now. Reporters were swarming him like ants on a Popsicle stick."

"I hope you knew enough to walk the other way."

He raised a corner of his mouth. "I knew enough to come get reinforcements."

Since the summer, the newspapers had been full of reports pitting the querulous Dr. Sabin against the earnest young Dr. Salk. The closer Jonas came to his nationwide trial, the more critical Albert became. On the train to Detroit, Dorothy had overheard a March of Dimes publicist tell a reporter that she would not defend Dr. Salk against Dr. Sabin's claims that his rival's vaccine was not ready. Nor would she take Dr. Salk's side and try to make Dr. Sabin look bad. She didn't need to. Albert Sabin was doing that all by himself.

"Maybe we should unite behind Jonas for the time being," she said. "He's giving the public what they want."

He blew out a breath. "What the public wants! If a kid wants to drink battery acid, would you let him?"

"That's a terrible analogy, Albert. His vaccine isn't bad for them, nor dangerous."

"It could be. If it's sloppily prepared."

"Just concentrate on preparing your own vaccine."

"I can't! He's got all the funding!"

The elevator stopped with a *ding*. The door shuffled open to Dr. Paul, complete with bow tie and briefcase, standing next to the operator. He glanced between Dorothy and Albert. "I see you found our girl."

Albert forced a smile. "Do you know what day it is?"

"No," said John. "And don't make me guess."

Albert held up his hands in mock surrender. "I won't! It's Nobel Prize Announcement Day."

"Oh. Well, then this is a good day!"

"Does the committee know how to reach Dorothy here?" Albert asked.

"You two!" she protested. "You're going to jinx me."

"You're going to win." Albert shrugged. "It only makes sense. Who else in medicine deserves it this year? Well, except maybe Bodian."

"She shouldn't share," John said. "Dorothy had proof of her theory months before he did—in November. But he caught up when she insisted on double-checking her results."

Dorothy stared at the back of the elevator operator's round red hat. She double-checked because Dr. Paul and the others had refuted her theory once and she was not going to let that happen again.

Never mind. All was forgiven. A Nobel, shared or otherwise, would take the sting out of any past injustices.

"Your discovery broke the back of polio," Albert said, patting her arm. "It's the most important medical finding of the century. I wish I'd made it."

"Enders's group figuring out how to grow the virus in a test tube is nothing to sneeze at," she said. Indeed, Enders's recent finding was a godsend. No longer needing to grow the virus in animal tissue saved thousands of monkeys' lives.

"Oh, Enders," Albert scoffed. "He was bound to discover *something*, as loaded as he is. He can afford to throw his own money at a problem until something sticks. Why is it that the guys who don't need all the funding get it?"

Albert wore his resentment of the wealthy on his sleeve—and to think she'd thought Albert was one of them. How blind we can be even when the truth is waving a flag at us.

The elevator deposited them in the lobby, where reporters had formed a tight circle around Jonas Salk. He appeared to be alternately rubbing his chin while frowning like a sage of yore and giggling as he made statements to the press.

"We should go over and talk to him," she said.

"Really?" said Albert.

"Yes."

"She's right," said John. "Swallow your pride, Albert. It's good for our cause. We are all in this together."

As they neared, a reporter asked, "Dr. Salk, what do you think about Russia having the hydrogen bomb?"

"As if he knows anything about that!" Albert muttered.

Dorothy winged him when some newsmen turned.

Jonas peered above the reporters to see who they were looking at. "I think if the Russian leaders want their people to love them, they'll forget the bomb and help us work on polio. They're having just as big a problem with the disease over there as we are here—Hello, Dr. Sabin, Dottie."

"Dr. Sabin!" The reporters' circle quickly morphed to include Albert in its nucleus and, because they were standing close to him, her and Dr. Paul.

Someone asked, "What do you say to Dr. Salk's announcement

that the March of Dimes was funding a nationwide trial of his vaccine starting in—" The reporter looked down at his notes.

"February." Jonas flashed his teeth.

"February?" Albert's face grew long, as if the reality of his rival's victory were pulling it down.

"Anything you want to say about it, Dr. Sabin?" The reporter glanced almost gleefully at a colleague.

Dorothy laid her hand on Albert's sleeve. He spoke anyway. "My only hope is that before the trial, Dr. Salk will reformulate his vaccine without the Mahoney strain—"

Jonas grinned. "I'm not worried about it. My inactivation process successfully kills it."

"—as," Albert continued coldly, "the Mahoney strain is the most virulent that we know of, paralyzing far more of its victims than any other, and if it's not rendered completely inactive—"

"But it will be!" Jonas stopped smiling. "My process is foolproof. Do you think I would endanger children with something that wasn't one hundred percent safe?"

"Inactivating it might be foolproof in your lab, Dr. Salk, but are you going to personally make every batch? You might be careful to kill all the strains that go into your recipe, but what if some laboratory contracted to make your stuff is not as meticulous as you are?"

"They will be!"

"Can you guarantee that?"

Jonas glanced at the reporters. "Yes. And do you have something better to offer? Because polio isn't waiting for you to reinvent the wheel. My vaccine is ready. Is yours?"

Albert's expression chilled into one of pure disdain. "Look, Jonas, I'm no fan of your killed-virus vaccine. Everyone here knows that. One, it doesn't give full protection—what is it, fifty-five, sixty percent effective? Two, it needs boosters, lots of them. Three, it doesn't help heighten immunity in the whole community, like my vaccine would. And four, syringes are required to administer it. A lot of places around the world don't have access to syringes—we will never be able to eradicate polio worldwide with your vaccine. But I could accept it as a stopgap measure, Jonas, if you would *just get rid of the damn Mahoney strain in it.*"

A willowy woman in a mint-colored twinset stepped from behind a sofa. "How dare you!" Her chin disappeared into her neck when she pulled it back in indignation. "Are you trying to discourage Dr. Salk? We might never have an epidemic again if you would just let him do his work. Imagine—a summer without polio!" she told the reporters. "Thanks to this man, that is now a possibility."

Jonas blushed. "All right, Lorraine, that's enough."

"Who's she?" a reporter asked.

"My secretary."

Everyone laughed.

Albert nudged Dorothy forward by the elbow. "If you fellows want a real scoop today, meet Dorothy Horstmann. She's about to be awarded the Nobel Prize."

The pressmen turned to her.

Dorothy could feel her cheeks burn. "There was a rumor that I was nominated. I haven't won it."

"*Yet*," said Albert. "They announce it today."

"What are you getting the prize for?" someone asked.

"Are you a doctor?"

"How tall are you?"

Dr. Paul put his hand up on her shoulder. "Dr. Horstmann has mapped out where we are to fight polio in the body. Some are calling what she has envisioned 'the Battle of the Blood.' Neither of these gentlemen would be as advanced in the development of their vaccines without Dr. Horstmann." He patted her. "We at Yale are proud of her."

"You her dad?" someone asked.

John winced.

“That’s Dr. John Paul,” said Jonas. “The Father of Epidemiology.”

“Huh. Then you are the father of something.”

Everyone laughed; John, uncomfortably.

Albert gently ushered him toward the edge of the circle. “Come on, Dad. The meetings are starting.”

He then reached back and grabbed Dorothy’s hand and didn’t let go of her until they were out the lobby door.

35

That evening, as the waiters brought in flaming platters of Cherries Jubilee, Dorothy realized with a start that she hadn't talked to Arne now for two full days. A cloud lowered over her excitement about a possible Nobel Prize as she thought of how little she'd seen him since April—the warm months were to a virologist specializing in polio what tax season was to an accountant. At least now that it was October, once she got home, she might begin to make up for lost time. She'd no longer constantly be on the road chasing outbreaks. Yes, her class load would increase, and yes, lots of conferences were coming up, and yes, she had statistics to compile on her most recent studies but— Oh, who was she kidding? There was never enough time. Arne could never count on her being around. He could never count on her, period.

Next to her, John cried, "Put it out!"

Their waiter lowered a domed lid over the blazing mound of cherries.

"I've seen too many burn patients in my time to enjoy flaming desserts," he told Dorothy as the waiter began to serve the confection. He tipped his head. "You're quiet."

"Am I?"

On her other side, Albert lit a cigarette. "I know what's on her mind." He pocketed his lighter. "And it's not the Nobel Prize."

"Then you are a better man than I am," said Dr. Paul. "I find our Dorothy to be inscrutable." He raised his cornflower-blue eyes to her. "Sometimes, dear, you worry me."

"Thank you, John," she said quietly. "I'm fine."

Albert pushed away from the table.

Dr. Paul tugged at his bow tie as he watched him leave. When Albert was gone, he said, "I guess I feel guilty that I let Dave Bodian catch up to you. I suppose you'll have to share your prize."

"That's okay."

"You should know," he said earnestly, "that I have put in for a full professorship for you. They won't be able to say no to a Nobel Prize winner."

Alfred had not returned by the time that the dessert plates were collected. She went back to the hotel with Dr. Paul, where she locked herself in her room, then dropped onto the bed.

The phone jangled, jilting her from her skin. She took a deep breath, then braced herself. This could be the phone call of her life.

"Hello?"

"*Elskede*, how are you this evening?"

She patted her throat. "Arne!"

"You sound so surprised. Have I been that inattentive?"

"Oh, Arne, no. You are an angel."

They exchanged reports on what they had seen that day, he on his new job as a translator for a Danish professor in the physics department at the university, she about the conflict between Drs. Sabin and Salk. Nerves wouldn't allow her to bring up the Nobel. He didn't know that today was announcement day.

They were wrapping up the call early (due to her exhaustion, she told herself, and not just because she didn't want to tie up the phone line), when a rapping sounded on the door.

Her heart flopped. She pictured a bellhop with a telegram.

"Arne, hold on a moment. Someone's at the door." Her pulse pounding in her ears, she laid the phone on the nightstand to go answer.

She swung the door open.

Albert put out his cigarette in the ashtray in the hall. "Can I come in?" His face was serious. Was he pulling a prank?

He sighed and walked past her.

"Now you're scaring me."

He turned around. "The Nobel was divided between two scientists this year."

"Bodian, too? That's great!"

He grimaced. "It was for the discovery of the citric acid cycle and the discovery of coenzyme A and its importance for intermediary metabolism."

"What?"

"Exactly. Two guys won, Krebs and Lipmann."

She stared at him.

"It wasn't you, Dorothy."

She eased herself down on the end of her bed.

He sat down next to her. "Who cares about citric acid! Have the judges never met a child battling polio for his life? You actually did something crucial to beat it."

"It's okay, Albert."

"It is not okay."

"Forget about it. Thanks for telling me."

He put his arm around her.

"I really don't care."

He pulled her under his shoulder. "It's all right to care, Dorothy. You were brilliant. They should have recognized you."

"It's stupid to care."

"You caring—about everything—is why I love you."

She glanced at him.

"I do love you, you know." He kissed her forehead, then kept his arm around her shoulders as the terrible news sank in.

A bolt went through her. She lunged for the receiver on the nightstand. "Arne. Are you still there?"

His voice was rigid. "Yes."

She waved Albert out of the room, then waited until he was gone. "Arne, Albert came to tell me about the Nobel Prize. I didn't win."

Tension radiated through the phone line. "I am sorry. Truly. I know how that must have hurt you."

What had he heard?

"It's not like it sounded. I'm sorry I kept you waiting."

He did not speak.

"Arne? Are you there?"

"We Danish may not be as demanding of our women. We do not require that our wives stay at home, raise the children, and cater to us husbands, as do Americans, if Americans are as they are depicted on the television. I do not want to imprison you in my house. But, *elskede*, I did hope you would love me best."

"But I do!"

"Do you?"

"There's nothing between Albert and me."

There was a sharp inhalation. "Did you think that I meant Albert?"

She was silent.

"*Elskede*. I meant your work."

WHEN SHE HUNG UP, HER GAZE SLID ACROSS THE ROOM to the vase of carnations that Albert had stolen from the front desk.

I did hope you would love me best.

She jumped up, then grabbed her hat and went to the elevator. In the lobby, two virologists from Ann Arbor were at a far table, arguing and scribbling on cocktail napkins, two bucks establishing their rank. She shook her head and stalked outside. Before her, the Henry Ford Hospital shone like a burning fortress in the night.

Inside its glistening halls smelling of disinfectant, she found herself searching for the newborn nursery.

SHE LOOKED THROUGH THE GLASS AT THE ROW OF COTTON-wrapped cocoons basking under lights blazing at all hours of the day. Normally, her heart was lifted by the sight of the babies' plump cheeks and eyes sealed as tight as newborn rabbits', or by the remembered feel of their bottoms, solid as five-pound sacks of sugar, resting in the crook of her arm. But not tonight. Tonight, they were a reminder of the dreams she'd failed to reach.

She'd turned forty-two in July. Her window for having a child was barely cracked open and closing fast. If she had a prayer of becoming a mother, she would have to buckle down with Arne now and get serious. Maybe even quit work. Why was she clinging to it anyhow? She, her accomplishments, would never be fairly recognized. She should be thankful to the Nobel Prize Committee for clarifying that.

If she were smart, she would do everything in her power to get pregnant and get dolled up in some big-bowed maternity top like Lucy Ricardo and become one of those American Madonnas worshipped in magazines and on television, before it was too late.

Dorothy left the row of sleeping chrysalises and rode the elevator, unmanned at that hour and empty save for a baggy-eyed orderly. When it stopped at a floor for her companion to make his exit, Dorothy could hear the groan and the wheeze of the iron lungs in the polio ward, even from the elevator car. She found herself getting off.

A washerwoman sat back on her heels as Dorothy picked across the wet tile of the hall, apologizing all the way. When she got to the front desk, she identified herself to the lone nurse, who then bent into the light of the single lamp to read her medical license.

Inside the glassed-in ward, the iron lungs clanged and wheezed in the near darkness like asthmatic prisoners rattling their chains in a dungeon. Through the window, she could see the patients sleeping, a skeleton crew of nurses floating in the dim between them. It struck Dorothy how the patients resembled the newborns she had just visited, helplessly cocooned, but within metal, not soft wrappings, with only their faces exposed. But while the newborns knew nothing other than their dependent state, the polio patients understood well the life that they were missing.

Anger flamed up. All she ever wanted was to stop this monster. And she nearly had—she'd found the beast in its lair. Whether the Nobel Committee cared or not, she had tracked it down and was ready to thrust a sword into its foul belly, but she couldn't do it alone. Alone, she was just a lady in a lab.

She looked up at her reflection in the window. *You could do it with Albert.*

The March of Dimes had all but shut the door on him. Didn't they see how rabid he was to kill the beast? He didn't just want to tamp down outbreaks like Jonah; he wanted polio *gone.* Wiped off the earth! Annihilated! He was as insane about it as she was. She loved him for that.

You could go to his room now. Who better understands your hopes, your work, your pain? Who better knew how badly she'd been crushed?

He'd let you in. You know he would.

A high-pitched whine jolted her. An alarm. Was one of the ventilators failing?

Inside the ward, the nurses were gathering around one of the machines. She went in to help.

She stayed until the situation was in hand. She was almost out of the ward when she detected a kind of chortling. Was someone laughing?

She followed the sound down a row of the clanging tanks, so intent upon it that she knocked into a small table. Righting it, she heard a soft click: a plastic marker falling onto a Candy Land board.

She edged to the closest ventilator, where the glow of a nightlight revealed the glitter of tears flowing down Mrs. Konkle's temple and into her bouffant hair. Even if she had been able to hear Dorothy over the manmade breathing of her machine, she couldn't have moved her head to see her.

Dorothy could leave now. Albert would receive her. He knew the anguish of being scorned by the scientific community. She'd find some kind of relief to the howling inside. Mrs. Konkle would never know. Nor would Arne.

PAT WAS THE FIRST NURSE TO ARRIVE THAT MORNING TO relieve the night shift. Her eyes smarted from a lack of sleep. She'd been up most of the evening, calming her three-year-old. She knew she should have hidden that new *Life* magazine with its cover depicting a saber-toothed tiger, a gigantic wolf, and a mastodon fighting it out, literally tooth and nail. "The Age of Mammals," indeed. A picture like that was just asking for nightmares. The child was terrified of creatures from the past.

Rubbing her left eye, Pat turned on the lights. She checked the seams on her white hose—straight enough, considering she'd walked a mile and a half to get there—then commenced her stroll along the three ventilators she was responsible for, to make sure that they were all working. Though the night shift was supposed to keep an eye on things, she was always terrified by the possibility of finding a malfunctioning machine that had gone undetected, even though these models were armed with alarms. That had happened to her when she was a student nurse, and she'd never gotten over it. Dying by self-suffocation seemed a terrible way to go.

Her heart in her throat, she was walking between the tanks, checking first this gauge, then that, when she saw her.

The woman was truly an Amazon in proportion—the tent created by her knees jutted out far beyond her chair. She had her cheek against Mrs. Konkle's tank and her arm inside the porthole, as if to hold hands. Both she and the patient were sound asleep.

THE NEXT EVENING, DOROTHY DROPPED HER BAGS INSIDE the kitchen. She glanced at the mail neatly stacked on the counter, on which her mixer, the canisters, and a new potted philodendron were arranged in a more orderly fashion than she'd ever kept them when she'd lived alone. She strode through to the living room, where Arne sat in the blue glow of the television.

He pushed off of the sofa. "*Elskede.*"

"Oh, Arne." She buried her face against his chest. The tears of disappointment that she had been holding in for the past twenty hours boiled into her eyes.

He stroked her hair and let her cry.

Her gaze went to the television, tuned, she saw, to *I Love Lucy*. On the show, Lucy and Ethel were petulantly demanding equal rights as men, drawing benevolent hoots from Ricky and Fred.

Dorothy's tears came harder. She had reduced Arne to watching *this*?

Her gaze drifted to the stairs. Arne's leather cases sat at the base of them, his overcoat folded neatly on top.

It was as if a styptic pencil had been applied to her eyes. Her tears, everything, dried.

She pulled away from him. "Arne? Are you leaving?"

"You must tell me, *elskede*—am I?"

She saw now that the light had gone out of his eyes. "Arne! I don't want you to go!"

His silence frightened her even more.

On the television, Lucy and Ricky were quarreling in a restaurant.

"Is it because I can't give you a baby?"

"A baby? No. Of course not." He shook his head slowly. "All I ever wanted was you."

She started to protest, then stopped. As much as she was gone, she had not even given him that.

He pushed her hair from her forehead. "If what we have now is satisfactory to you, I am willing to take it. It would be temporary, yes? Until you find the cure."

"There is no cure for polio, only prevention."

It was true—there was no curing polio, no softening its effects on its victims. There were only people like her, willing to stand at the bulwark against it. But once they snuffed it—and they would, so help her God, they would—would her work be over? As long as there were diseases that attacked little children, would she ever be done?

He heaved his chest, its warmth radiating through his sweater. "I knew who you were when I fell in love with you, *elskede*. That is why I fell for you. You care so much for other people."

"That's you, Arne. That's why I love you."

A terrible truth was unfurling. She'd never been so frightened in her life.

"Do you love Albert?" he asked gently.

"No!"

"Because he is married?"

"No. Because he's not you."

He wrapped his arms around her. "Shhh. Shh, *elskede*. Please do not cry."

Her heart, that muscular flower, began to fold in its petals. Because she loved him, she could not keep him.

"Dorte, please, it doesn't have to be this way."

But even he knew that it had to be.

She laid her cheek against his chest and, breathing in his scent to hold it forever, listened to his heart for the very last time.

1954–1956

A SECRETARY

1954

Lorraine Friedman cranked open the passenger-side vent window of the Chevy, directing a blast of humid heat upon herself, not that it did much good. When she resumed her perusal of the *Time* magazine, sweat continued to soak into her dress shields, but that's what they were there for, weren't they? To absorb the mess?

She stopped at a full-page Hart Schaffner & Marx advertisement. In it, a handsome dark-haired gentleman—who actually bore a great deal of resemblance to Jonas, if you filled in the gaps in his hairline and took off his glasses and changed his mouth, jaw, and ears—posed, frowning manfully while talking on the phone. She studied the model fellow's cool masculine side-glance, the confident tilt of his chin, his casual lean against the desk with his snowy cuffs shot just so. These advertisers knew what they were up to when presenting their product. Learn from the experts, she always said.

"This is a nice suit." She turned the ad toward Jonas. He glanced at it, grunted, then kept driving.

Well, it wasn't his job to worry about his image, was it? It was hers. Certainly, it was not his wife's. And why should it be? Donna had those three boys, little stairsteps, quite the handful. Lorraine could not blame her for his neglect. She was happy to fill in where Donna left off.

She knew Jonas Salk was going places from the moment they'd met, when she was twenty-five and he was not much older than that. It had been in his office in the hospital, if you wanted to call that little storage closet an office. He didn't even have a desk. They'd sat on two mismatched office chairs, a metal file cabinet between them, he in his lab coat with *Jonas Salk, MD* embroidered in blue, she in her straight skirt and sweater set and the pearls in which she had invested a good chunk of her WAVE earnings. Although she had a college degree, the first in her family, and had been in a typing pool during the war, she had no civilian work experience. All she had, as she had stated in the newspaper employment-wanted ad that he'd responded to, was her willingness to "work long, hard hours."

That description had got him. She saw why soon enough. All he did was work. Long, hard hours. He got by on little sleep and expected her to do the same.

He'd sat on his beat-up armchair that day, drumming the metal file cabinet with his jiggling foot. "Excuse the environs. I'm just getting started here. I've petitioned the dean for laboratory space—I found a conference room that was originally intended as a lab on the hospital blueprints. The hookups are already in the walls. It's perfect."

He'd gone to the length of combing the hospital blueprints to find himself a lab? But if the dean intended for him to have his own lab, wouldn't he have already given it to him?

"I also found a storage room on the second floor that could easily be converted to a place to house my lab animals, and a space by my laboratory that could be converted to my offices. Things will look different here soon, wait and see."

Then he had grinned that big grin, which was a disconcerting mix of shyness and naked ambition. It was the patented Jonas Salk smile, the one that made you do things that you didn't want to do before you realized you were doing them. Lorraine later heard Donna say that she'd had no intention of marrying him when they'd met, that there was *absolutely nothing* about him that had first appealed to her (she'd said with unnecessary harshness, Lorraine had thought). But Donna had been mowed down by the twin scythes of Jonas's sweetness and lethal determination. Everyone was, eventually.

Now Lorraine flipped through the *Time*. "Whichever suit we get you, Dr. Salk, it needs to be made of Dacron. I've seen three ads for it in here. It's a new material that's better than wool." She eyed an illustration of a dapper man trotting through a downpour. "Apparently, you can get soaked dashing between meetings and still appear fresh. Water sheds right off."

He kept driving.

Well, he did have *just a little bit* on his mind. After the success two years ago at the limited trial on the mentally incapacitated kids at the Polk State Home, he'd gotten the money to conduct one at the D.T. Watson Home for Crippled Children. Most of last year, he, personally, gave every shot and took every specimen, while she recorded *everything*. Without her keeping track of which vaccine he was giving to whom and whose blood they were testing for antibodies to polio, his work would have been for naught. The March of Dimes had given him a lot of money for that trial—a record-breaking amount. Lorraine wasn't even allowed to tell anyone how much—$255,472—and her records were the key. The lives of thousands of kids depended on them, and Jonas's future, too.

It worked. When Mr. O'Connor saw how successful that trial was, he'd heaped all of the March of Dimes's riches on Jonas. Jonas was given over a *million dollars* to set up a trial on schoolkids all across the nation.

It was going on now. The biggest drug trial *ever*! Parents had *begged* to sign their kids up. More than a million first, second, and third graders took part: 422,000 as actual vaccine recipients, 201,000 as placebo recipients, and 725,000 as control subjects. "Polio Pioneers," Jonas called them. They got their shots in April. Now, with polio season raging, all she and Jonas could do was wait.

Dabbing her neck with her handkerchief, she went back to the Hart Schaffner & Marx ad. "I don't care what you say, Dr. Salk, you look like this man." She held up the picture.

That got his attention. After another grunt—did she detect pleasure?—he said, "Which magazine is that?"

She showed him the cover with the baseball player on it.

His eyes flashed behind lenses pearly with magnification. "Where'd you get that?"

Well, he didn't have to snap! "It's an old one, from fifty-two. I got it from the waiting room at the hospital."

"Sorry, Lorraine. Guess I'm just tired. What I was getting at is that's the one with Bodian and Dorothy in it."

"Dorothy? Horstmann?"

"Look in the Medicine section."

He would remember a magazine from two years ago! His memory astonished her. She pushed the pages with her fingertip until she found it. The headline read, "The Battle in the Blood."

The picture of David Bodian from Johns Hopkins and that nice Dorothy Horstmann took up a good sixth of the page. In it, Dorothy looked to be taking dictation from Bodian. Actually, this would make a good setup for Jonas and her in an article. She could see the caption now: *Jonas Salk shares his findings with his secretary, Lorraine Friedman.*

He patted his shirt pocket, retrieved a pack of Lucky Strikes, knocked it against the steering wheel, then pulled out a cigarette with his mouth. "Too bad I was so busy," he said, his unlit cigarette bouncing in his lips. "I would have liked to have been at that meeting."

She put down the magazine and dug in her purse. He hadn't been at that meeting because he wasn't invited. It didn't make sense to her. Why did all the big scientists treat him as an inferior? Albert Sabin was the worst! Jonas had never gotten over the time when Sabin had shamed him in front of all their peers for asking a perfectly reasonable question. Sabin'd had the nerve to sneer, "You know better than to ask a question like that," like Jonas was an intern or a child. Unforgivable.

Well, let's just hear what tune old Albert Sabin sang once he saw the results of this trial! He was going to be sorry that he'd treated Jonas Salk with such disrespect.

She struck a match and held it to his cigarette. "Do you think Sabin and Dorothy Horstmann are having an affair?

He sucked in as his cigarette caught fire. "Nah."

"They share the same interests. That can be a powerful aphrodisiac."

He blew out smoke. "Have you seen her? She's a giant. No guy wants a girl who's taller than he is."

Lorraine swallowed. She was taller than Jonas by two and a half inches.

Well, that was not what she wanted from him, was it?

Her gaze trailed to the advertisement next to the article. Evidently, Viceroy cigarettes were better for your health. It said here that none of the nicotine and tars trapped by the filter got to your lungs. She would have to buy a pack for Jonas to try. She cared about his health, even if Donna didn't.

They were almost back to the lab. She drew in a breath. The first order of business now was to get him a new suit. Not just *Time* and other magazines and the newspapers would be clamoring for him as his trial went on, but radio and all three television networks, too. He couldn't just show up on Edward Murrow's program in a baggy old suit. She had to figure out a way to get him into Gimbels, stat. Because once the world saw that Jonas Salk's vaccine worked, all Hades was going to break loose, and she, Lorraine Friedman, would have him ready. Together, they were going to kick that SOB polio in the rear. Let Donna take care of those children.

36

NEW HAVEN, CONNECTICUT, 1955

Dorothy and the Yale boys had been huddled around the TV that Mrs. Beasley had lugged in, waiting for the announcement, but Tommy Francis hadn't even started his report, which, knowing Tommy's thoroughness, would be interminable. God knew how many more hours until Jonas announced the results of his trial to the nation. *Had* his vaccine proved to be safe and effective when given to hundreds of thousands of children? Could there be *at last* a weapon to slay the monster? Dorothy hadn't been able to take it a second longer. "Anyone need anything from the store?" she'd cried. "Coffee," Mrs. Beasley had said. Which was how Dorothy came to be at the supermarket a few blocks away, in line to check out with a can of Folgers, when the automatic entrance door wheezed open.

A woman ran in, her patent-leather purse whaling against her hip. "It's on all the TVs in Steinberg's window! Dr. Salk made his announcement! That vaccine all those kids got in school, those little Polio Pioneers—it works! Dr. Salk's shot works!"

The woman hadn't finished her proclamation when outside, cars started honking and church bells bonged. Through the plate-glass window, Dorothy could see people pouring into the street. It was V-J Day all over again.

Inside the Kroger, mothers clapped and exclaimed or broke into tears, their little ones looking up at them in wonder, their boxes of animal crackers dangling from their strings. Behind the meat counter, the cheeks of the butcher wettened as he dug into a red pile of ground beef—his son, a high school basketball star, was now in a wheelchair. It had come too late for him.

Everyone wanted to go home at once. The checkout line snaked into the cereal aisle, but people were extra polite, cheerful, even tender to one another, much like they'd been, Dorothy thought, in the days following the attack on Pearl Harbor—the behavior of fellow survivors. No one actually had protection against polio yet, unless they were one of the schoolchildren who'd participated in Salk's nationwide trial last summer, but just knowing that everyone would have it soon lifted the collective weight they'd tried so hard to ignore. In their entire lifetimes, many Americans had never known a summer without wondering: Which child was polio getting next?

The neighborhood was loud with the honking of horns and people sharing the good news out on the street as Dorothy loped through, cradling her can of coffee and grinning. When she got back to work, she delivered her prize to Mrs. Beasley, who jumped up from dabbing her eyes to embrace her, then she danced on into the inner office where Joe Melnick, Robbie (there from Baylor), and the others were where she'd left them—now with smelly cigars.

Joe blew out a blue cloud of smoke. "Dorothy!" He hugged her, then stepped back to let her receive the others like a bride in a very smoky reception line.

"Well, Dorothy," he said as the others were patting her back, "looks like you won."

"Me?"

The others laughed at her befuddlement.

"It was your discovery that opened the door."

"Wait, we all had a hand in this! This is all of our victory."

"Thanks!" Robbie puffed at his own cigar. "I'll buy that. We all have worked our tails off trying to nail down polio. I've only slept in my own bed eight times this month—Dottie, I know it has been even worse for you. Yeah, it's all of our victory, but tell that to our buddy Sabin." He grabbed his empty coffee mug and yelled toward the outer office. "Beryl! Is the coffee ready yet?"

Joe frowned, his widow's peak diving onto his forehead. "Dorothy, what do you think Albert will do?"

She was not Albert Sabin's spokesperson, no matter what they thought. Yes, he had been the first recipient of her research these past couple years. Yes, they put their heads together at conferences, too. He was her co-conspirator in planning the slaughter of polio, but that was all he was. "He'll keep working. Just like the rest of us. None of us are done yet."

Robbie ducked back into the room. "I bet Sabin is." He whistled. "I wouldn't want to be his wife tonight."

"I wouldn't *ever* want to be his wife," said Joe.

The guys laughed, flicking glances at Dorothy.

The phone rang in the outer office.

"There he is," said Joe. "Lover boy."

She shook her head. "Cute."

Mrs. Beasley's garbled voice came over the intercom. "Dr. Horstmann, it's Dr. Paul from Ann Arbor."

"John?" Dorothy said. "Great! Put him on speaker. We all want to celebrate."

A WIFE

Sylvia had worked all day for this hour. The kids had been bathed, pajamaed, read to, and watered. Now the house was quiet save for the swish of the heavy, colorized pages of a *Life* magazine as Sylvia turned them.

Here was the British prime minister, Sir Winston Churchill, at the London Zoo. Evidently, he had time to feed lions and to pet cheetahs now that the war was long over. There were Princess Margaret and the handsome—and divorced, alas—Mr. Townsend. He was holding a skinny snake over the laughing Princess Margaret on their picnic at one of her castles. The story was, the princess had to decide whether she wanted her man or her title. You'd think that at least royals could get what they wanted, Sylvia thought. It was bad news for the rest of us if even they didn't.

She lit a Winston, pocketed the lighter in her skirt pocket, then sluiced on through the glossy pages. She paused on an article about an actress who had the unenviable job of replacing Marilyn Monroe in a movie. At first glance, the accompanying picture was of two large white balloons. A closer look revealed that the poor girl had let herself be photographed from the rear in a pair of tight white pants. The poor thing was all haunches.

Sylvia looked for the photo credit. A man. It figured. Her idol, Margaret Bourke-White, would never photograph a woman in such a humiliating way. Miss Bourke-White's pictures often captured the quiet strength of women under unendurable circumstances. Sylvia had given up photography, but if she were at it now, she'd shoot pictures like that.

The next page featured home-movie stills of the girl in her underwear. In three frames, the girl bared just about everything, yet one's gaze went to the little two-by-three-inch photo above them, a copy of the famous shot of Marilyn Monroe stretched naked on satin sheets. How was this child—Sylvia squinted at the print—Sheree North, age twenty-two, ever going to top that? The next page revealed young Sheree's attempt: she assumed a Betty Grable over-the-shoulder gaze while posing in a negligee, fishnet stockings, and stilettos.

Sylvia drew in on the cigarette, letting the wet smoke rake her lungs. You did what you had to do when you knew you weren't the one.

The groan of a car climbing the driveway floated through the open window—it was April, early for windows to be open in Cincinnati, but Sylvia liked the cold, at least tonight she did. She wondered if Albert drove all the way back from Ann Arbor with the top down. She turned the page as his Cadillac roared into the garage like someone had stepped on a lion's tail.

The kitchen door banged open. The rap of wingtips neared, then her husband stormed into the living room, tossed his hat on the davenport, and flipped on the television. "My God, Sylvia, don't you know what happened today?" He tore out of his tie as the set warmed. "You're missing it! He's on with Edward R. Murrow now. I came home as fast as I could."

Sylvia reached for another cigarette.

Murrow's long grooved face filled the screen of the new Magnavox. "Today," the reporter was saying in his no-nonsense voice, "a great profession made a giant step forward, and the news that came out of this room lifted a sense of fear from the homes of millions of Americans."

The camera panned to Jonas Salk. He had the goofy overjoyed grin of a high school basketball team manager after the players had just won the regionals.

"Look at him!" Albert cried.

Sylvia smoked quietly. It was hard to hear the broadcast over her husband's agitated breathing.

Her husband held up a finger. "Wait—"

"Your figures go from sixty to ninety percent in effectiveness," Murrow was saying, "depending on the type of polio. What about going to ninety-five or a hundred percent?"

"Yes," Albert said, "what about that, Salk?"

Jonas's brow furrowed. "I think it's one of the things that would be very interesting to do something about."

Albert flung up his hands.

Murrow said, "Who owns the patent on this vaccine?"

Jonas's grin got even toothier. "Well, the people, I would say. There is no patent." He giggled. "Could you patent the sun?"

"Patent the sun!" Albert clasped his head. "Can you believe that? He can't patent his vaccine because there's nothing new to patent. He just tweaked the recipe for Isabel Morgan's vaccine and grew poliovirus in tissue that could be scaled up for production and it was Elsie Ward who figured out how to do that. He didn't even try to figure out how polio works in the body. That was Dorothy's doing."

"All women," Sylvia said.

"What?"

Upstairs, a child cried.

He was crouched at the television, turning the channels, when she returned. She dropped into the wingback across from him.

"I can't bear it," he said. "Millions of doses of Salk's vaccine are being shipped across the country tonight. It should have been mine!"

"Why don't you just go to her?"

"What?"

"To Dorothy Horstmann."

"Don't be absurd."

She shaded her eyes to look at him.

He sat back on his heels and stared at her. "I can't go to her, even if I wanted. If you must know, she's in love with someone else."

Upstairs, a child cried again. Sylvia's lungs ached as if she were already screaming. "I only meant for you to call her."

Inhaling deeply, he stood, then left the room.

Her hand was shaking as she got out another cigarette, with "Happy Days Are Here Again" spouting from the Magnavox. The whole world was celebrating.

37

The first sign of trouble with Jonas's vaccine came two weeks later. Dorothy was over in the Yale hospital nursery, evaluating a newborn with an organic heart murmur. She feared the child had damage to her valve. The infant also appeared to be deaf. Dorothy was gently re-swaddling the baby, asking the nurse if anyone had questioned the mother as to whether she'd had rubella in her first trimester of pregnancy, when the department secretary came to find her.

"Dr. Sabin wants you to call him immediately."

Dorothy cradled the baby to her chest. Albert had called every day since Jonas Salk had made his announcement. Each time it was about a new outrage: *Newsweek* had called "the quiet young man's victory" enough to "land him next to Jenner, Pasteur, and Lister in the medical dictionaries." Congress wanted to replace FDR's profile with Jonas's on the dime. Marlon Brando wanted to play Salk in Salk's life story on the silver screen.

Yesterday, Albert had been nearly apoplectic. He'd seen on the news that President Eisenhower had been reduced to tears when awarding Jonas the Congressional Medal of Honor. Old Ike had begun crying when he'd looked over at his little grandson, David, playing on the White House floor—saved, now, from polio. Old Ike, the battle-scarred general, Albert exclaimed, crying in front of the whole world over that grinning kitchen chemist!

She gave the baby to the nurse, then took her time in getting back to Albert.

She placed the call in her office, standing by her desk, too busy to sit down. "Yes, Albert."

"Dorothy, you aren't going to believe this."

She sighed. She wanted to look at the bloodwork from the mother of the baby with the defective heart. The distraught woman claimed that she hadn't had rubella, but Dorothy wondered if perhaps she'd had such a mild case that she hadn't noticed. Dorothy had seen too many babies damaged when their mothers caught this common childhood disease, often from their own kids. There really ought to be a vaccine for it.

She tried to keep the weariness out of her voice. "Albert, we should be supporting Jonas. I know the advantages of your vaccine. I'm just a wee bit partial to its principles—"

"It's based on your science!"

"—but until it's ready, we need to be encouraging the public to get their shot."

"We'll see about that," he said ominously.

"What do you mean?"

"Seven cases of paralysis have been reported from the killed-virus vaccine."

"Seven cases? What?"

"The surgeon general is shutting him down. All administration of the vaccine has been suspended. I just got word."

"Albert, this is a tragedy. How can this be?" She thought of Isabel Morgan, fearing even one death caused by the vaccine. She sat down. Nausea rose up her esophagus like mercury in a thermometer.

Silence flowed from the other end of the line.

At last, he sighed deeply. "Being right doesn't feel as good as I thought it would. In fact, it feels terrible."

TWO WEEKS LATER, SHE WAS AT A CONFERENCE TABLE AT the NIH, chafing under the rubberized band of a new brassiere. She looked around the table: John Enders, recently returned from Stockholm with his Nobel Prize for growing poliovirus in cell tissue instead of in animals (which made him a saint, in her book); the surgeon general, Leonard Scheele, a soft-mouthed man from Fort Wayne, Indiana; Bill Sebrell, the head of the NIH; Albert; John Paul; and a sweaty, despondent Jonas Salk. None of these leaders in public health had to ponder the vaccine crisis while suffering under the grip of a Playtex bra.

The group was waiting for the arrival of a few more scientists, Albert chatting with Enders and Sebrell, Scheele writing, and Jonas with his head in his hands, when John Paul slipped her an opened copy of *Business Week*. "From this week." He pointed to a paragraph.

> The nation, which mere weeks ago clamored with one voice for the Salk vaccine, now is skeptical. The faith of the reading, listening, and watching public has been severely shaken. The delays in school inoculation programs, the starts and stops in vaccine production, the cloak-and-dagger meetings in Washington—

She looked up at John. This was one of those meetings.

> —all this has raised doubts. Nobody seems to be giving straight answers. It has the look of a cover-up.

They exchanged grimaces. Confidence in a polio vaccine—any polio vaccine, killed or live, was eroding fast. As the heartbreaking toll mounted, 164 paralyzed, 10 dead, accusations were flying. In Congress, Democrats blamed Republicans. The NIH blamed the manufacturers. Scientists blamed the March of Dimes. O'Connor blamed Albert for undercutting the killed virus movement from the start.

The immediate root of the cause appeared to have been found: One of the manufacturers, Cutter Laboratories, had trimmed corners and produced batches in which the virus wasn't completely killed. The Mahoney strain, the strain that Albert had begged Salk not to use, survived the inactivation process to give polio to the recipients of those batches instead of protecting them against it. Albert had predicted all of this. Her whole body hurt from the horror of it.

Dr. Enders took his unlit pipe from his mouth with a click of teeth, then frowned at her and John over his bifocals. "What's that?"

John shook his head.

Dave Bodian blew into the room, his rubbery features sculpted by a frown. "Sorry I'm late. Traffic is miserable."

The NIH chief, Bill Sebrell, sharp-eyed male intensity in a tweed suit, stood as Dave took the only available seat, next to Jonas. "All right. Let's call this meeting to order. As we all know—"

The door burst open. A woman in a white lab coat pushed into the room.

"Bernice!" Dr. Sebrell exclaimed.

"Bill, forgive me for barging in, but I think these gentlemen"—she glanced at Dorothy, her dark French twist scraping on her collar—"and this lady need to know."

Dr. Sebrell stepped toward her. "This is not the time—"

"It is never the time, Bill. I've tried to tell you—"

He took her arm. "Bernice."

She swung around to face the startled gathering. "I'm Bernice Eddy. I was one of the inspectors the NIH sent to Cutter last year. And what I saw—" She fought to be freed. "I saw tanks containing live poliovirus and tanks containing virus being inactivated for the vaccine, *all in the same room*. It looked like contamination waiting to happen."

"Let's go." When she planted her feet, Dr. Sebrell cried, "Will someone help me?"

"When I got back here at the NIH—" She resisted well for a small young woman being tugged toward the door by a large angry male. "We had eighteen monkeys," she began again. "When we inoculated them with vaccine from Cutter, we started getting paralyzed monkeys. All eighteen of them."

"We all know Cutter's shortfalls," Dr. Sebrell said.

"I made a report. They released the vaccine anyway. The monkeys, they just discarded. Did you know this, Dr. Salk?" She shook loose, rubbing her arm. "I'm going now. I just wanted everyone to hear. Good day."

Dr. Sebrell shut the door behind her. "Sorry. This is the end of the line for her."

Dr. Enders stood, his pipe clenched in his hand. "Do not blame that woman, Bill. These deaths are not on her head. Some of us have been against a killed-virus vaccine with Mahoney in it from the start. But Basil O'Connor had to get a vaccine, any vaccine, out there, regardless of what we said."

Albert's grim smile all but shouted *I told you so*.

John Paul spoke up from next to Dorothy. "We allowed publicity experts at a philanthropy to take over our responsibilities. We let an ambitious promoter assume leadership in our affairs."

"We did," said Dr. Enders. "And that is our cross to bear. We must never again allow decisions about essentially scientific matters to be made for us by people without training or insight. That lesson must be learned and remembered."

Jonas ran his hand over his face.

Dr. Enders's impressive nostrils flared as he turned to Jonas. "Did you know?"

Jonas closed his eyes and shook his head.

"Did you?"

The anguish on Jonas's face made Dorothy want to weep. This could happen to any of them if they let their ambition run away with their sense.

Enders pointed his pipe at him. "It is quack medicine to pretend that this was a killed-virus vaccine if you knew there was any chance of live virus being in it."

Jonas groaned, his eyes still squeezed shut. He seemed to be shrinking, shrinking, into himself, until all that would be left would be his suit.

Enough. She stood up. "Jonas's science was sound. We now have learned, in the most painful way possible, the importance of tightly regulating manufacturers. The question is, gentleman, what do we do next?"

The men swiveled their glares from Jonas to her.

"We can't afford to squander the public's confidence another second. We cannot let polio win."

On her other side, Albert motioned for her to sit. "Thank you, Dr. Horstmann. You are correct, as always." He waited for her to take her chair before he stood. "Perhaps you all will be cheered by the news that I have been contacted by *Time* magazine."

Dorothy's scan of the room confirmed that the news wasn't as cheering as he thought.

"You must know that I spoke for all of us when I agreed to do this piece. It runs next week." He held up a galley, to which was clipped a photo of him in his lab coat, peering intelligently into the distance.

He read. "'While virologists are still trying to decide whether Dr. Salk's killed-virus vaccine was safe, or how it could be made safer—'" He glanced at Jonas, then stopped. "I'll skip to the meat. I said that instead of killing a virulent virus for use in my vaccine,

I am using a living virus that is nonvirulent to begin with. I'm planting the seed that we have a safe and effective alternative in the works."

Dr. Sebrell crossed his arms. "You could have run this by us first."

"You did right, Albert." John patted Dorothy's wrist. "As Dr. Horstmann says, we haven't a moment to spare in calming the public's nerves. They must be reassured that we *will* beat polio."

"Exactly how far along is your vaccine at this moment, Albert?" asked Dr. Enders.

"I've run a trial."

Dorothy looked up at him. As closely as they had worked, he hadn't told her this.

"Human?" someone asked.

"Yes."

"Where'd you get subjects?"

"Prisoners." Dorothy could feel him avoiding her. "At Chillicothe."

The men looked at one another. "How'd it go?" asked Dr. Enders.

"Yes," Dorothy said pointedly, "how'd it go?"

"It was a small group of lesser offenders, all volunteers—" Albert looked down at Dorothy. "Thirty of them, mostly fathers who wanted to protect their children. They wanted to do their part."

"That is a small sample," said John.

"But all of them showed robust antibodies. And when I challenged them—"

"You challenged them?" John exclaimed. "You gave them polio?"

"—not a one showed a single symptom. Gentlemen"—he smiled at Dorothy—"and dear lady, my vaccine works."

Whatever happened to "First, do no harm"? Those brave

imprisoned fathers, offering up their bodies to spare their children. How we underestimate the nobility of the reviled.

"We need a larger trial." Dr. Enders put his pipe between his teeth. "Now."

"Yes." Albert looked to Dorothy. "But where?"

38

CINCINNATI, OHIO, 1956

The Russian scientist's face had the rough, almost crystallized texture of homemade Play-Doh, Dorothy thought, its coarseness accentuated by his combed-back thatch of silky gray hair. He was stroking his grainy cheeks as Albert spoke.

"There is a reason why my vaccine was not ready for trial as soon as Dr. Salk's." Albert nodded at Sylvia as she brushed by him with a tray of hors d'oeuvres. She lowered the sound of Sinatra purring from the living room stereo; he continued. "It takes time and skill to deliver a virus that is potent enough to produce an infection in a recipient, yet mild enough to do no harm. The difference between making a killed-virus vaccine and a live one is like, well, the difference between slaughtering a bull and breeding it, or wringing a chicken's neck and teaching it tricks."

Albert glanced at Dorothy as the Russian's stocky blond interpreter relayed his words. He was selling his vaccine hard. Originally the Russians, experiencing one of the worst outbreaks in the world, were only interested in getting the Salk vaccine. Their interest lay chiefly in quelling the spread. But Albert, Dorothy knew, had bigger plans. He wanted to wipe out polio altogether, and in her, he had an ally. It was at his invitation that she and John Paul had come, as he put it, "to acquaint this guy with the beauty of the live-virus vaccine."

What might have looked like a private dinner at an eminent scientist's lovely home in a wooded suburb of Cincinnati was actually a government-sanctioned, much-red-tape-loosened official visit from Moscow. As Sylvia made the rounds with her tray, Dorothy marveled at the bizarreness of the scene before her. Albert was wooing a scientist from a country that wished to blast the US off the earth—the country whose soldiers had nearly blinded him as a child—while his wife offered nibbles to a woman she distrusted. Saving lives made for strange bedfellows.

Dr. Chumakov responded in Russian. "That seems like a lot of effort," the interpreter relayed. "Now that you know what went wrong with the Salk vaccine, it is safe and ready to go. Our children are dying. We cannot wait for you to teach the chicken tricks."

"Cocktail sausage?" said Sylvia, lifting her tray.

"Ah," Albert said as the Russian scientist plucked up a morsel on a toothpick, "but my vaccine is ready for trial. Its advantages are well known. My vaccine follows the same path as naturally occurring poliovirus, moving from the mouth, down the digestive system, and into the intestines to multiply, stimulating antibodies to be produced in the blood. Here is the scientist who discovered how this works, Dr. Dorothy Horstmann."

Dr. Chumakov listened to the translation, then took Dorothy's hand. He gazed at her, his large brown eyes eloquent with appreciation. "My wife is scientist," he said in halting English. "You are hero to her."

"Oh! My."

"You are woman who knows polio best." His hands were as rough as his eyes were soft. "My Marina wants to meet."

"Perhaps Dr. Horstmann could accompany me to Russia to set up a trial," Albert suggested. "Your wife could meet her then."

As the translator spoke, Sylvia turned her head slowly toward her husband.

Dorothy kept her smile in place. The possibility of her going to Russia was news to her. Even if the rigid new FDA restrictions had allowed it, there was no appetite for a vaccine trial in the US, small or large, after the "Cutter Incident" with Jonas's vaccine. Albert had been driven to seek a trial in a country that he mortally hated, during an escalating cold war. Did he really think the Russians would ever allow one, let alone two, American scientists behind the Iron Curtain?

"Dr. Horstmann knows my vaccine better than anyone," Albert said. "And the world health community knows *her* better than anyone, perhaps even me," he added with a modesty that he couldn't quite pull off. "She has certainly been to more outbreaks than anyone else."

Dorothy felt his wife's gaze upon her.

Enough.

"Sylvia?" she asked. "How is your photography coming along?"

Sylvia blinked as if blinded by a sudden light. "I don't do much anymore."

"Do you still have your workshop in the basement? I'd love to see it."

Albert glanced at them as he continued to court the Russian.

Drawing an unhappy breath, Sylvia led her downstairs.

They picked their way past dusty piles of boxes and shelves with jars of home-canned tomatoes and peaches. Dodging a dressmaker's dummy, Dorothy asked, "Didn't you once say that there was a passage to the Underground Railroad down here?"

The cold stone walls repelled Sylvia's curt words. "It's bricked up. Cave-in hazard."

Once through the darkroom door, she flipped on a red light, then folded her arms. "Sorry, only the safelight is working. Anyhow, there's not much to see."

Dorothy squinted through the crimson glow to the empty trays lined up on a table.

"I want you to know—" Sylvia began.

Dorothy turned.

"—I am willing to do what it takes to back my husband. I will forward his interests over my own. I have and I will sacrifice myself more than you can ever dream of."

"Oh." Dorothy nodded. "I know."

Sylvia, bathed in red, smiled grimly. "Good. Keep that in mind when you go with him to the USSR."

"I would, if I were going. His plan for me to go with him was a sudden whim, not likely possible nor representative of our relationship. We are not a package deal. We never have been."

Sylvia's frown was not of belief.

"I would go, don't get me wrong, if the Russian government or the WHO or suchlike asked me. You see, I am willing to do what it takes to fight polio. I will forward the fight's interests over my own."

Sylvia glanced at her.

"Sylvia, we're in this together."

Sylvia cupped her mouth, her chest rising and falling as she thought. Dorothy reached out to touch the empty clothesline strung over the table. How exciting it must have been for Sylvia to hang photographs here and admire what she'd caught on camera. Was she ever surprised by what she'd captured, things she hadn't seen when behind the lens, but that had been there all along?

Sylvia lowered her hand. "We look like a couple of red devils in this light."

Their eyes connected.

Dorothy chuckled. "Don't we, though?"

1959–1960

A GRANDMOTHER

1959

Mrs. Horstmann sat in the eye doctor's waiting room next to her husband. It was in the university hospital where Dorothy had worked, in a fancy clinic with clean upholstered chairs and music piped in over a speaker. She was glad that she had insisted on bathing Henry before they came, and had dressed him in his suit and best white shirt. She'd made the appointment at Dorothy's urging clear in Connecticut, before she had left to go to Russia.

Russia! Of all places to go! Mrs. Horstmann had seen their bully of a new leader on the television, arguing with the young US vice president, Richard Nixon, about whose country was best. This Khrushchev disagreed with Mr. Nixon about everything, even something as silly as whether American women needed electric dishwashers. She hoped that Dorothy kept far, far away from that tyrant, in whatever work she was doing there.

She looked up. "*Nein*, Henry!"

Her husband stopped in the act of giving a little child a peppermint wrapped in cellophane.

Mrs. Horstmann shook her head. "*Nein*."

The child's mother, a pale young woman who could use a

shampoo, whisked back her daughter, as if Henry were the one with the infectious red-rimmed eyes.

"You want it?" he asked Mrs. Horstmann in German. After all these years in America, he still could not say but "please" and "TV" and "hamburger" in English.

She shook her head again. "*Nein.*"

He pocketed the candy as he sat back, knocking her purse to the floor. She picked it up, that stiff spot catching in her hips.

He patted her hand with his leathery paw and smiled. Even with cataracts fogging his blue eyes, they were still as beautiful as those of the boy who had carried her through the stubbly hayfield.

She saw that the mother of the little red-eyed girl was watching them. Poor little child. Mrs. Horstmann didn't want her mother to think that she held the girl's illness against her by not being friendly. "My daughter used to work in this hospital," she offered.

The young mother half smiled, plucking the white Peter Pan collar of her green dress.

"Now she works for Yale. As a professor."

When this did not get as big of a response that she felt it deserved, she said, "She's the foremost expert on polio in the world. It's she who countries call when there are outbreaks. You may have heard of her—Dorothy Horstmann?"

The mother slapped her child's hand away from her nose.

Embarrassed for the mother for her inelegant behavior, she said brightly, "She's in Russia now. The World Health Organization asked her to oversee the trials of Dr. Sabin's vaccine, to see if the vaccine is safe or not. Whether or not we get the new Sabin vaccine here in the United States depends completely upon Dorothy." She smiled at the little red-eyed girl now sucking on a hank of hair. "Children will love it—Dorothy says that you take it by mouth. No shots! So if you ever get a sugar cube or teaspoon of syrup with a polio vaccine in it, know that it was because my daughter, Dorothy Horstmann, said it was okay."

The woman scooped up her child and plunked her onto her green-clothed lap. Clearly, she was not understanding something here.

Mrs. Horstmann opened her purse and began digging. "She's been in *Life* and *Time* magazine."

The blue plastic sleeve containing the clipping was next to her packaged rain bonnet. She pulled it out and lovingly unfolded it.

"Dorothy." Henry poked at the picture in *Life* of Dorothy drawing blood from a little boy. "Miracle of Hickory."

"That's right." Mrs. Horstmann beamed at him. He *did* know more English than "hamburger" and "TV."

The young mother stared pointedly at the receptionist's counter.

The realization thwacked Mrs. Horstmann like a wet bedsheet. The woman didn't believe her. She thought Henry and she were two nuts.

She tucked the clippings back into her purse, then took Henry's warm, thick hand.

She knew who she was. Dorothy Horstmann's mother. And that was enough for her.

39

MOSCOW, USSR, 1959

Dorothy smoothed the button-down collar of her shirtdress over her cardigan. Her outfit worked well enough on the road. Whether she was winging to Alabama or Albania, it was a staple in her suitcase, along with one small blue dish. Washed in rusting sinks and drip-dried in kitchens that were also bathrooms in dozens of households across the Soviet Union these past six weeks, the dress had reached its limit here in the drawing room of the Soviet premier's palace in Moscow.

She looked around the high-ceilinged room with its brocade chairs and gilt tables, a far cry from her interpreter's flat, by which they'd stopped earlier. Three generations of the family of her interpreter, Elena, were crammed into an apartment the size of an American two-car garage. Elena said Russians called the tiny one-bedroom flats *Khrushchyovkas*, and her family's was one of millions that honeycombed apartment blocks in cities across the USSR, the new Soviet premier's answer to the housing shortage after the war.

Cramped as Elena's *Khrushchyovka* was, Dorothy wished she were there now, having tea with Elena's smiling grandmother on this cold mid-October day. Sitting here on this elegant chair, outnumbered by glaring men in trench coats and underdressed, she almost laughed, and not just from the brain-numbing exhaustion that came from forty-five days of tramping across the biggest landmass on the globe to inspect its laboratories and clinics and their records. She, Henry Horstmann's daughter, was to tell the most important person in this behemoth country whether or not the vaccine that he'd allowed every person under the age of twenty in the USSR to take—a mind-boggling seventy-seven million young people—a vaccine given to him by a scientist from his archenemy, the US, was safe and effective?

If it was a flop, or if she misrepresented its efficacy, there would be world war. An army of scientists had been called to evaluate the trial of Jonas Salk's vaccine in America back in 1955, but to evaluate the design and execution of the hugest vaccine trial of all time, and the validity of its results, there was just her.

No pressure whatsoever.

Elena, perched next to her on a wildly mismatched brocade throne, noticed her expression. "Nervous?" she said in her excellent English.

Elena was strawberry blond, pretty, and thin, with the wrung-out, exhausted look common to many Russian women, as if they had just trudged from bed after delivering a twelve-pound baby. When she smiled, as she was doing now, it seemed as remarkable as a cactus flower bursting into bloom.

The World Health Organization promised Dorothy a top-notch interpreter when they'd asked her to go on this mission, and they'd delivered. The WHO had bent over backward on every aspect of this trip, as if the future of eradicating poliovirus depended on it.

It really did.

Elena tucked a wisp behind her ear as she smiled, waiting for Dorothy's response. "Nervous, no," Dorothy lied. "I've met heads of state before." She had. But the king of Morocco or the president of Egypt did not wish her and all her people dead. What had Albert Sabin gotten her into?

It wasn't anything that Albert hadn't put himself into, she thought, straightening her skirt. Three years ago, he'd sat on a plane with his coat pockets stuffed with vials of deadly poliovirus strains nailed in wooden boxes the size of playing cards. A fine, toxic, international mess it would have been if they'd broken. Together with his Russian friend Chumakov and his wife, the good doctor Marina Vorosjilova, they'd produced enough vaccine to inoculate ten million children. The distribution went so well that he and Drs. Chumakov and Vorosjilova got the idea they needn't content themselves with just tamping down outbreaks. They aimed to wipe out polio completely, a mission that Dorothy could love.

A tall, wiry dog padded into the salon, its nails clicking on the polished marble. She was petting it when a burly man plowed in on thick black shoes, his black suit straining across the white-shirted meat of his chest. She rose and put out her hand as she'd been instructed. He took it, then tipped back his snowy-furred slab of head.

Elena interpreted his growl. "'So you are the woman with the cure.'"

Dorothy opened her mouth to explain that she had no cure, but noticing Elena's glance, closed it.

"*Ty vysokiy,*" he growled.

Dorothy smiled, then looked at Elena.

"He said, 'You are tall.'"

"Tell him 'thank you.'"

He listened to Elena, then burst into rapid-fire speech, gesturing with hands as large and creased as baseball mitts.

"He says if you were sent here to make him think that all American women were as tall and beautiful as you, he knows better. He just got home from America, where he met Marilyn Monroe and Elizabeth Taylor in Hollywood."

He spoke again, making rounding motions with his mitts.

"He says they have breasts like the udders of the cows that he herded as a boy, but they were shorter than he was. Not such impressive specimens. You, however—"

He revealed a gap-toothed grin before continuing.

Elena blushed as she translated. "You, however, he would like to bed."

He widened his smile for Dorothy as if to verify this.

There was no slapping his face or rebuffing him. So much rode on this mission to Moscow.

For the kids of the world to run, jump, and play as they were born to do, she would stand here in a limp shirtdress in a former czar's palace and be propositioned by a randy dictator.

She gave him the friendly but firm smile that had worked on a chieftain in the Brazilian Amazon when he'd suggested that she marry him. "How did you like America?"

His thick lips fell in a fleshy curtain over his teeth. He crossed his arms over that barrel of a chest, a man seldom denied. Even in Russian, his tone was sulky.

"'They would not let me in Disneyland,'" Elena relayed, looking even more tired than usual. "'What are they afraid of? That I will make a better Mickey Mouse here?'"

He tossed his hands in disgust as he continued.

"'They took me instead to a place called San Jose, where they keep the IBM computer machine. I do not see the use for the thing. I have mathematicians to do that kind of work, the best in the world.'"

He waited for Elena to finish, then went on.

"'I did, however, eat at a "self-serve" cafeteria. Very clever, very efficient. I am setting up such a place to eat here in a factory. It will be better than the American model.'"

He squinted at her as Elena told her this, then barked something else.

"'Where are you from?'" Elena interpreted.

"San Francisco."

He nodded knowingly when Elena told him, then fired back.

"'I was taken there. A hilly city. I was shown what you call a "supermarket." This is another concept that I will improve upon. It will fit well with the housing for every citizen that I have provided in all my cities. You must come back soon, and I will show you what I have done. You will come back soon?'"

"Yes. Of course."

When Elena had finished, his smile was back. For such a rough and homely man, he could be surprisingly charming, even when speaking in a language Dorothy couldn't understand. Who could explain charisma?

Khrushchev fired more words at her. Elena raised one of the downturned corners of her mouth. "The premier wants to know, is your father a big man?"

"Well, yes."

"'Is he strong? Is he successful? Is he as powerful as me?'" He crooked his arm in a strongman's pose as Elena relayed his words.

Even as Dorothy opened her mouth to say no, she remembered her father those years ago, leaning to her in the theater as "Moonlight Sonata" rowed forth from the grand piano on stage. "I like that lower hand," he'd whispered. "It does not mind if the upper hand steals the show. It knows it is strong." How he had admired the constancy of the bass, giving freely of itself so that the other could soar. Was he not telling her the secret of life?

The premier puffed out his chest and watched Dorothy expectantly.

"Yes. In his way, he is."

The premier's expression soured. Standing before her with his mitts on his hips, he demanded her report on the trial.

He listened for several minutes, snorting like a bull until she said, "I have found that the oral polio vaccine used in the trials by Drs. Chumakov and Vorosjilova is essentially one hundred percent safe and effective."

He tossed his hands. "'My doctors say it is good?'"

"Mr. Khrushchev, this vaccine will change the world. Your success here just made history. We are on the road to polio eradication."

"'But *my* doctors like it?'"

To Elena's translation, Dorothy answered, "*Da*."

With a jerk of his head, he stormed from the room.

Only after she and Elena had left the palace and were standing on the street busy with rusting automobiles, their scarves dancing in the wind, she told Elena, "Well, we survived that."

Elena pulled her coat closer as she raised her narrow eyebrows.

"I guess I should have humored him and told him that my father was not strong."

"You were just telling the truth, not that he likes to hear it. But your father must be a wonderful man to have produced a woman as capable as you, Dr. Horstmann."

"Dorothy. Thank you. He is."

They waited for a mother to usher her stairstep brood of children across the street. Although dressed in layers of crazily mismatched clothing, all seven of them were rosy-cheeked, robust, and smiling as they chatted among themselves, unaware of their pale, thin mother, sandals on her wool-stockinged feet, watching them so proudly.

It struck Dorothy with the force of the buran whipping across the steppes: that was Mutter. Always giving, always loving, always sacrificing, with no thought of thanks or recognition—Mutter, to a T. All of Dorothy's childhood, Mutter had shouldered the bulk of the work both at home and at the bar so that she could send off Pop to be with Dorothy and for Dorothy to learn and delight in him. Ha! Mutter had even taken the mop out of Pop's hands to shoo them off to the theater to go hear "Moonlight Sonata." She had ensured that Dorothy, solid in Pop's love, could become another link in the chain of human goodness that encircled the world. How had Dorothy not known this? Like poliovirus lurking unseen in the blood, the truth had been there all along: behind her dear, strong father was an even stronger Mutter.

"Shall we go for some tea . . . Dorothy?" Elena's face lit with one of her cactus-flower smiles.

"I would like that. And after that, could you please help me with some changes I need to make in my travel itinerary? I'd like to book a flight to San Francisco, immediately."

40

CINCINNATI, OHIO, 1960

It was a carnival atmosphere. Children and their parents lined the sidewalk to the hospital as if queued up for the lion grotto at the zoo. The mothers, in dress hats and gloves, and not a few fathers chatted and laughed beneath the blooming cherry trees. The kids squatted together to look at stones or sang songs and swung hands. At the entrance of the Art Deco-style building, nurses tipped a spoonful of vaccine into the mouth of each child, who then skipped off with the pink plastic spoon as a souvenir.

Dorothy breathed in a lungful of grass-scented spring air. Imagining a sight like this was what had gotten her through the privations of her grueling expedition across the Soviet Union last fall.

On the street in front of the hospital, the newspaper reporter was saying to Albert, "Looks like people are really going for your 'Sabin on Sunday' vaccine."

Albert put his hands in his lab coat and grinned. Though his thick waves of hair had silvered and he now wore a pair of black-framed glasses, he was still the cocksure, riveting man that she'd met nineteen years ago. "SOS, we like to call it. I've been working most of my life for this."

"The children seem to like it."

"They should! The syrup tastes like cherries. Whether given in syrup or in sugar cubes, it's a far cry from a shot in the arm."

The reporter nodded as he wrote. "Why should we take your vaccine, Dr. Sabin, and not Dr. Salk's?"

Dorothy pulled her attention away from the children. Sylvia, at Albert's elbow, was watching her husband closely, too.

Albert took a hand from his pocket to push up his glasses. "My research shows that poliovirus can infect both the tissue of the nervous system and the small intestines. Because it is taken orally, my vaccine goes straight to the digestive tract, unlike the other vaccine, which is given, as I noted, by injection. My vaccine induces the body to make the antibodies that give natural and effective protection before it can reach the nervous system."

"It sets up a battle in the blood."

"Yes. That's one way of putting it."

The reporter tipped back his hat and whistled. "Super! But is it safe? Salk's vaccine killed people. How do you know yours won't?"

"Mine has been tested thoroughly."

"In the Soviet Union, I hear."

"Yes. It was the perfect place to find subjects who had not already received the Salk vaccine. In all, seventy-seven million children—"

"Seventy-seven million!"

Albert grinned. "That is right, seventy-seven million children and young adults have taken it, and there was not a single case of vaccine-induced polio among them."

"Look over here!" cried a photographer. Albert aimed himself at him and lifted his dimpled chin. A flashbulb popped and sizzled.

"Has this been verified?" the reporter asked.

Albert rocked on his heels, hands in pockets. "Yes. It has been stringently verified."

Dorothy poked at the clumps at the back of her head. She should have worn a better hat.

"How can we trust anything out of the Soviet Union?" said the reporter. "Who vouched for these results?"

Dorothy put on her smile. Ready to go!

Albert chuckled. "Who vouched for them? Why, my own kids did! I tried it on them."

The reporter laughed, his pencil scratching on his notepad. The photographer's flashbulb exploded.

A group of reporters strode up. "Say!" one of them shouted. "How does it feel to be like a god? You must feel like Prometheus giving fire to mankind."

A crowd formed around Albert, pushing Dorothy outside of their circle.

She felt a hand on her elbow: Sylvia was leading her to the far side of the street. She didn't stop until they were under some maples shaggy with red buds.

"Don't feel bad."

"I'm okay," Dorothy managed to murmur.

Sylvia opened her purse, then took a cigarette from its case. "Look, he didn't tell me that he'd vaccinated the kids until after the fact." She lit her cigarette, then blew out smoke. "My own kids. They're all I have. They're all he's left me. But he didn't even think to ask me."

"I'm sorry, Sylvia."

"Don't be. We got what we wanted, didn't we?"

They gazed across the street at a little girl opening her mouth for her dose, then trotting away with her spoon.

"Yes. We certainly did."

1963

A DAUGHTER

SAN FRANCISCO, CALIFORNIA

There was no wearing Mutter out. Not a drive through the forests of Golden Gate Park in Dorothy's Dodge Dart convertible, nor the white-knuckled (for Dorothy) trip across the big red bridge with the top down; not the cruise along the coast, nor the tramp through the sleeping giants of Muir Woods had put a dent in Mutter's energy. Now, she was stumping along in the foamy surf of Stinson Beach, as barefooted as a child.

Dorothy sat back on the tan sand and watched as Mutter stopped to talk to a child lugging a bucket half the size that he was. She bent to look into the bucket, then gasped and exclaimed as if she'd been shown the Hope Diamond. She always did know how to make people feel like they were champions.

Mutter's dress flapped in the salt air, hugging her sturdy frame. She had been losing weight since Pop had died last summer—Dorothy would have to help Catherine and Bernard to keep an eye on her. They all suffered from his absence. To Dorothy, Pop's decline and death had been like watching the grandest redwood being hacked to the ground. The aching hole left was unfillable.

But at least she'd gotten to spend as much time with Pop as she could wring from her life in his final years. She'd gotten in enough "Moonlight Sonata" playings with him, his face angelic with contentment, to tide her over on those tough nights on the pediatric ward or blinding hours on the microscope. Some might say that he was too simple to know what he'd done for her, but she knew that wasn't true. Even in his last days, when dementia had drawn its clouds around him, he knew what he was to her. She took comfort in that.

Next to where she sat on the shore, a family's Labrador retriever had nosed into their picnic basket and was gulping a sandwich, waxed paper and all.

The father laughed as he tried to take the remains from the dog's stiff jaws. "There goes my sandwich!" He then piled jackets and towels on top of the basket to prevent another canine heist. The way he lovingly stroked the dog's ears after he'd sat back down again made her think of Eugene Oakley. It seemed that her colleague's sympathy for animals had transferred to his younger son, Robert, who was now enrolled in veterinary school. Eugene himself had retired, and he and Viola were enjoying time with their grandkids.

Dorothy sighed. Her work was her grandkids. She wasn't leaving Yale anytime soon, at least not until she'd had her say with rubella, which was in her crosshairs now, and then with whatever other new pediatric virus that came along.

She sighed at the memory of her and Eugene in the lab, heads together over work that was supposed to change her life. It hadn't, in the way she'd hoped. His, neither. But in the long run, it did change the life of nearly every human on this planet. She may not have gotten her Nobel Prize, but her discovery had led to the vaccines that were halving polio cases by the year, and at her say-so, Albert's vaccine was being distributed to every child around the world. It seemed reasonable to believe that the poliovirus organism would soon be wiped from the earth, as extinct as the pterodactyl.

Mutter, farther down the beach now, shouted something at Dorothy.

"What?" Dorothy called back.

Mutter shouted again.

Dorothy got up and, brushing sand from her slacks, loped toward her mother. She strode by kids flying kites, teens listening to transistor radios, children jumping in the waves, toddlers waddling in sunhats and diapers.

It occurred to her that in the polio summers, this beach would have been empty. Children would be at home, waiting for the shadow of the disease to pass like sparrows hiding from the flight of a hawk. With the beach so full of kids now, it was hard to remember that. Strange how only what's before us seems real, yet she more than anybody knew that just because something was not visible didn't mean that it didn't exist. All the most powerful forces in this world were invisible to the naked eye. Like viruses. Like antibodies. Like love.

She had yearned for Arne over the years, kicked herself for letting him go. There were times that she feared she could not live this life without him. But then she pictured Sylvia Sabin waiting by the door, the phone, or the mailbox, her spirit crumbling away like sand through an hourglass. She'd spared Arne from that and herself from a lifetime of apologies, because, no matter her best intentions, crushing a disease would always be her first love.

Ha, Albert, yes, she was heartless, or at least ruthless, in that way.

She caught up with Mutter when she stopped to examine a shiny black stone. "Do you want to go home?"

Mutter straightened and gestured toward the yellow transistor radio blaring from its perch on a rock. "That is not Beethoven!"

Dorothy listened. It was the Beach Boys' new song, "Surfin' USA." She smiled. It seemed right to celebrate summer again.

"But I like it!" Mutter exclaimed.

"Me, too. Are you ready to go home now?"

"Ho-ome?" Mutter's eyes rounded behind thick lenses as she reared back as if being robbed. "Home, when there's so much to do?"

Dorothy laughed. "All right."

Mutter set off again, prodding the surf with a soggy stick, and Dorothy, her mother's daughter, followed.

ACKNOWLEDGMENTS

On December 31, 2019, Chinese scientists first officially notified the World Health Organization of an outbreak of pneumonia caused by an unknown virus in Wuhan. I was chilled six months later, while living under lockdown conditions due to the coronavirus pandemic, to hear the timing of this announcement. On December 31, 2019, I had first put my hands to my computer keyboard to start a novel about the pandemic caused by the poliovirus. I had never dreamed I'd be writing about a pandemic while living through one.

Putting those first words on paper came as a relief to me. My longtime walking partner, Karen Torghele, had been intriguing me with tales of medical pioneers since she began recording oral histories for the Centers for Disease Control and Prevention in 2015. I couldn't wait until our Friday hikes, when I would hear the next installment about the disease detectives. These people actually ran toward contagion instead of fleeing it! Then, when Karen starting telling me tales about the heroes in the race for the polio vaccine, my novel alarm went off. This was a book!

The work did not commence apace. There was the tricky matter of figuring out how to tell the story. As a writer of historical fiction, I construct a story around real people and actual historical events, but I'm acutely mindful, and my readers should be, too, that these are only the jumping-off points. What did I want to say through these real-life people and events? Ralph Waldo Emerson said, "Fiction reveals truth that reality obscures." What were the truths best told, then, through the spinning of this tale? In other words, what was the larger, albeit fictitious, story sparked by the facts?

Problematic for me, too, was the usual way in which the story about the race for the polio vaccine is framed. The traditional telling focuses upon two men, Albert Sabin and Jonas Salk, as if they had retired to their separate laboratories in search of the magic bullet and then emerged, decades later, bearing flasks of vaccine like Moses coming down the mountain with the Ten Commandments. But not since the days of Joseph Lister, who revolutionized surgery by introducing the antiseptic methods that he devised in his Victorian lab, has research been a solitary endeavor, and even he wasn't alone. His wife, Agnes, worked with him on his discoveries.

Even back in 1916, when the fear of poliomyelitis outbreaks first gripped Americans, teams in various laboratories around the country contributed to the research when there was a major problem to solve. Who were the others that brought Salk and Sabin to the finish line? I wondered. More importantly, to me, where were the women? Who were the Agnes Listers?

And then I found Dorothy Horstmann. Although she's rarely mentioned in the telling of the race for the polio vaccine, the development of the vaccine hinged on her discovery. She suspected that poliovirus was found in the blood and that was how it got from the gut to the nerve cells it destroyed. But her hunch went against the theory then embraced by the scientific community and was therefore discounted. It took ten long years of dogged persistence and meticulous research to confirm her hypothesis. How frustrated she must have been to share the honor of the discovery with David Bodian, who became interested in it many years after she did. Even more upsetting is thinking about how many children could have been saved had her work on the way poliovirus traveled through the body been encouraged earlier.

Dorothy's major contribution to ending polio didn't stop there. She was the scientist the WHO tapped to verify Sabin's mass oral polio vaccination program involving seventy-seven million recipients in the Soviet Union in 1959, essentially the biggest vaccine trial in history. Whether or not the live attenuated vaccine would be approved for use here in the United States by the Food and Drug Administration, as well as by public health organizations in other countries around the world in a step toward total polio eradication, came down to one person: Dorothy Horstmann. That yummy sugar cube that you were given in school in the '60s? It could be said that you got that on Dorothy's say-so. American babies received the oral live-virus vaccine until 2000, when polio in the wild had been eliminated from 99.9% of the world and the use of Salk's injectable killed-virus vaccine was then advised.

Other women began emerging from the shadows as my research deepened. There was Isabel Morgan, whose vaccine successfully induced immunity in monkeys and became the basis of Jonas Salk's entry in the race. We'd be talking about the Morgan vaccine instead of the Salk if not for her refusal to take the next step in the development of the vaccine: testing it on children. Feeling pushed to move forward before she was ready, she dropped out of the race to get married and to help raise her stepson.

And there was Elsie Ward, who perfected the technique for growing poliovirus outside of a living body. It was her technique that allowed Salk's lab to make enough of the virus to put in the vaccines for millions of children.

There was whistleblower Bernice Eddy, who reported that the test monkeys who got the vaccine from Cutter Laboratories were developing polio, thus alerting officials that Cutter would be releasing unsafe Salk vaccine for use. But her warning was ignored, and the vaccine manufactured by Cutter resulted in forty thousand cases of polio, leaving two hundred children with varying degrees of paralysis and ten dead. The tragic "Cutter Incident" led to the necessary tightening of federal regulation of vaccines, which is why we can rely on the safety of immunizations with such great confidence today.

One mustn't forget Sister Elizabeth Kenny, who developed the method of treating polio patients with hot wet packs applied to their affected muscles, freeing them from the excruciating and harmful practice of sealing them in body casts. Nor should we forget Jessie Wright, MD, an orthopedist who specialized in physical rehabilitation, in particular with polio and cerebral palsy patients, who innovated the use of the rocking bed as a less invasive (and less claustrophobia-producing) alternative, in some cases, to the dreaded respirators known as "iron lungs." Nor Barbara Johnson, the laboratory technician who, after developing poliomyelitis from contact with poliovirus-infused tissue in Sabin's lab, became Sabin's statistician. Nor Eleanor Abbott, who invented the game Candy Land to amuse polio patients during the long days, weeks, and months in the hospital after she herself was hospitalized for the disease. Nor the thousands of unnamed, unheralded nurses and physical therapists who dedicated their lives to mentally and physically healing their patients. This book could have easily been entitled *The* Women *with the Cure*. But my heart belonged to Dorothy.

While the Dorothy Horstmann you meet in this novel is based on what I could glean about her life from articles, letters, books, censuses, and oral sources, for this story she became my creation, as are all the other characters, whether drawn from real-life people or completely made-up. (Along those lines, Salk is *my* fictitious Salk, Sabin is *my* fictitious Sabin, and so on.) The majority of the scenes in the book are spun from documented events, but they are fictionalized, too, as is the case in novels. Even the scenes made up out of whole cloth happened within the actual timeline of the battle against polio, so ostensibly, they *could have* happened. But at all times, *The Woman with the Cure* is a novel, not a biography. For nonfiction reading about poliomyelitis and the race for the vaccine, I strongly recommend David M. Oshinsky's Pulitzer Prize–winning *Polio: An American Story*; Charlotte DeCroes Jacobs's *Jonas Salk: A Life*; Nina Gilden Seavey, Jane S. Smith, and Paul Wagner's *A Paralyzing Fear: The Triumph Over Polio in America*; Richard Carter's *Breakthrough: The Saga of Jonas Salk*; and *A History of Poliomyelitis* by John Rodman Paul.

Beyond my reading, grounding this story in the facts came courtesy of several generous contributors. First and foremost, I am grateful to Karen Torghele for lighting the fire in me to write this book, then, with weekly infusions of Albert Sabin and polio lore, fueling it into a three-year inferno. While I was tackling this novel, Karen's studies led her to become an authority on Sabin, resulting in her writing his definitive biography. Her *Albert Sabin: A Fierce Joy* (in press) is a must-read for those wanting an in-depth look at this notoriously difficult giant in medical history. Thank you, too, to Larry Anderson, MD, for his expert advice on virology and immunology, and Jamil Stetler, MD, for his insights into the medical world, although any mistakes made in explaining these areas in the book are my own.

My sincere thanks go to the renowned portraitist Alastair Adams for providing me with the dozens of photos of Dorothy Horstmann that unlocked my understanding of her personality. I had sought out Mr. Adams after examining his posthumous portrait of Dorothy commissioned in 2019 by Yale University. I was intrigued by how the portrait vibrated with kindness and intelligence, which was his reading of Dorothy after viewing her photos, a take on Dorothy that was common to everyone who had known her. But mostly, I was curious about a certain little blue-and-white dish in the foreground of the painting. Mr. Adams told me that he included the dish in the portrait because it appeared on her desk in photos over the years and must have held some importance to her. That's all one has to tell a novelist. A major plotline came of it.

I fondly thank my dear friend Dorte Glass for the use of her given name and for squiring me around Denmark for a lesson in hygge and Danish customs and lore. All the scenes in Denmark come from places we visited in spring 2019 BC (before Covid). I can't explain how this happened, but her kind and bright spirit came to infuse the book—an example of the magic that makes writing such a wonder and joy.

Also wondrous is my beloved agent, Margaret Sutherland Brown of Folio Literary. I'm grateful for her belief in this story through the many drafts it took for me to hack it out of a block of stone, then for her wise suggestions as the plot and characters slowly began to take shape.

The story next hugely benefited from the keen eye and great insights of my editor, Amanda Bergeron. I'm so grateful to have had her, a like mind who sweats the writing details as obsessively as I do, in charge of shepherding the book. And we had fun while we were at it! Amanda, I can't thank you enough. A huge thanks goes to Sareer Khader for her thoughtful editorial suggestions, as well.

The whole Berkley team has been fantastic. Thank you to Ivan Held, Christine Ball, Jeanne-Marie Hudson, Claire Zion, and Craig Burke for your belief in this book, and thank you to Christine Legon, Megan Elmore, and Courtney Vincento for taking such good care with it. A special thanks goes to sales genius Kate Whitman, marketing guru Jessica Plummer, intrepid publicists Tara O'Connor and Chelsea Pascoe, and Vikki Chu for the brilliant cover design.

I'm grateful, too, to those on the home front, from my daughters, Lauren Lynch, Megan Cayes, and Alison Stetler, to friends like Colleen Oakley, Jani Taylor, Jan Johnstone, and Alison Law, who all kindly let me ramble on about my book as we met for masked lunches or tramped around our neighborhoods during the long, strange years of Covid. Thanks to the women of my neighborhood book club of thirty-some years, who were patient listeners, as well. Heartfelt thank-yous go to my sister Margaret Edison, for her role as genealogist and comber of censuses; to my sister Jeanne, beloved provider of kindness and wit; to my sister Carolyn, my confidante and enabler during the research trip to Sabin's Cincinnati (and always), as well as a genuine Polio Pioneer; and to my sister Arlene, whose goodness has been a staple upon which I've depended my entire life.

And as always, my deepest thanks go to my husband, Mike, the steadfast bass whose calm, grounded, and unrelenting strength allows for the treble to sing.

THE WOMAN WITH THE CURE

LYNN CULLEN

BEHIND THE BOOK

WITH LYNN CULLEN

My buddy Rosie and I, age seven, were riding our bikes into new territory. Through a playground and past Johnny Appleseed's grave we pedaled, until, at the river's edge, we stopped. Straddling our Schwinns, we gaped past a dormant life-size checkerboard and fading picnic tables; past an elaborately tiled baby pool, long drained and collecting leaves; past a massive sandbox still filled with sand but devoid of toddlers to an empty sandy beach. I could almost hear kids splashing in the water and see mothers swatting sand from their babies' rubber-covered diapers. But the place was as vacant as if everyone had been beamed up by aliens.

"Polio," my mother told me when I got home. "They had to close down the beach." Visibly upset, she spoke of a boy at church who walked with braces and crutches. "He might have gotten it there."

Half a century later, that memory would find its way into my book. But because I was born the year that polio vaccines became available and cases dropped annually thereafter, by the time I was cognizant, polio was no longer a threat. I was completely unfamiliar with the fear felt by parents and children in those years of isolation and despair. And then came our own pandemic.

As we entered that first lockdown in March 2020, I was just beginning to write a book about the race to beat polio. Suddenly—in ways I never wanted—I could begin to understand the feeling of being trapped indoors during those anxious polio summers. Isolation was bad for me but worse for my daughters with young children. How did they entertain their kids while keeping them inside all summer without friends? A few more months into the COVID-19 pandemic, and my empathy for those mid-century parents who never knew a summer without fear for their children turned into deep respect. How did they get themselves and their children through it?

I had started writing my book thinking that it would focus on the famous competition between Jonas Salk and Albert Sabin to be the first with a polio vaccine. But the more COVID altered our way of life, the more I understood that polio was a much bigger story than the race between two ambitious men. I kept circling back to Dr. Dorothy Horstmann, who had only a walk-on part in my tale in the early months, but whose life was a crucial example of that which interested me most—the role of women in crushing polio.

With Salk and Sabin historically taking up so much of the limelight, it took some digging for me to fully understand the importance of Horstmann's game-changing discovery. It also took me a while to fully appreciate her role in evaluating the safety and efficacy of the oral polio vaccine, which led to the eradication of the disease in 99.9 percent of the world. She was a key player in the drive to end polio, yet who has heard of her?

It seems Dorothy was used to that. But the lack of acclaim never stopped her. After polio was conquered, she went on to be a major contributor to the rubella vaccine, which our children receive to this day. She didn't stop championing children through her work in stamping out childhood diseases until Alzheimer's disease felled her. She died at age eighty-nine, in 2001.

In my research, I was taken with something one of her colleagues said, that Dorothy felt she'd sacrificed much to her science and her career and she believed that it was difficult, if not impossible, for a woman to have it all. That resonated with me. What woman, even in young adulthood, isn't acutely aware of the choices she must make in balancing career, family, love, and personal interests? Oh, sure, we can have it all, but in what proportions? Something has to give. I wondered what gave for Dorothy.

As captivated as I was by Dorothy and as awestruck by her achievements, I was equally curious about life in the polio era in general, especially for women. I started to open my story to other women's voices. How did mid-twentieth-century mores and culture affect the choices they made?

Popular magazines from the era formed an important part of my research. (Indeed, magazines were my windows to the world when I was growing up.) Combing through the thick, slightly mildewy-smelling stack of magazines I'd accumulated, I was struck by how both articles and advertisements worked to reinforce the roles women were supposed to play. One article in *Good Housekeeping* enticingly entitled "Across a Crowded Room" ended up being a call for women to stop being critical of their husbands. Wives were told to look for ways to praise their men, such as to thank them for so wonderfully carving the chicken at dinner. I couldn't help but think, fair enough—if their husbands thanked them in return for planning and shopping for, preparing, and cleaning up after that wonderfully carved chicken.

Throughout the book, I mention many actual advertisements, one of the most telling of which pictured a sexy woman frozen within a block of ice in front of her vanity. It promoted a brand of air conditioners as well as the way that women were best kept in that era—on ice.

Even scientific articles contributed to defining a woman's place. It wasn't just by happenstance that when Dorothy was photographed with David Bodian in *Time* magazine at the conference where they announced their independently made discovery, the photographer positioned Dorothy to look like she was a secretary taking dictation from Bodian, although she'd unofficially made "their" discovery years before he did.

Ultimately, my story about the race to find the polio vaccine became so much more than that to me. It's a tale of women in many walks of life and in many roles under unbearable pressure, and the oft-unexamined marvel of their grace and strength. Whether the miracles they wrought changed the world like Dorothy Horstmann's discoveries or were of the everyday sort, both were vital. Both, as Arne might say, are truly a WON-der.

QUESTIONS FOR DISCUSSION

1. Polio touched everyone's lives in the decades that it reigned. Do you have family stories or personal recollections of the polio years?

2. Magazines, radio, and television reinforced traditional roles for women during the polio era. Think about some examples of television shows or ad campaigns from your youth that promoted the "ideal" woman. What are current examples in which contemporary media shapes our perception of women? Apply this thinking to a popular television series.

3. Examine the sacrifices made by the individual women in each lead-in chapter. Which of these women resonated with you the most?

4. Do you think Dorothy was right to end the relationship with Arne? What do you think their lives would have looked like if they'd stayed together?

5. Dorothy could not see her mother for who she was until Dorothy was far into adulthood. What important self-discoveries have you made only after having lived into adulthood?

6. As a reader, when did you understand Dorothy's mother's importance to Dorothy's success? How did her father contribute to building Dorothy's character? Who in your life has contributed to making you who you are, in quiet, easily unnoticeable ways?

7. In Denmark, Bente points out to Dorothy that all humankind is connected, and that we'd be kinder if we only realized this. What is a way in which we are connected that we usually don't take time to realize?

8. The author states in the essay above: "What woman, even in young adulthood, isn't acutely aware of the choices she must make in balancing career, family, love, and personal interests? Oh, sure, we can have it all, but in what proportions?" At what age were you first aware that you had to make choices? What choices did you make? Any regrets?

9. What parallels can be drawn from the polio years and recent COVID-19 pandemic times? Did you find yourself reflecting on these recent years and making any connections to your experiences while reading?

10. In the book, Sister Kenny states, "We are what we have willed ourselves to be, whether we realize it or not." Do you believe that there is some truth to this?

Author photo by Megan Cullen Cayes

LYNN CULLEN is the national bestselling author of historical novels *The Sisters of Summit Avenue*, *Twain's End*, *Mrs. Poe*, *Reign of Madness*, *The Creation of Eve*, and *I Am Rembrandt's Daughter*. *Twain's End* was an Indie Next List selection, a *People* magazine Book of the Week, and a Townsend Prize finalist. *Mrs. Poe* was an Indie Next List selection, a Target Book Club pick, an NPR Great Read, an Oprah.com Book of the Week, and a Costco "Pennie's Pick." Lynn's novels have been translated into seventeen languages. She lives in Atlanta, surrounded by her large family.

VISIT THE AUTHOR ONLINE

LynnCullen.com
AuthorLynnCullen
LynnCullenAuthor